SOMEBODY ELSE'S BOY

BY
JO BARTLETT

04393120

© 2016 Jo Bartlett

The right of Jo Bartlett to be identified as the author of this work has been asserted by her in accordance with the Copyright, Designs and Patents Act 1988.

The story contained within this book is a work of fiction. Names and characters are the product of the author's imagination and any resemblance to actual persons, living or dead, is entirely coincidental.

All rights reserved. No part of this book may be reproduced, stored in a retrieval system, or transmitted in any form or by any means, electronic, electrostatic, magnetic tape, mechanical, photocopying, recording or otherwise, without the written permission of the copyright holder.

Published by Accent Press Ltd 2016

Paperback ISBN: 9781786151117
Ebook ISBN: 9781786150554

For Lloyd, who made me realise that second chances at love are the best kind of all.

ACKNOWLEDGEMENTS

I'd like to start by thanking my fantastic editor at Accent Press, Rebecca Lloyd, for her tireless work in whipping *Somebody Else's Boy* into shape! As well as the rest of the team at Accent Press for their support and the faith they have shown in me.

I'd also like to thank my writing tribe, The Write Romantics – Alys West, Deirdre Palmer, Helen Phifer, Helen J. Rolfe, Jackie Ladbury, Jessica Redland, Lynne Pardoe, Rachael Thomas and Sharon Booth – for their constant encouragement, support and friendship, especially when the going gets tough!

To all my long-suffering family and friends, thank you for never complaining too much when I'm head down at the laptop and not really listening to what anyone is saying. Especially Toni Hazard for always offering to pick up the slack on the school runs. I promise to make it up to you all. And thanks to my mum for telling everyone how proud she is to have a daughter who writes and encouraging them to buy my books!

I especially want to thank Paula Stroud and Jeannie Monaghan for the years we spent sharing a staffroom at a certain FE college in Kent, which provided some of the inspiration for this novel. I'd like to thank all of my friends for making me laugh and giving me so many moments that help me capture the comedy element I just can't seem to leave out of my stories.

Most of all, I'd like to thank Lloyd, Anna, Harry, Jake and Ellie for being the most important people in my world. We might be a jigsaw family, but that's what makes us fit together like we do.

CHAPTER ONE

'Your father's been in bed with the vicar again.'

Nancy closed her eyes and gripped the handset a little harder. It was like a line from a bad sitcom, the sort with intermittent canned laughter helpfully positioned at the points you're supposed to find hilarious. Only she wasn't laughing.

'Have you told my mother?'

Forcing her eyes open, the index and middle fingers on her right hand involuntarily crossed – as though that kind of superstition might actually make a difference.

'Not yet. We've been trying to get hold of her, but …'

'*Please* don't. There's really no need now you've spoken to me, is there?'

'Well, it is our policy to inform next of kin when there's been,' there was a momentary pause at the other end of the line, 'an incident.'

'I think, if you check your records, you'll find we're both listed as next of kin.'

If she sounded curt, it was tough – she had to protect her mum. Especially now she could no longer help her dad; no one could really do that.

'Well, if you're sure? But there will have to be an investigation, you know, and there'll be a note on John's file.'

'Of course, I understand you've got things you have to do. What about Erica's husband?'

'Mr Parkinson already knows. He's even more upset this time.' The manager of the care home's monotone voice didn't lessen the impact of her words.

Gerald Parkinson had been heartbroken the first time his wife of forty years had been found in bed with Nancy's dad. No one knew if anything had actually happened, but it was betrayal enough. Even though neither Erica nor John remembered they were married to other people, it still hurt, and there was no need for her mum to go through it again.

There'd been a meeting at the care home that first time, with both sets of family there, but it hadn't achieved anything more than tears and pointless recriminations. Mr Parkinson had accused her father of being the instigator. After all, Erica had worked for the church all her life and been the vicar of Dayham parish for more than ten years before the Alzheimer's took hold.

Nancy had tried to reason with Gerald that it was no one's fault. Her father, whose hands now bore one or two liver spots (though far fewer than someone who'd lost every one of his memories should have) would never, *ever* have acted like that if he were not the shell of the person he used to be.

Those same hands had guided her on her bike from stabilisers to independence and had driven her home from parties at all hours of the night, just so she didn't have to get a cab. They weren't the hands of a man who would coerce anyone or deliberately cause hurt to another human being. But Mr Parkinson had never met the *real* John O'Brien.

'I'm sorry to hear that.' Uncrossing her fingers, Nancy shifted the phone to her other hand. 'Will you be taking any action to stop it happening again?'

'We can't lock them in, if that's what you mean. It's a violation of their human rights, *apparently*.'

Sue Lewis had been the manager of The Pines, a specialist care home for residents with Alzheimer's and dementia, for some fifteen years, or so she'd told them when Nancy's dad had first gone in for respite care. But she didn't sound all that convinced about human rights following the latest incident.

'The only exception is if they're a threat to themselves or someone else and, if I'm honest,' there was that uncomfortable pause again, 'they looked quite content when we found them.'

There was nothing Nancy could say to that.

Ending the call, she took a deep breath. The stress of having to keep another secret from her mother strained the muscles in her neck. She needed to speak to someone, to rail against the unfairness of it all. Her father was only sixty-two years old and yet he'd long since left them. How was that anything close to fair?

Twisting the ring that sat awkwardly on her engagement finger, she stared at the chunky sapphire. It had looked fine in the box – not really her taste, but fine. Yet on her finger it sat at a weird angle, like it was going to slide off.

Maybe she should phone David. You were supposed to lean on your fiancé at times like this, weren't you? Only he would just make some ill-judged joke about it. 'Way to go, John. Good for him, it's great to see there's life in the old dog yet,' that sort of thing.

No. There was only one person who could take her mind off things. Picking up the phone she dialled the number she knew by heart.

Having the police make a doorstep visit on a Saturday evening, in their part of Peckham, wasn't that unusual. It wasn't the toughest area of London, admittedly, but it still had its fair share of domestics, drug deals and massage parlours in private houses that offered all sorts of 'extras'.

Jack liked it, though, partly because it was gritty and real, but mainly because it was cheap in comparison to other boroughs. He hadn't been entirely honest with his aunt, when he'd said the only reason was because it helped him write: find the characters that would make people read his books, feel the truth in the stories. Having her throw money at the problem, as she'd see it, was the last thing he wanted. He could teach anywhere, but, if he was ever going to make it past the polite rejection slips he could paper his office wall with, he needed to immerse himself in the lives his characters lived and her offer to buy him a luxury flat in some soulless development wasn't going to cut it.

Alice had tried to convince him that his aunt's offer wasn't the charity he saw it as and for a while he'd wondered if their difference of opinion was going to be a deal breaker. He couldn't bear to let history repeat itself, determined to learn from his parents' mistakes. Luckily, although his wife might crave the lifestyle his aunt was offering, in the end it had been enough for them just to be together.

Only now there was a policeman at their door. Two officers in fact. And it was the WPC, with her head tilted on one side, who worried Jack the most. She had an unmistakable look of sympathy. He hugged Toby closer to his chest. Alice wouldn't leave them. Whatever it was that the police had come for, it couldn't be that.

'Mr Williams?' The young policeman didn't smile as Jack nodded. 'Can we come in?'

Without speaking, Jack moved to one side and ushered them through to the lounge. The TV was on, showing the highlights of the tennis at Wimbledon. Toby seemed to find the to and fro of the ball hypnotic, and Jack had watched his son's eyelids start to grow heavy as he drifted towards sleep.

'Shall we sit down?' The police officer's voice cracked, and Jack might have felt sorry for him if his heart hadn't felt like it was about to burst out of his chest. He'd seen the police officers' expressions on TV dramas – he'd described them in his own writing – but having such a look directed at him was something he'd never be able to capture with words.

'Of course.'

Jack's response was automatic, when the last thing in the world he wanted was for these people to sit down and tell him what every fibre in his body feared.

'There's no easy way to say this.' The constable, whose name Jack hadn't taken in, sat on the sofa opposite him. 'There's been an accident.'

'My wife is at work, at the theatre, she'll be there now ... on stage.'

If he could just explain why it couldn't be Alice, everything would be all right. But even as he tried to convince himself the skin on the back of his neck prickled.

Toby, thinking it was some sort of a game, clapped his chubby hands together, giving his father the benefit of a gummy grin.

'I'm afraid this concerns your wife, Alice.'

Silently, like a sympathy ninja, the WPC had moved to sit next to him and put her hands over his, at the point where they knitted together around Toby's waist.

'Several of her colleagues at the theatre identified the

bod ...' The constable caught himself and exchanged a horrified look with his colleague, which Jack desperately wished he hadn't seen. 'She was identified at the scene of the accident.'

'She's dead,' Jack said. It wasn't a question and he didn't want an answer; didn't want the truth confirmed.

'I'm afraid there was nothing they could do. There'll have to be an investigation. It looks as though one of the cables used in a lifting scene got trapped and she was helping a stagehand to free it when it suddenly unjammed. It took her with it as it recoiled and sent her flying upwards. She hit her head when she fell and the paramedics couldn't revive her.'

'How long did they try?'

It was an odd question, but nothing seemed real. It was like being underwater. He wanted to know how hard they'd tried to save the girl who'd been his everything for years – *his* girl.

'About forty-five minutes we were told.' The constable consulted his notebook; he was obviously new to this. 'And they closed the theatre for the evening, of course.'

'That was big of them.' Jack stood up and moved towards the window, Toby still in his arms, gabbling in that indistinct language of the very young. 'Why was she the one helping?'

'Her colleagues said it could've been any of them, that she was just in the wrong place at the wrong time.'

The WPC said the words as though they might help, as if anything could.

'It *should* have been someone else.'

He spoke quietly. If it was wrong to wish someone else dead, he couldn't help it.

'Can we take you to the hospital? So you can see her?'

'I promised I'd get Toby to sleep.' Jack kept his back to them. Lights twinkled in a thousand households stretched out beyond their flat, full of ordinary people, getting on with their ordinary lives. Did they know how lucky they were? 'She thought that way she wouldn't miss it.'

'Miss what?'

The WPC was at his side again. Her saccharine-sweet voice made him want to scream, his arms involuntarily tightening around his son, until the boy moaned in protest and Jack forced himself to relax his grip.

'We watched him all afternoon, lying on his stomach on the playmat. A hundred times we were sure he was going to move, that he had a fraction, but he hadn't, of course.'

He had to move back to the sofa, the bones in his legs seeming to dissolve. History appeared determined to repeat itself, one way or another. Toby would be motherless, just like him.

'She was terrified that he would crawl for the first time when she wasn't here, that she'd miss it, wouldn't be part of it. I promised to get him to sleep, so that he wouldn't try again until tomorrow when she'd be here to see it.'

The WPC's eyes filled with the tears Jack had yet to find.

'I wouldn't have told her even if he had. I'd have kept quiet and pretended and it would all have been all right. So she's got to come back, because Toby's waiting for her. We both are, just like I promised ...'

CHAPTER TWO

'Thanks for dropping everything. I just needed to get out and think about something other than the situation with Dad for half an hour.'

Nancy spoke as they weaved through the café towards their favourite spot by the window, negotiating the shopping bags that surrounded most of the occupied chairs.

'No David today, then? I thought you two lovebirds would want to spend your day off together.' Olivia's eyes widened at the sight of the double chocolate muffin which Nancy had set on the table alongside the skinny latte she'd asked for. 'I'll only eat half of that – I'll stay within my points that way.'

'It's Saturday, and it's against the law to count points on a Saturday.'

Pulling out a chair, Nancy sat opposite her friend at one of the bleached pine tables in Tea Four Two, St Nicholas Bay's quirkiest coffee shop. The balance between shabby and chic had perhaps swung in favour of the former, but she loved it, and its position at number 42 in the high street lent it a distinctive name, which unlike most of the local businesses didn't play on the town's Dickens connection.

'And to answer your question, David is playing golf.'

'Ooh, quite the networker these days, isn't he?'

When Olivia laughed, her sleek blonde bob shook so that it threatened to fall out of place, but then settled back into that just-stepped-out-of-a-salon look which Nancy's red curls never achieved.

'Has he taken the van?'

'Yep.' Despite her mood, Nancy's mouth curled slightly upward. 'Bet they won't know what's hit them when they see Electrical Dave's white transit van parked next to the club captain's BMW!'

'Oh my God! He didn't actually go through with it, did he?'

'Uh huh.' Nancy grimaced as she swallowed the hot coffee, pausing before she could explain the full horror of the situation. 'He thought I was being serious when I told him he should use Electrical Dave as the name of his business. I'll have to make it clear when I'm joking in future.'

'I suppose it does do what it says on the tin. You couldn't mistake him for a plumber!'

'That's true, but sometimes I wish he wasn't quite so obvious ... about everything. His idea of romance is to jump on me as soon as I get through the door. There I was growing up thinking I'd find my Mr Darcy, never dreaming I'd end up with Electrical Dave!'

'It could be worse, he could be like Miles. At least with David what you see is what you get.'

Olivia's blue eyes twinkled, but it was difficult to tell whether it was laughter or the tears that often seemed just below the surface with her lately.

'That never would have been enough for you, though, would it? Do you remember your ten-point checklist?'

'Yeah, and a fat lot of good that did me.' As she drew the second half of the muffin closer to her, Olivia's painted-on smile wobbled. 'No chance of romance *or* sex for me these days.'

'I'm sure we can put that right. David keeps telling me he can fix you up any time.' Nancy grinned, something else her fiancé had said suddenly popping into her head. 'In fact, we might have found just the man for you. David got the idea for the signwriting on his van from one of his mates at the club and he's newly single – Alan the Magic Man, or something.'

'The kids' entertainer?' Olivia's eyebrows shot up. 'He did Sophie's seventh birthday party in that God-awful harlequin waistcoat. You must remember!'

'Christ, was that him?' It was a memory that Nancy would rather not hold on to. Even the kids had been embarrassed at how amateurish the whole thing was. 'Well, we can rule him out for a date, definitely. Even Al Cadabra would have been a better name than Alan the Magic Man.'

'I think it's a sign. I'd rather spend time deciding on a name for our business than fixing up a blind date with one of David's dodgy mates! I was thinking that we could go for something like The Dramatic Duo?' Olivia grinned and gave the napkin a flourish much like Alan the Magic Man might have done. 'Or maybe The Drama Queens would be more appropriate?'

'Well, I guess if you want us to be remembered for all the wrong reasons, that could work. But I thought The Merry Players might be good. Then we could have the Mini Merries for the kids.'

'Flattered as I am that you'd consider using my maiden name, it makes me sound like the founder and that hardly seems fair when you're the one putting in all the groundwork.'

'You quite like the idea, though, don't you? And it's

not like you go by the surname Merry these days, so it wouldn't look like you were self-obsessed or anything.' Nancy ducked to one side as Olivia flicked a chocolate chip in her direction.

'I wish I'd never shown you those old head-shots now! I must admit there's something quite appealing about using my old name for the business, though. It would show Miles that I haven't collapsed in a heap, just because he's shagging a stewardess young enough to be his daughter.'

'Being a pilot called Miles is almost worse than Electrical Dave, and the whole stewardess thing is such a cliché. I'd have been much more sympathetic if he'd taken up with a burly baggage-handler called Clive.'

'Cliché is one name for him.' Olivia raised an eyebrow. 'But I think Grade-A arsehole suits him better.'

'Goes without saying.' It was Nancy's turn to smile. 'So we're agreed, then? If we get the go-ahead, we're going for The Merry Players?' She paused as the other woman nodded, her mouth far too full of chocolate muffin to reply. 'There is one condition, though.'

'What's that?' Little bits of sponge danced through the air as Olivia spoke.

'If I have to sleep with Bernard to get the okay, then we're naming the business after me.'

Ruth hesitated. Maybe she still had time to duck into the Cancer Research shop before she was seen? Although she might stand a better chance of hiding by blending in with the crowd of pensioners and young mums with buggies waiting to board the bus.

Damn. It was too late. Philly had already spotted her. She was waving and giving Ruth the benefit of one of her trademark inane smiles, so indicative of the lack of any real substance.

Bracing herself against the expected onslaught, Ruth arranged her face into an expression so unnatural it actually hurt. 'Philly. It's good to see you.' The lie had barely left her lips before the other woman enveloped her in an over-the-top embrace, heavy layers of Elizabeth Arden perfume threatening to cut off Ruth's oxygen supply.

'Oh, Ruth, you look *dreadful*, so tired.'

There was more than a hint of judgement in Philly's tone. The smile still firmly fixed on her face was anchored in the corners by lip liner that looked strong enough to mark lines in the middle of the road.

'Well, it's been difficult, you know.'

'Oh yes, of course, it must be.'

Philly nodded, but her hair didn't move, and Ruth self-consciously ran a hand through her own frizzy curls, still damp from the shower and six months on the wrong side of their last visit to a hairdresser – untameable locks that ran in her family. An uncomfortable moment passed where neither of them spoke. There was no way Philly understood; her life was a constant round of hair appointments and her biggest worry was the 'absolute drama', as she described it, of her son's forthcoming wedding.

'So how is *John*?'

Breaking the silence, Philly pronounced his name as if describing an embarrassing condition in a busy chemist's shop. Much in the way that you might ask for piles cream if there was a long queue of people behind you.

Ruth wanted to confront her with the truth, to say he wasn't John at all. That he was a hopeless, helpless remnant of the man she'd married, now that the illness had progressed to the stage that it had. She wanted to say it was exhausting, unfair, and that a big part of her wished it could have happened to Philly's husband instead. Anyone's husband, in fact, just not John.

'He's fine.'

Her cheeks were really hurting now. Perhaps it was worth thinking about scrawling a happy expression on her own face using industrial-strength lip liner. After all, most people didn't *really* want to know the truth or hear how you *really* felt.

'Good, good.'

Philly didn't press for more, even though it was blatantly obvious that John was anything but fine. And neither was Ruth.

'We must have you over to dinner soon. It's just that things are so busy what with Josh's wedding and – I don't know if you've heard – but Nigel has been elected as the captain of the club this year! It's like being royalty, one event after another!'

'Sounds great. Anyway, must dash, lots to do too, you know.'

She couldn't bear to listen to any more. This had once been due to be John's year as golf club captain. Not that Ruth had ever really looked forward to the prospect, but it was just a reminder that everyone else in the world seemed to have filled the void, as though he'd never been there at all.

She was half way up the hill on St Nicholas Bay's high street before Philly even had a chance to respond. It would give them more to gossip about down at the club, no doubt, how Ruth was as big a screwball as her husband. Surely she must have lost her marbles, too? Why else would she be so rude?

The bald truth was that it *would* have been easier if

she'd been the one to get ill. Or if John had just died suddenly in some terrible accident. Then the grief could have come all at once – instead of this terrible erosion, losing him bit by bit, day after day. Perhaps Philly and her type would've been more sympathetic to that, instead of expecting her to carry on as though nothing had happened, just because John was still alive.

There were moments so dark, Ruth really believed she couldn't make it through another day. Her only comfort was that Nancy felt the loss of John as keenly as she did. Her daughter was the one person she could phone in the middle of the night, when it all got too much and the fear threatened to overwhelm her.

Nancy had texted earlier to say she was meeting Olivia for coffee in town, and Ruth had been determined to stay away to give her daughter some space, but the encounter with Philly had left her rattled.

Pushing open the door of Tea Four Two, she smiled, and this time it didn't hurt. As long as she had Nancy, she could bear it. And even the Phillys of this world couldn't take that away.

CHAPTER THREE

The pub garden was packed and it was one of those beautiful blue-sky days. A buzz of conversation and laughter carried on the light summer breeze. No one who happened upon the group, dressed as they were in a sea of Alice's favourite colour, would have realised that they were at a wake.

'She was a special girl, mate. She even got me wearing turquoise.'

Craig's distinctive accent roused Jack from the trance he slipped into in every quiet moment.

'She was.'

Jack took the beer his best friend was offering, the same friend who'd revelled in his best-man duties only two years before at the church where they'd just buried Alice.

'Toby looks like he's bearing up okay.'

'I wouldn't know.' Jack gestured to where his mother-in-law stood cradling his son against her chest, as if he could somehow stop her broken heart from shattering into a thousand pieces. 'I've barely been able to get near him, since … you know.'

'It's understandable, though. He gives her something else to think about and a link back to Lissy. Pam's bound to want to stay close to him.'

Craig was always upbeat, always wanted to think the best of people, to give them a reason for acting the way they did. Jack sometimes wondered how they were such good friends.

'Yeah, I know it's a normal reaction, but I feel suffocated and I need Toby too.'

'Give her time. She'll ease off a bit when things get back to …'

'Normal? Only they won't for me and Pam, will they?'

Jack dug his nails into his palm. Craig didn't mean anything by it. But, as loved as Alice was, most of the other two hundred people who'd packed out the church would go home and get on with their lives.

'I'm sorry.'

'I know you are, but whatever way I look at it, there's no such thing as normal any more. I can't stay around here, not now.' Jack surprised himself with his words; the snap decision was as clear in his mind as if he'd weighed up the pros and cons for days rather than come to it in the last ten seconds. 'Everything reminds me of her.'

'I wish there was something I could do to make this less awful for you.'

Even the determinedly cheerful Aussie couldn't sort this one out and it was clearly torturing him.

'Thanks for everything, for all this. I don't know how I'd have done it without you.' Jack met Craig's eyes for a moment and had to look away, his throat raw with the urge to cry. He still hadn't. He just couldn't. Not even when he'd seen Alice in the hospital morgue, her body cold and lifeless, but curiously unmarked.

'I think me and Tobes need some time on our own. He might not be able to say it, but he misses her as much as I do. He hasn't slept through the night since she died, and every time I get up to comfort him, Pam's already there.'

He'd caught his mother-in-law the night before standing over a sound-asleep Toby, sobbing quietly and stroking the velvety soft skin on his chubby legs.

'It could be a great idea, Jack. A holiday for the two of you might do you the world of good.'

There was that relentless optimism again.

'I wasn't thinking about a holiday, more of a trial run at living outside London.'

'Right …' Craig stretched out the word until it became oddly distorted. 'Have you thought about where?'

'I've not decided on anything, but we took Toby down to the coast on the last weekend that Alice had off work. She loved the place where we stopped for lunch – it was a little seaside village called St Something's Bay. She said, if she didn't need to be in London for work, she'd have loved to bring up a family there.'

'Don't rush into anything. We're all here for you, you know.'

'I do, but I think maybe I should get away. Pam is pushing for a court case, she wants compensation, and it would put The Old Granville out of business. It couldn't take that sort of hit.' Jack took another sip of his beer.

'Don't you want them to pay for what happened?'

'Why? It won't bring her back and it would feel wrong, like I'm profiting from her death or something. She'd never have forgiven me if she thought I'd been involved in getting them closed down.' Jack could imagine Alice's reaction. She'd loved performing so much and had been due to audition for a main role – her dreams finally starting to come true. Acting had been her passion, long before he'd come along.

Watching Alice's friend, Selena, finally wrestle Toby from Pam's grasp, he made up his mind. Escaping was their only hope.

The flat was quiet and so claustrophobic it was as though the walls were closing in. Alice had always had music playing and he'd sometimes seen her practising dance steps, when she hadn't known he was watching. She could never hear a song she loved and keep still. Since she'd gone, he hadn't been able to listen to any music. Pam had chosen it for the funeral, she'd chosen the flowers and organised just about every detail of the whole damn thing. He had only been determined to choose the pub where they'd held the wake, the same place they'd spent their first date.

It was partly Pam who was making him feel claustrophobic in his own home. She'd started making up Toby's bottles as soon as they got home from the pub, and pouring cups of tea that would never be drunk, just to keep busy.

'Have you thought any more about me taking Toby back to mine for a while? Giving you a bit of time to yourself?'

She sprayed the kitchen worktop with anti-bacterial fluid, wiping it down as though she meant business. Pam had the same slim dancer's figure as her daughter, probably because she never sat still. Even when she was holding Toby, she'd be walking him up and down or rocking him back and forth, as if she was scared to stop for a moment and let reality sink in.

'I don't need time to myself, at least not away from Toby.'

Jack tipped his tea down the sink. It was no good telling her that he didn't want a drink; she'd just make it anyway.

'You must have some writing to do, or some marking?'

Taking the cup out of his hand, before he even had a

chance to place it on the drainer, she dried it with her customary vigour and hung it on the chrome mug-tree that she'd insisted on buying the day after she'd arrived. He'd heard her muttering something about it not being any wonder they had such an untidy kitchen when they didn't have any of the right equipment.

'Not at the moment.'

He didn't add that he couldn't write, hadn't felt the slightest urge to since Alice's accident, since he'd become a *widower*. It was a horrible word, one that belonged to a much older man than he.

'Maybe you should try? Doing something might make you feel better.' Her voice was half muffled as she reached inside one of the kitchen cabinets, emerging with a mixing bowl and a rolling pin. 'I'm going to do some baking before the baby wakes up and then I'll take him out in his buggy, get some fresh air. Why don't you go along to your office and see if you can get a couple of hours' work done?'

Feeling like he was on the receiving end of a royal command, he left her to the baking and walked past what had been his and Alice's room. He'd given it to Pam to stay in, on the basis that it would be more comfortable for her, even though the truth was that he couldn't bear to go in there. It smelt of Alice's perfume as he walked past and her silk dressing gown would be hanging on the back of the door, as if she might still come home and put it on. Energetic as she was, even Pam hadn't managed to tackle packing her daughter's stuff away. So Jack had lain on the sofa for the last ten nights, barely sleeping, and Toby had slept in his little box room – missing the comfort of his mum's arms when he woke in the night.

The study was at the end of the hall, the door pulled firmly shut. He didn't think he'd be able to work, but getting away from Pam was something he needed to do if they were going to survive sharing the same flat for another minute. He'd hoped she'd make firm plans to go home once the funeral was over, but when she'd suggested that she take Toby with her to allow him to work, he'd put his foot down. That was never going to happen. They were at an impasse and somehow he couldn't find the words to tell her she *had* to go. After all, she'd lost a huge part of her life too.

There was no way he could write; hiding out in his study didn't change that. But maybe he should contact the university, let them know he could only keep tutoring the online students. He wouldn't be going back to the campus. He was moving away, even if he would never be able to move on.

The late afternoon sun was still strong, and a thin layer of dust had settled on the desk in less than two weeks since he'd last been in there.

There were Post-it notes stuck all around the computer screen, showing plotlines and ideas for his latest book, and a love heart scrawled in red pen, with *Lissy loves Jack* written inside it. He peeled it off, opened the top drawer of his desk, and dropped it inside.

There were postcards pinned on the noticeboard next to his desk, one from his aunt in New York. She hadn't come to the funeral, although she'd wanted to. The previous year, she suffered a thrombosis on a transatlantic flight so the risk in travelling was too great. And on top of that, her presence would bring more unwanted press attention. It was bad enough that the local reporters had been poking around, loving the headlines that the young mum's death had given them.

There was another postcard, which they'd bought on their day at the beach. Alice had drawn a second love heart around the name of the town. It was St Nicholas Bay. He'd forgotten all about the postcard and couldn't help feeling that its presence was a sign that Alice approved of his plan.

'Where are you, Lissy?' Saying the words out loud, he closed his eyes. When he did, he could still see her, hear the sound of her voice. The way she always came to the study to find him when she got home from work. Toby would already be in bed and they'd talk about their days, Alice with her feet tucked under her on the battered leather chair in the corner of his office. They'd dream about Jack finally getting a book deal or Alice at last being cast in a lead role. They'd moan about demanding students and impatient directors, and sometimes even argue about Jack not taking advantage of his aunt's connections. Now he would give anything to have the worst students in the world, if only he could have Alice back to hear about it.

When he opened his eyes, her chair's emptiness was like a fresh wound; it was like losing her all over again. He ran his hands over the imprint pressed into the seat, tracing the curve her body had made. He would never touch her again. An emotion he hadn't been able to release racked his body, the sound he made barely human. Sinking into the physical space that his wife had left behind, he was broken, terrified that nothing and no one would ever fill the aching void – for him, but most of all for Toby.

CHAPTER FOUR

Nancy smoothed down her dress. Did it set the right tone? She had to look girl-next-door enough to get certain members of the town council onside, but business-like enough to convince the rest that she knew what she was talking about.

It would have to do either way. She'd changed her outfit three times already, and every time she pulled a dress or a jumper over her head, static electricity was injected into her hair making it wilder than ever. If looking like Ronald McDonald was likely to sway the committee, then she was on to a winner.

Unfortunately the others who should have been part of the pitch had suddenly found far more urgent things to do. Olivia had called to say that her elderly aunt was unwell, and David had a contract with a large chain of pharmacies, which required him to carry out the electrical work in the evenings when they were closed for business.

Gathering her bag and her copy of the business plan she'd sent to the Town Clerk for The Merry Players, she opened the door of the cottage, the late summer evening warm on her skin.

The sweet aroma from the honeysuckle bushes that draped across the wall in front of the cottage filled the air. She would have given almost anything to sink down onto the garden bench with a Pimm's and a feel-good book. Her responsibilities weaved their way into her life, like the vines on the honeysuckle, almost threatening to overpower the crumbly stone wall that supported it.

The population of St Nicholas Bay almost doubled at the weekends and school holidays, when the holiday lets were filled and the 'Down from London' types, known locally as the DFLs, took up residence. St Nicholas Bay's fame had grown out of its connection to Charles Dickens who was supposed to have penned much of *A Christmas Carol* while staying in the town. The Bay was dotted with aptly named businesses as a result – Tiny Tim's Toys, Fezziwig's Wine Bar and Nancy's father's old business, Marley's Chains, a DIY store, to name a few. It came into its own at Christmas, but its prettiness and golden sand made it almost as popular in summer. Only an hour from London, it was a popular choice for second-home owners, and there was building resentment among residents who didn't make their living from tourism.

Nancy was hoping to use this tension to her advantage. Some of the DFLs had approached the council about turning the old community centre into an art gallery. The theory was it would bring a bit of culture to the Bay and encourage more tourists. If Nancy could persuade the councillors who were anti-DFL to side with her plan for a community theatre instead, then she might just pull it off. She had nothing against the DFLs or the opening of an art gallery, but since The Merry Players were low on funds and needed a venue, it was the old community centre or nothing at all.

'Nancy, the members are ready for you now.' She was waiting nervously outside the council chamber in the new lottery-funded town hall when Dilys Hamilton, the clerk to the council, who was also prop forward for the local women's rugby club, came for her. Dilys's broad shoulders were supporting a densely patterned nylon dress and, as always, she had a smile on her face. Nancy couldn't recall ever seeing her look miserable.

'Thanks, Dilys. I read in the paper that the team look like they might make it all the way to the county championships this year.' Nancy smiled at the other woman, who had cheeks like two rosy-red apples and a surprisingly tinkling laugh always ready to escape.

'Ooh, Nance, it's so exciting!' Dilys linked arms with her conspiratorially as they made their way down the corridor. 'It's all down to that new girl, Kirsty Galway. She's got legs like a racehorse and a charge like a buffalo, that one.' Dilys's cheeks flushed redder still with excitement. 'You must know her anyway, love. She teaches sports science up at your college, she said.'

'Yes, we've met. In fact she's interested in being part of the project that I'm putting forward to the committee.' Nancy couldn't help smiling at the thought. If Kirsty's singing voice came close to the volume her bellowing reached when she was shouting at students on the sports field, the old community centre would need a new roof before panto season was over.

'Excellent, excellent, but you mustn't tell me anything about that before we get inside. I don't want anyone thinking we've been engaging in espionage.' For once, Dilys looked deadly serious. 'After all, we can't risk blowing your chances by anyone thinking I'm trying to influence the vote in some way, can we?' Giving Nancy's arm another squeeze, which went right down to her toes, Dilys propelled her through the door and into the lion's den.

'Miss O'Brien, come in, come in, take a seat.' Bernard Nicholson stood, pulling himself up to his full five feet two inches, his moustache twitching as he greeted Nancy.

'Thank you.' She smiled shyly – years of studying drama came in handy from time to time. Taking a meek, grateful and, if needs be, grovelling approach to the committee was more likely to work than brash confidence. Using the old community centre for The Merry Players was a good plan, but that wasn't enough. Pushing her idea down their throats *Dragon's Den* style was just about the worst thing she could do. Most of them were on the council because they were nosey, had way too much time on their hands, and liked to have their say in what could and couldn't go on in the town. So she'd play a role, let them think it was their idea. That was definitely the way to handle it. At least she hoped so.

'Do you want to tell us a bit about this little idea you've had?' Bernard raised a bushy eyebrow. He could condescend for England if the need arose and Nancy had to bite her lip to stop herself slipping out of character. There was only so much holding back that one person could do and she'd had just about enough of it over the last year.

'I'd love to, Bernard. May I call you Bernard?' He nodded in response and Nancy looked through her eyelashes at him. 'Thank you all for taking the time to consider the idea that Olivia and I are proposing.'

'Yes, where is Olivia?' Nerys Cooper, who until five years before, and a disastrous Ofsted report, had been the head teacher of St Nicholas Bay primary school, looked over her half-moon glasses and gave Nancy an appraising stare.

'Oh, she was desperate to be here.' Nancy was on the edge of over-acting. The big movements and actions required on stage didn't translate as well close up. It was why she'd ended up teaching drama instead of doing it for real. She didn't have the subtlety that it took to be *really* good. 'Unfortunately she was called upon to tend to her elderly aunt.'

'Really?' There was that unblinking stare over the half-moon spectacles again; Anne Robinson had nothing on her. 'Well, her aunt must appreciate Olivia making an effort, because I saw her getting into her car earlier and she was dressed like ...' Nerys appeared to struggle for the right phrase for a moment or two and very nearly blinked, '... a show girl.'

Nancy shook her head; she had to win the support of the council at all costs, but right at that moment she was tempted to join in a character assassination of Olivia who, not for the first time, had dropped Nancy in it.

'That's just Olivia, she *always* looks fabulous.' Dilys's tone was insistent as she stepped in to save Nancy, all attempts to remain unbiased clearly forgotten.

'Not *that* fabulous, if her husband left her.' Alison Morton, the town's Community Support Officer, who'd gone to school with Olivia and Nancy, revelled in making the dig. Nancy had witnessed Alison suffering from Olivia's biting remarks at school. She'd probably waited years to get her own back. It was almost a shame Olivia wasn't there to hear it.

'Now, now, ladies. All of this is hardly relevant to this discussion, is it?' Bernard raised his wooden gavel in the air as he spoke. The threat he might be forced to bang it on to the table to call order was apparently enough to silence the other council members. 'Let's hear what this young lady has to say.'

There were no interruptions following Bernard's brandishing of the gavel. Nancy could stay in character as she quietly outlined the plan to start a community-theatre group that would bring together the residents of St Nicholas Bay and also provide a children's drama workshop for some evenings, weekends and school holidays to help working parents struggling with childcare in the town.

'And how exactly would you like the committee to help you with this?' Sandy Bond, a local builder who was almost certainly on the council because of his vested interest in planning decisions, smiled warmly at her. He was the least likely member to be anti-DFL, because they had plenty of money for the renovation projects that were his bread and butter, but she had to play her hand anyway.

'We were hoping that the council might help us to identify a suitable venue. One which means we could keep the costs as low as possible. And, almost as importantly, to ensure that there are shows, plays and musicals available in the town for all residents, so that a night at the theatre doesn't mean taking out a small mortgage for a trip up to London.'

'Hear, hear!' Dilys lost all pretence at objectivity. 'It would show those bloody DFLs that we're just as good as they are and that they can keep London and stay up there, too. Some of them only tried to join the team, you know!' She looked as though she'd found them squatting in her downstairs loo.

'What about the old community centre? Have you thought about that?' Bernard smiled, clearly delighted with his ingenuity, and Nancy bit her lip again to stop herself smiling.

'Well, of course we allowed ourselves to dream about it, but we didn't believe it was ever really an option. We couldn't compete with the plans for the art gallery.'

'Nonsense! If you were able to make use of the old

community centre, it would stop them opening one. The town is bursting at the seams with galleries and souvenir outlets as it is. Between them and the charity shops popping up everywhere it's getting so it's almost impossible to buy an ounce of tobacco and the *Daily Mail* without having to get into your car.' Bernard's moustache bristled again. 'Right, all those in favour of giving The Merry Players a one-year lease of the old community centre, at a nominal rent of a hundred pounds per annum, raise your hands.'

Bernard lifted his gavel into the air once more and a six-to-two majority raised their hands. Dilys, who didn't actually get a vote, looked as though she was having to sit on her hands to stop her arm shooting upwards. Even Sandy, who did so well from the DFL income, gave an emphatic nod and wave of his hand. Only Alison and an elderly gentleman, who Nancy didn't recognise and who'd been asleep for most of the meeting, kept their hands down.

'Motion carried!'

Finally bringing down his gavel with such force that the table in front of him wobbled, Bernard sealed the deal. There was no going back. For better or for worse Nancy was going into business with Olivia.

CHAPTER FIVE

Most of the packing cases had been wedged by the removal company into the front room. The letting agent had described it as cosy but this was clearly code for tiny. Maybe it wouldn't have felt as small if Jack's furniture had been suited to a house of this type. The London flat had been part of a converted Georgian building with high ceilings and big sash windows that let in lots of light and were the perfect backdrop for their modern oversized sofas. The cottage, on the other hand, had low beamed ceilings. The smaller of the two sofas had been shoe-horned under the front window; the larger sofa straddled the corner of the room, too long to fit against either of the walls. It was something else that would have to go; something else that would have to be sorted. It was crazy really, but the small things like this made him miss Alice more than ever. The day-to-day hassles of life felt almost overwhelming when there was no one to share them with.

The packing cases would never have ended up stuffed in the front room if Alice had still been alive. She'd have labelled them room-by-room, and unpacked them in a flurry of activity, so they'd have felt settled within hours of moving in. Setting down Toby in his car seat in the middle of the chaos, Jack sighed and wondered if he'd ever manage to make it feel like home.

'What do you think then, Tobes? Have we done the right thing?' His son was still sleeping peacefully, his long dark lashes sweeping onto his cheeks, just as his mother's had done. For the first two weeks after she died, Toby had looked at the door every time it opened, as if he was waiting for his mother to walk through it. He'd just started sleeping properly again, something which Jack could only envy.

The thought of unpacking the cases was exhausting and he badly needed a drink. He didn't want to go down that path though, drinking to blot things out. His stomach rumbled. He'd forgotten how to feel hunger in the past few weeks and his clothes were hanging off him. He made sure Toby was fed three times a day, but only picked at his own food. Everything tasted of nothing. He knew he needed energy to help him face what had to be done, which was the only thing that made him eat at all.

Leaving Toby asleep in the front room, Jack went through to the kitchen. Thankfully, Pam had packed up the kitchen at the flat. She'd been sobbing while she did it, about how she was losing her grandson as well as her daughter, but somehow she'd still managed to label all the boxes correctly. She'd even packed one large plastic tub, for immediate opening, which contained the kettle, tea, coffee and milk and a packet of chocolate biscuits.

As he walked back across the hallway with a mug of tea and the unopened biscuits, the letterbox rattled and a newspaper was shoved half through. Jack pulled it out and took it into the front room. He'd barely read a word since Alice had died and he still couldn't write, but maybe the free local paper would be manageable. He needed to find out a bit more about what went on in St Nicholas Bay, for Toby's sake at least.

The front page of the newspaper heralded St Nicholas

Bay's forthcoming carnival and reported damage to the beach huts on the sea front, due to unexpectedly high winds the week before. Peckham seemed a world away.

Flicking past the obituaries, so he didn't have to acknowledge anyone else's loss, Jack found himself pausing at the job section. He didn't actually *need* any more work; his online teaching would pay the bills and Alice's accident had been covered by her life insurance, meaning that the mortgage on the London flat had been paid off straight away. He'd felt terrible about that at first, not wanting any profit to come from her death, no matter how irrational it was. Craig had made him see sense when he'd talked about refusing to accept it. It was for Toby and it would make his future more secure.

The flat had been easy to rent out and he was using less than half of the income it generated to rent the cottage in St Nicholas Bay. So there was money left over after that which, with his online teaching, would make life reasonably comfortable for them – financially at least. Scanning through the ads, he saw clearly that nothing local would suit him. He didn't have any experience working in a café or gift shop and caring for the elderly definitely wasn't something he was cut out for.

On the last page of the jobs, though, something took him by surprise – a large advertisement for the local college. Among the requests for learning support assistants, a chef and a human resources officer, there was a vacancy for sessional lecturers and a list of the specialisms the college was after. One of them was for a creative-writing tutor and, although the hourly rate was a lot less than he was used to, something about it made him read on.

By the time Toby started to stir, and before he had

time to change his mind, Jack had completed the online application on his laptop. It was only for a few hours a week, split over two days, and he might not even get it, but it would be good for him to have a reason to get outside the four walls of the cottage at least a couple of times a week. It would be good for Toby, too. Jack would find him somewhere to go for those few hours, if he got the job – somewhere Toby could mix with other children and not have to spend all his time with a dad who cried more often than he did.

�֍

Nancy was lying full length along the sofa, luxuriating in being alone, when she heard David's key in the lock. She'd been watching one of the real-life medical programmes that she loved, about accident and emergency, which David always said put him off his dinner. Instead they'd usually end up watching some action movie that had far more blood and guts than any of the documentaries she wanted to watch. That was life in a couple, though; it was all about compromise.

'How was the meeting, Nance?' David kissed her forehead and somehow managed to shove her into an upright seated position in a single manoeuvre. 'Turn this rubbish off, love.' The remote was already in his hand and the screen was instantly filled by twenty-two men chasing a ball around a football pitch.

'They went for it.' She smiled, despite the flash of irritation prickling her skin at the interruption to what had been a pretty perfect night up until then. 'They're going to rent the old community centre to us for a hundred pounds.'

'What a week? That'll be a bit steep to cover, won't it?' He was looking around her, even as he spoke, his mind already more on the football than on what she was saying.

'No, for the whole of the first year.'

'Wow, that's brilliant!' David actually gave her the benefit of his full attention for a minute. 'Even Princess Olivia should be pleased about that.'

'Don't call her that.' Digging him in the ribs, she shuffled down the sofa a bit. He had a habit of draping himself all over her rather than just sitting next to her, and lately she'd had to fight the urge to push him away.

'Why not? She acts like a princess and you're her Cinderella.' Taking advantage of her moving further away, he stretched out, resting his feet on her lap. 'Well done though, babe.'

That was it, the end of the conversation – her thirty seconds at the centre of David's attention over, losing out to a bunch of sweaty men in polyester shorts. She shut her eyes and drifted off.

✤

'You awake, babe?' David was nuzzling her neck, disturbing the brilliant dream she'd been having.

'I am *now*.' She pulled away, the nibbling of her ear getting more insistent.

'Shall we go up then or do it down here?' He'd moved so he was straddling her and pushing his groin into hers.

'Do what?' She knew exactly what he meant, but she was stalling, searching her recently awoken brain for an excuse to get out of sex.

'Come on, babe, you know you enjoy it when we get going.' His hand slid up her body inside her top, unhooking her bra before she even had a chance to protest.

'And they say romance is dead.'

He stood up and unbuttoned his jeans, the next move in a repertoire he followed like clockwork. When she had more time, and The Merry Players were up and running, maybe she'd have more energy to think about how to inject something different into their sex life. If they were going to be doing it for the next forty years, they'd definitely have to work on it. But right now it was easier just to go with it. Closing her eyes again, she felt his weight move back on top of her and her mind drifted back to the community theatre plans.

CHAPTER SIX

'Morning Mrs O'Brien.' Barbara was by far the nicest care assistant at the home. When she looked up at Ruth, her plump cheeks were bright red from the exertion of wiping the breakfast table down. 'Your John's certainly doing all right for visitors today. You're the second this morning.'

'Really? Let me guess, did the Prime Minister pop down to see how the care-home system is taking the strain? And I've told you a hundred times to call me Ruth – we've known each other long enough, for goodness sake.'

'Don't be daft, *Ruth*. Who else would it be but your Nancy?' Barbara straightened up and smiled. 'She was in before work to give John his breakfast. I wish my Carys was a bit more like her – never comes near or by unless she wants to cadge a bit of cash to pay the bills. She went to school with your Nancy, too, but they must have learnt very different things.'

'She's a great girl.' Ruth returned the smile. There wasn't much she liked about going to the home to visit John, but Barbara always managed to cheer her up a bit. 'I don't know what I'd do without my daughter, but if it was down to my Mark…'

'Ooh, I'd almost forgotten you had a son.'

'You and me both, Barbara, you and me both.' Giving her a quick wave, Ruth forced herself to push through the double doors that led from the dining area into the day room.

The grey room might have been a better name for it. Three of the four walls in the room were lined with faux-leather chairs, easy to wipe down, and every one of them was beige or a muted grey. The walls were off white and most of the residents wore zip up cardigans in yet more shades of grey or beige.

A host of grey heads, and one or two bald ones, turned to look at Ruth as she entered the room. Not one of them acknowledged her, their faces as blank as if she had never visited before, despite seeing her every other day. Worst of all, the head of the man she'd come to see, whose hair was still dark with only the odd fleck of grey, didn't even turn. He was so noticeable in the room, a good ten years younger than almost all the other residents. He shouldn't be there – he didn't belong.

'John?' She moved across the room to stand next to his chair. He was looking out into the sunroom that led off from the dayroom, but there was nobody in there. Breakfast was only just over and it would be several hours before the care assistants moved the residents out of the dayroom and into the sunshine. It didn't really matter, though; every one of the patients was in a world on their own. They didn't care which room they were in.

John turned to look at her and there was a brief leap of optimism that today would be the day he remembered her. It had been months since he'd given even a hint of that. But there was something in his eyes every time he looked at her for the first time, as though the memory was imprinted somewhere, even if it had long since left his consciousness.

'Your hair's pretty.' John smiled and Ruth smoothed down her fading red hair. Most of its colour came out of a bottle these days, but he'd always loved the burnished auburn it had been when they'd first met.

'Thank you, darling.' She kissed the top of his head like she might a child's. If she tried to kiss his cheek it would sometimes upset him. She'd learnt that from experience; she was a stranger to him, after all.

'My girl's coming today.' He pulled away from her, uncomfortable at her show of affection.

'Nancy's been already, love.' Pulling up the chair next to him, Ruth fought the urge to take one of his large hands in her own. Those hands had worked so hard to give his family the life that he'd wanted for them. They still looked young enough to work, as though nothing had changed – in fact, the change had been so quick and so drastic that Ruth was still in shock.

'No, my girl's coming. She's coming and we're going to the beach.' John was getting distressed, the strong hands clenching the arms of his horrible beige chair.

Ruth knew better than to argue with him. It didn't do either of them any good. All it caused was more upset and it didn't help John remember. If anything it just intensified the fog of confusion.

'That'll be nice. What will you do on the beach?'

'I'm going to hold her hand, take her for a swim and ask her to be my girl for ever.' He smiled, and it took every ounce of her self-control not to take his hand in hers, as she'd been fighting to do for the past five minutes. She remembered that day well enough for both of them.

'It sounds lovely. She's a lucky girl.' And she had been. She hadn't realised how much at the time, of course. Perhaps no one ever does until it's too late.

41

'I've got a ring here.' John patted his pocket, a sudden look of panic flashing across his sky-blue eyes when he realised there was nothing there. 'I had it, I had it!' Before she could stop him, he'd got to his feet and was pacing, still searching through his pockets.

'It's all right, John. It'll be in your room. We'll look together, don't panic, *please*.' Tears blurred Ruth's vision as she placed her hand on his arm, desperate to calm him down and take away the pain that his confusion caused him.

'Are you sure?' Turning towards her, he gave her a look of hope which replaced the panic. She nodded.

'I like you.' John smiled and sat back down, his relief tangible.

'I like you, too.' This time Ruth didn't fight the urge to hold his hand. For a moment he was hers again and she'd cherish every second.

❈

'Morning.' Nancy entered the performing-arts staffroom, negotiating her way around a piece of scenery that Trevor from art and design had kindly prepared for her, but didn't have space to store.

It had been a week since she'd got the go-ahead to use the old community centre as a theatre. She couldn't wait to have her own venue – her own space to dress for shows and set up the way she wanted – instead of working round a college principal who seemed to believe that performing arts were a total waste of time and money.

'Morning!' Maisie popped up from behind the two-foot-high divider that separated their desks, supposedly to allow them to concentrate on their marking. Whoever designed them had clearly never worked in the same space as a group of drama and music lecturers. They'd have needed lead-lined offices to get any quiet work done.

'What are you looking so upbeat about?' Dumping her bag on her desk, Nancy walked over to the little kitchen area behind Maisie's chair. 'Did no one tell you it was Monday?'

'I know, and you can make me another coffee just for reminding me.' Maisie shoved her cup into Nancy's hand before she had a chance to argue. 'But they've finally appointed a scriptwriting tutor, who apparently has experience coming out of his ears. Even Principal Trunchball is excited!' Maisie grinned. The nickname for their humourless principal had entertained them through hours of boring meetings about exam results and student-retention data.

'That's great, but it's not going to lessen your workload, is it?' Nancy handed the cup back to her friend. Maisie was as enthusiastic about teaching music as she was about the band she spent most of her free time playing in, The Beachcombers. But between the two she barely had time for a life. Like every public-sector organisation, the college had wanted more and more in recent years out of fewer and fewer staff. So another music lecturer might have warranted Maisie's display of enthusiasm, but not a scriptwriter.

'No, it won't lessen my load, that's true, but you keep nagging me to get a private life and apparently he is H-O-T – hot!' Maisie grinned and licked her lips. 'Imagine, someone hot at Bay College? Come on, we've both been working here over five years and there hasn't been a single hottie in all that time!'

'I wouldn't know, what with being an engaged woman and all.' Nancy affected an innocent expression and took a sip of coffee, trying not to think about Fraser. As close as she was to Maisie, the breakdown of her relationship with her friend's brother was something they just didn't discuss. And, let's face it, no one wanted to hear their brother described as hot, did they?

'Yeah right, and I'm sure David never notices a pretty face either.' Maisie grinned again. 'Still at least we won't be competing for the new guy's attention.'

'Only you would say something like that out loud! Where is he anyway?' Nancy glanced around the empty staffroom. 'I know everyone else is teaching, but surely they haven't put him to work already?'

'Apparently Trunchball is showing him around campus. *Personally*, would you believe?' Maisie shuddered. 'We'll just have to hope that doesn't send him running for the hills before he even makes it as far as the staffroom.'

Almost as soon as the words were out of her mouth, the staffroom door swung open, framing Principal Jefferies in the doorway.

'Just Nancy and Maisie in at the moment, I'm afraid, but I'm sure they'll show you where to find everything.' Mary Jefferies ushered a tall, slim man into the room. He had dark wavy hair and even darker shadows under his eyes. Maisie's gossip was spot on: he would have been really good-looking if he lost the haunted look, and a smile certainly wouldn't have gone amiss.

'I'll leave you to it then, Jack.' Trunchball didn't bother addressing them, her smile directed entirely at the new lecturer. Turning on her stilettoed heel, she left the staffroom – seemingly the only person in the world who didn't realise oversized shoulder pads had gone out of fashion.

'Nice to meet you, Jack.' Maisie launched herself from behind her desk and was shaking his hand enthusiastically. 'I'm Maisie. I teach music.'

'Right.' For a moment he just looked at her and then seemed to shake himself, as though remembering he was supposed to be polite and make the effort to engage in conversation. 'That's nice. It must be rewarding to teach a subject like that.' Maisie just nodded in response, in danger of looking like the village idiot if Nancy didn't step in.

'And I'm Nancy. I teach drama.' Holding out her hand, she looked at him again. The air of sadness around him was palpable.

'I guess we might be working together then.' Jack finally managed a smile, but there wasn't an ounce of enthusiasm in his voice. It looked like it was going to be a *very* long term.

CHAPTER SEVEN

Jack walked back along the seafront from the college, hoping it would clear his head of the unwanted thoughts that crowded in as soon as he had a moment to himself. The Indian summer had lasted all of two weeks, and a mid-September wind was making up for its late arrival by driving the waves towards the beach with such force that it sent them crashing against the sea wall of the small harbour.

The golden triangle of sand was almost covered by the high tide, and flanked on all sides by brightly coloured beach huts. There were a few late holidaymakers braving a walk along the small pier which stuck out from the harbour, just past the little chapel dedicated to the patron saint of sailors – St Nicholas himself. Alice had dragged them along the pier, when the three of them had come down a couple of weeks before she'd died, and Toby had eaten several handfuls of sand on the beach. Had it really only been a few months ago? It felt like at least as many lifetimes.

If he could just talk to her now and ask her if he'd done the right thing by taking the job. The staff he'd met at the college seemed friendly enough, and it was only for a couple of days a week, but friendship was the last thing he wanted. He just wanted a distraction for a few hours a week, a brief respite from thinking about what was and what might have been.

'Sorry, mate.' As he rounded the bend past the old lighthouse, the narrowest point of the promenade, a lad in his twenties glanced Jack's shoulder with his own. The younger man was holding tightly to the hand of a pretty girl, seemingly oblivious to everyone else until the moment his shoulder made contact with Jack's.

'No problem,' said Jack. He swallowed a gulp of salty air as he spoke. Maybe he'd have a beer with Craig when he got in. There was friendship that needed no explanations about Alice or what had happened to her. Talking about it to strangers and having to see the looks that crossed their faces was part of meeting new people now. The sympathetic tone of their voices or, worse still, that rabbit-in-the-headlights look they got when they had absolutely no idea what to say in response.

Craig had taken time off work and come down to look after Toby for Jack's first couple of days in the job. He was staying on for the weekend, too, and Jack had actually looked forward to it for the five days since they'd organised it – the first time he'd looked forward to anything since the accident.

The path up from the beach to the end of the road where his rented home nestled in a row of former fisherman's cottages was steep. Jack enjoyed climbing it, though; it robbed him of his breath and that, along with the sting of the wind on his face, made him feel alive.

'Honey, I'm home!' Walking through to the lounge, he called out, using the greeting the two of them had jokingly perfected when they'd shared a flat a decade before, after Craig had first come over from Australia. They'd struck up a friendship when Jack had been on a gap year and, travelling through Perth, had found a casual job in a fish-gutting factory to help pay his way on to Sydney. Craig, a hard-up student on a summer break from university, had already been doing the job for a week when they met. Spending a month together, day in day out, ankle deep in fish guts, had forged a bond of friendship that neither of them expected.

'Jack!' Craig sprang away from another body on the sofa with whom his arms and legs had been entangled until a split second before. He looked like an adulterous husband caught in the act by the unanticipated arrival of his wife. 'We weren't expecting you home so ... early.'

'Clearly.' Jack's voice sounded flat even to his own ears. 'I had no idea that you and Selena were ...' He wasn't sure how to finish the sentence, so he didn't bother. 'I didn't even realise you were down here, Selena.' His wife's best friend and his closest mate were together. If Alice had still been alive she'd have been delighted and, back then, Jack probably would have been too. As it was he didn't know what he felt. Probably nothing. That seemed his default setting of late.

'She's staying in one of the rooms above Fezziwig's. We were just going to spend the time you were working together. We didn't want you to know.' Craig looked at his bare feet; at least the rest of him was still clothed. That was something. Jack had made love to Alice on that sofa and the thought that someone else could impose themselves on that memory made his chest go tight.

'Didn't want me to know what?'

'What Craig is trying to say, not very well, admittedly,' Selena had got to her feet and was squeezing Jack's shoulder, 'is that since we got together we haven't wanted to rush to tell you, in case it made things worse.'

'Things couldn't be worse. I'm guessing you got together at Alice's funeral? Let's face it, there's not much that's worse than burying your wife. But it doesn't mean I want everyone else to be as miserable as I am.' He put his hand over hers, the feel of a woman's hand in his own triggering another memory, before he gently slid her hand off his shoulder. 'I'm going up to see Toby.'

'He's asleep. We've got the monitor on, we weren't just sidelining him, mate.' Craig still looked mortified and Jack wanted to shake him. If even his oldest friend couldn't be natural around him, what hope was there for life to get back to some sort of normality again?

'I know. It's fine, really.' Taking the monitor, he climbed the stairs to his son's tiny box room at the back of the cottage. It had a warmer feeling than the bigger second bedroom, which Jack had made up for Craig. It felt like a place that would keep Toby safe.

He wanted to talk to Alice, tell her about Craig and Selena, ask her what she thought about the chances of it working out. A thousand times since she'd gone he'd thought of something he wanted to say to her, something so simple, and it knocked the wind out of him every time he remembered he couldn't. Instead, Jack sank into the small armchair next to Toby's cot, watching the boy's chest rise and fall – swallowing against his emotions until it felt like a golf ball-sized lump had lodged in his windpipe.

'Explain to me again why you've spent almost a month's maintenance money on underwear.' Nancy lay on Olivia's bed, watching her best friend twirl round and look at herself in the mirror, almost £300 worth of black silk barely covering her bum.

'I'm going on a second date with Greg and it's time to prove to myself and Miles that there are plenty of men out there who still would.' Olivia smoothed the fabric down. 'It's almost a shame to put my dress on, it cost a fraction of what these French knickers did. Actually, that's a point. Can you take a photo of me before I get dressed?'

'Dare I ask why?' Nancy took the iPhone off the bedside table. 'Do you want me to use this? Are you planning on sending it somewhere?'

'Sure am!'

'Please be careful, Liv. You don't know enough about this Greg. If you split up, he might end up posting it all over the internet.'

'Oh, don't worry. I'm going to write a text to Greg to go with it, but I'm actually going to send it to Miles and then pretend I did it by accident! Let him see what he's missing.'

'Well, I'll give David some credit – since he set you up with Greg you're like a different woman!'

Nancy smiled. It was brilliant to see Olivia back to her old self, even if that meant she was spending money like she still had full access to Miles's bank account and whiling away half the evening looking at herself in the mirror. Back in the pre-divorce days she'd been vain but fun, the life and soul of every party. Nancy had always known where she stood. Olivia was someone to have a great night with, but not necessarily someone you could rely on. Since the divorce, and Nancy's dad falling ill, they'd been much more to each other, and hopefully this new phase in their relationship wouldn't change that.

'It's so good to dress up like I used to,' Olivia said in a muffled voice as she pulled a sequinned cocktail dress over her head. 'Even if it's only for a dinner and dance at the golf club.' She finally emerged from the neck of the dress. 'I wish you were coming though, Nance.'

'I'm far more use to you as a babysitter.' Nancy

winked at her and sneaked a quick spray of Olivia's favourite Chanel perfume, which stood on her bedside cabinet. 'Anyway, I hate those golf club dos at the best of times, and I'm certainly not going to go to one on my own, just to wait and see if David finishes work in time to turn up. Not even to keep you company. I'd much rather play Monopoly with the kids.'

'Thanks for agreeing to stay the night, you know, *just in case.*' Olivia grinned, spraying herself liberally with perfume and making them both cough. 'I'll tell you all about it in the morning.'

'Damn right you will!' Nancy lay back against the pillows, the bitter taste of perfume in the back of her throat. 'It's the very least you can do!'

CHAPTER EIGHT

'I've called you all here to make a very important announcement.' Principal Jefferies pulled her lips into a sinister smile; the Joker had nothing on her.

'Probably to tell us we're working Christmas Day this year,' Maisie whispered not very discreetly into Nancy's ear, causing sniggers in the row in front.

'More likely another round of redundancies so that she can pay herself more than the paltry hundred k she's getting at the moment. Mind you, with a mouth like hers, she must spend that on lipstick alone.' Trevor, from the art department, turned and winked at Nancy, sending a shower of dandruff swirling into the air around him – like a snow globe nobody wants. Lovely though he was, it paid to hold your breath when Trevor was around.

Principal Jefferies, clearly unamused by the outbreak of giggling towards the back of the staff restaurant, paused for effect – ever the teacher in front of a class full of naughty children.

'As I was saying, I am sure there has been a lot of conjecture about the purpose of today's meeting.' Mary Jefferies's mouth deflated like a punctured tyre. 'I'm afraid it's bad news.'

'Told you.' Trevor thankfully didn't turn his head again, so it was safe to take a deep breath.

Maisie was wringing her hands in her lap and Nancy had to fight the urge not to follow suit. They all had bills to pay and, even though she was quite keen to drop some of her hours at the college to build up the community theatre, she was reliant on a regular salary to give them some security. David's earnings weren't fixed and it could be famine or feast with him. They needed some guaranteed income.

The only person who didn't look worried was Jack Williams, but then they were hardly likely to make him redundant, were they? He'd only been appointed a few days before.

'Some of you may have heard,' Mary Jefferies clutched a hand to her chest and Nancy wondered briefly if she should ask her to audition for The Merry Players, 'but for those of you that haven't, I have a feeling that this is going to be an awful shock. You see, I'm leaving.' She paused and a ripple went around the room. How many people were, like Nancy, barely resisting the urge to punch the air?

'The governors haven't yet decided who to appoint to take over my legacy of continuous improvement at the college.' Mary's ego had its own shadow. 'It's a difficult decision and so they've decided to appoint an acting principal for now. I am sure that some of you will be pleased to hear that your former colleague, Fraser James, who was previously head of the performing-arts department, has been seconded back to the college to take on the role.' She said the words *performing arts* like they were something she'd discovered stuck to the bottom of her shoe and Nancy felt her short-lived joy dissipate almost as quickly as it had arrived.

'When did she say she was going?' Struggling to make herself heard over Trevor and his colleagues from the art department, Nancy grimaced. The art lecturers, who were second on Mary Jefferies's hit-list of expendable staff, were loudly singing 'Ding, Dong, The Witch is Dead' as they walked back to their staff room.

'At Christmas, apparently.' Maisie gave Nancy a knowing look. She was probably the only person who understood how torn she felt about Fraser coming back. 'You okay, Nance?'

'Just a bit shocked, that's all, that Fraser's coming back and that he agreed to be seconded here after he was so keen to get out of the Bay. Did you know?'

'Oh come on, you know my brother better than that. He didn't say a word! Anyway, you've moved on now. You've got David.' Even Maisie didn't sound convinced.

'I suppose it'll give me the push I need to move on from other stuff too.' Nancy was desperately trying to do some mental arithmetic without resorting to counting on her fingers. Maths had never been a strong point.

'You're not going to leave, are you?' Maisie caught hold of her arm. 'You can't leave me here with this lot. You're the only person that keeps me sane. Having my big brother as your boss is hardly something to look forward to either!'

'Don't worry, I'm not planning on leaving altogether, but I was working out if I could drop some of my hours now that I'm going to have some income from the community theatre. I'm sure Sarah-Jane would take them on.'

'Yuck, don't make me spend more time with Sarah-Jane. She's forgotten how to get around the campus on her own, she's spent so long with her head up Trunchball's arse!'

'I can't be around Fraser five days a week. I know he's your brother, but things between us didn't end that easily.' She didn't add that she could hardly rely on Olivia to do the practical, boring jobs at theatre that would ensure bills were paid and subscriptions collected.

'I suppose it would be difficult,' Maisie said. 'I told Fraser he was being a total arse at the time.'

'What's this Fraser guy like then?' A voice behind them made Nancy jump. It was Jack Williams, and she wondered how much he'd heard.

'Oh, you know,' Maisie giggled, linking her other arm through his, forcing them to step out at a uniformed pace, as if they were in some strange five-legged race, 'tall, blond, but nothing special.' She winked at Nancy. Only a sister could describe Fraser like that.

'At least his background is in performing arts. Most principals these days seem to be all about the money.' Jack didn't sound as though he cared much either way and Nancy found herself wondering why he was working at the college – what his story was.

'You'd think so.' She struggled to keep her voice even, memories of the final day before Fraser had left the college flooding her emotions. 'But his ambition is stronger than pretty much any other alliance he might have. So I wouldn't count your chickens, or your teaching hours.' If she sounded bitter, she didn't much care about that either. Maisie would understand and she had a feeling that Jack wouldn't be around long enough for it to matter.

❋

Jack took the coastal path home again. Part of him would have liked to join the others for a drink to celebrate Principal Jefferies's departure. Not because he had any particular axe to grind or because he wanted the company of his new colleagues, but because he didn't want to go back to his empty house. Pam had taken Toby to her place for the week, Craig and Selena had left, and Toby wouldn't be back until the following afternoon. He hadn't wanted to let his son go, even for a minute, but the childcare situation for his slightly odd hours at the college hadn't been resolved as easily as expected and he couldn't keep Toby to himself all the time – as much as he wanted to.

In the end he stayed on at the college, working on his session plans, as late as he could while the evening classes were being held. At about nine o'clock the caretaker had turfed him out of the staffroom, saying he needed to lock up and jokingly asking Jack if he had a home to go to. He'd wanted to say no, that he had *a house* to go to not a home, but he doubted if the elderly caretaker would have wanted to hear all that.

The sea was calm and metallic in the fading light. On the corner of the last avenue that led down to the coastal path, before the hotels and restaurants, a car was parked and was rocking slightly from side to side. Jack grinned despite the heaviness in his chest. It didn't take a detective to work out what was going on. Young love, probably. Or an illicit liaison.

Alice would have laughed if he'd told her about the rocking car when he got home. Jack shook his head; he had to accept he was no longer part of a pair. There was no one waiting at home for him to talk to and no mates locally he could meet for a drink and laugh about it with over a pint. At some point he'd need to make a life for himself again, if they were going to stay here. Toby would need friends, and perhaps one day he would too. Maybe he'd take up Maisie's invitation to go and see her band play in a few weeks' time, and take the risk that a familiar tune might make him break down. He had to start somewhere.

Nancy had barely got in from Fezziwig's when the phone rang. Her head was fuzzy from the double whammy of celebrating Mary Jefferies's departure and drowning her worries about Fraser's return. She vaguely recalled firing off an email to Mary saying that she was formally giving notice on the personal-tutor role that made up half of her hours. Automatically crossing her fingers that the call wasn't something to do with her dad, she picked up the handset.

'It's me, babe.' David sounded like he was in a pub. 'I need you to pick me up.'

'I can't drive. I've been drinking.' She couldn't for the life of her work out why he would need picking up. He was supposed to be working late again, pulling an all-nighter.

'It's okay. I don't need you to drive. I just need you to come with your credit card. My car's been clamped and I've left my wallet at work.' His tone was impatient, as if she was already supposed to have met with him and had forgotten.

'Where are you?' She picked up the pen beside the phone and doodled on the notepad. If he was out of town she'd have to get a taxi to wherever the car had been clamped and she could barely remember her own name, let alone an unfamiliar address.

'I'm at the police station. In town.'

'The police clamped your car?' Nancy's brain definitely wasn't processing properly.

'Yeah, it was causing an obstruction across some old bloke's driveway or something and when they came to have a go at me about it, I got a bit lairy.' Part of Nancy wanted to put the phone down and leave him to take responsibility for his actions, but she didn't.

'Can't you come and get it yourself?'

'They're not going to let me use your credit card, are they?' He didn't actually call her stupid, but it was definitely implied.

'Okay, I'll be there in ten minutes.' She replaced the handset, not waiting for the thanks that she knew she probably wouldn't get. Was this really the man she wanted to have kids with? He'd have to grow up a hell of a lot himself first, though it was hard to imagine that happening.

Pulling on her boots, Nancy trudged out of the front door, taking the alleyway at the end of the road that led down the steep hill to the coastal path. She passed Olivia's car as she reached the avenues and wondered which house Greg lived in. Either way it looked like Olivia had decided to spend the night at his. She certainly seemed to be making up for lost time.

St Nicholas Bay still had its own police station. It was hardly *CSI Las Vegas*, though. Clamping David's car had probably been the biggest thing that had happened all day. She checked her pockets again, to make sure the credit card hadn't jumped out, and popped another mint into her mouth. Smelling of the vodka martinis she'd been downing was unlikely to impress the duty sergeant when she turned up at his desk.

The strip lighting in the police station reception area buzzed like an angry wasp. It took a moment or two for Nancy's eyes to adjust to the brightness.

She'd met the burly sergeant before when he'd come in to talk to her tutor group about the perils of drink-driving. He was talking to two colleagues who leant against one end of the reception desk. They were so engrossed in their conversation that none of them noticed her.

'You mean they were actually full-on naked?' The young WPC giggled and the officer next to her laughed too.

'Yeah. Apparently they were so busy doing it, John had to knock on the window three times. He was quite surprised there were only two of them in there, the way the car was rocking..' The sergeant turned slightly and caught sight of Nancy, straightened up and arranged his face into a professional smile.

'Can I help you, madam?' His colleagues melted away from the reception desk, but she could still hear them laughing after they'd disappeared through a side door.

'I had a telephone call from David Thornton to come and pay the fee to get his car released from your clampers.' The sergeant's lips twitched as she spoke; he was having serious trouble maintaining his professional stance.

'And did you bring him some trousers, madam? The ones he'd taken off got badly ripped during his arrest.' The sergeant, who didn't seem to recognise her from their meeting at the college, looked as though laughter was bubbling inches from the surface.

'He wasn't wearing any trousers? I don't understand ...' She paused, slowly putting two and two together. But that couldn't be right. If David had been caught without any clothes on, it would have been because he was getting changed in his van for his night shift. She knew he'd done that before when he was running late for something. It couldn't be David caught *doing it* with someone else. He didn't have it in him. He was far too lazy to go out looking for a start.

'I think I should let him explain, madam.' The sergeant had looked down at her hand and couldn't have missed the chunky sapphire ring she still wasn't used to. 'I'll just check whether they've finished with him and we can sort out the paperwork for the car. He's been lent a pair of overalls that the CSIs normally wear for now, so he'll be fine to go home in those.'

Nancy didn't know what to say, so said nothing at all. She didn't really feel anything either. There was a strong possibility that David had been caught shagging another woman, but there was just a kind of numbness. There was none of that powder keg of emotion that had exploded on the day Fraser had told her he was leaving St Nicholas Bay, and her, behind.

Sinking onto one of the orange plastic seats, she waited, the clock ticking in a way that seemed louder than she'd ever noticed before.

Eventually the door beside the reception desk opened and David emerged, dressed in an overall that looked like it was made from dishcloth material. Nancy could see along the corridor. She didn't hear what David was saying to her, but something crossed her eye line and suddenly everything was crystal clear. About twenty feet away and dressed much more as she was used to seeing her, Nancy saw the other half of the equation.

'Looks like you and Olivia have been having fun.' Standing up, she yanked the engagement ring off her finger and handed it to David. 'You've got three choices as to what you can do with this ...' He started to protest, offer some weak excuse, but she waved her newly naked hand at him. 'You can (a) put it back in the Christmas cracker you got it from, (b) see if they'll take it in exchange for getting your van unclamped or (c) shove it up your arse!'

Turning on her heel and so angry that she was oblivious to any response from him, she stormed out of the police station, slamming the door behind her.

CHAPTER NINE

Maisie's sofa was lumpy. Uncomfortable didn't even begin to describe the experience of sleeping – or more accurately not-sleeping – on it. Nancy couldn't complain. She was just grateful that her friend had still been awake when she'd knocked on her door at almost midnight, and that she'd given up her sofa without asking a thousand questions about what had happened. Nancy could have gone to her mum's house, but there a thousand questions would have been just the tip of the iceberg. Maisie had taken the holdall, hastily stuffed with the clothes Nancy had managed to grab from the cottage after running back from the police station, and accepted a potted version of the story without further interrogation. As far as she was concerned, David was a complete prat anyway, so she didn't seem that surprised.

'Breakfast?' Maisie poked her head around the living-room door and Nancy fought the urge to throw the covers over her head and lie there, possibly forever.

'I'm not sure I can face it.'

'Rubbish.' Maisie plonked herself down on the end of the sofa, squashing Nancy's feet. Her Batman onesie wasn't the most calming sight first thing in the morning. 'This calls for a breakfast at Gav's.'

Gav's was an old-fashioned café, right on the seafront,

at the end of St Nicholas Bay's promenade. The owner looked about a hundred years old but did the best fry-ups in the known world, and had resisted calls to rename Gav's Caff to fit the Dickens theme, like most other places in the Bay.

'I should get out of your hair.' Nancy sat up and almost tipped Maisie onto the floor.

'Nope, what you should do is sort out your own hair. You look like you've been caught in a tsunami.' Maisie grinned. 'And then, my girl, we'll go down to Gav's, eat twelve-million calories each and work out what the hell you're going to do next.'

Nancy put a hand up to her head. Even she had to admit the wildness of her red curls had risen to a new level. Maybe she could sell some of it to make wigs. She'd need to get hold of some money fast, one way or the other. Catching sight of her reflection in Maisie's TV, she shuddered. On second thoughts, not even the desperately bald wanted hair like hers.

❀

Half an hour later, showered and with hair more or less under control, they were on their way down to the beachside café. The small mercy was that it was a Saturday. Having to go into work and start explaining to everyone where the 'bling ring' – as her colleagues had christened it – had disappeared to was not something Nancy wanted to face.

'So what did he say?' Maisie linked her arm through Nancy's and propelled her towards Gav's Caff.

'Not a lot.' Screwing up her face, she tried to remember. 'Well, he might have done, but I wasn't really listening.'

'Was that him when your phone was constantly

pinging with text messages this morning?'

'Yes, sorry. I switched it off last night, but I thought I'd better switch it on this morning in case there was anything about Dad, you know. It was just filled with messages from him, and *her*, saying it was a one-off and how sorry they were.' Nancy shrugged. Talk – much like the look of her discarded engagement ring – was cheap.

'And how did that make you feel?' Maisie had recently undertaken an Introduction to Counselling course as part of her personal-tutor training, and was much more in the mood to ask questions in the cold light of day. She had her head cocked to one side and was using the gentle but slightly patronising tone she reserved for the more needy of her students.

'Like I was listening to a load of bollocks.' Nancy managed a grin. 'I did get the whole story at least, which resolved a few questions, because I couldn't work out last night why his van had been clamped but they were talking about the two of them being caught naked in a *car*. Apparently, in their rush to get it on, or as David put it, "the moment of madness they both regretted", he parked his van over a disabled man's driveway and he couldn't get in or unload his wheelchair. His wife called the police to tow the van away and, when they came down to sort it out, they saw some "suspicious activity" in Olivia's people carrier. The police must actually have caught them having sex. David lost the plot a bit, I think, and had a right go at them and it all escalated from there. From what the police said, they were carted off to the station in the nude and the van ended up being impounded.'

'I know I shouldn't laugh,' Maisie's cheeks were already red with the effort of suppressing it, 'but I honestly don't think I can help it!'

'It's like something out of a farce, isn't it?' Nancy

sighed. 'Part of me is relieved to be out of things with David, and in a way I don't even blame him. If I'm honest, I never really loved him. He was a reaction to Fraser leaving and I think he knew it too. So what can I expect?'

'The decency for him to dump you before he has sex with someone else?' Maisie shook her head, as though Nancy had just asked her the most obvious question in the world.

'Well yes, there is that. But it's what Olivia did that hurts the most. Even worse, if Trunchball forces me to stick by my resignation, then I've got no choice but to carry on working with her at the drama group. I can't afford the rent on the cottage by myself. I can't live there with David. I'll have to move back in with Mum and you know what happened last time I went down that route. It's all of that that bothers me much more than splitting up with David. That says a lot about our relationship, doesn't it? If he'd chosen anyone but Olivia I might even have thanked him for giving us both a way out of something that was never going to work.'

'You know I'd let you live with me if I had a spare room, don't you?' Maisie squeezed her arm. 'And you can stay on the sofa in the meantime, for as long as you want.'

'Thanks, but you've done enough already. Anyway, Mum's got tons of room and she'll be thrilled to have me back.'

Maisie smiled, looking relieved the sofa surfing wouldn't last too long after all. 'She won't want to let you go.'

'I know and that's exactly what worries me.'

Gav's Caff was wall-to-wall vinyl and a marked contrast to the other cafés in town which were all shabby chic and reclaimed driftwood. It was no-nonsense and down to earth and, as a consequence, it was a struggle to find a free table, especially on a Saturday morning. There was a small patio area at the side of the café with one free table when Maisie and Nancy arrived. As the weather was dry and mild for September, and since they weren't in the mood for waiting for someone else to finish eating, they decided to sit outside. Their table was the closest one to the edge of the small wall at the front of the patio, giving them a sea view.

'The usual, ladies?' Gav's son, Alfie, came to their table, his blue-and-white apron straining where it tied around his ample girth. Nancy liked the fact that he looked as though he lived off the café's speciality breakfasts. You should never trust a skinny chef.

'God, has it come to that? We eat breakfast here so often that you know our orders by heart?' Maisie sucked in her cheeks, as though looking thinner might change the fact they'd consumed too many fry-ups in the past year.

'Not really.' Alfie winked, already walking away from their table. 'There's hardly anyone who doesn't ask for a full English, that's all. Tea or coffee?'

'One of each please, and make the coffee as strong as you can.' Nancy twisted the paper napkin in front of her into a tight ball.

'So, what are you going to do first?' Her friend leant forward, resting her elbows on the table.

'Wait until David heads for the golf club later and then go back to the cottage and pack up the rest of my stuff.' She felt tired at the thought of it. 'Will you give me a hand?'

'Of course. I'll even help you cut the crotches out of

all of his trousers if you like, and pour all his booze down the sink, but I don't know if my little Fiat will be up to the job. Won't you need a van?'

'That's the sad part. I'm twenty-eight years old and I think all my worldly goods will probably fit into four black bin bags. He can keep the furniture, and all my really personal bits – books, old photos and my stuff from uni – are still at Mum's.' Nancy sighed. 'I can't believe I'm moving back home again.'

'Do you have to?' Maisie paused as Alfie's wife made her way to their table with a tray of drinks.

'Yep, financially I'm in just about as tight a spot as possible.' Nancy took a big swig of coffee. 'Trunchball is bound to accept my resignation from the tutoring post. She hates me anyway and it'll be good for the budget if she can squeeze a bit more out of the rest of you.'

'Maybe. But when Fraser gets back, he'll up your hours for sure.'

'I wouldn't be so certain about that. Anyway, spending more time with Fraser is *not* a good idea in my current state. I know he's your brother and it's not that he isn't a decent guy, but going back there, well …' Trailing off, she warmed her hands on the cup for a minute. 'If I think my life has hit rock bottom now, how am I going to feel begging and grovelling to my ex-boyfriend to give me a few extra hours at the college?'

'Fair point.' Maisie's stomach gave a loud rumble as the smell of bacon drifted across the patio. 'But are you really going to be able to work with Olivia?'

'I'll have to. I thought about it for half the night, but if I don't do the community theatre project now, I'll never get another chance. Olivia won't be able to run it by herself, but she will bring in the other yummy-mummies. It's like a mafia down at that school. If I tell Olivia that she's out of the business, she'll persuade the rest of them to steer clear of the kids' club and that's where most of the income is going to come from.' Nancy leant back as their breakfasts arrived – no one did crispy bacon like Gav. 'One thing I do regret though is naming the bloody thing after her.'

They fell silent as they ate their breakfast. Maisie ploughed through hers as though she hadn't eaten for a week, and Nancy was lost in thought, passing most of the food on her plate over to her friend.

They ordered another drink and other diners came and went from the terrace. Nancy barely noticed what was going on around her and, from her seat near the wall, she couldn't see the other diners without turning round. Usually she loved nothing more than people watching, but her mind was too busy. The thought of being back at her mum's already felt suffocating, and guilt at feeling like that added to the boulder that seemed to have settled in her chest.

It wouldn't be easy telling her mum she was coming home while making it clear that it wouldn't be for ever. Ruth was lonely, and she might grab on to the possibility, even though at twenty-eight it was hardly likely Nancy would be moving home for good.

'What you need is a part-time job where you get accommodation thrown in. That would be the best solution.' Maisie furrowed her brow. Nancy could imagine the cogs whirring round her brain as she spoke.

'Not a lot of those about in St Nicholas Bay though, are there? Not unless I want to work in the care home where Dad lives or take a job housekeeping in one of the hotels. Even building up and then crushing Mum's hopes has got to be better than that. I know she doesn't want to be on her own, but I'm worried that she'll get too used to having me around to fill the void now Dad's not there. And after everything that happened when my grandmother died, I really don't want to put either of us through that again.'

'There might be one suitable job.'

A voice from the table behind them almost made Nancy drop her coffee cup. She hadn't noticed Jack Williams sit down on the terrace, but he'd clearly heard every word they'd been saying for some time. Nancy's face burnt as he folded over the newspaper he'd been reading. 'I'm sorry. I didn't mean to eavesdrop and I wasn't going to say anything, but I think we could maybe help each other out.'

'I don't know, I'm not looking for ...' She stumbled over her words, keen not to embarrass herself any further. She couldn't really respond when she hadn't given him a chance to explain.

'It's okay, don't panic.'

He smiled. Nancy had hardly seen him do that before and it changed his whole face.

'I know I'm almost a total stranger, but I've got a spare room and a very part-time job going. It might work out. Even if it just tides you over for a bit.'

'A job?' Maisie interjected and Nancy forced herself to close her mouth. He was almost the last person on earth she would have expected to offer to share his house with someone he barely knew. He seemed far too measured and closed-up for that.

'Of sorts.' Jack took a deep breath, as though bracing himself for a revelation. 'My son Toby's nine months old and I just need someone to look after him for a few hours a week and take him to and from nursery on the mornings that I'm working at college. My first classes on both days start at nine and the nursery hasn't got space for another baby until half past ten. They don't have the ratio of staff to children until after that apparently.'

'What about your wife?' Maisie was doing all the talking, something Nancy was grateful for.

'She's dead.' Jack's face was almost as deadpan as his voice.

'I'm sorry.' For the first time, Nancy managed to speak. A lot about Jack suddenly made sense. She didn't need to ask for details; with such a young child, the loss of his wife must have been very recent and it had clearly devastated him. It was written in his eyes.

'You'd be helping me out and you could live rent free in return.'

He didn't acknowledge her condolences and she was glad; she wouldn't have known what to say next anyway.

'But you don't know me. I might be a horrible housemate.' Nancy managed a rueful smile. 'In fact, I can almost guarantee it. I never put the top back on the toothpaste and I leave coffee rings like a gingerbread trail behind me, wherever I go.'

'I've been through worse. It would give Toby some stability, and as soon as the nursery has an earlier slot available you'd be free to move on if you wanted to.' Jack picked up his paper and stood up. 'I live in the same road as you, I think – 3 Elderberry Cottages, Maple Street.'

'I live at the other end.' Nancy caught herself a second too late. 'Well at least, *I did*.'

'Why don't you pop round this afternoon, after three? Toby will be back from my mother-in-law's by then and you can have a look around, get to know us a bit and decide if you want to give it a go.' Jack's dark eyes met hers briefly. 'See you later.' It should have been a question, not a statement. But he clearly knew she'd turn up and, much to her surprise, so did she.

71

'Well, that was ... *odd*.' Nancy sipped her coffee, which was nowhere near as appealing once it had gone cold.

'*I* wouldn't say no.' Maisie pulled a face, but she didn't sound bitter. 'After all, what's the worst that can happen?'

✳

'It's lovely to see you, darling, I wasn't expecting you.' Ruth looked up from where she was sitting on the sofa, the sight of her daughter lifting her spirits immediately. They always had Sunday lunch together, without fail, but seeing her on a Saturday afternoon was an unexpected bonus.

'I'm not interrupting, am I?' Nancy crossed the room and sat down heavily on the sofa, right next to Ruth.

'You could never interrupt, sweetheart, and let's face it, this Sudoku puzzle isn't going anywhere.' Ruth cast it to one side and looked at her daughter. Something was wrong.

'You're not still doing ten of those things a day, are you, Mum?'

'I read somewhere they keep your brain active, and if you do at least fifty of them a week they can stop you getting Alzheimer's.' The ugly word caught in her throat. She'd always thought it sounded like the name of a concentration camp, and the disease was almost as evil.

'I've told you before, if you take every bit of advice about how to stop you getting it, you'll be living off bananas and drinking filtered water while standing on your head.' Nancy squeezed her hand and Ruth knew it was because she really cared, even if she did sound a bit impatient from time to time.

'You didn't come here to give me a lecture about the

dangers of Sudoku though, did you? I'm your mother, I can tell there's something wrong.'

'I'm surprised you haven't heard.' Nancy sighed. 'It's the best bit of gossip they've had in St Nicholas Bay for years.'

'It's not your dad, is it?' Ruth wondered if her heart had actually skipped a beat. If he'd been caught in someone's bed again, she didn't think she could stand it. As much as she knew he couldn't help himself, the thought that other people might find it funny made her feel sick.

'No, it's not Dad. It's David.'

'Another woman?'

'Was it that obvious?'

Nancy looked troubled as she met Ruth's gaze and Ruth ached to take her daughter into her arms, to make it all better like she'd done when Nancy was small.

'He was always aiming too high with you. It's bound to make a man insecure and a fling is the ultimate confidence boost for men like that.' Ruth had half a mind to track David down and throttle him for hurting her daughter, but the other half of her wanted to shake his hand for setting her free.

'It was Olivia.' The words were bald, but Ruth didn't miss the catch of emotion in Nancy's voice.

'That bitch!' Ruth stood up, her fists curling into two tight balls. There was no question in her mind what she'd have liked to do to Olivia.

'Mum, don't get wound up about it. It won't do any good.' Nancy sounded so tired it broke a little bit of Ruth's heart. 'We've both got to get past it – you, but especially me. I'm going to have to carry on working with her.'

'You don't have to. You could come home, live with

me.' Ruth tried to keep her voice steady, but she couldn't keep the glimmer of hope from it. 'Two can live almost as cheaply as one. It would be great, just like the old days.'

'I would have loved to, Mum, you know that, but it would be even harder on both of us when I leave again, and you know I'd have to one day.' There was such honesty in Nancy's eyes that Ruth had to fight to keep the tears out of her own.

Nancy had come home once before when her grandmother died and it had ended up changing her life beyond all recognition when Ruth had needed her too much to let her leave. No wonder her daughter looked terrified at the prospect of doing it again.

'Anyway, I've promised to stay with a friend who's lost his wife and needs some help looking after his son. We can help each other out, a bit of childminding for some free rent. To be honest, I think he's lonely.'

Ruth nodded and smiled in all the right places, somehow resisting the urge to scream, 'Me too'.

CHAPTER TEN

'So what are your plans for taking care of Toby now that you're going out to work?' Pam made it sound like he'd be hanging out in a lap-dancing club.

'It's sorted. Don't worry about it.' Jack had wanted to take Toby from her at the door, but she had made a three-hour round trip and it was too rude not to at least invite Pam in for a coffee. Unfortunately, she was only too keen to accept.

'Well, of course *I* worry about him. He's my grandson and the only thing I've got left of Alice.' She gave him a look that spoke volumes about her opinion of his parenting capabilities, as if he couldn't be trusted to make a safe decision. Perhaps best not to tell her about his rash solution to the problem. After all, he still couldn't quite believe the arrangement he'd made himself.

'A friend of mine is going to look after him for a couple of hours a week and she's a qualified teacher, so he'll be in perfectly safe hands.' He didn't mention the fact that she'd be moving in, in lieu of wages. His mother-in-law's head exploding all over the living room would definitely affect his tenancy deposit.

'And how long have you known this *friend*?' Pam's lip curled as she said the word. This inquisition wasn't going away just yet.

'Long enough. She's an old friend of mine from uni.' He'd have to brief Nancy about all of this later, in case she was ever stuck in a room with Pam on her own.

'So why haven't I ever met her? Why wasn't she at the wedding or Alice's funeral?' If he looked closely enough, Jack was sure he'd actually be able to see her skin bristling as she spoke.

'She's been working in Africa. Teaching in some schools out there.' The lies were getting out of hand now. 'We've been in contact by email and letter though.'

'What? And she just happened to settle in a place like St Nicholas Bay? That's a bit of a coincidence, isn't it?'

'No. It's one of the reasons I came here.' Even Jack knew that lying about a million-to-one coincidence would only make things worse.

'Are you telling me that you and she are …?' There was a mad look in Pam's eyes and he wouldn't have put it past her to grab Toby and run back to her car, if she thought it was true.

'Of course not!' His anger was genuine. How could she think he'd move on that quickly? No one could replace Alice. 'She's just a friend and she's due to get married next year.' Pam needn't know that the engagement had just been broken off.

'I'm sorry.' Pam looked genuinely contrite. 'It's just that I can't bear the thought of someone else taking her place, holding Toby in her arms when it should be Alice. Or Alice missing out on life with you. I can't stand it.'

'Nor can I, Pam, but it's not like that. I'll never let Toby forget her, I promise.'

Pam was a bit calmer by the time she finally left. She burst into tears when she kissed Toby goodbye, but Jack understood why. A few days without his son in the house had made his own constant aching loneliness tip into something almost unbearable.

'Are you ready for this then, Tobes? We've got a new friend to meet.' Jack's stomach contracted as his son looked at him. His eyes were exactly the same shape as Alice's and, as Toby grabbed his finger with his tiny hand, it was like she was back with them for a moment.

The house was already a chaos of toys, changing mats and half-eaten bowls of baby food and they only had half an hour before Nancy was due. Jack decided not to tidy up. She'd said she was untidy and he didn't want to make her uneasy by thinking the cottage was some sort of show home. There was little chance of that with Toby around anyway. He was at the stage where he was pulling himself up on the furniture and chucking his plastic bricks around with the skill of an Olympic shot-putter.

By the time she arrived, Jack had talked himself in and out of the house-sharing idea about ten times. It would sound crazy to anyone listening to it objectively, but what choice did he have? He could have sent Toby to a childminder, but would that have been any better? A childminder would be a stranger, too, though admittedly not living in the same house. He couldn't afford a live-in nanny, but even if he could, Jack would know no more about them than he knew about Nancy. So maybe it wasn't that crazy after all.

'Thanks for coming.' Jack opened the door for Nancy and then froze. How was he supposed to greet her? A kiss on the cheek or shake her hand?

'No problem. Can I come in then?' Nancy was looking at him; he'd have to do something.

'Of course. Sorry.' He stepped to one side. The hallway was so narrow there was barely room for her to squeeze by and she had to brush up against him to get past. She probably thought he was a nutter or, worse still, a pervert.

Toby was sitting in the middle of the lounge, hitting some of his building bricks with a plastic hammer. He looked up as they came into the room and gave them one of his trademark gummy grins. If Jack had been looking for a sign, his son had just given it.

'Hello, gorgeous.' Nancy crouched down next to him and Toby offered her a red brick.

'Ummm.' Toby raised his other hand towards Jack, as though he was inviting him to join them.

'Is he speaking already?' Nancy began adding extra bricks to the haphazard pile in front of them. Perhaps Toby would end up going into demolition.

'Just the odd word ...' Jack smiled and for once he didn't have to force it. 'Mainly gog. He says that an awful lot when we're out and about.' He picked up Toby's toy dog to make a point, but his son was far too engrossed in his building project. 'Honestly, he does. It's his attempt at dog.'

'It's all right, I believe you.' Nancy returned his smile and her green eyes crinkled at the corners. 'It'll be nice to have a break from making conversation all the time. I think we'll get along fine, won't we, darling?' She suddenly looked embarrassed. 'I'm so sorry. I've just realised I don't know his name.'

'Toby.' Jack picked him up and pulled him onto his lap. 'Meet Nancy.' Toby held out another brick. He definitely approved so far.

'He's lovely.' Nancy looked at Jack as she spoke and it was obvious she meant it. 'Can I ask you what happened to his mum?'

'Are you worried I might be an axe murderer? I can

promise you she's not buried under the floorboards.' His attempt to be flippant backfired a bit, his voice cracking as it always did when he spoke about Alice.

'I know. I can see how much losing her has hurt you.' Nancy managed the neat trick of sounding like she genuinely cared, without slipping into the patronising, sickly-sweet tone that most people seemed to do. 'I just thought it might be better for us both to get it all out in the open. Rather than me walking around, treading on eggshells, petrified I might say something awful and totally put my foot in it.'

'She was an actress, in the supporting cast at The Old Granville theatre.' He took a deep breath and fiddled with one of the plastic bricks so he didn't have to make eye contact. 'Alice was one of those people who loved to be popular. She'd always stay late after a performance to sign autographs even though people didn't know her name. She hoped that one day they would and they'd be glad they'd got her signature before she made it big. She was always helping out the crew, wanting to be everyone's favourite actress. On the day she died, she was giving a hand with the cable for a flying scene when it suddenly recoiled, and took her with it. She fell from about thirty feet and hit her head so badly the paramedics couldn't revive her.'

His voice sounded robotic, even to his own ears, but it was the only way he could manage to get the words out. Maybe if he'd been able to make her feel more like the centre of his world, she wouldn't have kept chasing popularity, or if he'd taken up his aunt on her offer ... The 'what ifs' just wouldn't leave him alone.

'There's nothing I can say that will make any difference to you.' Nancy placed a hand on his arm. 'But I really am sorry, for you and for Toby.'

'Thank you. You were right – it'll be easier now I've told you.' He briefly touched her hand, before she moved it away. 'Maybe you should tell me why you are so reluctant to go and stay with your mum, so I can avoid putting my foot in that situation.' He didn't want to talk about Alice any more. It was easier not to mention her, so changing the subject felt like the best thing to do.

'Fair enough, it's a reasonable question. I hope you've got half an hour spare if you really want the whole story.' Nancy ran a hand through her hair. 'I love my mum, don't get me wrong, and she'd like nothing better than for me to move back home. The trouble is that if I do that, she'd be devastated all over again when I left.'

'All over again?'

'It happened once before, when my grandmother died. I was just finishing my first year at university in Bath. Loving life and living exactly the way a student should.'

'Pot noodles and cheap booze, if I remember correctly?' Jack smiled and she nodded, the smile on her lips dying almost instantly.

'That's it. But, when gran died, Mum had a breakdown. I came home for the holidays to be with her, hoping by the time term started again in October, she'd be able to cope.'

'But she couldn't?'

'She completely fell apart. She was on anti-depressants, but she couldn't bear to be left on her own. She'd have panic attacks and someone had to be with her all the time. Dad and Mark were working, so …'

'So it fell to you to take the load, I'm guessing?'

'Uh huh.' Nancy nodded and passed Toby another brick; he rewarded her with another gummy grin. 'I gave up my place at Bath and transferred to a part-time course in Canterbury, studying in the evenings, which meant it took me three years to finish what would have taken two at Bath. Luckily, by the time I got to my final year, she was a lot better and I was able to go back to day classes. But I was still living at home and still on tenterhooks every time I got a call in case my mum was having a bad day. I gave up a rite of passage and I'd do the same thing all over again, I really would, but there were times when I felt like I was going to suffocate and, at one point, I didn't think I'd ever be able to leave.'

'So what changed?' Jack looked up as her eyes flickered in his direction.

'Things seemed to get back on an even keel. Dad's business was doing okay – or at least we all thought so – and I got a job at the college after graduating, got together with another lecturer and we ended up moving in together. I thought everything was falling into place. Then Dad started to forget things, stupid things at first, but it was obvious after a while that something was really wrong. I split up with my boyfriend and, I suppose, if I hadn't met David so quickly afterwards, the natural choice would have been for me to go home. I just couldn't do it again and I feel guilty for that, but I know Mum doesn't want to be alone, and going back for a little while would be worse than never going back. You probably think I'm a heartless cow not to go back to be with her.'

'Not at all. No one could expect you to give up your own life completely.'

'I honestly think she's the better for me not going back. She's been stronger this time around, maybe because she had to be, without me there all the time. I don't know, perhaps I'm just making excuses for myself, but I really think supporting her, but not going home full-time, is best for us both.'

'So your dad's passed away?'

'Losing Dad broke Mum's heart.' She held up a hand, shaking her head as he opened his mouth to speak. 'He's not dead, but we've still lost him. He's got Alzheimer's. It took him really quickly and in the end she couldn't keep him at home any more. He's in The Pines Care Home now, and between us we see him most days, even though there isn't a lot of point.'

'Were you close before he was ill?' Jack had lost his parents, years before. A story for another day.

'Really close. Even now there are things I want to do for him and protect Mum from that mean I'm stuck keeping secrets that aren't mine to keep.' She didn't elaborate and he didn't push her. They'd both said enough for now; it was time to get back to business.

'Shall I show you where you'll be sleeping?' In different circumstances it might have qualified as the world's worst chat-up line.

Scooping up Toby, who screwed up his little face in protest at being taken away from his building bricks, Jack led the way out of the lounge, back into the hallway and up the steep staircase.

'This will be your room.' He stepped back to let her go through the doorway first. 'If you're still up for it, of course.'

'I haven't got a lot of choice.' As she turned, he could see she was smiling. 'Sorry, that didn't come out the way I meant it to. It's actually incredibly kind of you to make the offer and I am grateful, honestly. I'm happy to take the smaller room, though, if you want to put Toby in here.'

'The smaller room?'

'Your cottage has got exactly the same layout as the one that David and I were renting, so I know the third bedroom is just about wide enough to stretch out your arms and touch the walls on either side.'

'I think that might be why Toby likes it. Somehow the two rooms at the back of the house feel warmer. Not that there's a bad atmosphere in here or anything.'

'It's great and you've got a much nicer view from here than we have. I mean *had*. You can actually see the sea.' Her face shone, like a tourist unused to seeing the sea on a daily basis.

'Have you always lived here?'

'Apart from the year at uni. I'm St Nicholas Bay born and bred and I think I'd have come back here eventually, even without everything that happened. It's a place that has that kind of draw – there have always been more reasons to stay than to leave.' There was a hint of something in her voice, as though she hadn't quite told the whole story.

'Housemates then?' Jack fished a key out of his pocket with his spare hand. Toby, who was perched on his other hip, gave a gurgle which Jack took for approval as Nancy took the key. If it was a crazy idea to invite a stranger to share their new home, there was no going back now.

CHAPTER ELEVEN

'So you're definitely going to do it then?' Maisie was leaning forward in her tiny Fiat as it snaked up the hill towards Maple Street, almost as if she were riding a horse and easing her weight to the front, and Nancy couldn't help smiling. For a day when she should have been nursing a broken heart, she'd smiled more than she had in a long time.

'Yes, Jack's a lot nicer than I thought. I think a lot of what looks like being standoffish is actually grief. And Toby is heavenly.'

'Making you broody?' Maisie shot her a sideways glance as she pulled up outside what was now David's cottage. Although perhaps it was his and Olivia's – who knew?

'A fat lot of good it would do me, even if I was broody. I'd have to find myself a sperm donor.' Nancy looked past her friend as she spoke. There was no sign of David's van in the street outside the cottage. He must have gone to the golf club, as he always did on a Saturday, and she felt a flash of irritation that he hadn't changed his plans. Surely he should have been too upset to play eighteen holes as though nothing had happened? 'Anyway, after David and Fraser, I think I might be off men for good.'

'I *never* want kids.' Maisie unclipped her seatbelt. 'When I'm an internationally famous music megastar, I might think again and adopt some babies like Brangelina – if I can pay someone else to look after them.'

'Remind me never to ask you to babysit, if the time comes.'

'Oh, don't worry. I will!'

Nancy got out of the car and walked through the walled front garden that had convinced her this was the house she and David should rent. At the time, she'd thought they'd end up buying it, maybe even start their married life there. Had she ever really believed she could make a life with David, though?

'He hasn't changed the locks then?' Maisie whispered as they stood on the doorstep like they were breaking and entering.

'Nope, but I really don't want to have to see him if I can help it. So let's be quick.' The hallway was cold, as if the temperature reflected recent events. Maybe it had always been like that and she just hadn't noticed. If she was honest she'd buried her head, along with her real feelings, deep into the sand a long time ago.

'What shall I do? I don't know which stuff is yours.' Maisie was panicking.

'You take the main bedroom. It's not rocket science. All the girly stuff is going to be mine.' Nancy felt another smile twitching at the corner of her lips. 'Well, at least most of it. There are a pair of lilac silk pyjamas that David would never forgive me if I took.'

'Please tell me you're joking.' Maisie grimaced when Nancy shook her head. 'And am I putting pin pricks in all his condoms and pouring his Stella down the sink?'

'I couldn't possibly condone such behaviour,' Nancy

winked, 'unless we've got time, of course!'

Maisie disappeared upstairs and Nancy moved from room to room downstairs, collecting only the things that really mattered to her. There was the photograph of her with her parents on her graduation day, a painting which Fraser had bought her on their first holiday in Cornwall and a mac hanging on the hook in the hallway – the last thing that her dad had bought her before he lost the ability to make a rational decision. She still remembered him saying he was worried about her getting wet and cold on her walk to college. No man ever cared about you like your dad did. The last few days had brought that home even more sharply.

'You're not really packing, are you?' David's voice made her jump and the silver picture frame almost slipped out of her fingers.

'I texted you and told you I was.' She'd been worried that some suppressed emotion might come bubbling to the surface when she saw him again, but there was nothing.

'Yeah, but I didn't think you meant it.' David took two paces towards her. 'I thought you were just angry, babe, that you'd calm down.'

'I'm perfectly calm.' Nancy looked around to see if there was anything else she needed to take. She wasn't about to start wrangling with him over possessions that didn't really matter; Take That CDs were easy to replace.

'Babe, come on. It didn't mean anything. We can get past this.' Another two paces and Nancy tensed. What was she supposed to do if he tried to touch her?

'Do you know what?' Taking two steps backwards, she clutched her bag a little tighter. 'I think that's the worst thing. If your fiancé and your friend decide to sleep together – sorry, I mean shag themselves senseless in the back of her car and get arrested – you would at least hope that it *did* mean something. If the two of you were madly in love, maybe I could accept that you couldn't help yourselves and that you'd never meant to hurt me. A meaningless quickie, on the other hand, shows exactly what you think of me.'

'Nance, you know men don't think like that.' His voice had gone all thin and reedy. 'Olivia threw herself at me and I didn't think you'd ever find out.'

'Oh, that's all right then. As long as you didn't mean to humiliate me – and blaming Olivia for it all is *really* classy. Begging for forgiveness might be the way to go.'

'Would it make a difference if I did?' David lunged forward, looking like he might drop down on to his knees at any moment. He'd done that once before and that hadn't ended well either.

'No. I don't love you, David.' Despite everything he'd done, she couldn't bring herself to tell him that she never had, even though she knew for sure now it was true. 'And maybe part of this is my fault, because you must have picked up on it. But choosing Olivia was what really hurt. I thought she was one of my closest friends. Neither of us is blameless, but the best thing we can do now is walk away from this with a bit of dignity.'

'You don't mean that, babe. We can make it work.'

'Is this yours?' Maisie appeared in the doorway and Nancy and David span round to look at her. She was gingerly holding a frilly 'peep-hole' baby-doll nightdress, which almost perfectly matched the lilac pyjamas she'd been told to look out for.

'Nope, it isn't mine.' Nancy shoved two more photos into her bag as she spoke. 'And we're done here.' Swinging her bag on to her shoulder, she swept past David, more aware than ever that she'd just had a narrow escape.

'Was that nightdress really David's?' Maisie hadn't asked the obvious question on the ludicrously short drive between Nancy's old home and her new one. But now that they were back in the car, having dropped off all of Nancy's worldly goods, it was the first thing Maisie said.

'It was either his or another of his conquests'.'

'I'm not sure which is worse!' Maisie pulled a face. 'The things I do for our friendship.'

'I know and I'm grateful, believe me. It's times like this when you find out who your real friends are. If you ever need me to expose your ex-fiancé's kinky bedroom habits by waving his baby-doll nightdress around like a semaphore, then I'm your girl.' Nancy giggled again. This was more like fun than it should be – until she thought about Olivia's part in it.

'Are you sure you don't want to come for a drink after you've seen your dad tomorrow?' It was nice of Maisie to offer. Nancy knew she was meeting up with the rest of her band and she doubted that they'd want her hanging around while they were trying to plan world domination.

'Thanks, but I'll give it a miss if that's okay? I'm going to see Mum afterwards and I've got to get a bit of work done for Monday's lessons. I couldn't concentrate on anything yesterday, after I heard about Fraser coming back. I've also got to see whether Trunchball will let me tweak my timetable to take Toby to nursery. Although she'll probably accept my resignation from the tutoring post straight away and I'll have plenty of time on my hands.'

'Are you going to be okay to carry your shopping back?' Maisie took the corner at the bottom of Maple Street, which led out to Sea Street, a bit too quickly and Nancy was thrown against her.

'I'll be fine, and it's more likely to stay intact if I walk anyway!'

'Cheeky cow. Just for that I'm going to tell Trevor first thing on Monday that you're single again.' Maisie grinned as she pulled into the car park behind the high street.

Nancy returned her smile and winked. 'And there I was thinking Olivia was the bitch!'

Nancy needed to move into Jack's with a few supplies. Maybe it would end up being like her old student digs in Bath again. Half the residents of the flat had written their names on their food and had their own shelves in the fridge, while the rest of them had ignored the labels and eaten everybody else's food anyway. She never thought she'd miss that when she moved back home to look after her mum.

It was seven-thirty and the high street had long since emptied by the time she'd finished stocking up at the supermarket. Along with her food, Nancy had bought Toby a toy garage and some cars in the same bright shades as the building blocks he liked so much. The box it came in was much larger than she'd realised, so it was unwieldy and difficult to carry back up the hill to Jack's place.

When she was about a hundred feet from the cottage, Jack emerged from the front door and jogged down towards her.

'I saw you struggling from the window. What on earth have you got in there? It looks like it weighs a ton.' Jack took most of the bags from her.

'Just a bit of shopping. I didn't want to empty your cupboards and I like a lot of biscuits with my tea. And I got this for Toby.' As she went inside, Nancy got out the box containing the toy garage.

'You didn't need to do that. I've just put him down for the night, but he'll love it.' Jack turned to look at her. The smile that changed his whole face was back again. 'But if you've really only got biscuits in these bags then we might want to get the hallway widened.'

By the time they'd unpacked the shopping together and Jack had made them both a cup of tea, the tight knot of nerves that had been gripping Nancy's insides since Maisie had dropped her off had all but disappeared. Jack was all right. Wandering around the supermarket was the first bit of time of any significance she'd had on her own since she'd found out about David and Olivia, never mind since the impetuous decision to move in with Jack. That so much had happened in less than twenty-four hours was overwhelming. She might not have been heartbroken, but in the neon-lit harshness of the supermarket, surrounded by families doing their weekend shop, she had wondered what the hell she was doing moving in with a stranger. She'd heard of people having drastic haircuts after a break-up, or splurging out on a whole new wardrobe, but this was something else.

'Have you got any plans for tonight?' Jack sat on one of the red sofas which he'd obviously bought for a very different house and, not wanting to seem overfamiliar, she sat on the one opposite. The space in the middle of the room, which had been dominated by Toby's building blocks earlier in the day, had been cleared and the coffee table that had previously been shoved to one side of the room was back in place.

'I wasn't planning on doing anything, but if you want time to yourself I can go up to my room and read. I've got a TV at Mum's, and I can pick that up so we don't get on top of each other too much. I'll have to wait until Maisie can lend me a hand, though, as I never bothered with a car living this close to the college. The parking is a nightmare in this road anyway, and David's van takes up half the street, as you probably know.'

'Electrical Dave?' Jack couldn't seem to keep the face-changing smile at bay and Nancy felt more relieved every time she saw it. It was going to be okay, it really was.

'That's the one. Let's just say it wasn't his creativity that won me over. Like I said before it was more about being in the right place at the wrong time than anything.'

'It's none of my business,' Jack put his tea down and looked straight at her, 'but if you ever feel like talking about it, I'm more than happy to listen.'

'I'm not going to end up in one of your books, am I?' It was her turn to smile. 'I take it you write yourself, as well as teaching?'

'I try, but not in a way that anyone would notice, so your secret's safe with me. Even if I write your story, no one would ever read it.' He leant back on the sofa as though he was settling in for the night.

'I might as well tell you. It'll be the hot topic of the college once Fraser comes back.' Nancy shifted uncomfortably in her seat. It was never easy talking about her ex. She was already over the man who'd been her fiancé less than a day before and yet the pain of losing Fraser was still raw.

'That's the interim principal, isn't it?'

'Yes, he used to be a lecturer and then head of our department and we went out for a couple of years.'

'So that's the guy you were living with before your dad started to get ill?'

Jack was looking at her intensely, as if trying to take in not just what she said but the way she said it. He was definitely a writer.

'It was, and I really thought he might be … God, this

sounds cheesy.' She wrinkled her nose, but decided just to tell it as it was, cheese and all. 'Oh sod it, I thought he was the one.'

'It's not cheesy. It's what we all want.' There was something in his tone that made Nancy want to reach out to him, but that might give him totally the wrong impression and ruin the friendship that seemed to be building.

'He was everything I wanted. At least I thought so.'

'What happened?'

'Dad had started to go downhill fast and I knew Mum wouldn't be able to cope with him at home full-time in the long term. Fraser was offered a promotion as one of three deputy principals at another college, down in Cornwall, and he wanted me to go with him.' Sighing, she paused and took a sip of her tea, remembering just how torn she'd felt at the time. 'There was no way I could. It was the wrong time and too far away. If it had been a commutable distance, or even somewhere I could get back from at weekends, I would have gone with him.'

'Did you ask him to stay with you instead?'

'I didn't just ask him, I begged him. I go hot now just thinking about it. He had to walk out of the door with me virtually hanging on to his leg.' She hadn't been lying when she said it made her feel hot; she was still mortified about the way she had handled the final days of their relationship.

'He couldn't do that?'

'He said it was hard for him, sure.' Nancy shrugged her shoulders. 'But not so hard that he would consider us seeing each other when we could on a long distance basis.'

'Sounds like a prat to me.' Jack dunked one of the chocolate biscuits she'd bought into his tea. 'Sorry, I shouldn't have said that.'

'Fine by me.' Nancy laughed – in fact, she was liking him more and more. Maybe she wouldn't miss Olivia much after all – it looked like she had a new friend. 'But, to be fair, things are rarely as simple as it all being down to one person. I should probably warn you, too, that he's Maisie's brother, so perhaps best not to voice that opinion around her.'

'Enough said.'

'The truth is, I was really broken up about it, and then David came along and I guess he was only ever a rebound. I needed to find a new place to rent, so we ended up moving in together really quickly because it gave me a reason not to go back to Mum's, and then he proposed.'

'And you said yes?' He made it sound as though she'd agreed to a frontal lobotomy without an anaesthetic, and she was beginning to wonder if he was right.

'Crazy but true. Some people might say I've got a habit of making rash decisions when it comes to my living arrangements.' She paused for a moment as Jack smiled. 'It seems mad to me now, but with everything that had happened with Mum when Gran died, getting together with David seemed like the least terrible option.'

'Sounds like a catch!' Jack ducked as she threw a cushion at him.

'That's it! I'm definitely off to read a book in my room now.' She was surprised by how little the idea appealed, but she didn't want to outstay her welcome.

'Don't. I mean don't on *my* account. I've had more than enough space over the past few weeks and I was only planning to watch a bit of trashy TV.'

'What were you thinking of?' She couldn't see him as a fan of reality TV or talent shows.

'As it's your first night here, I'll let you pick.' He

passed her the remote control. 'As long as it's not football.' It was all she could do to stop herself kissing him.

Expecting him to protest, she finally settled on a documentary following an infertile couple on their quest to adopt a baby from rural India. She couldn't believe it when, not only did he not moan about her choice of programme, he really seemed to get into it. So much so that when she looked across at him through a haze of tears as the couple finally got to take their little girl home, she could have sworn that he had a tear rolling down his face too.

CHAPTER TWELVE

The walk to the care home had been unexpectedly invigorating. Jack, who had offered her a lift since he was taking Toby swimming in one of the hotels just down the road from The Pines, had warned her it was really windy. Nancy had always loved the weather as autumn turned to winter. The biting squalls that rolled off the sea made her feel alive, so she'd turned down Jack's offer. The strength of the wind had made it hard to breathe, and her hair was beyond wild by the time she stood in the porch of the care home waiting to be let in. She could see it reflected in the glass door, like giant ginger candyfloss.

'Good morning, Nancy. You've missed your dad's breakfast today and he's already in the day room.' Barbara, who was everyone's favourite care assistant, didn't sound accusatory. She was just stating a fact, but Nancy felt guilty all the same.

'Thanks, I'll go straight through. How is he today?'

'A bit down, actually, but I'm sure he'll be all the better for seeing you.' Barbara smiled, perhaps sensing the irony in her own words. 'I know he doesn't recognise you, but he's calmer after your visits all the same.'

Nancy walked through to the dayroom and found one of the residents counting from one to ten over and over again, wedged into the corner behind the door, playing some never-ending game of hide and seek.

'Are you okay, Doreen?' When Nancy took her hand, the old lady jumped like she'd been burnt.

'Got to count, got to count, got to count.'

Doreen's eyes flew open, as if surprised by what had come out of her mouth.

'What have you got to count?' Nancy stroked her arm. Poor Doreen was shaking.

'The money. I've got to make it add up or I can't go home.' She began thumping the palm of her hand against her forehead in distress.

'Why don't we sit down and try to work it out together?' Leading Doreen towards an empty seat, Nancy passed a group of the newer residents who were in a far less advanced state of dementia than either her father or the woman whose elbow she was gently guiding.

'I want to go HOME!' Doreen suddenly screamed the word and one of the newer residents turned and looked in their direction.

'Don't we all, love.'

By the time Barbara came to see what all of the fuss was about, Nancy had already managed to calm Doreen down considerably.

'Was she counting again?' Barbara was clearly exhausted, but it was obvious how much she cared. A lot of the other staff seemed to be more detached from their jobs, as though seeing the residents in such distress had become as familiar and mundane as the muted furnishings. It didn't help that Sue Lewis, the care home manager, had left suddenly the week before so they were short staffed.

'She didn't seem able to stop counting. It was like she was playing a game from her childhood. But then she said something about money and wanting to go home.' Nancy glanced at Doreen again, who was still mumbling about numbers under her breath.

'She used to work in the bank, met her husband there so he tells me.' Barbara sighed again. 'It's like the poor old poppet is constantly stuck with the memory of trying to balance the accounts at the end of the day and all she wants to do is go home, but she can't, not ever.'

'I don't know how you do it, Barbara, it would break my heart every single day.'

'It does, love, believe me. But it makes you realise that you've got to grab life by the short and curlies too. I've done more with my time off since I've worked here than I ever did before.'

'You deserve a medal.' Nancy leant forward and gave her a hug. 'I'd better go and see Dad, but don't think that we don't appreciate everything you do for him.'

John O'Brien was in his usual spot in the dayroom, staring into space as if he'd gone off somewhere else a long time ago, leaving just a shell behind. A big part of Nancy hoped he had and that it was somewhere nice.

'Dad?' She pulled up the empty chair beside him and he turned to look at her – not even the faintest hint of recognition in his expression.

'He's not here.' He looked confused and she didn't want to push him. Sometimes he seemed to think he was a child himself and he remembered memories from the past as though they were yesterday, with a clarity at odds with everything else. Most of the time, though, his memories were shattered fragments that didn't make any sense at all, and trying to get him to explain only made things worse.

'It's okay. Shall I talk to you instead?' She saw a small

shrug of his shoulders, but he wasn't agitated like Doreen, and if he didn't want to talk she wouldn't make him. Sometimes it was easier that way. He looked almost the same as he used to, perhaps a bit more stooped, a little greyer and with a vacant air; it was only when he spoke that he gave the game away. Silence was as golden in many ways as it promised to be.

She would normally have taken him out into the garden. It encouraged him to talk about the flowers or a passing butterfly. His favourite thing of all was when she took him out for a walk and he could read signs: road signs, shopfronts, anything that caught his eye. He would read them out loud and for a moment or two he sounded totally normal. Of course he had no idea what the meaning of the words was and couldn't recall them a second later – but he could still read. The human brain was as amazing as it was incomprehensible. There would be no going out today, though. The weather was too wild for her to support his weight against the wind, so they had to be content with a move to the sunroom.

'It's warm.' John settled into another chair, the short walk seeming to tire him out. She tried not to think about how long his body would last. She couldn't wish the end for him, not even with things the way they were.

'You're not too hot, are you, Da…?' Nancy just managed to stop herself from saying the word.

'Just right, sweetpea.' He patted her leg and smiled. It was his term of endearment, not just for her, but for everyone. It didn't herald a miraculous recognition, but it was lovely to hear him say it all the same.

They sat like that, looking out at the garden for a good hour. Occasionally he would notice something outside and make a comment, more often than not the same thing over and over again. If he'd asked once whether or not anyone had put some bread on the bird table, he must have asked ten times.

'I thought I'd find you here.' The voice was so familiar and yet so unexpected that Nancy's head jolted back with shock.

'That's funny, because it's just about the last place on earth that I would have expected to see you.'

She looked up at Olivia, her former friend. How strange that being in her company was now more uncomfortable than sharing a confined space with a near-total stranger.

'All the more reason for me to choose here to speak to you. Some idiotic young girl let me in without even bothering to check who I was. You really should have been more careful about where you and your mum dumped your dad when you couldn't be bothered to look after him any more.'

As Olivia spoke it was like years of denial on Nancy's part had peeled away. Her mother had always said the friendship was one-sided and she'd always defended Olivia, but there was no denying it any more.

'If you had even one thought in your head about someone other than yourself, you'd realise just how cruel that is. I don't care what you think about me, but no one can criticise Mum. She never wanted to let Dad go, but he's so much calmer here that *she* made the sacrifice. Although God knows why I'm even trying to explain that concept to you.' Nancy's hands tightened around the arm of the chair as she struggled to remain dignified. A Jeremy-Kyle-type showdown was not really her style, and definitely not in the sunroom of her father's care home. 'Judging by the deluge of texts you sent me, the only thing you're interested in is making excuses.'

'They weren't excuses, they were reasons.' Olivia,

who clearly wasn't going to be put off her stride that easily, sat down on the other side of John. 'Things between you and David were rubbish. You told me as much and, let's face it, you can't sit there and promise me you aren't happy to have got out of marrying him.'

'That's hardly the point!' Nancy's voice had gone several octaves higher, but as much as she tried to control it, she couldn't help it.

'What *is* the point then? David didn't mean anything to you and he didn't mean anything to me either.'

'Maybe he didn't, but *you* did. You were one of my best friends and you betrayed me for a meaningless fling.' Nancy could taste the bitterness in her mouth. 'So, go on, tell me exactly why did you do it?'

'To prove I could.' Olivia smiled so smugly that Nancy barely resisted the urge to smack the look off her face. 'I was flattered and it gave me a boost. You wanted shot of him and so I did us both a favour. Come on, admit it. Let's kiss and make up, be best friends again. We've got to work together after all.' The sheer audacity shocked Nancy so much that, for a moment or two, she didn't say anything.

'You're right, we've got to work together and we'll have to find some way to do that, but as for the rest of it,' Nancy looked her straight in the eye so Olivia would know she meant business, 'you can get stuffed.'

For a few seconds Olivia mouthed silently, as though she was going to say something, but then she stood and walked out, not looking back.

'I don't like her.' John turned to look at Nancy and she smiled. He might not remember his own daughter, but he was still a better judge of character than she'd been.

CHAPTER THIRTEEN

Half way home from the supermarket, Ruth wished she'd taken the car. She only had a few bits of shopping and she'd fancied a walk in the fresh air to clear her head of the thoughts that had been plaguing her for half the night. Unfortunately the blustery day had blown in some unexpected clouds, which were now pelting her with the sort of fine rain that got her soaked through in minutes, and felt like a million tiny needles bouncing off her head.

A huge black car was heading in her direction and she inched away from the edge of the pavement. The last thing she needed was to be drenched as its tyres hit the puddle in the road. It was a considerate driver, though. The car slowed down as it approached. Then, when it drew level with her, it stopped altogether. The electric window slid down silently and immediately she knew who was leaning across from the driver's side.

'Ruth, let me give you a lift.' The voice was assured. He wasn't used to hearing the word 'no', but if she'd ever been tempted to shout the F-word in the street, it was now.

'You're going in the other direction.' Her nails cut into her palms as she spoke, the pain distracting her from her emotion. Without saying any more, she started walking. Even someone as arrogant as Daniel Chapman surely wouldn't reverse up the high street just to keep the conversation going.

Within a minute he was back, having turned the car around. He drove slowly past her, but this time the window was shut. Pulling up on the side of the road, thirty feet or so in front of where she was walking, he got out of the car and walked across. She wanted to cross the road to avoid him, but why should she? He was such a thick-skinned pig, he'd just keep following her. If he was going to push it, she might as well say what needed saying.

'I'm going in the right direction now, in case you hadn't noticed.' The lazy smile, which he probably thought could charm the birds out of the trees, made her hate him more than ever.

'Where you're going is straight to hell.'

Stalking straight past him, she didn't miss a beat, even as he reached out to grab her arm.

'I don't know what you've got against me.'

He was walking with her now, still holding on to her arm as she contemplated shouting out 'rape'. Except that since everyone in St Nicholas Bay thought he was some kind of hero, she'd look like the crazy one.

'Oh, I don't know. The fact that you run The Pines like it's a sweatshop with underpaid and overworked staff, most of whom couldn't give a damn about the residents. Christ knows why Barbara sticks with you, but thank God she does.'

'I'm trying to improve things there, you know that. And I started with letting Sue Lewis go.' Daniel turned so that he was blocking her path, a hand on each of her arms to stop her dodging past him. 'I've only had the place six months and I'm desperate to make it better, but you can't just sack the whole staff and start again, you know that as well as I do.'

'So you say, but you're hardly hands on, are you? I can't imagine you're there for more than five minutes a week, you've got your fingers in so many pies.' Her face twisted as she spoke, the bitterness she felt about everything that had happened making the muscles contract.

'Has something happened with John?'

If she hadn't known him better, she might have mistaken the tone in his voice for genuine concern – but she *did* know better.

'Nothing happens with John, not any more, and we both know why he ended up in The Pines. Isn't it bad enough that you put him there in the first place, but now you're profiting from it too?'

'I bought his business off him. It isn't a crime, Ruth.'

'It should be. The way you did it, virtually forcing him out of business so he had no choice but to sell. He wasn't right after that – the light went out of him and then the Alzheimer's took hold. It seems like an amazing coincidence to me.'

'No, it wasn't a coincidence.' Daniel released the grip on her arms. 'It was a tragedy. The two of you should be enjoying the profit he made from selling the business after so many years of working hard to make it a success. But it wasn't me who robbed you of that, Ruth, it was that horrible disease.'

'If that helps you sleep at night, then carry on believing it, but I *never* will.'

�֍

'How was lunch with your mum?'

Jack was lying on the sofa with a sleeping Toby in the crook of his arm when Nancy arrived back at the cottage. She looked tired, but it wasn't surprising. She'd had a hell of a weekend.

'It was okay. She seemed distracted though.'

Nancy unzipped her boots as she spoke and he tried not to notice her long legs as she curled them under her on the sofa opposite him.

'She got soaked going into town to get some blackberries for the dessert. She arrived back at her place at the same time as me, after I'd spent the morning with Dad. She looked like she was ready to burst into tears.'

'I guess it's not surprising with everything that's going on with your dad. How was he by the way?' Jack shifted slightly in his seat, keen not to wake Toby up yet. The feel of his son's solid little body in his arms was the highlight of his life these days.

'He was like he always is. But it was certainly more eventful than normal. Olivia turned up.'

'Is that the girl that your ex was caught with?' He was struggling to get to grips with the names of everyone at the college, let alone the dramas in his new housemate's life. He knew her ex-fiancé was called David, aka Electrical Dave – you couldn't miss his van, unfortunately. And of course he knew about Fraser, who was about to become their boss, but he wondered if he'd have to write a character plan, like he did with his novels, to keep up with rest of it.

'That's the one. I think she turned up there because she thought I wouldn't make a scene.'

'And did you?'

'No. I just about held it together, but working together is going to be a bit more difficult than I thought. I need to get the members of the community theatre organised, and make sure there are lots of them so they dilute her presence as much as possible.'

'Do you think there'll be a lot of interest?' Toby was

starting to stir and arching his body as he stretched against Jack's arm.

'I hope so. I printed off flyers at Mum's place and then walked off her blackberry and double-cream Eton mess by delivering them to almost every house in town. I put posters up on all the notice boards I could find, too. We've not long to go if we're going to get a passable panto put on in time.' Nancy sighed, revealing just how tired she was. It went beyond the physical. He'd seen that drained look before – in the mirror.

'Do you fancy a drink?' There was a decent bottle of champagne in the fridge. Craig and Selena had brought it down for him as a moving in present, but he hadn't felt right about opening it. What was there to celebrate, when the reason for the move was to run away from memories of his dead wife? This weekend had brought with it some pivotal moments, though, which were worth marking, even if 'celebration' didn't seem the right word. He had a new housemate and she'd launched a new business, and lost a fiancé and a close friend. If that didn't warrant a drink, then he wasn't sure what did.

'Do you want a cup of tea? I can do it, as you've got Toby.'

Nancy moved to stand up and Toby sat bolt upright at the mention of his name, already squirming to get out of Jack's arms and desperate to get back to his new garage in the middle of the floor. Admittedly he'd been sending his bricks down the ramp instead of the cars, but he loved it.

'I was thinking of champagne actually, but I can get it, if you don't mind keeping an eye on Toby?'

'Champagne? I think I'm going to like it here.'

She smiled and Jack found himself hoping she was right.

'I can't promise it's an everyday occurrence, but it's

been a fairly remarkable weekend, one way or another, and I think it's as good a time as any to open it.'

His unpacking wasn't quite complete and as a result there were several boxes still stacked in the shed in the small walled garden. Most of the glasses were among them and, if he'd ever owned champagne flutes, he didn't have anything remotely appropriate to hand. Two tumblers would have to do the job.

He'd just walked back out to the hallway when the doorbell rang.

'Shall I get it?' Nancy called out from the lounge, where he could see her kneeling next to Toby, showing him how to push the cars along the wooden floor and crash into his piles of bricks. In return, Toby was grinning and waving his arms around.

'No, it's fine. I'm here now anyway.' Wedging the champagne bottle under his arm and holding the tumblers in one hand, he used his other hand to open the door. A hall table suddenly seemed like it might be a useful thing to have.

'Can I help you?' On the doorstep was a stocky man with a military-style moustache and florid cheeks, with a stern looking woman in half-moon glasses on one side and, on the other, a well-built woman with a grin to rival Toby's. If they were Jehovah's Witnesses, they were certainly not what he would have expected, but he was more than ready to slam the door in their faces anyway.

'I've got a feeling we can help each other.' The man smiled in a way that made Jack distinctly uncomfortable. 'Is it true that Nancy has moved in?'

Jack was feeling more uncomfortable than ever about the way the conversation was going. They clearly knew a lot more about his situation than he did about them.

'Are you friends of hers?'

'Of course we are.' The larger of the women breezed past him with a surprising turn of speed before he had a chance to respond.

'You'd better come in then.' They were on their way in already.

'What on earth are you all doing here?' The car in Nancy's hand was dangling in mid-air.

'We saw your advert about the theatre group and the news is all over the town about you and David, so I rang your mum to see how you were. I'm Dilys Hamilton, by the way, the town clerk.' The tall woman held out her hand to Jack.

'Nice to meet you. I'm Nancy's housemate, Jack Williams.'

'Yes, we know who *you* are.' Dilys was blushing as she turned to the other two. 'This is Bernard Nicholson, chair of the town council, and Nerys Cooper, one of our other councillors.'

'Right, well do you want to sit down?' Jack still didn't have a clue what these people were doing in his front room, but that many bodies standing up in such a small space felt incredibly awkward.

'Thank you.' As if reading his mind, Bernard sat down and took charge of the situation – once a chairperson, always a chairperson. 'I'm sure you're wondering why we are here.'

'Well, *I* certainly am.' Whoever they were to Nancy, she didn't look that pleased to see them.

'I'm not sure if Nancy has told you, but it was the town council who approved her application to run the community theatre, and when we saw her posters on one of our noticeboards we thought it was only right to come up here.'

Jack couldn't tell if Bernard was smiling or grimacing;

his moustache seemed to have taken over the bottom half of his face.

'Look, Bernard, I'm sorry if I should have asked your permission to put the posters on the noticeboard first, but ...'

'It's not that.' Dilys cut Nancy off mid-flow. 'We thought we should be the first to sign up.'

'That's great. She was just saying how keen she was to get lots of talent signed up.' Jack couldn't supress a grin as he caught her eye. There were enough characters in the room to fill the cast of his next book. Maybe a decent publisher might even want that one.

'And, as founder members, we thought we might also have some say in the first production that we put on.' Nerys looked over her glasses at him and he was sure he saw her wink. 'We thought maybe one of yours?'

Jack was glad he was sitting down or he might have fallen over. He'd written a couple of plays straight out of university, when he'd thought that was going to be his thing, but they'd been self-published and obscure. He'd only ever known a couple of small rep theatre groups put them on – to dire reviews, he suspected. So, if they'd found out about his plays, God only knew how. Since then he'd had a couple of novels accepted by a tiny publishing house as e-books and had earned a pittance in royalties, but he hadn't written a play in for ever, so his brain couldn't quite process what was going on.

'I googled you, after I was at the college governors' meeting last week and Mary introduced all the new staff. In fact, I googled everyone, but you were the only one to turn up something *interesting*.'

Bernard's smile was more sinister than friendly.

'I found an article about Josephine Williams in the *Mail on Sunday* from a couple of weeks back which mentions her nephew Jack moving into the Bay that Dickens made famous. I can't believe we've got the nephew of a Broadway playwright in our midst. I mean everyone knows who she is since that alleged dalliance with a certain former US president ...'

'I'm flattered, but you're mistaken. Jack Williams is a horribly common name, there must be hundreds of us trying to make it as writers.' Jack tried to keep his voice level. It was the last thing he'd expected to happen.

'If that's the way you want to play it.' Bernard wasn't going to be put off. 'But I managed to find a couple of your plays online and we thought it would be great to put on the work of a local writer. Of course, if your aunt wanted to come and watch, that would be a bonus.'

'Even if I was related to someone as well-known as that, my stuff isn't right for Nancy's project. I'm sure you want what's best for the children here and so it was always going to be a panto first.' Jack fixed Bernard with a stare. It was a while since he'd had someone wanting to get to his aunt through him and he hadn't expected it to be an issue in St Nicholas Bay.

'Of course, of course.' Bernard smoothed his moustache. 'It was just a thought, and your aunt would be most welcome to pay a visit either way.'

'Unfortunately, I think you'll be disappointed, since the only aunt I have is a whist-whizz living in Penrith.' Jack was starting to enjoy himself as a look of abject disappointment crossed Bernard's face. 'Still, I'll let her know, and I'd be more than happy to help Nancy with anything else.'

His housemate smiled in response and stood up from where she'd been sitting with Toby, a determined look on her face.

'Well, thanks for coming, guys, and we can have a

111

chat about a panto that might suit the cast when we've got a few more members in the group, but I'll certainly bear in mind what you've said about Jack's plays for the future.'

She had gone into teacher mode and was ushering them out firmly, but without being rude.

'Yes, I really think you should.' Bernard was not quite ready to give up. 'And I presume we have your assurance that the recent events involving Olivia won't put the project at risk?'

'Of course. It won't be a problem.' Nancy had her hand on the small of his back, and if Bernard was used to dominating other people to get his own way, it looked as though he'd met his match.

When she'd finally seen them out and had closed the door behind them, Nancy leant her back against it and looked straight at him.

'Is Josephine Williams your aunt?'

For a moment or two he hesitated, but he didn't want to lie to her.

'Yes.'

'I take it I'm not the only one with complex family dynamics.'

She walked towards him and curled her fingers around his wrist, a jolt of desire taking him by surprise, and guilt washing over him at his response to her touch.

'I think we both need that drink more than ever, don't you?'

'I suppose you want to know all about it? It usually fascinates people.' Jack sank down onto the sofa.

'Like you said to me before, it's your business and you only have to tell me what you want to.' Nancy was already filling up their glasses. 'I'm happy to have a drink and pretend the town council mafia didn't turn up.' She passed him a glass. 'I wouldn't mind, but I deliberately avoided posting leaflets through their doors.'

'I really think I could get used to you, you know.' Jack took a swig of his drink and hoped it hadn't come out wrong, because he meant it as a compliment. Unlike most people, she seemed to know when to back off with the questions. He'd expected to gain a housemate but he'd found a friend.

'That's just as well, because it looks like you're stuck with me.'

CHAPTER FOURTEEN

'Are you sure you don't mind helping me out with this?' Nancy turned to look at Maisie and Jack, who were busy moving furniture around the old community centre to make the most of the space. Toby was asleep in his buggy in the corner and she wondered if anywhere had ever looked less like a theatre so close to opening its doors.

'Having met Bernard, I wasn't about to miss his audition piece.' Jack lifted up an oak table and carried it to the centre of the room with ease. In the seven days that they'd lived together, he had proved to be a constant surprise.

'I'm looking forward to that, too, but even more than that I don't want to miss out if Olivia shows up.' Maisie was leaning against a pillar that looked like it could do with steam-cleaning, it was so dusty, and Nancy wondered for the hundredth time how the hell they were going to make the space work. The town council had given them a small grant to cover the cost of some portable staging, but the rest would be down to her.

'Your guess is as good as mine.' Nancy pushed the ancient piano against the wall. It weighed a ton, and what it was doing there in the first place was a mystery. 'I sent her an email after I blocked her number on my phone, but she didn't reply.'

'Oh, she'll be here.' Maisie, who had been on a couple of nights out with Nancy and Olivia, grimaced. 'There's no way she'll miss out on being the centre of attention, or on having the power to make decisions about who gets cast first time around.'

'It's a community theatre, so we won't be turning anyone away.' Nancy metaphorically crossed her fingers that she wouldn't have to find some way of letting down anyone who turned out to be really dire. There were other ways people could get involved after all – prompting, helping out backstage, selling programmes once the shows got put on. 'What about you two? Are you going to try out?'

'I'd love to, but I've got no one to look after Tobes.' Jack gave her a wry smile. 'Added to which, in my experience, nearly all actors are self-obsessed tossers. In fact, my wife was the only one of them I've ever really liked, and even she wasn't above elbowing me out of the way to get into the limelight. As for the first actress I ever met, she left me scarred for life!'

He smiled, but it didn't convince Nancy. They were very different. She'd told him almost everything there was to know about her life in the first twenty-four hours of moving in, but Jack wasn't quite so open. She suspected she'd only just begun to get to know her housemate.

'That's true. They are generally egomaniacs.' Maisie nodded in agreement. 'Although if any of the blokes that turn up are lookers, I might still give it a go.'

'Great to know you'll be committed to the project, then.' Nancy grinned despite herself. Maisie and Jack had both been brilliant over the past week. Among other things they had reassured her that she'd manage for money even when, as expected, Trunchball gleefully accepted her resignation.

People started arriving on the dot of 4 p.m. It was a Saturday afternoon and Nancy hadn't been sure whether anyone would turn up; in fact, nerves had kept her awake for half the night before. She needn't have worried; there was a steady stream of St Nicholas Bay locals of all ages. Among the usual suspects were two total surprises. The first was her mother, and the second was Daniel Chapman. The look on Ruth's face, when he arrived five minutes after her, didn't need explanation. Livid didn't even come close.

'How dare he turn up here and waltz in. Like you would dream in a million years of letting him join!' Ruth's hands were on her hips and, as soon as she'd finished making her point, her lips returned to the thin line they'd been set in since his arrival.

'I'll have to give him a fair try like everyone, Mum. And even if he doesn't get a part, I'll have to offer him a job backstage.' Nancy was tempted to say that she'd find it a lot easier to get on working alongside Daniel than she would with Olivia, but Ruth hated him with a passion, and she couldn't be the one to set her mother straight. Some time ago she'd made a promise to her father, as had Daniel and her brother, Mark. Now she doubted her mother would ever know the truth, because no one wanted to break their word to John O'Brien.

'Get real. He's a glory hunter. He won't stick around if he doesn't get a lead role. So just make sure you don't give him one.' Her mother fixed her with the sort of look that went with being grounded back when she was a teenager.

'Looks like it won't just be my decision. I'm sorry, Mum, but can we talk about this later? Can you and Maisie ask the others to wait at the back of the hall, please, and I'll call you when we're ready.' Nancy caught her breath as Olivia swept towards her. She was wearing a tight red dress and boots with a ludicrously high heel that left small pock marks in the parquet as she crossed the floor. 'You got my email then?'

'Obviously.' Despite not having lifted a finger to help, Olivia immediately set herself down on one of the three chairs behind the old oak table, which Jack had set up in the centre of the room as a makeshift judges' panel.

'So, how do you want to do this?' Jack took the seat next to Olivia, so that Nancy could take the one on the end.

'What's it got to do with you?'

Olivia looked at him as though he were something she'd stepped in and Nancy barely resisted the urge to lean across and tell her exactly where she could shove her attitude.

'Is this the way you're playing it now?' Olivia was definitely spoiling for a fight. 'Taking your new boyfriend with you everywhere, like some sort of lap dog?'

Nancy could have explained that Jack wasn't her boyfriend, but it would drive her ex-friend crazy imagining what was really going on; the look on Olivia's face said as much. She only hoped he didn't mind being a pawn in their game.

'Actually Jack's got significant experience of directing and can make changes to the script where we need to, so I think he's got every right to help us decide on the cast.'

'So you've already decided on which pantomime then?' Olivia sniffed. She was amazing, really, acting like the wounded party after all she'd done.

'Cinderella with a twist.' Nancy smiled.

'What sort of twist?' Olivia's eyes flickered in her direction. 'The ugly sister gets her man?'

'No, we've decided to have a reformed Scrooge taking

the role of the Fairy Godmother.' Jack put an arm around Nancy as he spoke. 'We thought it was the perfect way to tie in everything St Nicholas Bay is famous for, without being completely *obvious*.' If Jack had intended to direct the last word at Olivia, it clearly hit home. Never had Nancy wanted to kiss someone so much.

'And what about my script approval?' Olivia looked like she was sucking on a lemon.

'You missed out on that when you didn't respond to my email, and everyone has been sent the audition scenes now, so we'll just have to go with it.'

Jack had stuck to the traditional flow of the fairy tale in the couple of scenes he'd had time to rewrite for the audition, but they'd been given more than just the twist of Scrooge with a magic wand. The scene which featured the wicked stepmother was a lot more sinister than Nancy remembered, and Cinderella's father leaving for business was really quite emotional. It touched Nancy at any rate. Maybe it was the situation with her own father that was making her sentimental over a pantomime. Watching Jack, though, she was sure the rewrites had come from the heart. He could have drawn on the loss of Alice, but she couldn't help thinking it went further back than that.

Of course, the question of who would play the role of Fairy God-Scrooge was the key decision of the night and, when Bernard was the last called forward to audition, Nancy couldn't help but be impressed at the effort he'd made.

'Am I going mad or is he sporting fairy wings?' Jack turned to look at her, more than a hint of a smile playing around his mouth, and she had to press her lips together for a moment.

'I wonder if he bought them especially for the occasion. Although, I suppose it's more worrying if he didn't!' Nancy whispered back.

'Will you two shut up? Some of us are trying to take this seriously.' Olivia's snapping drew far more attention to them than the initial whispering had.

'Is there a problem?' Bernard puffed up his chest. If his sense of self-importance was anything to go by, he was about to give an Oscar-winning performance.

'No, sorry, Bernard. I've just spotted a glitch in the script that I hadn't noticed before, but it doesn't affect the scene, so please go on.' Jack flicked the pages of his script over and Nancy caught sight of his wedding ring. He'd been through so much, and so recently too. He kept stepping in to defend her, to help her out and steer her away from trouble, and yet it was Jack who really needed the support.

'Jack's right, Bernard. Apologies, we can talk about it later. Go on, please.'

'Cinderella, you shall go to the ball!'

As Bernard shouted, Dilys, who was auditioning for a lead role too, stepped on to the stage.

'There's no way I'll ever be able to go to the ball. I'm nothing more than a servant since my stepmother arrived. My step-sisters tell me the best I can hope for is to dress them for the ball and count myself lucky that they're allowing me to do that when my hands are so rough and worn. Besides, they'd never let me inside the palace dressed like this.'

Dilys delivered the line with conviction, and although she was not the obvious choice for the role of Cinders, it looked like she had the makings of a capable actress.

'But I'm here to grant your wish. I have seen with my own eyes what the magic of Christmas can do. Making a pumpkin into a carriage will barely ruffle my nightgown in comparison.'

Bernard delivered the line with the monotone expression of a station announcer. Striding across the stage, he prepared to change her rags into a ballgown. The stage direction said that he was supposed to twirl her around, and he wrapped his one arm around her. But Bernard being eighteen inches shorter than Dilys meant that his arm ended up just below her ample bust, and in drawing her backwards he was inadvertently acting like some sort of human Wonderbra.

Dilys started to spin, just as directed in the script, and Bernard's character was supposed to guide her behind the screens to the left of the stage for a quick change, which would be masked by a smoke machine in the show itself. The balance of power was completely the wrong way round, however, and Dilys had clearly underestimated how much stronger she was than Bernard. She appeared to be dragging him across the stage while he clung to her like the world's oldest toddler having a tantrum.

'I know pantos are supposed to be funny, but this wasn't quite what I intended!' Jack lost the battle, his shoulders shaking as he spoke.

'Thank you, Bernard, Dilys.' Nancy stood up, hoping the change of position would stop her from joining Jack, who had tears streaming from his eyes. 'We'll be letting everyone know which parts have been allocated once the auditions are over and we've had time to deliberate. You've certainly entertained us though.' It must have been the years of practice at the college that had done it, giving students some positive feedback for even the most dire of performances. Somehow she managed to say it with a straight face, her insides aching from the effort.

'It was entertaining all right.' Having regained a

modicum of composure, Jack leant back as if he wanted to make sure Olivia heard everything he was about to say to Nancy. 'I think we've earned a drink after that, gorgeous. Your place or mine?'

It was getting on for six by the time they left the auditions and set off towards home, and Toby had woken up. He was in his buggy, happily alternating between sucking on a rusk and drinking milk out of his supposedly un-spill-able cup, waving it around spraying milk into the air while babbling a little song of his own creation.

'You almost gave me a heart attack for a moment with that gorgeous stuff.' Nancy dodged to one side as Toby sent a spray of milk out from the side of his buggy that would otherwise have been a direct hit.

'I know. I would say that I was sorry, but the look on Olivia's face made it all worthwhile.'

'It was quite something.'

All in all it had been a good afternoon. She'd faced Olivia and, with Jack on her side, she'd got through it and managed to get her own way about the auditions. She knew he wouldn't be able to hold her hand through all of it, but it had made the difference today. Even having her mum and Daniel in the same room hadn't exploded in the way that she thought it might.

'How about if I treat you to fish and chips to celebrate?' she suggested.

The smell of cooking from Charlie D's fish bar was wafting towards them and Nancy realised she was starving. The name of the restaurant might have been one of the worst attempts to work the Bay's Dickens connection, but the food was great.

'I can't let you do that. I know money's tight after

losing the hours at the college, but I think it's a great idea. How about I treat you instead?' Jack was quickening the pace as he pushed the buggy nearer the fish shop, trying to race Nancy to beat her to the till.

'No way! If things get so bad that I can't afford two portions of fish and chips then I might as well give up altogether.'

In the end, she persuaded him to let her buy dinner and they settled down in front of the TV and ate out of the paper. Toby was straight back to his garage, deciding what it really needed was a tower of bricks – well more of an abstract pile really – on the roof of the building.

Afterwards Jack managed to feed him some sort of pureed mixture, until Toby started to reject more of it than was going in.

'Can I ask you something?' He didn't look up as he spoke and she wondered if he didn't want to make eye contact, or if Toby's chin actually needed as much attention as he was paying it.

'When people say that, they usually ask anyway, so go for it.'

'You and Olivia.' He paused, finally looking up at her. 'I'm struggling to work out what the two of you ever had in common.'

'It's almost hard to remember after what she did, but we were at St Nicholas Bay High at the same time. She was a couple of years older and always one of the cool kids. We were both always into acting, though, and so I knew her through the drama club. I suppose I wanted to be her back then, even though she wasn't the nicest person in the world.'

'It doesn't sound like an awful lot's changed then.'

'Put it this way, she wasn't the sort of person you wanted to get on the wrong side of. Nothing physical, but she and her group of friends seemed to pick a new person to victimise each term and I suppose I was just glad it was never me. I was never what you'd call cool and I mostly hung out with the other kids in the drama club, but all the girls wanted to be Olivia at some point, I think. She was slim, pretty, and used to get picked up from school when she was in the sixth form in her boyfriend's sports car.' Nancy laughed at the look on Jack's face. 'You can mock, but these things were important at the time!'

'Okay, so maybe I can buy the allure of the mean girls to a naïve schoolgirl, but why did you stay friends?'

'I suppose circumstances threw us together. She married Miles just after she turned twenty-one and was soon left at home with her first baby, with Miles away for weeks at a time working as a pilot. I came home a year or so later, after leaving Bath, and our friendship sort of grew from there. Her old gang were all still single and childless and my friends were away at uni, so I'd babysit sometimes for her and Miles so that I could get out of the house once Dad was home from work to keep an eye on Mum, and we started to hang out a bit more.'

'And was she there for you when your dad got ill and you split up with Fraser?' He raised an eyebrow, suggesting he already knew her answer.

'She was busy with the kids.' Nancy held up her hands. 'All right, if I'm honest, not nearly as much as she could have been, and certainly not as much as I was for her when she found out Miles was having an affair with one of the stewardesses. I suppose it's always been out of kilter and that's why Mum never liked her.'

'It seems like you've got a habit of putting yourself last.' Jack's dark eyes held her gaze for a moment. All this was starting to feel uncomfortably like she was being profiled, like a character in one of his books. 'You don't have to do it, you know, just to make people like you or so you feel worthwhile.'

'Is that what you think I'm doing?' It was none of his business even if she was; he hardly knew her.

'It's what it looks like from where I'm standing. I'm just worried about Olivia finding a way to manipulate you, to play you like she has before.'

'I'm not an idiot or – what was it you called me? – a naïve schoolgirl any more …' She moved away as he reached out to touch her hand.

'Look, I'm sorry, that probably came out wrong. I saw it with Alice, that desire for everyone to love you, but you don't get it from letting people walk all over you.'

She was tempted to tell him what she really thought – that she wasn't Alice and she wasn't the doormat he seemed to have her down as either. But the truth was he'd touched a nerve. It would have been easy to open his wounds by telling him she wasn't a stand-in for his dead wife, but that would be a cheap shot, just because he'd made her feel uncomfortable. Instead, she forced a tight smile that made her ears ache.

'Thanks for your wisdom. I'll bear it in mind.' Piling the plates on top of one another, she shivered. 'I'm off to bed.' By the time she got to the sink, the tension in her jaw was painful and, for the first time since she'd moved in, she wondered if she'd made a mistake.

CHAPTER FIFTEEN

The week hadn't got off to the best of starts. There was tension in the house all day on Sunday and Jack was aware that the blame lay with him. His interpretation of Nancy's friendship with Olivia was mostly based on his own baggage. It was Nancy's way to put herself out for others and, unlike Alice, she didn't seem to have an ulterior motive. Alice had needed to be adored, to feel like she had fans. She had thrived on the promise that maybe one day her name really would be up in lights. Nancy had a different motivation, but stepping in to protect her – even if she didn't want him to – was about easing his guilt that he hadn't been able to prevent Alice paying the ultimate price. He'd wanted to apologise, but having stomped all over such a sensitive subject once, he couldn't quite bring himself to stir it up again. He'd need a therapist at this rate.

On Monday, Craig had phoned and left a message asking Jack to call him when he had a break from teaching.

'Good to hear from you, mate.' Craig, who had his own plumbing business, sounded as though he was taking the call in a bathroom, his voice echoing off tiled walls.

'Not in the middle of working, are you?' Jack had often envied his best friend's lifestyle but, looking down at his own hands, he suppressed a smile. He'd never had a talent for mending things and Craig had christened him Bob the Bodger when he'd tried to fit some kitchen units in the flat. It had ended up costing him more to replace them than he'd have spent on hiring a kitchen fitter in the first place.

'No, Selena and I have got the morning off, just taking in a few sights.'

'How the other half live, eh?'

Did Craig know how lucky he was, having someone to spend his morning off with?

'Yeah, yeah, it's one long party in the world of plumbing, you know. Nothing like those long summer holidays you teacher-types have to slog through.'

'Well, clearly you've got time to skive off for the morning, on a Monday no less, and phone up a hardworking teacher – taking me away from the very important business of crushing people's hopes and dreams … Sorry, I mean marking their creative-writing assignments.'

'You said it, mate! You know what, I think I need to get down there and insult you in person. It just isn't the same over the phone.' Craig paused for a moment and took a breath before he spoke again. 'Selena and I were thinking of coming down for the weekend and staying at a hotel, now you've got a lodger.'

'Oh, okay.' It wasn't that Jack didn't want to see Craig again, but it had only been a couple of weeks and he felt awkward about merging his new life with the old one now that Nancy was living in his house.

'Look, if you've got plans just say, mate. We can do it another weekend. It's just we've got something we want to talk to you about and it'd be great to see you.' There was something in Craig's tone that made up Jack's mind.

If it was what he suspected, he didn't want to hear it over the phone any more than they wanted to announce it that way. Life was moving on without Alice, whether he wanted it to or not.

'No, no plans. It would be great to see you, and you can meet Nancy and see how good she is for Toby.' Although there was no certainty Nancy would still be there by the weekend after the way he'd put his foot in it.

✳

'You all right, Nance? You look lost in thought.' Maisie plonked a cup of coffee in front of her, sending some sloshing out of the cup so Nancy had to whip the pile of scripts on her desk out of the way.

'Thanks, I was just thinking about work.'

'Liar! I know that look.' Maisie swivelled the base of Nancy's chair so that she couldn't avoid looking at her friend. 'Come on, is your mood down to my brother or your gorgeous but brooding housemate?'

'Am I a doormat?'

'Is this a drama question? Like when your class act out being trees? Are you supposed to be a doormat?' Maisie grinned as Nancy shook her head. 'I wouldn't say you were a doormat by a long stretch, but if you mean are you sometimes too nice for your own good, then I'd have to say yes.'

'Right.' Nancy picked up her lesson plan and the pile of scripts she'd just saved from a drenching. 'And that's a bad thing?'

'Well, no ...' Maisie looked like she was going to say something else, but then shook her head. 'What's brought this on?'

'Just something Jack said about me being friends with Olivia.'

'I was right then, it was the gorgeous housemate, in the library with a candlestick.' Maisie gave her leg a squeeze. 'Don't change, Nancy, just because there are people like Olivia out there. I'm sure Jack doesn't really think you should change either.'

'I wouldn't be so sure about that.' Nancy put the scripts and lesson plans into a box file. Sometimes the urge to put herself first rose to the surface, but there was always something or someone she was responsible for – this time it was her second-year diploma students. 'I'm teaching in five minutes, but we'll catch up later and I'll let you know which part you got in the panto.' She couldn't help smiling at the look of excitement that crossed her friend's face.

'You can't do that, Nance! Tell me now, please!' Maisie gave her an imploring look.

'Sorry, got to stick to protocol. I can't tell you until I've emailed everyone who auditioned.'

'I take it all back.' Maisie crossed her arms, looking every bit as stroppy as one of Nancy's seventeen-year-old students. 'You're nowhere near as nice as I thought you were!'

'Well done, everyone. That was a great read-through.' Nancy smiled at the group of teenagers on the stage of the lecture theatre and braced herself for their response to what she had to say next. 'We need to devote the next couple of lessons to working with the art department on set construction.'

'Oh Miss!' Laura, who had perfect Kate Middleton hair, stuck out her bottom lip. 'Do we have to do all that other stuff? I just wanna be an actress, not get covered in paint and get splinters in my arse lugging scenery about.'

Nancy suppressed a smile, knowing she shouldn't laugh. Principal Jefferies insisted that students call the lecturers Sir or Miss, even though most colleges operated on a first-name basis. She had a feeling it would be one of the first things Fraser would change. All the same, it didn't do to laugh when one of the students said 'arse'.

'Yep, Laura, you do. As I've told you at least a hundred times over the last term, scenery construction is a key part of your diploma.' She met the younger woman's gaze. 'And clearly you need a lot more practice if you're managing to end up with splinters in your bum.'

The smile that had crept across her face disappeared as she caught sight of a figure through the glass pane in the door.

'Okay, guys, thanks again for today. You've all worked really hard to learn your lines and you'll be word perfect long before the spring revue. I'll see some of you at The Merry Players rehearsals later in the week and the emails will go out tonight about parts in the panto for those of you who auditioned.'

Dropping their scripts into the box file, Nancy's students began to leave the lecture theatre, almost immediately glued to the mobiles she'd insisted were turned off and left at the back for the lesson. If she'd had any doubt about who'd been watching them through the glass pane, it was quickly dashed. Fraser held open the door for the students as they filed out, causing a group of the girls to start giggling and whispering. Having a principal as good-looking as Fraser was likely to liven college life up for some of the students, not to mention the staff.

'You've still got it, Nance. Those kids are doing great.' Fraser crossed the space between them as soon as the last of the students had left the room.

'How much of it did you see?' Nancy spent far longer than she needed straightening up the scripts. He wasn't supposed to be here. Not yet.

'Ten minutes or so.' He touched the sleeve of her jumper, but she wasn't ready to be around him. She'd had it all planned out and this wasn't the way she'd rehearsed it.

'I didn't think you were taking over until after Christmas.'

'I'm not. I'm contracted down in Cornwall until then, but I was at a conference in London over the weekend and so I told the governors I'd pop in today before heading home. To check out the lie of the land, see what's changed.' He ran a hand through his hair – the colour of wet sand, just as she'd remembered.

'Not much has changed here as you can see. We're still having to sneak the odd rehearsal session in the lecture theatre and put the shows on here because we don't have a proper drama studio.' She shot him a look, daring him to trot out the same line Trunchball would have about them being lucky to have funding for the course at all.

'We'll have to see what we can do about that.'

'Don't make promises you can't keep, Fraser.'

'Are we still talking about the drama studio?' His hand was on her arm again and it was all she could do to look up at him instead of running out of the lecture theatre and never coming back.

'What else would I be talking about?'

'Maisie told me about what happened with you and David … and Olivia.'

Sympathy from Fraser was the last thing she needed.

'Did she?' Blabbermouth.

'Look, do you want to go for a coffee, off campus,

somewhere we can talk?'

'I can't.' Nancy lifted the box file up to her chest, wrapping her arms around it like a makeshift shield. 'I'm picking Toby up from nursery.'

'Toby?'

'Oh, did Maisie neglect to tell you that bit?' Nancy moved past him towards the door. 'Maybe she's the one you should take for coffee. I'm sure she'll be only too willing to fill you in on the guy I've moved in with. Toby's his little boy. I'll see you in the New Year, Fraser.'

If it was childish to leave Fraser open-mouthed and let him think Jack was more than just a housemate, then that's what she was. Maybe Maisie was right. She wasn't that nice at all.

CHAPTER SIXTEEN

'You look better, Jack, more like the old you.'

Craig was leaning against the work surface in the small kitchen of the cottage as Jack put the finishing touches to his famous chicken curry. He wasn't the best chef in the world, but there were one or two meals he could cook which always went down well.

'It's been a lot better since Nancy moved in.' He shook his head at the look that crossed Craig's face. 'Not like that. I just mean having another adult to talk to, even if it's as mundane as discussing what we're watching on TV. It stops me having to think all the time. The flipside is I feel guilty sometimes that I don't miss Alice in quite that same gut-wrenching way as I did in those first few weeks. It's not like I've replaced her obviously, but maybe it's wrong that having company somehow takes the edge off.'

'I'm sorry I haven't been around more, mate. It's just with work and everything.' Craig took a swig from his can of beer.

'You've always been at the end of the phone, and it was me that moved miles away, not the other way round.'

'You've nothing to feel guilty about, you know that, don't you?' Craig put the can down and looked directly at him. 'It's not any reflection on how you felt about Alice to want to take the edge off things by surrounding yourself with new people. Alice loved being the life and soul of every party we ever had and she wouldn't have wanted you to make yourself more miserable by being lonely.'

'I know. If it had been the other way round I've got a feeling she'd have grabbed life by the throat all the more because of what she'd lost, but it's hard to know what you're supposed to do.'

'You're not *supposed* to do anything. You can't live your life to prove some kind of point to Alice's mum, or anyone else for that matter. What you've been through is shitty enough without feeling guilty about everything.'

'Thanks, mate. I know you're right, but I seem to be all over the place at the moment. I even started giving Nancy advice about her life the other night, like I'm in any kind of position to do that sort of thing!' Jack managed a wry smile. 'I think she was close to packing her bags and I wouldn't have blamed her.'

'She put up with listening to *your* advice?' Craig laughed as Jack nodded his head. 'Jeez, mate, then she's a keeper as a housemate!'

'Thank God, because Toby loves her and she's brilliant with him.' Even as he said it, the guilt Craig had encouraged him to let go of surged up again. Would Alice have wanted another woman to have such a bond with her son?

'Toby's shaping up to be a great kid. Lissy would have been proud of you.' Craig seemed to read his mind, crossing the small room to pat him on the back, making his eyes water, a fact he'd have to blame on the curry if his old friend noticed.

'This needs to simmer for another twenty minutes or so. Shall we go and see if Toby's mastered that new puzzle you bought him yet?' Replacing the lid on the saucepan, Jack led the way through to the front room, where Toby had Nancy and Selena at his beck and call. His son certainly had a way with the women in his life. Craig was right, Alice would have been so proud of him.

'Looks like he's got you right where he wants you.' Jack looked down at Selena who had her hands cupped in front of her, where Toby was placing brick after brick as though she was a human dumper-truck.

'He's very persuasive.' Selena grinned. 'He might not have the words, but he has a very effective way of letting you know what he wants all the same.' As if to illustrate the point, Toby pulled down on her wrist so the bricks she'd been holding were tipped into a pile next to his garage. As she moved, Jack noticed the ring on her left hand catch the light. If there'd been any doubt about what Craig and Selena wanted to say, there wasn't any more.

'Da, da, da, da.' Toby held a brick out to him.

'So, come on then. What's this big news you've trudged all the way down to the sticks to share?' Jack fixed a smile on his face. Perhaps he should ask Nancy for a part in her show, although acting was a lot harder than it looked.

'We wanted to ask you what you're doing on June twentieth next year.' Selena, who'd been released from her dumper-truck duties, stood up and moved to join Craig on the sofa, her fingers interlacing with his like they belonged there.

'Oh, I don't know. Probably fighting for a parking space with the influx of tourists to St Nicholas Bay.' He tried not to think about the fact that next June would also mark a year without Alice. Life trudged on.

'Nothing you can't dump for a wedding then?' Craig's smile could have graced a toothpaste ad.

'Nothing would keep me away.' Jack stood and hugged them both, auto-pilot kicking in. 'You two don't hang about, do you!'

Craig shrugged in that wonderfully casual way he had. 'My folks had already booked to come over from Oz next summer, so we thought it would be good to tie it all in.'

'Congratulations!' Nancy was beaming, but it must have stirred some emotion in her too. She'd been quiet all week, even though they'd cleared the air. The thought that things might not be fully resolved between her and David didn't do anything to cheer Jack up.

'Thank you.' Selena returned Nancy's smile and Toby looked up at them both before returning to his pile of bricks. If only Jack could have got away with doing the same.

'I need more detail. It's a girl thing.'

At least Nancy was managing to say all the right things.

'It's been such a whirlwind, I have to think for a minute to remember how it all happened.' Selena giggled and held out her ring finger. 'You can't miss this, though. He chose it himself.' The ring was a simple diamond solitaire, almost exactly like the one that Jack had given Alice three years before. Would anyone but he remember that?

'I picked it myself.' There was definitely a note of pride in Craig's voice. 'I got down on one knee, did the whole works. I even asked her dad first!'

'Who'd have thought you'd go all traditional.' Jack's voice was monotone, despite his best attempt at enthusiasm. He was happy for them but, with the best days of his life already behind him, would he have something to celebrate again?

'In some ways, I guess we are.' Craig grinned and

wrapped an arm around his fiancée's shoulders. 'Although I reckon some people might think we're crazy and it's too fast, but neither of us have ever felt this way before … Why wait?'

'And, what the heck, it's not until June.' Selena planted a quick kiss on his lips. 'I've still got plenty of time to change my mind!'

'As if!' Craig pulled her closer still and looked up at Jack. 'We knew you'd understand that life's too short to hang around waiting for the right time just because other people think you should. That's why we wanted to tell you first, straight after our families.'

Craig's eyes were scanning Jack's face. He had to keep his feelings in check and focus on their news.

'I think it's brilliant and Lissy would have loved it. You know she'd have been getting involved in organising everything, sorting out Selena's hen night and insisting on being chief bridesmaid.' Jack smiled despite the pain twisting his insides, knowing it was exactly what she'd have done.

'Talking of which, if you're up for it, we'd love you to be best man.' Craig's words were heavy with expectation and Jack managed a nod.

'Honoured.' It was all he could say, the word catching against his throat like sandpaper.

'I'm so glad that you're okay with it, Jack.'

Fishing a thick cream envelope out of her bag, Selena handed it to him – invitations already.

He pulled out the card, a black and white photograph on the front. It was clearly a selfie, taken on the balcony of Craig's flat, the two of them beaming and Selena flashing her sparkling ring at the camera, probably straight after he'd proposed. It was all the nicer for that though; no posed studio shots – just the happiest moment of their lives. He and Alice hadn't taken any photographs on the day they'd got engaged but, God, he wished now they had. In fact he wished he'd taken more photographs of every aspect of their lives together. He was terrified he was going to forget things about her – how she'd looked first thing in the morning, without her make-up. She'd have hated being photographed like that, but he needed to see her like that again – even if it was just in a picture. Anything would be better than nothing at all.

'Great picture,' he managed to say.

'I'll put it above the fireplace for you.' Nancy had to prise the invitation out of his hands. He'd disappeared into his own world for a moment and she'd realised.

'Thanks. It'll be something to look forward to. Good food, wine, dancing, my best friends tying the knot, but for now,' Jack stood up again and moved towards the door, 'I'm afraid you'll just have to settle for my chicken curry.'

By the time Selena and Craig headed back to their hotel a few hours later, Jack was exhausted.

When he walked through to the lounge, after seeing them out, Nancy was reading the wedding invitation. Turning to look at him, she had tears in her eyes.

'Hard, isn't it?' He was weighed down by the mixed emotions he'd been desperately trying to keep in all night, but they were kindred spirits, he and Nancy, in many ways. 'Does it make you think about what might have been, with David?'

'No, it's not that and I shouldn't be so self-indulgent. You've got far more reason to be emotional about it than I have.' Nancy tried to smile.

'Hey, you've got every right to be upset. I don't have

the monopoly on a broken heart, unfortunately. Even if I do sometimes mentally pull rank if other people complain about their lives.'

He leant down and topped up both their glasses before joining Nancy who'd moved to the sofa, the invitation still in her hand.

'It's this picture on the other side.'

She turned the invitation over and there was a picture on the back he hadn't even noticed before.

'It must be Selena and her dad.'

It was definitely Selena – she had the same dark wavy hair and the big, dark eyes were unmistakeable, her head on one side leaning against her dad's chest as they danced together. She looked about ten years old. There was a caption underneath with the date of the wedding and the words, *Please come and see me dance with my dad again.*

'It's about your dad then?'

'I'm being stupid.' Her eyes filled with tears again as she looked at him. 'Sometimes I surprise myself with what hurts me about losing him. It's not the things you imagine, but having the shell of him still there is worse than anything.'

'You're not being stupid at all. I can't begin to imagine what it's like. Did your dad know you were engaged?' He hoped he wasn't saying the wrong thing, especially after the way their last meaningful conversation had ended.

'No, he was too far gone by then. It's funny, whenever I thought about getting married, before David and I had even met, I could visualise Dad walking me down the aisle, making a speech to say how proud he was, and most of all dancing with me at my wedding. The image of the groom was always fuzzy in my mind, but I could picture Dad so clearly and I know he'd have loved that role. Only now I'll never have that. I'll *never* dance with my dad again, never have a photo to treasure like Selena will. It's mad to be jealous of a moment she hasn't even had yet, but the might-have-beens hurt like hell.'

Without thinking, Jack put his arm around her shoulder and pulled her towards him until her head was resting on his chest, their losses bringing them together. They didn't need to say anything, but there was comfort in their understanding that just about made it bearable.

CHAPTER SEVENTEEN

'You want to do what?'

Ruth looked at her daughter as though she was mad. Nancy was racing around, setting up for The Merry Players' first official rehearsal. Irritated didn't quite cover Ruth's emotions, having seen the cast list on the noticeboard. She didn't read her emails any more, not since the last one from Philly at the golf club, which was filled with self-congratulation and news about social events she and John were no longer part of. So the list on the noticeboard was the first she knew about who'd secured which role. Nancy casting Daniel as Scrooge meant Ruth would be forced to act in a scene with him. To say this hadn't put her in the best of moods was a considerable understatement. She was still contemplating whether to pull out, and now her daughter had sprung this on her. The one person she could usually rely on seemed to be turning against her, too.

'You heard me, Mum. I want to put on a tea dance at The Pines.'

Nancy looked up briefly from setting up the collapsible stage. A small part of Ruth acknowledged she was doing an amazing job without much help from Olivia. Before finding out about Daniel's lead role, she'd been determined to help out more. Nancy would appreciate it and she could use something to occupy her time to distract her from becoming too bitter.

'And whose bright idea was that?' She couldn't seem to stop herself snapping.

'Jack thought it might be nice.'

'Oh did he, indeed? And when was the last time he was at The Pines and saw what they're like? It's just what they need, a tea dance for a bunch of vegetables.' As the word escaped from her lips, she shocked herself, and she had to sit down.

'Mum! You can't say that! He's still Dad, they're all still people. They're just trapped inside a body, a brain, that's let them down.'

'I know, love, I'm sorry. I don't know why I said something so horrible. I just don't know how much more I can take, and then I came here and saw what you'd decided about Daniel and I lost it.' Tears stung her eyes. It was so unfair that a good man like John had lost everything, from his memories to his dignity, and a bastard like Daniel was lording it up as the star of the show.

'I had to cast Daniel. He was the only man with the right comic timing and a decent-enough singing voice at the auditions, but you shouldn't let yourself get eaten up with hatred towards him. Dad was happy with the deal and we have to trust his judgement.'

Nancy sat beside her and placed a hand on her arm, the maternal role shifting between them.

'Yes, but looking back now, his judgement was already impaired and I'm convinced Daniel knew and took advantage of that. The way he operates, your father probably had no choice but to sell the shop to him or be driven out of business anyway. I hate going past the old place now and I bet the service is nothing like it used to be when we had it.'

'Maybe not, Mum, but that's his way and he's already opened a second branch in Copplestone. You know that was always Dad's dream and Daniel has even called the new place O'Brien's. I think Dad would have liked it.'

If Nancy's words were meant to offer Ruth some comfort, they'd fallen a long way short. The fact Daniel had taken John's name and used it to his advantage made Ruth sick to her stomach. Marley's Chains would always be called that because of its location in the Bay and the Dickens connection, but John had longed for a second shop with the family name – a place their son Mark could run as his own. But Mark had disappeared along with the dream.

'So tell me about this tea dance then.' Desperate to change the subject and stop taking things out on her daughter, Ruth forced a smile. 'I'm sorry for being such a horrible old cow. It's a lovely idea.'

'It's all right. I know Dad won't remember it and he won't even know he's dancing with his daughter, but *I will*. And even if he enjoys it for the few moments we're actually dancing together, it'll be worth it, won't it?'

There was so much hope in Nancy's eyes that Ruth couldn't bear to crush it.

It was definitely going to be one of those nights for Nancy. It was bad enough that her mum seemed to have been tipped over the edge by Daniel's casting, but Bernard, Dilys and some of the others were also moaning about the roles they'd been assigned, despite numerous email exchanges. She hated this bit; even with her classes at college there was always someone who felt put out because they hadn't won the role they thought they deserved.

Maisie, who had been given the role of Cinderella, was one of the few who was smiling. Kate and Will, two teachers from the Bay's primary school, had originally come along just to help out with Mini Merries, the children had been given roles as the mice who would be turned into horses or as dancers at the royal ball. They had a natural camaraderie that came from years of friendship, so eventually Nancy had persuaded them to take on the role of the ugly sisters. Watching them round up the kids they spent all week teaching, Nancy crossed her fingers that Kate and Will wouldn't decide to back out. After all, it wasn't everyone who'd want to extend their working day into their spare time.

Even Daniel didn't seem that delighted, despite having the coveted role of Scrooge.

'I thought your mum might have a bigger part.'

He ran a hand through his hair. It was obvious from his appearance that he had money. His clothes screamed quality, even the casual linen shirt and jeans he was wearing. The Rolex on his wrist was an even bigger clue, but Nancy was well aware there was a soft heart beating below his façade. She wished more than ever that she could share this knowledge with her mother.

'Mum had to be persuaded quite forcefully to take a speaking part at all.' Nancy shrugged and decided not to tell him how close Ruth had come to quitting because of him.

'It's a shame. I thought maybe working together on the play would help her to see that I'm not the ogre she thinks I am. I'd never tell her what happened with John, of course, but I can't help hoping she might come to the conclusion herself that I'm not all bad.'

He looked genuinely disappointed. It wouldn't have surprised her if that had been his sole reason for joining The Merry Players.

'I keep singing your praises.' She squeezed his hand briefly. 'Thanks for keeping the promise to Dad. I know he'd thank you for it if he could.'

'I'll take it to my grave.' Daniel smiled.

Nancy didn't doubt him for a second.

'It really means a lot. I suppose we'd better get down to the business of rehearsing if we're ever going to put this show on. Would you mind handing these scripts out to the others? I thought we might do a read-through of the first scene.'

Nancy reached out to pass them to him just as the doors at the back of the building swung open and Olivia stood motionless, as if she was waiting for some acknowledgement of her arrival. Nancy could think of a few things to say, but just about managed to keep them in.

'Looks like the princess has arrived.' Daniel winked at Nancy as he took the scripts. 'Don't worry, we know who does all the work around here.'

'What do you want me to do?' Olivia walked towards her and Nancy fought the urge to give her an honest answer.

'I've just given Daniel the scripts to hand out, so I thought we'd do a read-through of the first scene. Do you want to follow a script and prompt them for emphasis in the dialogue while I direct the action?' She couldn't quite bring herself to look her ex-friend in the eyes, even though it should have been Olivia dropping her gaze with embarrassment.

'Oh, I see. So you get to be the director and I'm the prompt?' Olivia wrinkled her nose.

'We're both directing. You're doing the dialogue and

I'm doing the action, that's all. If it makes you feel better, though, I'm happy to swap with you.' Nancy finally forced herself to look at the other woman, who shook her head.

'No, it's fine. As long as you're not trying to marginalise me again.' Olivia gave her a tight little smile. 'Where is your side-kick today, anyway? At home washing his hair?'

'His mother-in-law has come down to pick up Toby for the weekend.' Part of Nancy wanted to tell Olivia to mind her own business. Whatever Nancy said, Olivia was bound to cheapen it, judging everyone by her standards.

'That's nice. Cosy it being just the two of you. I'm sure you're glad to get the kid out of the way.'

'Where do you want to sit, or are you going to stand to direct the dialogue?'

Nancy didn't want to let the remark about Toby go. She loved being around him and missed him almost as much as Jack did when he was away at Pam's, but Olivia wasn't worth the effort. She'd believe what she wanted to believe, either way, and it was a perverse sort of fun to let her work herself up imagining Nancy's wonderful new life. Olivia and David's relationship was over and, according to what Maisie had heard, he was already dating one of the barmaids from the golf club – so Olivia was obviously feeling left behind.

'Where are you going to stand?' Olivia looked at her pointedly. It was like she had to be in competition with Nancy on every little point. It was strange to think how quickly the irretrievable breakdown in their friendship had happened. Had it been built on such shallow foundations? Despite how difficult it had been to hear, Jack was probably right that the friendship had always been all one way. Olivia was choosing to act like they were back in the playground, but it was a hard lesson to learn at any age that her friend had never cared about her.

'I'm going to stand back from the stage, so I can see the interaction from the audience's viewpoint.' Nancy paused. 'I think you'll need to be considerably closer to direct the speech.' It didn't really make any difference where Olivia stood, as long as it wasn't next to her.

Going with tradition, they'd decided the wicked stepmother should be a pantomime dame. Despite his initial reluctance, Bernard was soon camping it up with considerable style. Daniel, on the other hand, was making half-hearted efforts at best. Scrooge had much more of a role than the fairy godmother normally would, as Jack's hybrid version of *Cinderella* had him disguised as the family's butler so he could appear in almost every scene. It had seemed like a good idea when Daniel had given such a convincing audition; now Nancy wasn't so sure.

'Daniel, you need to project more.' Olivia strode across the stage, a look of determination in her eyes like a predator on the hunt. Nancy had a horrible feeling that Olivia was up to her old tricks. She was leaning in to Daniel, her body almost pressed up against his, placing one hand on the front of his shirt. 'You need to project from your diaphragm and not your throat.'

'Okay, thanks.' Daniel shifted back slightly, his eyes flitting towards where Ruth was standing, her arms folded tightly across her chest.

'Olivia's right, Daniel. If you could project a bit more it would lift the scene and ensure you're the focal point when you're speaking. Bernard, you're doing a great job. Looks like you were born for the role!' Nancy felt the tension leave her shoulders when Bernard smiled in response. It had been the right decision to cast him, and thankfully it looked like he finally agreed. 'Kate and Will, it's great you're interacting as you really might with a sister, laughing and bickering, but we need to make sure that it doesn't overpower the other actors when you aren't the focal point in the scene.'

'This is all sounding very professional.'

A loud voice from the back of the hall commanded immediate attention and made Nancy jump. She looked round, a sense of dread washing over her.

'Am I too late to get a part?'

'Miles, what on earth are you doing here?' Olivia moved away from Daniel as fast as if he had burst into flames.

'I need to talk to you, Liv, to put things right.' He looked directly at his estranged wife and Olivia put an arm out to steady herself against the wall. If she'd still been a friend, Nancy would have done whatever it took, shaken her if needs be, and told her not to run back to Miles at the click of his fingers after all he'd put her through. Instead she watched her walk towards him like she was in a trance.

'There's no hurry. If Nancy can't spare you now, I can wait for a bit.' Miles might have been playing the Mr Nice card, but it wasn't fooling Nancy.

'No, it's fine, they can manage without me, I'm sure.' Without even looking in her direction, Olivia swept past, her simpering tone somewhere between sickening and sad. A tiny part of Nancy actually felt sorry for her.

'You're doing a great job, you know. The rehearsal was better as soon as *she* shoved off to chase after Miles.'

Ruth smiled at her daughter, wishing she could find the words to tell her how proud she was. She had two children and loved them in equal measure as a mother had to, but while she barely saw Mark, she couldn't imagine life without seeing Nancy on a regular basis. Knowing how much that had cost Nancy in the past, though, made it hard to say what she wanted to sometimes without putting more pressure on her daughter. Ruth was determined to stop sniping at Daniel, at least in front of Nancy. It wasn't fair on her when Olivia had predictably left her in the lurch at the first opportunity.

'Do you really think it was okay?'

Nancy looked up from where she'd been scribbling notes into the margin of one of the scripts.

'It was really funny. Kate and Will are hilarious together, although like you said they're in danger of stealing the show.' Ruth smiled. 'Although, that said, I never thought Bernard would come into his own quite so much as the dame. I think you've created a star there.'

'Or maybe a monster!' Nancy squeezed her hand. 'Thanks, Mum.'

'For what?'

'For being here, for doing your best to get on with Daniel. I saw you trying not to look quite so daggers at him after Olivia left. He's not a bad guy, you know.'

'Let's not talk about that as we'll only disagree.' Ruth returned the squeeze of the hand. 'But I promise to be on my best behaviour. We've already got one diva in Olivia and that's more than enough.'

'I was so shocked when Miles turned up, although less so when she dropped everything to be with him.' Nancy sighed. 'Two unexpected arrivals in a week.'

'What was the other one?' Ruth hadn't missed the look that crossed Nancy's face.

'Fraser came to the college on a flying visit to check things out.'

'You didn't say ... How was he?'

'Just the same, and I wanted to play it cool, convince myself as much as him that I was okay with him coming back and that we can be friends.' Nancy's eyes were glassy as she looked up at Ruth. 'Instead I acted like a stroppy teenager to try and hide my feelings.'

'And? How did you feel, seeing him again?' Ruth had never got the full story about why Nancy and Fraser had split and she'd hated herself for being glad they had; glad that Nancy had chosen to stay in the Bay when Fraser left.

'Awkward, almost like we were strangers, but I'm not sure. Maybe if he'd shown the slightest hint of interest I'd have been like Olivia and been at his beck and call, no questions asked.' Nancy shrugged. 'I guess I'll find out if we can get along as colleagues when he's back for good. If not, there's always the checkout at the Co-op.'

'You'll make the right decision, love.' Ruth squeezed her shoulders. Nancy had always made the right decision as far as she was concerned, because she'd always come home to the Bay. Pushing down the feeling that it might not always have been the right decision for her daughter, Ruth pulled her close, wishing she never had to let go.

CHAPTER EIGHTEEN

Aunt Josie's Facetime call had come through as regular as clockwork since they'd lived on opposite sides of the Atlantic. Jack had resisted her attempts to call more frequently in the early days after Alice's death. He didn't want to look into his aunt's eyes, even through the medium of modern technology, and to have to answer her probing questions about how he was feeling or listen to her concerns about how thin he looked, or her constant threats to drop everything and fly over. She'd sent plane tickets for him and Toby to visit too, but he wasn't ready for a face-to-face meeting. Text messages were easier to deal with – easier to hide the truth in – and so they'd kept to the once-a-week call, despite Josie's protests. Since she'd had the blood clot on that last flight, it was much more difficult for her to travel out of the States. Which was maybe just as well.

'My darling boys!' Josie grinned out from the screen of his iPad.

'What have you done to your hair?' Jack narrowed his eyes. She was definitely going Hollywood since she'd signed a deal for one of her plays to be made into a film and had made the temporary move from her home in New York.

'Extensions. What do you think?' Toby let out a loud

burp as Josie spoke, having finished his dinner just before the call.

'I think my son's about summed it up!'

'Everyone's a critic. Don't I get enough of those as a playwright?' She was laughing, though. 'Okay, so maybe at my age I should be a bit past long hair, but everyone does it out here.'

'It's nothing to do with your age.' For a moment Jack wished they were face-to-face and he could give her a hug. 'It's just you don't look like my auntie Josie so much these days.'

'But the good news is you're looking more like my Jack-Jack.' Josie used the pet name only she could get away with. 'Having Nancy around looks like it's suiting you.'

'Don't.' Jack pulled a face and saw it reflected back in the corner of his iPad screen. 'I know you want a happy ending like all the best stories, but we're really just friends. Toby loves her and it has definitely made things easier for me having someone to talk to and not having to go back to a house that radiates emptiness without Alice. But that's it.'

'That's more than good enough and I'm not suggesting anyone could replace Alice. I just want to see you happy. Since Nancy came there's been a lot less of you having to look away from the screen, thinking I don't see you wiping your eyes.' Josie laughed. 'You should know better than to think you can hide anything from me. I can read you like a book. I've seen you trying and failing to hide those pesky emotions of yours for years.'

'Okay, you got me.' Jack smiled, determined to change the subject. 'Enough about me, though. Make me jealous with your life of glamour.'

'I've never been able to do that, Jack, and you know it.' Josie shrugged. 'It's like everyone says, it's a lot less glamorous than you think it's going to be. There are lots of meetings, script reviews and lots of standing around even when you make it on to set.'

'Any chance of a new leading man in your life?'

'None whatsoever, despite the rumours. You and Toby are the only men I need in my life and, since I meet mainly actors, it's a definite no-no.' Josie paused for a moment. 'Let's face it, your dad's experience of getting involved with an actress would be enough to put anyone off.'

'I still fell for Alice.' Jack pulled Toby, who was drifting into an after-dinner snooze, closer into the crook of his arm. 'Even after I swore the last person in the world I'd ever date was an actress.'

'But you made it work and you've got Toby.' Josie was beaming again. 'Look at him there, sleeping like an angel. I wish I could give him a squeeze. He's changing so much; he was tiny last time we were together.'

'He was.' Jack dropped his eyes from the screen for a moment, thinking about his aunt's last visit. Toby had only been a few weeks old and she and Alice had talked at length about how America would be a brilliant place for a young family like theirs. His aunt had her own agenda, wanting her boys close to her, and Alice had seen the chance to grab *her* dream. Maybe if Jack had given into the two of them, she'd still be alive. But would they have ended up apart all the same? She'd wanted to be famous so badly, to take advantage of Josie's connections, and he'd fought it all the way. He didn't want that for Toby – history repeating itself. Despite it all, like his father before him, Toby was now motherless. Jack and Alice had made it work against the odds, but whether they'd have lasted the distance – the tension of her ambition against the demons of his past – was anyone's guess.

It had been six weeks since Miles had returned and Olivia hadn't shown her face at any of The Merry Players' rehearsals or the Mini Merries' workshops. Thankfully, Ruth had been on hand to help her daughter out, but as far as Olivia knew or cared it could have all fallen apart.

The next time they'd bumped into each other had been in town in the first week of December. There were scenes from *A Christmas Carol* strung out across the high street in bright white lights – the three ghosts who visited Scrooge each telling their story above Nancy's head as she walked. Crowds were drifting up from the craft shops on the pier and there was a Christmas market in the pedestrianised area of the town. The smell of gingerbread, mulled wine and slowly roasting chestnuts filled the air, and for the first time Nancy felt like Christmas was really on its way.

Stopping to sample the mulled wine with a view to buying a few bottles to spice up the tea dance at The Pines, Nancy turned round at a familiar voice behind her.

'I'm glad you're here. I've been wanting to talk to you.' Olivia had dark circles under her eyes and her skin was almost china-white. She looked like she'd lost about a stone in weight. Either she was living on love or things weren't going well.

'You could have called me, or failing that you know where I live.'

Nancy had been relieved not to hear from Olivia. Although it had been hard running both drama groups, it was preferable to working alongside her. Ruth and Jack had been of far more use than she'd ever have been. Maybe Olivia wanted to give up her involvement with The Merry Players altogether. Nancy could only hope.

'I didn't want to talk to you at your place or have Miles ask where I was going. We've been spending most of our time together while he hasn't been working.' Olivia frowned.

'He's not working?'

'He's been offered a job with another airline, so Zenoc didn't want him working for them any more. He's on garden leave until he's worked his notice out.'

'Oh.' Nancy wasn't sure what else to say. There'd been a time when she and Olivia could have talked for hours on end, but those days were long gone.

'So obviously he's been around *a lot*.' Olivia pushed a strand of hair behind her ear and Nancy noticed a red mark on her neck. It didn't look like a love bite, but she wasn't going to ask.

'What did you want to talk to me about?'

'I need to ask you a favour.' Olivia took in a big breath, as though even she realised asking Nancy for a favour was a liberty. 'I need you to cover for me.'

'You want me to *what*?' She wondered if she'd heard correctly and nearly dropped the bottle of mulled wine she was holding. The stallholder watched her nervously.

'Miles has heard some gossip about me and David. You know what St Nicholas Bay's like.' Olivia's eyes widened. 'So if he asks you, or you see him, I don't want you to mention it.'

'I wouldn't do that anyway. Miles was difficult to talk to at the best of times, so I'm hardly going to bring up that sort of thing, am I?' Nancy was still gripping the neck of the bottle, wondering if there was any way she could get away with smashing it over Olivia's head. She could hardly believe they were having this conversation.

'It goes a bit further than that.' There was a hint of a blush on Olivia's cheekbones. 'I need you to tell him that it isn't true, that it's just idle gossip from the Bay and that people are jealous we're back together.'

'So you actually want me to lie for you?' Nancy shook her head. 'What about all the others? And that photograph of you in your underwear you texted to make Miles jealous?' She knew Olivia had been on dates with at least two other men.

'I didn't send him the photo in the end. That was for … someone else. I know I haven't been the best friend in the world.'

Olivia had quite a talent for understatement given that the photo she'd asked Nancy to take had almost certainly been sent to David. But then she played her trump card.

'If you can't bring yourself to do it for me, think about Sophie and Jasper. They've been so thrilled to have their mummy and daddy back together, but unless I can convince him that it's all just a malicious rumour, we'll be on our own again and they'll be heartbroken.'

Nancy wanted to tell Olivia that the children would be better off not being raised by a misogynistic pig like Miles in a household built on a bed of lies – but the mention of the children had pushed the right buttons, just as Olivia had known it would.

'And what opportunity is going to present itself for me to do that? In any case, wasn't he the one who left you to shack up with one of his air stewardesses? He's hardly got a leg to stand on taking the moral high ground, has he?'

'Miles doesn't see it like that.' Olivia paused, but if she'd been planning to say something else, she'd obviously changed her mind.

'You know if I do it that it's only for Sophie and

Jasper, don't you? It doesn't mean anything has changed between us.'

Nancy looked at her levelly. The fact Miles had been such an arse did make the prospect of lying to him quite appealing. But she needed Olivia to know that they were never going to be friends.

'Oh, thank you!' Olivia flung her arms around Nancy, who still had the wine in her hand and stood as rigid as a postbox in the unwelcome embrace – thankfully as brief as it was inappropriate. 'I thought I might pop down to the next rehearsal.'

'That's nice of you.' She couldn't keep the sarcasm out of her voice. 'The cast members have been wondering where you've got to and Bernard has made a few acid comments about thinking this was supposed to be a partnership.'

'Oh, no, I meant with Miles, not to get involved with the drama group again. Now that he's home, he's made it clear that he doesn't want me to be out working. Don't worry, though, I'm not expecting any share of the profits, even though my name is on it. Oh, and that's another thing, now I come to think of it. I don't want Miles to know that The Merry Players were called that as a way of me asserting my independence. It would just inflame things. So I told him we chose the name because the aim of the community theatre was to make people happy and the connection is just a coincidence.'

'And he bought that?'

'I think so. Or maybe he just decided to let it go. We're both going to have to do that if we're going to make this work.'

'Are you sure this is the right thing to do? Getting back with him?' Nancy couldn't help herself. As much as part of her wanted to see Olivia have a horrible time back with

Miles, there was another part of her that couldn't help speaking out.

'I'm a grown-up and I know what's right for me and for the children.' Olivia scowled, attack clearly her favoured form of defence.

'You're right. Your life is none of my business. I'd lie to Miles any day of the week though, and at least it means all that drama training didn't go to waste.'

Setting the bottle of mulled wine down on the stall, Nancy turned away from Olivia and pulled out another two bottles.

'So I'll see you at the rehearsal on Wednesday, then?'

'Yes.' Nancy took the money out of her purse, still not turning around. Her friendship with Olivia, like the woman herself, was well and truly behind her.

It was the afternoon of the first Saturday in December and everywhere Jack looked the world seemed to have gone Christmas mad. Every advert showed happy families, gathered around the hearth, celebrating Christmas surrounded by beautiful things with snow falling outside the window. The Christmas card image of family life had never, as far as he knew, portrayed a widowed single father spending Christmas alone with his son. It wasn't like he hadn't had invitations, but spending Christmas with Pam or any of his old friends wasn't something that appealed. Perhaps if Craig hadn't been spending it entertaining his new fiancée's family, Jack would have felt more inclined to take him up on his offer to spend the day with him and Selena. His aunt had begged them to come to California and stay in the beach house she was renting. When he'd refused, she'd been determined to come back to the UK, but after a series of lengthy conversations he'd persuaded her to stay put. Maybe part of it was him punishing himself. Why should he enjoy Christmas when Alice wasn't around? He had to find a way to face the season without her to prepare for all the others that were to come. Running away to California from everything that reminded him of Christmases with Alice was appealing, but he knew he had to face it head on – even if that meant being miserable and alone.

'What have you been buying? You look like you've bought half the stock in town.'

Jack went to the door as Nancy came in, taking some of her bags. They'd settled into a comfortable routine and the cottage had begun to feel like home as a result.

'Alcohol and lots of it!' Nancy grinned but her eyes were red-rimmed. He'd seen her look like that when she came back from visiting her father, but she wasn't due up there until the next day.

'That stressful, was it, your Christmas shopping?' Jack raised his eyebrows.

'I bumped into Olivia.'

'Oh.' He couldn't help smiling at the look on her face. 'Do you think it's too early to open some of that drink? You look like you need it.'

'Yeah, but if we start down that path trying to out-drown each other's sorrow, who knows where we'll end up!'

'Perhaps you're right. Anyway you don't want to mess up your dance steps for later.'

'Do you think I'm mad to be doing all this, just to dance with someone who doesn't know me from Adam? And who won't even remember what we've done by the time we sit down?'

'I don't think you're mad at all. When you talk about your dad, it's how I want Toby to think of me when he grows up and looks back on his childhood.' Jack wished he could think of his own father like that. 'It's only natural if you want to get a bit of that back. It's nice to see you doing something for yourself too.'

'Thanks, it means a lot that you understand. I'm sure most people don't. Are you sure you don't mind driving me up there? Only coming up from the town with all this mulled wine has already stretched my arms and I don't want to be walking around like an orang-utan by tomorrow.'

'Of course I don't mind. What did Olivia say, by the way?'

Something flitted across her eyes as he spoke.

'She wanted me to understand how things stood between her and Miles now and not to rock the boat.' Nancy sighed heavily and Jack wanted to tell Olivia exactly what he thought of her.

'I hope you told her to get stuffed.'

'She knows our friendship's over for good, if that's what you mean.'

There was something Nancy wasn't saying; she was far too keen to change the subject.

'I'm going to get ready as we need to be up there for four, if that's okay?'

Jack nodded and wished for a moment he wasn't driving so he could have a drink. Why did all this crap have to happen to someone as nice as Nancy?

Ruth had agreed to go to the tea dance against her better judgement. Since Daniel had got involved, it had moved from a low-key idea that Nancy had come up with, just for her and John, to a social event that would probably end up being covered by the local press. Daniel didn't do anything unless there was something in it for him, as far as she could tell. He'd use it as an opportunity to spread more false propaganda about what a nice guy he was. If only they knew. If it was anything to do with her, one day, when she had enough proof, they would. Then let the press come running, hear about how he'd driven John out of business and over the edge.

'Trust him to organise a twenty-piece band when a bloody CD would have done.'

Ruth was being a misery, but she couldn't seem to stop it. Nancy didn't answer, just shot her an exasperated look in response. Jack was with her, as he so often seemed to be these days. They obviously got on really well, but Ruth didn't hold out any hope for a romance. Jack was definitely damaged goods in that respect. She liked him, but sometimes he got such a haunted look in his eyes. Ruth knew his wife had died in a tragic accident, but if Jack had revealed any more about his past to Nancy, she was certainly keeping counsel.

'I'm sorry, love, I promise to be on my best behaviour from now on.' Ruth slapped the back of her own hand. 'You look great, by the way.'

'You both do.' Jack smiled and Toby waved his hands around excitedly to the music. 'I'm sure John would be proud of you.'

It was funny how people often spoke about him in the past tense, even though he was very much alive and, at that moment, sitting across the room from them in one of the beige armchairs, tapping his feet to the music. It didn't offend Ruth, though; the real John had gone a long time ago. It was worse when people didn't acknowledge the change in him, or tried to avoid her altogether because it was an uncomfortable conversation for them.

'Are you going to ask Dad to dance first, Mum?'

'I'm not sure, maybe we should see how he is.' Glancing over at her husband again, Ruth sighed. Sometimes he reacted badly if she tried to show him any affection. After all, she was a stranger to him. She couldn't bear him to reject her, not in front of Daniel. It was bad enough that he was there, standing in the corner of the room balancing his tea and cake and laughing with some of the other relatives. No. She wouldn't give him the satisfaction of seeing what he'd done to them.

'Looks like Dad's enjoying it to me. He hasn't stopped tapping his feet. Go on, Mum, *please*.' Nancy could still turn on the puppy dog eyes when she wanted to, as if she was five years old again. And she'd gone to so much trouble that Ruth couldn't bear to say no. Daniel was moving on to talk to another group, further away from where John was sitting, and she decided to grab her opportunity while he wasn't there to witness the outcome.

'Are you enjoying the music?' She sat down next to her husband of thirty-five years and he looked at her with a smile on his face.

'It reminds me of dancing with my girl. I'm hoping she might be here soon.' He looked past Ruth and shook his head.

'I'm sure she'll make it.' Tentatively Ruth reached out and squeezed his hand. If he snatched it away it would be a sign, but he just smiled again. The music was definitely having a calming effect and he seemed less troubled by the fight with his memory than he had in a long time. 'Do you think she'd mind if we had a dance first? It would be good practice, so you can sweep her off her feet when she arrives.'

'You're a bit old for me.'

John was still smiling and she couldn't help but join in. 'So is that a yes?'

Ruth stood up and held out her hand as John nodded in response. They were the first to get up and dance and she tried not to think about the eyes around the room looking at them, or notice how frail John's body felt through his clothes compared to the man he'd once been. Day after day of sitting around meant he'd lost all of the muscle tone he'd once had. He might not be the man he used to be, but she buried her head in his shoulder, careful not to place too much pressure there, and let herself remember for a moment what it felt like to be in his arms. Of course, he wouldn't stroke her hair the way he used to or whisper in her ear and he didn't even smell the same, but it was still nice to be held.

✷

'Your mum and dad look like they're enjoying themselves.'

Daniel had been working his way around the room, talking to all of the families, and Nancy noticed him walk towards her before he spoke.

'They do, don't they? Thanks for putting all this on. The band is great.'

'They played at my silver wedding, so I knew they'd be just right for this sort of thing. My wife was in remission then, but six months later, it was all over.' Daniel's eyes clouded over.

'I'm sorry.'

She'd heard that Daniel was widowed, but she hadn't known much about the circumstances and now it seemed it was still pretty raw.

'You know Jack from The Merry Players, don't you?'

She'd been about to add that Jack had lost his wife too, but it seemed crass, like she was trying to create some sort of exclusive club that nobody wanted to join.

'Of course. Good to see you again, Jack, and Toby too.' Something about the dance definitely seemed to have brought Daniel's emotions to the surface. Nancy felt it too – watching her parents dance together had moved her. It was a strange sense of love and loss that mingled together in the room, almost as though the emotions were engaging in a dance of their own.

'I hope it was okay to bring him here?' Jack looked apologetically at Daniel. Toby was clinging to his dad shyly, surrounded by so many unfamiliar people.

'Of course. It's lovely for the residents to have a child here. Lovely for us all, in fact.'

Daniel was swallowing hard and Nancy wanted to comfort him, but was aware it might make things worse.

'It's my one regret that Cheryl and I never had a family.'

More than ever Nancy wanted to tell her mother just what Daniel had done for the family. They could both use a good friend and they had much more in common with each other than her mother would ever know. But the promise she'd made to her father had to take precedence, so she just leant forward to kiss Daniel's cheek instead – a silent thank you would have to do.

'Thank you for suggesting this, Nancy.' He cleared his throat, acknowledging the unspoken message with a small nod, and gave an apologetic look. 'I've got to go and mingle, but I'll catch up with you both later, okay?'

'Shall we go and sit down for a bit?' Jack said as they watched Daniel move on to another set of relatives. 'Toby's getting incredibly heavy. Either that or it's a sign that I need to work out a bit more.'

'Do you want me to see if they've got any spaces for you here?' Nancy winked and he laughed in response.

'It's a good job you're the best childminder Toby has

ever had. Well, the *only* childminder come to that.' Jack smiled and they took their seats to the right of where the band was playing while a few more couples joined Ruth and John on the dance floor.

'Can I get you a glass of that mulled wine? It smells like they've started to warm it up.' Toby slithered off Jack's lap and Nancy caught a hint of the distinctive aroma of cinnamon and cloves. It was definitely the smell of Christmas.

'Yes please. I think a large one is called for after this afternoon.' Nancy kept an eye on Toby, who was using the chairs to support himself as he moved down the line a bit and then back up towards her. He still wasn't quite walking unsupported, even though it looked as if it would be any day now.

'Well, you certainly know how to throw a party.' Barbara, the care assistant, plopped down onto the next chair, her toddler granddaughter waddling towards Toby with a plastic doll wedged under her arm. 'I can't believe I'm here on my day off, but the residents look like they're loving it. Thankfully someone shoved this mulled wine into my hand as soon as I walked in the door. God knows what's in it, though. I can feel it burning the skin off my throat on the way down!'

'I bought it from the Christmas market. Although I thought I spotted one of your colleagues slipping some brandy in.'

'Probably from some long-dead resident. Still, what doesn't kill you makes you stronger!'

'Not interrupting anything deep and meaningful, am I?' Jack sat down on the other side of Nancy and passed her the promised mulled wine. He was obviously sticking to tea and he smiled at the sight of Barbara's granddaughter and Toby, apparently playing with her doll together. 'It seems he's a fast worker, my son. Looks like he's already picked up a girlfriend.'

'She could certainly do worse.' Barbara was staring at Jack, and Nancy suppressed a grin. She'd seen how other women reacted to him around college and at the drama group, and she had to admit he was looking the best he had since she'd known him. That drawn look seemed to have gone. He smiled more, too. Of course there were still days that hit him hard, but only she really saw that; thankfully, Toby was too little to understand.

'I think I'll leave you two to plan the children's wedding!'

Confident that Barbara could keep Jack entertained, Nancy wanted to do the thing she'd arranged the tea dance for in the first place, before her father got too tired. Her mother had broken off from dancing with him a few moments earlier and he was standing at the edge of the room, swaying gently to the music. As a teenager she'd complained about how embarrassing her father's so-called 'dad dancing' at parties had been, but she hadn't realised back then how lucky she'd been.

'Do you like this song?' She stopped at her father's side, his blue eyes flitting between the dancers.

'It's my favourite.' It was a swing number, 'I've Got You Under My Skin', and something deep inside him obviously remembered what it felt like to dance to it. His feet were moving from side to side and he held his arms as though the woman he always waited for was already in them. Her parents had danced to this song at their wedding.

'It's my favourite, too. Do you think you could show me how?' She placed her hands gently on his upper arms so that she could turn him towards her.

'Okay, but only until my girl arrives.' He smiled and

the twinkle in his eyes could have given old blue eyes himself a run for his money.

As they took to the dance floor, she wanted to cry. It was so strange and frustrating that he could remember the steps to a dance routine, but couldn't remember his only daughter. She shook her head, refusing to dwell on that for the next three minutes. He was her father and, even if he didn't know it, she was going to relish every moment of dancing with him. Pretending was better than nothing at all, and maybe that's what all the acting training had been for – to fool no one but herself.

Her father didn't speak, which made it easier to keep up the pretence, but he hummed along to the music instead.

'I love you, Dad.' She whispered the words so quietly into his chest that she wasn't entirely sure she'd said them out loud.

CHAPTER NINETEEN

Jack watched Nancy dancing with her father and felt a twist of guilt at not allowing his aunt to come over to spend Christmas with him and Toby. She'd been mother and father to him over the years and he owed her more than he could ever repay. Sometimes it was all too easy to forget that it wasn't just about the way he was feeling. He'd make it up to her next year, though, and take Toby to see her. His son needed to get to know his great-aunt. In a family as small as theirs had become, it was all the more important.

He'd been glad when Nancy's friend, Barbara, had gone to take photos of the dancers. She was pleasant enough and his initial fear that she might be interested in more than conversation, despite being much older than him, had been alleviated when she'd begun talking about her husband. It was when she started asking about Toby's mother that things became difficult. He still found not talking about Alice easier than telling the whole sorry tale – especially to a stranger.

'How are you doing? Not finding it all too much of a bore, are you?'

Ruth had crossed the room to sit next to him. At least she already knew what had happened to Alice – so there were no unspoken questions hanging in the air.

'Actually, not at all.' Jack smiled, realising he meant it. 'If you'd told me six months ago that sitting in a dementia care home, watching the residents enjoy a tea dance, would be the highlight of my week, I'd have laughed.' He smiled again. 'Actually, I'd have cried, because it's quite tragic really, but you know what I mean!'

'I do know where you're coming from. It's not how you picture your life, is it?' Ruth looked tired as she spoke and he reminded himself again that he wasn't the only one going through a bad time. At least his memories of Alice were untainted. It must have been so hard for Ruth to remember the man she'd loved now that he treated like a stranger.

'Nothing's how I thought it would be. The things I used to think were important just aren't. I was desperate to get a publishing deal with one of the major houses or persuade an agent to sign me. It was my greatest wish back when Alice was here. Now I'd give up that for ever just to have her back for a day to tell her all the things I never got to say.'

It sounded like a cliché, but it was true.

'Do you find that writing helps? I always imagined that doing something like that must be quite cathartic. I always cook when I'm stressed or upset, it's the only creative thing I can do. But there are only so many Victoria sponges that you can eat!' Ruth pointed towards a table that was groaning under the weight of the cakes sitting on top of it. 'Half of those are mine for a start!'

'I hoped that writing would work for me, but I haven't wanted to write anything emotional since she died. It's only thanks to Nancy's panto that I managed to start writing anything again. But today's the first time that I've had an idea for a completely new story, with the sort of emotional storyline I've always gone for in the past. I actually feel that tingle that makes me want to run to the nearest laptop and start typing.' He meant it. He'd felt the story form almost completely in his head as he watched Nancy move across the makeshift dance floor with her father.

'That's great! I can watch Toby for a while if you want to shoot off and get writing.'

'I doubt it's half as exciting as I think it is, so it can definitely wait, but thanks for offering. I'm just so glad that I actually feel like doing it.'

He smiled at Ruth; she had the same lively green eyes as Nancy.

'I thought maybe that part of me had died with Alice.'

Jack's stomach gurgled; he was hungry. It was a stupid thing to feel pleased about, but most of the time, since the accident, he'd had to remind himself to eat. Living with Nancy had given him a routine, but for the first time in a long time he wanted to eat something for the sake of it and Ruth's baking seemed to be calling his name.

'Can I get you a piece of cake or another drink, if you don't mind watching Toby for a minute or two?'

'I'd love a coffee.' Ruth laughed. 'Only I don't think I'd better have any more cake or they'll have to take a wall down to get me out of here!'

His days as a waiter in a coffee shop, when he'd been at university, had paid off and he could balance the cake on his forearm while carrying two drinks. It was funny how things you hadn't done for years came back to you when the need arose. As he walked back towards Ruth, he could see she was bouncing Toby on her knee with one arm wrapped around his waist.

'Everything okay? I hope Toby hasn't been a pest.' Jack set down the drinks and cake on a small table a few chairs away from Toby so he wouldn't knock them over.

'Not at all, he's a delight.'

'Not trying to steal my job, are you, Mum?' Nancy was suddenly beside him, her perfume mingling with the smell of cinnamon and cloves that wafted from the direction of the kitchen every few moments.

'Well, if you ever feel like giving it up, just let me know. After all, I'm still waiting on grandchildren.' Ruth tickled Toby's belly, making him giggle and squirm at the same time.

'Sorry, Mum, I don't think I'll be able to sort that out for you any time soon.' Nancy smiled as Toby reached up and wrapped his chubby hand around her finger.

'Well, you're not getting any younger, so don't leave it too long.'

The irony of Ruth's words weren't lost on Jack. Maybe if Nancy hadn't stayed around to support her family and had left with Fraser, those grandchildren would have been on the horizon by now. Poor Nancy, she really was expected to meet the needs of everyone around her.

'Maybe Mark will oblige.'

There was an edge to Nancy's voice Jack had never heard before.

'I'd ask if he ever got in touch.'

As Ruth spoke, Toby released his grip on Nancy's finger, holding his arms up towards Jack, and he lifted his son off Ruth's lap. Perhaps Toby was sensing the same atmosphere Jack did.

'You still haven't heard from him then?'

There was a barely noticeable twitch in Nancy's lower eyelid, as if she was battling to hold something back.

'No, it's been nearly six months now since he said he needed some space to think, but he'll get in touch when he's ready, I suppose.'

Ruth's mood had visibly dipped and Jack was suddenly desperate to fill the awkward silence.

'Us boys can be a bit like that sometimes. I don't always contact my aunt as much as I should, but I'm always thinking about her.' It was none of his business, but he had to say something.

'It's not an excuse, though, is it? Just being a boy.'

Nancy had folded her arms across her chest and her body language spoke volumes. Whatever Mark had or hadn't done since the last time she'd seen him, she clearly wasn't in the mood to forgive that easily.

'I just want us all to be together again. So whatever's stopping him from coming home or getting in touch, I hope he gets over it soon.' Ruth twisted the paper napkin that had been left on the seat beside her in her hands.

'So we can play happy families and pretend everything's like it used to be? We're never all going to be together again, not without Dad!'

There was no mistaking the emotion in Nancy's voice. If Jack felt uncomfortable, all this was much worse for her.

'I know it's not just going to all fall into place like it did before, if and when he ever decides to come home.' Ruth sighed. 'But it's not Mark who's to blame for all this. If you want to have a go at someone I suggest you start with Daniel, not your brother.'

'Mum, don't! If you want to know why Mark doesn't come home, then, yes, Daniel's involved, but not in the way you think.' Nancy stopped and looked at her mother for a long moment before turning around to where her dad was now dancing with Barbara.

'What do you mean?'

'Nothing, it doesn't matter.' Nancy shrugged. 'I'm just

angry at Mark, that's all, and I don't think you should take it out on Daniel.'

'One day you'll understand why I feel like I do and why I'd do anything to protect the people I love.' Ruth stood up and squeezed her daughter's arm before moving back across the dance floor towards John.

Nancy spoke so quietly Jack could barely hear. 'Believe me, I already know only too well.'

'Are you okay?' Jack glanced across at Nancy as they drove away from The Pines. After the raking over of the situation with her brother, the party seemed to be over for her. When he'd asked if she was ready to leave, she'd almost trampled on him to head out of the door.

'Yes, sorry. It's just that Mum wanting to break out the bunting and welcome Mark home drives me mad. She's the reason he doesn't come back, and blaming Daniel for all of it only makes things worse.'

'Did they have a difficult relationship then, Mark and your mum?'

There was clearly a lot of undercurrent in Nancy's family; she'd told him about protecting her mum in the past, but she'd never said that much about her brother.

'I need to tell you this because I have to get it off my chest after today.' Nancy was clenching and unclenching her hands as she spoke. 'I can trust you, can't I?'

'Absolutely.'

'When Dad started to get the first symptoms of Alzheimer's, but was still more or less his old self, the business was already in trouble. We'd had Marley's Chains for years, but Dad was stuck in the old way of doing things and he absolutely refused to use cheap imports from China, so he just couldn't compete any more. At some point, Mark realised how bad things were and had it out with Dad. The only option, to avoid losing the business altogether and the house with it, was to sell up.'

'I take it your mum doesn't know this?' Jack kept his eyes on the road as he spoke.

'Not a clue. Daniel was kind enough to step in and buy the business for far more than it was worth given the state it was in. He was an old friend of Dad's and played golf with Mark sometimes too, so he just wanted to help out.' Nancy gave a hollow laugh. 'Only Mum's decided he's the villain of the piece and I can't tell you the times I've wanted to set her straight, to tell her how close we came to losing everything. But Dad made us promise – me, Mark and Daniel – that we *never* would.'

'Is that why Mark left?'

'He couldn't stand to stay in the Bay and not work at the shop, although I'm sure Daniel would have let him stay on. He can't face Mum either in case he gives the secret away. He emails me every now and again from wherever it is he's backpacking at the moment, like some overgrown gap-year student, to ask if she's found out yet. It's easy for him, though, he just ducks out of it all and I'm left, keeping a secret for Dad and being there for Mum, when half the time I think it would do her the world of good to know what really happened.'

'Would it be so awful if you told her?'

'It was the last promise I made to Dad before things got really bad. I know it probably sounds ridiculous to an outsider, but I love him and I can't break that trust, even now.' Nancy's voice cracked.

'Love can make you do stuff that seems strange to other people, I know that.'

Jack hesitated; he'd been wondering for a while if he

should tell Nancy more about his own parents. Now that Alice was gone, only Craig and his aunt really knew the whole story, but his new housemate had quickly come to be one of the most important people in his life.

'My father did stuff that would seem insane to anyone else because of the way he felt about my mother. Time and time again he repeated the same pattern and every time she just let him down, until it wrung the life out of him. That's a definition of madness, repeating the same thing and expecting a different outcome. Trouble was he loved her and I think that was a kind of madness, too, in a way.'

'You've never really spoken about them before.'

'I don't often.'

Pulling up outside the house, he stopped the car. Toby had fallen asleep in his car seat and Jack was reluctant to wake him just yet.

'If you're happy to sit out here for a bit, I'd like to tell you about them. If you don't mind listening, that is?'

'Of course not.'

Nancy put a hand over his and a familiar guilt surged through his veins as he realised he wished she'd leave it there.

'Mum was an actress, determined to make it big, and Dad was training to be a cameraman when they met. My mother, Evelyn, was sharing a house with Aunt Josie, having met her at drama school. It was love at first sight for Dad when he went to lodge with them for a bit during his training. I think he was only ever meant to be a way to pass time for Evelyn, or so Josie tells me, only she fell pregnant with me.'

Jack shrugged. It used to be harder to talk about his childhood when it had felt like the worst thing that would ever happen to him – having parents who put him last –

but that had been before he lost Alice.

'And that changed her plans?'

'To an extent. She agreed to marry Dad, but I think it was only ever a stop-gap because she found out about the pregnancy too late to get rid of me.'

'Your aunt told you that?' Nancy gasped.

'No, my mother did.'

'Oh, Jack, I'm sorry. I've been banging on about my family's issues, when they aren't a patch on what you've been through.'

'I'm not saying it to make you feel like that.' Jack reached out and she took his hand in hers again, this time not letting go straight away.

'I know, it's just I had no idea.'

'I put it to the back of my mind most of the time, because Josie's been great, but seeing you with your dad today makes me realise all the things I want to be for Toby. My father was so obsessed with my mum he'd follow her wherever she wanted to go. From time to time, when she dropped him for someone else, he'd come home and spend a bit of time with me and Josie, but then he'd go again as soon as she called. In the end, when she told him she was marrying a director who had all the right connections, he couldn't take it any more and he killed himself.' The words sounded matter-of-fact even to Jack, as if he were reading someone else's life story.

'Oh God, Jack. I'm so sorry.'

'It was all a long time ago and my mother's been married and divorced three times since then. I haven't seen her for years.'

'Did she get the career she wanted?'

Nancy was still holding his hand and it was like they were in their own little bubble, sitting in the car, sharing secrets – the closest of friends.

'She got what she deserved. Nothing much at all. No career to speak of, and if she's lonely, I can't say I'm sorry.' Jack managed a wry smile. 'Luckily for me, Josie stepped in when my parents lost interest in me. She might not always have got things right, but I always knew she loved me and that was all I needed.'

'Are you spending Christmas with her?'

'Not this year. She wanted to but it's not that easy for her to travel any more, and I ...' He couldn't finish the sentence, unsure if his desire to maximise his misery would make sense to anyone else.

'So what *are* you doing for Christmas? You've got to do something for Toby'

'I don't know ...' There it was again, that reminder not everything was about him. He hadn't thought about how it might all affect his son. 'Why?'

'Because I *really* want you and Toby to spend it with me and Mum.'

'Are you sure you wouldn't rather spend it as a family?'

'God, yes. Having you and Toby there might be the only thing that can get me through. If you can stand it, that is?'

'On two conditions.' Jack allowed himself a small smile. 'The first one is that you don't come to physical blows with your mum if she starts bad-mouthing Daniel. I don't want Toby to need counselling in years to come from witnessing that.'

'Okay, I promise.' He could hear the smile in Nancy's voice, despite her straight face. 'What's the other condition?'

'You don't move out after Christmas. I know we agreed on a trial period when you moved in, but I don't think Toby and I can cope without you just yet.'

'I thought you'd never ask.'

Nancy kissed him briefly on the cheek and Toby laughed at something in his sleep. He was such a happy little boy and at least part of that came from having Nancy in his life. Whatever the New Year held, Jack was grateful for that and the decision he'd taken to make a new life for them in St Nicholas Bay.

Chapter Twenty

Winter had definitely arrived by the night of the final rehearsal. The headlights of passing cars made the frost shine on the pavement like millions of tiny fairy lights, and the sharp night air caught in her chest as Nancy walked to the venue. But with the effort of lugging her bag of props, she was as warm as if she'd run a marathon by the time she'd got there.

'Not too shabby.'

The room that had once been used for public meetings and to count the votes on election nights had now been transformed into a theatre – of sorts. Since they had at least a year's lease, Daniel had arranged for some builders to clad the front of the portable staging so it looked more like the real thing. Ruth had made some sarcastic comment, of course, about it not exactly being a huge gesture since Daniel's main business was property development and he had a team of builders constantly employed. Regardless of the secret they'd kept from her, Nancy hoped her mother wouldn't end up destroyed by bitterness. She needed to make a new life for herself. John O'Brien was never coming home.

Daniel had also donated a lighting and sound system. Not to be outdone, Bernard had donated a large artificial Christmas tree that looked like it had seen better days. Not wanting to upset him, Maisie and Nancy had bought two cans of fake snow and sprayed the tree to within an inch of its life. They'd also persuaded Trevor from the college art department to get his students to make Christmas decorations as part of their project work. The tree was so over-decorated as a result, it actually looked pretty impressive. It ticked the boxes for the theatre's engagement with the community, too. The students had been photographed for the local paper, standing by the tree with Bernard in his pantomime-dame costume. He might not have got the main part, but he was certainly relishing the public attention. Daniel, on the other hand, absolutely refused any publicity for his donations and Nancy liked him all the more.

Maisie and Jack had helped her to set out the chairs for the audience and, while they would never be West End stall seats, they had managed to arrange them in curved rows that made it look a bit less like a show in a school hall.

'I can't believe we're about to go live.'

Maisie had arrived only minutes behind Nancy and she was already shaking, even though it was just a dress rehearsal.

'I didn't think you'd get nervous, all the times you've performed with the band.' Nancy was checking the props which a group of her students had volunteered to move between scenes. They'd had one run-through before and it had been a bit messy to say the least. This was their last chance to get it right. There was still over a week until the show opened on the thirtieth, but with Christmas just around the corner, there wasn't a single other evening when all of the cast could rehearse. It was less than ideal, but the last thing anyone needed to see was how worried Nancy was.

'It's not the same when I'm with the band. There are so many of us that if I mess up my bit, someone else can always cover for me. Up there, if I forget my lines, it's just me – exposed as the useless actress I am.'

Maisie looked ready to bolt for the door at any minute.

'Hey you.' Nancy stopped what she was doing, straightened up and took hold of her friend's hands, as much to stop her running as anything else. 'You're the best in this group and, trust me, this panto would fall apart without you. Daniel is okay, but he only comes alive when you're on stage with him.'

Nancy looked furtively around to double-check that no one else had arrived.

'As for the rest, apart from Dilys, I don't think there's a person between them who could take on the role of Cinderella. And since she's our principal boy, there's not a chance in hell of me letting you duck out of this!'

'But what if I forget the words? I'll look like a total idiot! I was running through them on the way down here and I could barely remember the way here let alone anything else.' Maisie's voice had gone high and reedy, and her eyes widened as someone pushed the door open at the back of the hall.

'Barbara is going to be the prompt and she'll be there every moment of the big night itself.' Nancy grinned. 'If all else fails, say *something* and you can pick up again when Barbara prompts you. Jack will be on hand, too. He's coming down once he's finished online with some of his uni students. It'll be fine, but the more you think about it, the more it will cripple you.'

'Thanks.' Maisie managed a wobbly smile. 'I think I'll be okay once I start, it's more the thought of it. The others are starting to arrive now and I don't want them to know how nervous I am. Bernard will start doing that "I told you so" tutting about casting me in the first place.'

Maisie moved away to join the rest of the arrivals, all of whom had speaking roles. There was Bernard and Dilys, along with Daniel who looked even paler and shakier than Maisie, and, of course, Ruth. Kate and Will from the primary school were there, too, along with a group of their pupils, all of whom were in the Mini Merries. Mo, who had once been the cleaner at the old community centre, and who was playing Prince Charming's mother, had also arrived. She told Nancy that she'd spent most of her time, outside of her cleaning job, looking after her elderly parents, both of whom had died in the last couple of years and she'd found herself at a very loose end. Hearing from Mo how much difference being in The Merry Players had made to her life made it all worthwhile for Nancy, even when everything happened with Olivia and she'd felt like walking away.

'Right, I think perhaps we all need a bit of a pep talk before we start.'

Bernard pulled himself up to his full five feet two and looked most of the cast squarely in the neck. He didn't appear to have an *indoor* voice.

'Okay, well I ...' Nancy was cut off before she had even begun.

'I've got this.'

Bernard held up a hand to stop her and she was shocked into silence.

'I don't want anyone trying to act the diva tonight or hogging the limelight.'

Bernard's eyes flickered between Maisie and Daniel as he spoke, two people who couldn't have been less diva-like if they'd tried. Bernard's lecture was perhaps the definition of irony.

'Thank you, Bernard.' Nancy could still turn on her teacher's voice when the occasion called for it. 'I just want to say thank you to you all for supporting the community theatre with your time and the subs that helped to fund the project. I also want especially to thank Daniel,' she paused for a moment, forcing herself to add, 'and Bernard for their kind donations, without which this place wouldn't be looking or sounding half as professional, or half as festive.'

'It's us who should be thanking you.' Daniel looked around at the others, who all nodded in agreement. Even Bernard.

'Too right. I'd be sitting at home slowly boring myself to death if it wasn't for this group of people.'

Mo, who rarely spoke when she wasn't one-on-one, flushed shyly and no one seemed to notice the door opening again. Nancy certainly didn't.

'I'm sure you'll want to include my wife in some of those thanks. After all, she's a founding member of The Merry Players and some people appear to be labouring under the false impression that it was named after her.'

Miles was smiling, but his eyes told a different story. Olivia stood slightly behind him, wrapped up in a winter coat that was by now far too big for her.

'Of course. The thanks was directed at us both.'

Regardless of the truth, there was something in the way Olivia was positioned that made Nancy want to protect her, even after everything they'd been through.

'Right, well enough of the mutual appreciation society! If you guys want to get changed, the rest of the cast and the prop movers should be here in the next ten minutes. As soon as Barbara arrives to prompt and Jack gets here, we'll get started.'

As the main cast started to filter behind the stage

towards some of the old store rooms, which were now dressing rooms, Olivia finally spoke up.

'Is there anything I can do to help?'

Olivia took off her coat, a crop of dark fingertip sized bruises visible on her wrist.

'We're not staying. Put your coat back on.'

The charming version of Miles observed by the group all those weeks ago was evidently long gone. It was no surprise to Nancy that all the sweetness and light had been an act to get his wife back where he wanted her. Olivia just did as she was told, without saying a word, and Nancy's eyes stung with the threat of tears as she looked at her former friend.

'Was there something you wanted then?'

Determined to stand her ground, Nancy looked directly at Miles.

'Olivia's name, her married name, will be acknowledged in the programme if that's what you're worried about.'

'What I'm *worried* about, as you so sarcastically put it, are these rumours flying around about my wife and, it seems, half the men in St Nicholas Bay. One of which apparently involves sex in a car with your ex-fiancé.'

He was almost snarling, the cold smile he wore like a mask still painted on his face.

'Oh, come on, Miles, you know better than to believe the rumours in the Bay.' Nancy paused, deliberately looking him up and down. 'After all, you should have heard what they were saying about you and the way you abandoned your wife and children when you left. Not to mention the way you treated them before that, and I'm sure that's not true either.'

As she spoke, Miles clenched his right hand, drawing it backwards. For one horrible moment, she thought he might be going to hit her.

'Everything okay?' Jack suddenly skidded to a halt beside her, breathing rapidly, and she wondered how much he'd heard.

'Yes, thanks.' Nancy fought to sound calm. She wasn't going to give Miles the satisfaction of knowing he'd shaken her. 'I was just explaining to Miles that the only reason people are talking about Olivia is because some idiot found out the woman David was sleeping with was also called Olivia and jumped to the wrong conclusion. The fact that the other woman is from Copplestone, and is *at least* ten years younger, apparently means nothing to them.' If she couldn't resist the slight dig, she was only human.

'And how do I know you're not lying?'

Miles took a step towards her, trying to intimidate her again. He knew all the tactics of a bully.

'Because she said so.'

Jack's tone was flat, but it brooked no argument. When Nancy turned to look at him, there was a muscle going in his cheek.

'Why would I lie? Do you really think I would want to protect Olivia if she'd slept with David?' Nancy raised an eyebrow, still refusing to take a step backwards, even though Miles looked as though he'd like nothing better than to headbutt her. He was close enough to do it too.

'Right, that's all I needed to hear.'

Whatever his words, Miles's body language said otherwise and Nancy wished Olivia would stay.

'Come on, we're going.'

He circled his wife's bruised wrist with his hand and Nancy saw her wince, but she still didn't say anything, following like a lamb to the slaughter.

'What an arsehole.' Jack turned to Nancy as they left,

the tension in the room tangible. 'Are you sure you're okay?'

'Yes, but I don't think she is. And I'm worried about the kids.' The back of Nancy's throat was burning.

'What can you do, if she doesn't want to leave him?' Jack sighed; he must have felt as helpless as she did.

'Nothing I suppose. Although I could hold out an olive branch in case she wants to talk.'

She was torn. Doing nothing felt like allowing a tragedy to unfold while she watched from the side-lines, but their friendship had been irretrievably broken, smashed to pieces by Olivia herself.

'We'll work something out tonight to help her, when Claire and Neil have gone home.'

Claire, who was one of the secretaries from the college, had begged for the chance to babysit Toby, desperate to persuade her new husband that now was the right time to try for a baby. Nancy had laughed at her excitement when Jack had finally agreed to let her do the honours so he could get to the rehearsal.

'We'll be able to think of something between us, I'm sure.' Jack gave her a reassuring smile.

'I suppose the show must go on.' She forced herself to focus on the task in hand. 'We can sort out Olivia's life when all of this is over.'

But by the time the dress rehearsal had drawn to a close, things had already changed beyond all recognition.

'There are a lot of sirens tonight. I hope there hasn't been an accident. The roads look lethal now, they're so icy.'

Maisie stood by her car in the fuzzy orange glow from the street lamp, fumbling for her car keys.

'Do you guys want a lift?'

Nancy looked at Jack and read his expression.

'Thanks, but I think we'll walk.'

'The rehearsal was okay, wasn't it?' Maisie quickly regained the worried expression she'd managed to lose during the run-through of the show.

'You were great. Exactly as I imagined our version of Cinders would be.'

Jack gave Maisie a reassuring smile and it was obvious how much his comments meant to her.

'Do you think people will come, what with it being on between Christmas and New Year?'

Maisie's ability to switch her expression between ecstatic and terrified suggested she'd found her vocation in acting.

It was Nancy's turn to smile. 'Trust me. People will be desperate to escape the enforced family time by Boxing Day. By the thirtieth they'll definitely be looking for a distraction and what better one than our play? Anyway, Mum tells me three quarters of the tickets have already sold.'

'And who said the spirit of Christmas was dead!' Maisie wlaughed. 'Mind you, I wouldn't be surprised if Daniel hasn't booked and paid for the audience himself.'

'Now you're in danger of sounding like my mother and, much as I love her, one Ruth O'Brien is definitely enough!' Nancy gave her friend a quick hug. It was far too cold to stand around chatting for long and definitely time to start walking home.

'Only three sleeps until Santa now!' Maisie gave a cheery wave and slipped inside her car.

Stamping her feet, which were quickly going numb, Nancy wondered if they'd made the right decision to walk as another siren pierced the thin night air.

'So what did you really think of the performance tonight?'

Nancy's breath billowed like a cloud of smoke in front of her as she spoke, the eerily calm sea inky black as they rounded the corner to take the path along the seafront, past some of the bigger houses in St Nicholas Bay. Olivia had hung on to hers by her well-manicured fingernails until Miles's recent return. Jasper and Sophie had moved from their private school to St Nicholas Bay Primary and Olivia's fingernails had to go from salon beautiful to home styled. Nancy had admired her back then for giving the kids that bit of stability and ensuring that, no matter what, they woke up in their old bedrooms surrounded by all that was familiar.

'I thought most of them did okay. I did think Bernard was close to high kicking it across the stage at one point, though.'

Jack laughed and Nancy thought briefly how nice that was to see. He was such a different man from the one she'd met at college a few months earlier.

'You know Bernard, he'd do anything to build up his part, but I can't believe how good he is, actually. He was made to play a dame.'

'I think it's the high heels he likes!'

Jack's laughter died. A split second later, Nancy realised why.

An ambulance was up ahead and paramedics were steadying a stretcher while two children hung off the blankets that covered the patient. They made no sound. The children should have been crying out for their mother, but Sophie and Jasper just clung on desperately.

Nancy ran. She needed to get to Olivia, had to, though a part of her was terrified to find out how bad it was.

'Oh my God.' Olivia's face was purple and looked twice its normal size. Her eyes were so swollen there was no way she could see what was going on around her. The only evidence that she was still alive was a soft moaning escaping her swollen lips.

'Liv? It's me, Nancy.'

As she got closer, the paramedics eyed her suspiciously and the policeman standing at the end of Olivia's driveway began walking towards her.

'Nancy? Help me.'

It must have been an effort for Olivia to speak, but the children had already loosened their grip on the blanket that was wrapped over her body and Sophie's little hand snaked its way into Nancy's.

'What do you want me to do? Shall I take the kids home with me?'

'Come with me, *please*.'

Olivia half-sobbed as she forced the words, crying out as a cough shook her battered body. What other terrible injuries was the blanket hiding?

'Do you want Jack to take the children to my mum's, until your mum or someone can have them?'

Nancy looked towards Jack, who gave a quick nod of his head. Sophie and Jasper knew him from the Mini Merries, and Ruth had been like a second nan to them over the years as Miles's parents were long dead and Olivia's mum lived three hours away.

'Please.' It was all Olivia could manage.

Nancy turned to the young policeman, who looked distinctly relieved not to have to find someone to look after the children. Nancy couldn't bear the thought they might have to go into the care of social services – even for one night.

'Jack, can you take them to Mum's, please? I'll text her to let her know you're on the way and I'll give Olivia's mum a ring from the hospital when we know …' She paused and looked down at the children's frightened faces. 'When we know how long it will be before she can come home.'

'Is Mummy going to be okay?' Jasper asked, a big fat tear rolling silently down his cheek. God only knew what the children had been witness to. Nancy bent down to give him a quick cuddle, knowing that the paramedics were keen to get away.

'Don't worry, she'll be fine. You go with Jack and he'll take you to Auntie Ruth's until Nanny can get here. Okay?'

Jasper nodded and she turned back towards Sophie.

'The policemen won't let Daddy back home tonight, will they?'

The little girl's eyes were round with fear and Nancy shook her head. If there was any justice in the world, it would be a bloody long time before they let that bastard go anywhere.

'No darling, and I'll ask Auntie Ruth to make you a lovely hot chocolate with extra cream and marshmallows tonight, okay?'

'You remembered!' Sophie managed a wobbly smile. 'I'm so happy you're still Mummy's friend. She said you were cross with her.'

'It was just a silly squabble like you sometimes have with your friends at school.' Nancy gave the little girl a hug. 'I've got to go with Mummy now, darling, because they're waiting to go to the hospital to make her all better. You go with Jack and I'll tell Auntie Ruth to leave your night light on for you tonight and to read you a story until you fall asleep, okay?'

Sophie nodded and obediently took hold of Jack's hand, her older brother already grasping his other one.

'I'll ring you.' She mouthed the words to Jack who nodded and began leading the children along the pavement to where the policeman had opened the back door of his patrol car.

Jumping into the back of the ambulance, Nancy sat down and quickly fired off a text to her mum, explaining what had happened. Looking down at Olivia seconds later, she felt a wave of nausea about what Miles had done swirl in her stomach. She placed a hand on the edge of the stretcher and Olivia's hand mimicked her daughter's minutes before, finding Nancy's fingers with her own and curling their hands together.

'She is going to be okay, isn't she?'

Turning to the paramedic who was monitoring Olivia's blood pressure, Nancy shivered, and the look in his eyes did nothing to reassure her.

'She's sustained some head injuries and one of her pupils has …' He stopped, looking down at Olivia again. 'We'll know more when we get to the hospital.'

Nancy couldn't stop shivering now she'd started. Suddenly all of this seemed impossible – Olivia's injuries might be something that couldn't be fixed – it didn't bear thinking about.

CHAPTER TWENTY-ONE

Being in the back of the patrol car held painful memories for Jack. When the police had driven him to formally identify Alice's body at the hospital morgue, he'd been on some weird auto-pilot, a kind of coping mechanism. At the time he didn't think he'd taken anything in, but he must have done. The look, the feel, even the smell of the police car was inextricably linked with his memories of that night.

The children beside him were so quiet that it heightened the sense of trauma that hung in the air, just as it had on the night his wife had died. Even if Olivia completely recovered from her physical scars, these children's lives would never be the same again. They'd witnessed things no child should ever have to see; they must have heard their mother's screams for help and seen their father bundled into the back of a police car.

'How are you doing, guys?'

He wasn't going to ask the kids if they were okay, because he already knew the answer to that.

'I'm glad I called the police.' Jasper spoke quietly. 'It was the right thing to do, wasn't it?'

'Oh mate, yes. And don't you ever, *ever* doubt that.' Jack instinctively put his arm around the boy, feeling him relax a bit. 'What you've done means your mum will get better a lot more quickly.' He wanted to tell Jasper that he'd probably saved his mum's life, but he was choosing his words carefully. The last thing he wanted to do was make a terrible situation even worse.

'Why did Daddy want to hurt Mummy so much and shout horrid names at her?'

Sophie asked the question he'd been dreading and he wished he was better equipped to deal with it.

'I don't know, sweetheart. Sometimes people do things we don't understand, and if you ask them why they did it, sometimes they don't even know themselves.'

Jack, who was sitting between the two children, put his other arm around Sophie. Words just weren't enough.

As the police car began to wind its way up the hill away from the beach, Jack asked the children more mundane questions about school and the Mini Merries workshop. He almost asked what they wanted for Christmas, but what these kids wanted wasn't a wish Santa could grant. Even to the untrained eye, it was obvious Olivia was pretty badly beaten and Maisie's reminder about it being only three sleeps until Christmas meant there almost certainly weren't enough days for her to recover in time.

Thankfully Ruth was standing at her garden gate by the time they pulled up, ready to take over. She held her arms out to the children, who ran into them without hesitation, recognising a safe haven when they saw one. She and Jack had a brief exchange, not wanting to say too much within earshot of the children. It was clear she'd been put in the picture by Nancy.

'Can I drop you home, sir?' the young policeman asked as soon as the children had gone inside with Ruth.

'Yes please. It's 3 Elderberry Cottages, Maple Street.'

Sinking back into his seat, he was too exhausted to

face the walk. He needed to see Toby. Once he'd seen Claire and Neil out, he'd lift the little boy out of his cot and feel the solid reassurance of having his son in his arms, safe and exactly where he was meant to be. Then he would wait for Nancy to come home.

Hospitals had such unforgiving lighting. Olivia's face, once they got inside the accident and emergency department, looked even worse than it had in the ambulance. When she went to the toilets, Nancy's own reflection wasn't a pretty sight either. She seemed to have aged about ten years in the last two hours. Maybe she had. Sitting by Olivia's bed while she waited for the results of a CT scan to show what sort of internal damage her loving husband had inflicted upon her, Nancy had time for every emotion to run through her.

She'd forgiven Olivia now. There was no question about it. It didn't mean they'd ever be able to have the sort of friendship they once had – sharing everything. But she couldn't discard all of that history so easily. Much to her surprise she still cared about what happened to Olivia. Most of all she wanted to be there for her children. If she'd ever really loved David maybe she'd have felt differently – she might have been glad to see Olivia lying broken and battered in her hospital bed – but instead she wanted to cry.

The phone call to Olivia's mother, Louisa, had been really difficult. The police constable who'd turned up at the hospital in Canterbury just after the ambulance, to see whether Olivia was well enough to make a statement, had offered to get a Family Liaison Officer to make the call. But Nancy had wanted to do it. Getting a phone call from a police officer late in the evening was every mother's nightmare and there was no need to put Louisa through that.

'Louisa, it's Nancy.'

She was standing outside the doors to the accident and emergency department, shivering with a mixture of cold and shock.

'Darling!'

The older woman sounded genuinely delighted to hear from her and she wondered how much Olivia had told her about what had happened between the two of them.

'Long time, no hear. Now tell me all about this gorgeous new chap of yours who's been keeping you so busy!' Louisa was a larger-than-life character, all dangly jewellery and big hair, but heaps of fun and someone who loved nothing more than a good gossip. Nancy guessed that Olivia had explained away their lack of contact by inventing a romance with Jack.

'Early days.' Now really wasn't the time to try to explain. 'But, Louisa, I'm so sorry. Something has happened.'

'No! Oh dear, it's not your father, is it?' It was a reasonable question and, as awful as she felt for even thinking it, Nancy found herself wishing it was. John was a man ready to go, but Olivia had two small children and she shouldn't be lying in a hospital bed.

'It's not Dad, it's Olivia. We're at the hospital and ...'

'Oh my God! What has that bastard done? Is she all right? What's he done to her? I told her not to go back to him. She said he'd changed but I knew it. Tell me she's not dead. Where are the children?'

Louisa was sobbing and shouting and Nancy had to hold the phone slightly away from her ear so she could understand what was being said.

'She's alive.'

The word 'barely' almost slipped out of Nancy's mouth but she didn't let it. The journey over to the hospital was going to be traumatic enough for Louisa without every mile feeling like a race against time.

'They've just sent her for a scan to see what's what, but she'll want you here when she starts to wake up properly.'

'Has she said anything about what happened?'

'She spoke to me very briefly when the ambulance arrived and the police had taken Miles away. Jasper phoned them and told them what he was doing to Olivia, so they're piecing together what they can for now. They need to talk to her when she's ready, but they've given her lots of drugs to make her comfortable and so she hasn't really been awake or said anything since we got here.'

Nancy had been told that Olivia was in a drug-induced coma to allow any swelling on her brain to go down as much as possible, but until the CT scan results were in, they wouldn't know how bad the damage was. She didn't want to tell Louisa the whole story just yet.

'Oh my God, my poor darlings.' Louisa began sobbing again. 'Where are the children now?'

'They're with my mum and they've been incredibly brave. You've got two absolutely wonderful grandchildren there, you know.'

'I do. And to think their father is that evil pig. If I saw him now, I'd kill him with my bare hands. I swear I would!'

Louisa's tone left Nancy in no doubt she meant it. She'd have liked nothing more than for Miles to be given a taste of his own medicine by his mother-in-law.

'I think we all feel like that. Will you be able to get down tonight, do you think? Or do you want to wait until tomorrow?'

'I'm coming now. I'll get a taxi, I can't think straight to drive there myself.'

'It'll cost you a fortune at this time of night and you're a hundred and fifty miles away. I can stay with her tonight, if you like?'

Despite the offer, Nancy hoped Louisa didn't take her up on it. There might be difficult decisions to make, ones that could only be made by Olivia's next of kin, and the waiting in the meantime was something she wasn't sure she could bear.

'I don't care how much it costs. You've been a darling and I know you'll be there for her too, but she needs her mum. I should be there within three hours.'

'Okay.'

Nancy slumped with relief, her body aching all over. The nurses had told her someone could stay with Olivia all night. When things like normal visiting hours went out of the window so easily, it was never a good sign.

After the CT scan, the nurses moved Olivia to the ICU where all of the rooms were private. It was just as well since she looked like something from a horror movie. If Nancy hadn't seen the children clinging to her back at the house, she wouldn't have been a hundred per cent sure the body on the stretcher was her friend.

There was a relatives' room, with a narrow bed, a sink, and facilities for making a cup of tea, where Nancy had been told to have a lie down. She wouldn't, though, until someone else was there to hold Olivia's hand while the machines bleeped away and did her breathing for her.

The consultant had explained the initial results of the CT scan. There was some swelling on her brain and a skull fracture, which he said had probably saved her life –

giving the brain room to swell without causing the catastrophic damage it might otherwise have done. She also had four broken ribs and some broken fingers in her left hand where she'd tried to defend herself. There was bruising to both kidneys, where Miles had apparently kicked her in the back as she lay on the ground. Her nose and eye socket were also fractured and she'd lost several teeth. He seemed confident that she would at least survive, but the police constable had used the phrase 'attempted murder' and the consultant had said he couldn't be sure how long-lasting the after-effects would be.

Louisa arrived just after 1 a.m. in a flurry of perfume and clattering high heels. She had the same immaculately coiffured blonde bob as her daughter usually did, although that was now a matted mess stuck to her forehead with blood. Louisa was clearly in a panic, but still looked glamorous. Unlike Nancy who suspected she looked as bad as she felt.

'Darling, how is she?' Olivia's mother kissed Nancy on both cheeks, her perfume so strong that Nancy could taste it.

'The consultant's looked at her CT scan results and he's confident there's nothing life-threatening, so it's just a matter of time.'

Louisa would hear from the doctors about the swelling on her brain and hopefully, by that time, they'd know more about what the implications were.

'She looks so fragile, like a broken doll.'

Louisa stood for a moment at the edge of the bed, as if she was frightened to touch her daughter.

'Olivia's always been tougher than she looks and she's bound to benefit from having you here. Come and sit beside her – that's what she needs, to know that someone she loves is waiting for her to wake up.'

'God, I hope so.' Louisa pulled the other plastic chair up next to her and took hold of her hand. 'You must be exhausted, Nancy. I can never thank you enough.'

'Anyone would have done the same.'

'I want you to go and get some rest now.'

Nancy didn't argue. There were probably things Louisa wanted to say to her daughter, even in her comatose state, that she wouldn't want another person to hear.

Letting go of her hand, Nancy stood up. 'I'll come back tomorrow. But call me if you need me, okay? I'll leave my phone on, just in case.'

Jack jolted awake when he heard a key turning in the lock. He'd arrived back at the house just after ten, which felt weirdly early, given how much had gone on that night. Having thanked Claire and Neil for babysitting, he'd cuddled a sleeping Toby for a good half an hour. Unable to sleep, he'd gone back to the lounge and stared unseeingly at the TV. He hadn't meant to fall asleep, but his eyes must have closed at some point. The clock said it was nearly 2 a.m. and the inane American comedy show he'd been watching was still playing, the irritating canned laughter sounding even more out of place now. He pressed the stand-by button on the remote and turned to look at Nancy as she walked through the door. It had only been a few hours since the rehearsal had ended, but she looked as though she'd lived a lifetime since then.

'How's Olivia?'

'She's alive.' Nancy grimaced. 'And they seem to think she'll stay that way, but there's no way of knowing yet how much damage has been done. Her mother's with her now, so I felt okay to leave her.'

'And are you okay?'

'I am now.'

She looked at Jack and something in her eyes stirred an emotion he'd been fighting to suppress for weeks. Alice wasn't here, he couldn't protect her any more, but Nancy needed him and, despite the guilt that came with it, he wanted to be there for her more than anything.

'Come here.'

He held his arms out and she moved into them without hesitation, resting her head against his chest. He stroked her hair as silent sobs wracked her. Her breath was warm against his skin as her body shuddered. It couldn't have been more wrong at that moment to think what he was thinking. Never mind Alice having been gone less than six months, Nancy was distraught, so he was horrified by how much he wanted to kiss her.

'Do you know you're the best thing to have happened to me in the whole of this last year?' Nancy said, looking up at him, her eyes red raw as she attempted a wobbly smile.

'God, you must've had a shit year!' Jack grinned. He tried really hard not to think about what it would be like to comfort her in the way he wanted to.

'Not as bad as yours.'

If she'd read his mind and had deliberately set out to crush his libido, then she couldn't have done a better job. He was supposed to be a grieving widower, for Christ's sake, and here he was thinking what it might be like to sleep with Nancy. He was an arsehole who'd never deserved someone as wonderful as Alice in the first place. That was probably why she'd been taken from him. He had to believe there was some reason for it, but if it was supposed to have made him into a better human being then it was a total failure so far.

'Yeah, the New Year can't come quick enough.'

Jack sighed. Part of him wanted to say so much more, but he owed it to Alice to put those feelings to one side. Sleeping with Nancy, if that was even a prospect, might stop the aching loneliness for one night, but it would probably just do more damage in the end. He had to keep things in the right context. She was a friend and that was really important to him right now, something he wasn't about to risk.

'Coming here was the best thing I could have done and finding a friend like you, for me and for Toby, was something I never expected.'

She moved her face towards his, but there was nothing predatory or passionate in it. It was gentle and affectionate and their lips only touched for the briefest of moments. The faintest trace of her perfume jolted him again. This wasn't going to be easy. The events of the last few hours had somehow lowered his guard, and now that they had, he didn't seem able to go back again, even though she'd just reminded him of the hell of losing Alice. It made him feel guiltier than ever.

'I love Toby, you know.'

Nancy had dropped her head back onto his chest, but he was suddenly desperate to pull away from her so she wouldn't feel just how much he wanted her. He'd find some way to get through it. He had to; he couldn't lose her friendship. But for now he just had to cover it up and deal with the rest later.

'And he loves you. But he won't give you any leeway in the morning, you know.' Jack smiled, forcing his feelings aside. 'He'll be bouncing around by six o'clock and looking out for you if you're not down here for breakfast.'

'I know. I suppose we ought to get to bed.'

Nancy's eyes lit up at the mention of Toby's name, making it all the harder for Jack to resist her. For a moment he didn't dare speak, in case he revealed how much he wanted that – for them to go to bed. She obviously had no idea what a terrible person he was.

'You go up and use the bathroom first. I'll lock up down here and follow you up in a few minutes.'

Jack dropped a kiss on the top of her head. This was so hard.

'Night, Jack. You're the best, you know that, don't you?'

She smiled at him. When he finally met Fraser next term, he was going to struggle not to tell the guy what a complete idiot he'd been to let her go.

'If I didn't know better, I'd think you'd been drinking.'

He stepped back from her and cut himself a break. He might not be the best, but there were certainly far worse men around. Miles had proved that beyond a shadow of a doubt. He was only human and he didn't want to feel the way he did about Nancy, but at least he hadn't acted on it. Thank God. He could still look his son in the face tomorrow without feeling like the world's biggest jerk.

As Nancy headed towards the staircase, Jack knew he wouldn't be able to sleep any time soon. Pouring a brandy, he flicked the TV on again and sank back into the armchair, turning the volume down so it was barely audible. Out of the corner of his eye, he caught sight of the Christmas tree. There was the bauble, hanging in pride of place at the front, which he and Alice had bought the previous December. She'd been almost eight months pregnant and they'd spent the day at Winter Wonderland in Hyde Park, watching excited kids all around them and talking about what their next Christmas would be like as a family. Written on the bauble was 'Baby's first Christmas'. Alice was missing it. He had to fight his attraction to Nancy, no matter how much he wanted to give in. It might mean some difficult decisions in the coming weeks, but he wouldn't think about that for now. All he wanted was for sleep to take him for a few hours, so he could forget how messed up his life had become. Taking another slug of brandy, he waited for oblivion to wash over him.

CHAPTER TWENTY-TWO

'You're up early.'

Jack's voice startled Nancy and she stopped staring at the mug of tea she'd started to make ten minutes earlier and turned to look at him.

'Sorry, I was miles away. I seem to have gone into a zombie-like state today.'

Somehow she managed a smile in response to Toby's ever-reliable grin. He leant towards her, holding out his arms, almost toppling out of his father's in the process.

'Someone's missed you.' Jack passed the little boy to Nancy and she pulled him to her, breathing in the smell of talcum powder and baby shampoo as he wrapped his chubby fingers around her tangled hair. A restless night had made her curls spiral out of all control.

'I missed you, too,' she said to him.

'Shall I make us both that cup of tea? Or maybe a shot of espresso would be better in the circumstances?'

Jack smiled and she nodded, her eyes hurting with the effort of moving her head.

'I had a text from Louisa at about 4 a.m.'

Nancy walked across to the small table in front of the kitchen window and winced as the weak winter sun met her eyes.

'Does she know any more?'

Jack was fiddling with the coffee machine and she noticed his broad shoulders, which he'd offered her to cry on more than once. If only she could have fallen for a man like him – instead of David, the professional idiot, or Fraser, who'd returned her love by breaking her heart.

'She said Olivia's been incredibly lucky. There was a small bleed on the brain, as well as the swelling, but they don't think she'll need an operation. They've got to keep scanning her to make sure the bleeding doesn't start again and to monitor whether there are likely to be any long-term effects, but like I said to Louisa, she's tougher than she looks.'

'She always looked pretty tough to me.'

Jack passed her a tiny cup of ridiculously strong coffee.

'What about me? Do I look tough?' She felt anything but. Months of holding it all together for everyone else was threatening finally to pull her apart at the seams.

'You look lovely.' He looked away, as if embarrassed by what he'd said. 'Toast?'

She nodded, even though she wasn't hungry.

'I'm going up to Mum's this morning to see how the children are doing. Louisa's going to move in with her to look after them until Olivia's out of hospital. I think she'll probably need Mum's help and mine, at least while she's in and out visiting.'

'I can help too if you need me to. You only have to say the word.'

It was obvious Jack meant it. She'd fallen in love with Toby weeks ago and it would be all too easy to do the same with his dad. It was never going to happen, though, even if Jack hadn't been a devastated widower. If David hadn't put her off relationships for good, then Miles had just about sealed the deal.

Having lain down next to the children in the spare bedroom until they were finally asleep, Ruth had woken up almost hourly throughout the night, startled by everything from the noise of a seagull attempting to break in to the bin to Jasper screaming out, in the early hours of the morning, that his father was coming to get him. When she'd settled him back down, it had gone eerily quiet, which had almost been worse. The sound of the clock ticking on her bedside cabinet seemed much louder than it ever had before.

Given the appalling night she'd had, the last thing she'd wanted was for Daniel to turn up on her doorstep, laden down with presents. Like Father Christmas, forty-eight hours too early.

'What do you want?'

Ruth didn't bother with niceties. The only person she would have been glad to see on her doorstep was Nancy, and Daniel was barely a step up from Miles as far as she was concerned.

'People actually say you're friendly, you know.'

Daniel grinned and her fingers itched to slap the self-satisfied smile off his face.

'I am when people deserve it.'

Ruth held firmly on to the edge of the door. How would he react if she slammed it in his face? When Nancy was around to witness it, she had to moderate her behaviour towards Daniel, but she was free to do exactly as she chose this morning. After recent events, and with the lack of sleep, she felt justified in doing so.

'Are you going to let me in?'

He looked hurt. His acting had obviously come on in leaps and bounds since he'd joined The Merry Players. She'd bet the only thing he really felt was frustration at not getting his own way for once.

'I have absolutely no intention of *ever* inviting you into my house.'

She closed the door a fraction and he held out his hand to stop her shutting it altogether. If his business interests ever went horribly wrong, he had serious potential as a door-to-door salesman.

'I've brought some presents for Jasper and Sophie.'

'What on earth possessed you to do that?'

Ruth shivered despite her bravado. If Daniel had heard what happened the night before, and knew the children were staying with her, it must have been common knowledge on the St Nicholas Bay grapevine. She was almost sure the police wouldn't release Miles, but the fact he had the money to hire a hot-shot lawyer, and was just the sort who might be able to wangle the impossible, filled her with dread. Suddenly Daniel didn't seem in the same league at all and she drew back the door.

'I suppose you'd better come in. We can talk about this inside. I don't want the whole street taking pleasure in hearing about those poor kids.'

'How are they doing?'

Daniel looked so concerned he almost convinced her he was genuine.

'Still sleeping.'

Ruth's front door led straight into her cosy sitting room and now Daniel hovered awkwardly in front of an armchair. Was it wrong to enjoy his discomfort so much? He was right to be embarrassed. They'd lived in a much bigger house, just along the road from Olivia's, before John had been forced to sell the business to Daniel. He must have ripped John off badly, because the money from the sale seemed to go nowhere and they'd needed to sell the house, too, just before John began retreating into his own world on a permanent basis.

She'd never been able to find the paperwork detailing how much John had sold Marley's Chains for. Mark must have known the truth. Maybe that was why he didn't come home – he was too ashamed. He should have stood up for John and the family firm; it was his birthright after all, but somehow the men in the family had let the business slip through their hands, selling out to a shark just waiting to take advantage.

She couldn't blame John, he was already in the grip of the Alzheimer's. Mark had apparently wanted a quick escape. He'd left as soon as the business was sold and only Nancy had been there for her. Sometimes she felt a frisson of guilt that Nancy had given up so much. But that guilt rightly belonged with the man who was now such an unwelcome visitor in her home. She was sure the stress of selling off Marley's Chains had triggered John's series of mini-strokes.

Daniel was first to crack.

'Can I sit down?'

He'd already placed a large bag of toys at the side of the armchair and, without waiting to hear her response, he sank into the seat.

'It would appear you already are.'

Ruth folded her arms across her chest. She'd die before she offered him a cup of tea.

'And how are you coping? It can't be easy?' There was that look in those brown eyes of his again – warm and friendly. By God, appearances could be deceptive. Lots of women her age would find him attractive, younger women even, especially with his flashy cars and bulging bank account. She experienced an altogether different emotion when she was around him, one she'd never had in her life before. Pure hatred. Sometimes she'd lie awake at night and fantasise about him being crushed on one of his development sites by a falling building or a runaway digger, but she knew only too well what they said about the devil's luck.

'Why how *I'm* feeling should be any of your concern, I don't know.'

Ruth couldn't look him in the eyes; she didn't trust herself not to cry and she wouldn't give him the satisfaction.

'In fact I can't for the life of me think why you're here at all. Olivia and those kids are nothing to do with you. Unless you've got your fingers in more pies than even I dreamed possible.'

Bitterness filled her mouth and she couldn't seem to stop the venom pouring out.

'I know Olivia from The Merry Players and Jasper's best friend at school is my nephew, Tom. What I don't understand is why you look at me as though I'm a lower form of life than someone like Miles.'

His tone was reasonable and she realised she must sound like a fish-wife, but there was nothing she could do about it.

'If you don't feel even a shred of guilt about what you did, then I'm not going to try to explain it to you. I've kept quiet at The Merry Players for these past few weeks and even up at the home, because Nancy has begged me again and again not to make a scene. But when you have the brass neck to turn up on my doorstep and sit yourself down in my front room, like we're old friends, then I'm afraid I just can't keep up the ridiculous charade of civility for a single second longer!'

With the words finally out, she was breathless and had to lean against the mantelpiece. Daniel stared at her for a moment and let out a long breath, the sound of one of the children crying out momentarily breaking the tension.

'I'll just leave these and go.'

Daniel sighed again as he got to his feet and shook his head.

'The last thing they need to be subjected to is yet more shouting.'

He took a step towards Ruth and she flinched as if her cheeks were red from the imprint of his hand rather than the strength of her emotion.

'But I'll just say this. I'm sorry, whatever it is you think I've done. But if you really believe I forced John's hand in any way then you're wrong. I can't say any more, but Mark knows the truth.'

'Just get out!' The sting of him mentioning Mark's name was worse than any slap. The prodigal son. 'Don't you dare talk about my son, or any of my family!'

He didn't say anything else, just quietly closed the door behind him and she pushed both locks across. She leant her back against the door for a second, but Jasper was calling again. If exhaustion had made her overreact with Daniel and finally tell him what she thought of him, then she wasn't sorry. He deserved it and, despite his protestations to the contrary, she didn't doubt her views for a second.

It was one of those typical December days, where the whole world looked to Nancy like it was painted in shades of grey and never got fully light. The hospital entrance's peeling 1920s façade made the day even more depressing. At least it was warm inside, but the smell of institutional food mingling with disinfectant caught at the back of her throat as she made her way down the corridor to the ICU.

'Nancy, darling!'

Louisa embraced her enthusiastically, still as perfectly made-up and as heavily perfumed as she had been the night before. Sitting in another chair next to the bed was Bernard, of all people.

'I didn't expect to see you here, Bernard. How's Olivia doing?'

Nancy moved to the opposite side of the bed and took the plastic chair there.

'She's still unconscious, but they want to start weaning her off the meds today so they can make sure she's functioning as they expect her to. If she's not, they might still have to operate, but it's all looking positive so far.' Louisa's relief was tangible.

'I came in to see if there was anything I could do and Louisa invited me to stay.'

Bernard smirked as though he'd got one up on Nancy in a competition to see who could be the most involved in the drama. He was clearly still after that starring role. She knew he meant well, deep down, but he had to get involved in everything, probably because his own life was quite empty. Still, whatever floated his boat, it certainly didn't bother her. If Louisa had other support, it would take the burden off Nancy. She wanted to be there for Jasper and Sophie.

'I really appreciate his company.' Louisa's bejewelled hand closed over Bernard's thigh and his face's red deepened to burgundy.

'Did you want me to have the children stay with me for Christmas?'

Nancy smiled to herself, imagining Toby unwrapping the presents she'd bought for him from Tiny Tim's toy store. Maybe there were already presents back at the house for Olivia's children, but it didn't matter; she could hit the shops in Canterbury on the way home if she needed too. The last thing she wanted was for the kids to be any more upset than they already were. Finding out that Santa Claus was a myth might well be the final straw for a traumatised seven-year-old.

Louisa frowned. 'If you can keep them until tonight that would be wonderful. I'm not sure if it's entirely a good thing, but I was due to spend Christmas with my sisters and they've both decided to come down and spend it here instead, at Olivia's place. Between us we can take care of the children and make sure Olivia's never on her own, but my sisters are a bit loud.'

Louisa shook her head and her platinum blonde hair moved ever so slightly, just enough to offer a glimpse of the obscenely large diamond earrings she was wearing.

'It must be hard to cope with for someone as graceful as you.'

Bernard smiled so broadly the edges of his moustache threatened to tickle his ears. His chat-up lines were less than subtle, but his eagerness to please Louisa was really quite sweet. Nancy had to press her lips together for a moment to stop herself laughing.

'That's great news. I'm sure Jasper and Sophie will be delighted that they get to spend Christmas with their grandma and their great-aunts.'

'I prefer Lou-Lou to Grandma!' Louisa's tone was suddenly sharp, but she quickly smiled to cover it.

Nancy returned her smile, keen to break the awkwardness. 'Duly noted. If I can't do anything here, then I think I'll head home and see if I can organise something fun to do with the children this afternoon to see if we can take their minds off things a bit.'

Scooping up her bag, she glanced briefly at Olivia. Her face was still swollen and so unnatural in colour she could have been a Picasso portrait.

'That's a lovely idea. I've got Bernard here to keep me company,' Louisa was squeezing his thigh again, 'and Livvy won't be awake for a good while yet.'

'I take it you don't want the children coming in, until Olivia is more … I mean, yet?'

Nancy wasn't sure how to put it, but the idea of the children seeing their mum in that state was unbearable.

'No, no, I suppose best not to for a while yet.' The thought didn't seem to have occurred to Louisa. 'I'll let you know when she starts to wake up. I'm sure she'll want to see you.'

Nancy just nodded.

'I can always text Nancy with an update.'

Bernard smiled again. He was definitely enjoying being at the centre of things and he would relish not only knowing what was going on before everyone else, but also passing on the latest news to as many people as he could.

'That's great. Give her my love when she wakes up.'

Nancy said what was expected, despite feeling a complete fraud. She couldn't get back to Toby and Jack soon enough.

CHAPTER TWENTY-THREE

Nancy spent most of the afternoon of the twenty-third of December in the ancient cinema in St Nicholas Bay, with its lumpy seats and carpet sticky with the spilled drinks and dropped popcorn of at least three generations. And she couldn't have been happier.

She and Jack decided to take Toby and Olivia's children to see the sing-along version of *Frozen*, which was being screened again for the festive season. It was cheesy, but full of a much-needed feel-good factor.

Toby was remarkably well-behaved and sat contentedly on his father's lap for most of the film, before crawling across the arm of the seat to fall asleep in Nancy's arms. Jasper cuddled up to her too, and in the dim light she could see Sophie leaning on Jack's arm. She realised how completely happy she was and then it came to her like a body blow: this was what she wanted more than anything. A family of her own. Maybe it was Olivia dancing so close to death, so suddenly, which put the passing of time into such sharp perspective, or the realisation, with her dad's deterioration, that nothing was for ever. Whatever it was, she wanted the New Year to bring her closer to all of this.

'Did you enjoy that?'

As she emerged from the cinema, Nancy's eyes

struggled to adjust to the winter sunlight. Toby was back in his buggy and Jasper and Sophie were holding on to either side of it. To anyone passing, they must look like the perfect family. No one would guess that she wasn't the mother to any of the children or what the older two had just been through.

'It was smultzy,' Jack grinned, 'but if I'm honest I loved it!'

'It was great to escape for a bit, wasn't it?'

They took the path through the park towards Olivia's house, where they were due to drop the children back to their great-aunts.

It's a shame the light's fading so fast. We could have let the kids run around in the playground for a bit.'

Jack sounded as if he didn't want the afternoon to end either.

'I know, maybe another time.'

Nancy sighed. Tomorrow was going to be a more difficult day for both of them. She was spending Christmas Eve with her father to give her mum a break, and she was going to try to take him out for the day. Ruth had gone over to The Pines as soon as Nancy and Jack had picked the children up and she'd be there on Christmas morning, too. They'd agreed between them that Nancy wouldn't go up on Christmas Day so she could cook the meal at Ruth's place. At least now that Jack and Toby would be joining them, there seemed more point in going all out with a Christmas dinner and all the trimmings. Maisie and her band had been offered a gig on Boxing Day at a pub they'd wanted to play at for months, so she had ditched her plans to spend Christmas in Cornwall with Fraser and their parents, and would be going to Ruth's instead. Maisie was guaranteed to provide some entertainment to lighten the mood, which they'd all need after the last few days.

Jack had more trauma to face first though: a Christmas Eve meal with his mother-in-law and a trip to the cemetery to visit his wife's grave. A day at The Pines, with a father who thought Nancy was a stranger, was small fry in comparison.

They walked in companionable silence towards Olivia's house, lost in their own thoughts.

'Bye, kids.' Jack ruffled Jasper's hair as they reached the front gate.

'I don't want to go back in! I wish you were my daddy.'

Sophie clung around Jack's neck for a moment and Nancy tried to swallow the lump in her throat.

'You've got Father Christmas's visit to look forward to, sweetheart, so you need to make sure you're at home in your own bed so he knows exactly where to put all your presents.'

Jack spoke softly and Sophie nodded slowly, seeming to weigh up her options and decide that, much as she liked Jack, Father Christmas probably did have more to offer.

Nancy took her hand and they followed Jasper, who was already ringing the doorbell, up the path towards the house, leaving Jack standing with Toby's buggy just outside the gate.

'It's Sophie-Pops and JJ!' One of the children's great-aunts came to the front door and flung her arms around them. Unlike her sister, Louisa, she cut a stereotypical grandma figure, with large tortoiseshell-framed glasses and a halo of tight grey curls.

'Auntie Joan!' Both children looked equally pleased to see her and Nancy let out the breath she'd been holding, worried that leaving them was going to be difficult.

'Thank you so much for having them. Louisa has told

me what a Godsend you've been while our darling Livvy's been going through so much.'

Auntie Joan straightened up and smiled warmly at her. Nancy had never met Olivia's aunts, but Olivia had told her they doted on her and that she'd always been spoilt, since neither of them had children of their own. She was the sole focus of attention in the family. Perhaps that was why she was the way she was, but none of that mattered now.

'It was our pleasure.'

Nancy turned back towards where Jack was waiting, a strange heaviness in her chest. Her own family seemed to be shrinking to almost nothing and she envied Olivia the devotion of so many relatives. Her father was gone to all intents and purposes and her brother hadn't come home in ages. He'd barely even contacted her for the last six months. She had aunts and uncles, but not this level of closeness with any of them. She'd hated Mark for walking out on them when their father first got ill and leaving her to bear the burden of the secret they'd promised to keep from Ruth. She missed him, though, despite all that.

'You okay?'

Jack looked at her and she forced a smile. The poor sod didn't need her bringing him down with a bad case of self-pity. He had far more reason to feel miserable, facing his first Christmas without Alice.

'I'm fine. I just feel a bit shivery, that's all, nothing a hot cup of cocoa and a warm-up by the fire won't solve.'

'Would you like me to get your crochet out for you and make sure your copy of *Age Concern Monthly* is on the arm of your chair?'

He raised his eyebrows and this time her smile was genuine.

'All right, maybe a hot toddy then. I don't want you to tell everyone what a boring housemate you've got.'

If this was what boring looked like, then Jack could more than happily live with it. Back at the house he'd gone through to make the drinks and Toby had settled with Nancy on the sofa in the lounge, his eyes doing that drooping and suddenly shooting open thing they always did when he was desperately fighting sleep.

When Jack came back through with the drinks, Toby was lying against Nancy's chest, their legs covered by a crocheted blanket which her grandmother had made when she'd been a baby. *The Muppets Christmas Carol* was playing on the TV and Toby had given in to sleep. It was a perfect scene, but it shouldn't be. He still missed Alice, but the strength of it had faded – more than he wanted to admit to anyone, even himself. Pushing away the urge to sit with Nancy, he sat opposite instead, burying what he really wanted to say under small talk.

'I had a great time with the kids today.'

Jack took a sip of liqueur coffee, which was still far too hot.

'Me too.' Nancy laughed as he spluttered. 'What on earth have you put in those things?'

'Irish whiskey, but I'm not sure I got the measure quite right!'

'Ah, well, if my dad was still his old self, he could have given you a tutorial. He was a dab hand at those, and whiskey macs now I come to think of it. Proper winter warmers he called them.'

She smiled at the memory.

'So is that how you spent your Christmases, in a haze of hot toddies?'

'I was only ever allowed one of his special coffees in the last five or six years before he got ill. Before that, it was all about us kids. Dad would dress up as Father Christmas and do the rounds of all our friends' houses in the Bay before finishing at ours. Of course we knew he wasn't the real deal, but it didn't make it any less special. He really went for it, too. He had a red velvet suit handmade and even hired a pony and trap to take him round with all the presents loaded on the back.'

'It must have cost him a fortune.' Jack smiled. Maybe by next year Toby would be in to the whole Santa thing.

'It did, but he was always far too generous. I'm sure that's why he was in so much debt in the end. But Christmas is big in St Nicholas Bay. We'd all go down to the chapel on the harbour for the carol service on Christmas Eve and then we'd be allowed to come home and choose just one present to open.'

Nancy looked up at him and another unwelcome surge of attraction twisted in his stomach.

'What about you, have you got any traditions you want to pass on to Toby?'

'Singalong Disney movies now!' He found himself watching her lips as they curved upwards in response. 'And maybe we'll do the Harrods thing when he's old enough to appreciate it. Aunt Josie always took me to the Christmas parade and then to see Santa there. I don't suppose he was a patch on your dad, but he was one of the best store Santas around at least. Then, a bit like you, we'd go around the store and I'd be allowed to pick one thing that I really wanted to take home right there and then. After that we always went to Covent Garden to have hot chocolate by the big Christmas tree and we'd walk through town to Trafalgar Square and look at all the lights and shop windows. A bit more commercial than

Christmas here, but she always did her best to make it really special. I just hope she knows I appreciated it.'

'You could always tell her.'

Nancy grinned at the face he must have pulled.

'I thought sentiment was supposed to be easier for you writers!'

'On paper. In practice it's often much harder to say what you want to.'

He stopped. There was so much he could have said to Nancy if he'd let himself. Maybe it was time to start writing some more. The way he was feeling could be worked through on paper, poured into a story, so he could stop this tightness in his chest every time he looked at his housemate and the guilt that kicked him in the gut as a result.

'I should tell Josie what she did for a little boy who longed for his mum and dad to be there at Christmas. I might have felt sorry for myself at the time, but I realise now I'm lucky. Maybe I'll send her an email ...'

He laughed as she wagged a finger at him.

'Tell her when you speak to her on Christmas Day. It might even make up for the fact she can't be with you and Toby.'

Suddenly serious, she fixed him with that teacher's look he knew so well.

'We both know there isn't always a next time to say the things you want to say. There are so many things that I want to say to Dad that he doesn't understand any more. I'm sure there are things you want to say to Alice.'

'I do.'

Right now he wanted to apologise to her for feeling something so strongly about someone else when she'd barely left him. But Nancy was right. Life was short and unpredictable. Maybe he should tell her how he felt.

'There's something I wanted to mention, actually ...'
He paused, unsure how to go on, and Toby squirmed in
his sleep, pursing his lips in a way that was so like Alice it
was almost as if she was telling him something.

'Go on.'

Nancy's voice made him look up in surprise. He had to
stop feeding himself this bullshit that life was short, using
it to appease his guilt. Alice's had been short, not his, and
she deserved better than for him to do the easy thing, even
if it felt right a lot of the time.

'I just wanted to say that if you want any help with the
dinner tomorrow, I'm a sous-chef at your disposal.'

'You might regret that. I go all Gordon Ramsey when
I'm under pressure.'

She laughed, her eyes crinkling in the corners, and he
repeated the silent mantra that Alice deserved better from
him. Now he had a new Christmas wish – that he'd wake
up and find his feelings for Nancy had conveniently
disappeared.

CHAPTER TWENTY-FOUR

The prospect of spending a day with Pam, and the guilt he was already wrestling with, turned out not to be conducive to a good night's sleep. Jack had finally drifted off at about three. At least it had been around then when he'd last looked at the clock on the bedside table, willing the hours to speed past. Toby had woken him not long after five and the little boy was full of beans, as if he knew it was the day before Christmas. He'd half hoped that his son's crying would have woken Nancy too and that they'd meet, as they sometimes did, passing bleary-eyed in the corridor before heading down for an early breakfast. She was clearly still asleep when he carried Toby past her room, though. The door was slightly ajar and she was wrapped tightly in her duvet, like a caterpillar in its cocoon. She wouldn't be waking any time soon and, given the way he was feeling, it suddenly seemed a good idea to make sure they'd already headed off to Pam's by the time she did. Today was going to be hard enough as it was.

It took him less than half an hour in the end to make sure he and Toby were ready for their lunch date with Alice's mother. They were meeting at her flat just around the corner from where they'd once lived. Had it really only been a handful of months ago? God, he was a total bastard. He was beginning to forget the day-to-day details of life with Alice. What she looked like in the morning, even stupid things like what she would have chosen to eat for breakfast. He'd been making coffee the week before and suddenly couldn't remember whether she'd taken sugar in hers. He'd driven himself half mad trying to visualise her making them both a drink, and then woken in the night with the sudden recollection that she'd given up having sugar in her coffee when she'd been trying to lose weight after Toby had been born.

The familiar streets of London were thronging with people and they made slower and slower progress the closer they got to their destination, weaving through the traffic and Christmas shoppers. It might have been easier to take the train up, but having the car was a security blanket. Something he and Toby could dive back in to and head home if it all got too intense.

'My boy!' Pam wrestled Toby out of his father's arms as soon as she opened the door and the little boy, shocked by being suddenly snatched, burst into noisy sobs.

'Look, he barely knows me. It's like I'm a stranger. His only grandparent!'

She shot Jack an accusatory look and the sharpness of her tone made Toby cry all the louder.

'He's just a bit grumpy because he was up early this morning and he's teething again.'

Jack sighed. He wasn't about to remind Pam that she wasn't the boy's only grandparent, not as far as he was concerned. It really wasn't worth getting into an argument over, and Aunt Josie had never needed him to fight her corner – it had always been the other way around.

'Have you tried Bonjela?' Her tone softened a little, but she was still looking at Jack as though he was inflicting the pain on Toby's teeth himself. She'd already shoved a finger into the baby's mouth, looking for proof that it really was his teeth which were causing all the trouble.

'He virtually lives on the stuff!'

Jack immediately regretted his attempt at a joke and sighed again. On the best of days an hour could pass like a minute, but he had a feeling that every moment he spent with Pam would feel like a day all of its own.

His mother-in-law sat on the sofa and took off her grandson's coat, stroking his soft hair until the crying finally subsided. Jack sat opposite her, not knowing what to say for the best. They'd been okay in each other's company once upon a time, before the accident. Never exactly the best of friends, but it hadn't been like this. He'd overheard her once telling Alice that he was a dreamer, what with his crazy fantasy of making it as a writer and all that nonsense, and that he'd never be able to give her the lifestyle she wanted. It hadn't bothered him, because they were both dreamers once upon a time. Back then they'd had years ahead to give up on those dreams and settle down to focusing on proper careers as Pam put it. At least they'd thought they had.

'Shall I make us all a drink? I need to warm up Toby's bottle too.'

Jack got to his feet, the atmosphere in the lounge already stifling. He was so glad he'd booked a restaurant for lunch. They had to get through the cemetery visit first, but at least in a public place the atmosphere between them would be diluted.

He strung out making the coffee and warming Toby's milk for as long as he could, but she was like a predator, waiting for him to return so she could pounce.

'I can see you've not packed to stay.' Pam gestured towards the one small bag that held all Toby's paraphernalia for a day out – everything from teething gel to a change of clothes. 'I thought at least you'd be here for a couple of days.'

'We're spending Christmas with friends.'

Jack had known this was coming and he braced himself.

'Not Craig, surely? Selena told me they were with her family this Christmas when she sent me an invitation to the wedding.' She narrowed her eyes as he shook his head. 'So other friends in London then?'

'We'll be with Nancy and her family.' There was no point in him lying. He had nothing to hide and it would only make things worse in the long run.

Her mouth formed an O-shape, but she didn't say anything, just looked at him for a moment that felt like it might never pass.

'I can bring Toby to see you again, between Christmas and New Year, if you like?'

He didn't expect it to appease her and he was right.

'You'll make time for that, will you? Won't you be far too busy playing happy families with my grandson and some tart who'd like nothing better than to dance on my daughter's grave?'

'Pam, you're going too far there.'

He'd promised himself he wouldn't argue with her, but his own emotions were bubbling to the surface.

'Why on earth would you say something like that about Nancy? You don't even know her. And, if you did, you'd realise she was the last person in the world you could say something like that about.'

'I expect she's jumped in your bed as quickly. She must be delighted to find herself a widower, and one who's got a brilliant case for some hefty compensation too. Lucky for her that my daughter's dead and the path is clear. Or maybe you were seeing her before that even happened. You said she was a friend from way back.'

Pam stood up, Toby still in her arms, and started pacing the floor.

'Yes, that would make more sense. You moving so quickly, as if my baby had never even existed.'

'Pam.'

Jack stood in front of her and forced her to stop pacing.

'I've put up with some crap from you since Alice died. Made excuses for the way you've spoken to me and you criticising the way I've been raising Toby, but enough now. Enough.'

'I can't stand that you've moved on so quickly. It's barely been six months and I just don't know how you can …'

She trailed off, sobbing. He took Toby from her arms, guiding her gently back to the sofa where she buried her face into a cushion and wept until her body finally stopped shaking.

Setting Toby down on the floor, happily munching on his teething ring, Jack knelt down beside her as the pitiful sound of her sorrow finally began to ebb away.

'I haven't forgotten her. She's in my thoughts every moment, and don't think for a second that I don't miss her.'

Jack wanted to reassure Pam that there was nothing between him and Nancy, but something stopped him, the gnawing feeling of guilt turning his stomach.

'I'm sorry. I know I'm a horrible old bitch sometimes, but I just miss her so much, Jack.'

She moved towards him and he wrapped his arms around her. She felt as brittle and fragile as glass; one more blow would break her, and he couldn't be responsible for that. He'd grown closer to Nancy than he'd wanted to. But there was more than just him to consider. More even than his loyalty to Alice. It affected anyone who had ever loved her and he had to remember that.

The ground in the cemetery sparkled with frost. It was oddly beautiful for a place filled with such loss. It was quiet, too. Most of the bereaved had been kept away by the cold or the nearness of their Christmas celebrations. Nearly all the other graves were much older, the loss of other families perhaps less raw, or at least less new. How many other families would grieve tomorrow for that empty place at the table and the aching void in their chest? Pam had been wrong to react the way she did; none of this was Nancy's fault. Yet his mother-in-law's pain was so tangible, his own sense of loss had been renewed.

There were a handful of other people making a Christmas Eve visit to the cemetery and they passed one middle-aged woman kneeling at the side of an ornately decorated grave. The headstone was embossed with pink swirly writing and two cherubs flanked either side. Maybe some people would call it tacky. He could almost guarantee the word was at that very moment turning itself over in Pam's head, but thankfully she didn't say anything. Whatever gave bereaved family members comfort was right, as far as Jack was concerned. After all, it was Pam who'd insisted on Alice being buried within walking distance of her home, and it was she who'd chosen the headstone, with a picture of Alice in the centre, which had finally been secured after settling of the disturbed ground. He didn't like the headstone at all. He'd have to be pretty sick to like anything that marked his dead wife's grave, but he actually hated it. The photo Pam had chosen didn't even look like her, and Alice was no more at the spot where she'd been laid to rest than she was anywhere else. He didn't need to kneel next to her grave to think about her and he didn't want to imagine her bones lying beneath mounds of cold, wet clay. It had taken months to picture her as anything other than a dead body lying in the hospital morgue. But now, when he closed his eyes, he could see her dancing, remember the way her body moved and how she tossed her hair when she really laughed. Sometimes when he looked at Toby, like he had the night before, he saw her so clearly too. Coming here to look at the marble headstone, which had been erected just the week before, didn't mean nearly so much.

'It's lovely, don't you think?' Pam ran her hand along the top edge of Alice's headstone and Jack shuddered. She seemed calm now, after the earlier hysterics.

'It's … nice.'

He squeezed her shoulder. Pam seemed to relish the opportunity to do this small thing for her daughter.

'You've done a great job.'

'I think she'd have liked it.' She polished a non-existent mark on the marble, obviously not realising the irony of her words.

'Shall I put the flowers down now?'

Jack peered over the hood of the buggy to check that Toby was still asleep. He'd dropped off almost as soon as they'd left Pam's house and Jack was grateful. Not that the boy would remember any of this, of course, but he'd rather his son slept through it. Jack only wished he had the luxury of doing the same.

'Yes, please.' Pam was still buffing the stone, even though it already shone like glass. 'And I've put a teddy bear in the bottom of Toby's pram. I want to put that on too.'

'Right …' He stretched out the word, unsure of what to say.

'Oh, I know you probably think this is ridiculous, Jack, but I can't give my daughter a Christmas present, and at least this way she'll know I'm thinking of her.'

'Okay.' It was all he could say. If it made Pam feel better that was great, as long as she didn't expect him to have brought anything.

'I did think about bringing her a little Christmas tree, but it's too soon even to pretend we're still celebrating all that.'

'Maybe next year.'

He forced himself to agree. God knows what he'd find the next time he felt he had to bring Toby up for a duty visit. He supressed a rueful smile, despite the circumstances. With Pam pouring all her energies into it, Alice was likely to end up with the most immaculate grave around and a monument that could be seen from space.

After they left the cemetery and headed for the restaurant, Jack began to bump the buggy more vigorously in the hope Toby would wake up before they got there. Keeping him entertained during the meal would distract them both and make something he'd dreaded for weeks just about bearable.

In the end, though, it wasn't nearly as bad as he'd thought. Toby had done him proud and woken in a cheerful mood. He sat contentedly on his grandmother's lap and sucked on a rusk, grinning at the pretty waitress who'd been assigned to their table every time she went past. He and Pam had managed to talk about Alice and how much she'd always loved Christmas, and for once it didn't dissolve into tears. They'd talked about the panto that Alice had appeared in, how she and Jack had first met and even their last Christmas together, when she'd been just over a week away from giving birth, and had hung a present on the tree from the unborn Toby to Jack. The label had read, 'To the best daddy in the world' and Jack swallowed hard at the memory as he told Pam the story. It had helped him get his head straight and put any feelings he might think he had for Nancy into perspective. Alice was Toby's mum and Jack's wife – she couldn't be replaced.

Nancy had woken to find the house empty and felt oddly bereft not to be able to share a morning cuddle with Toby. He was such a happy little boy and he'd crept into her heart, so much so that her arms now ached to hold him. She shook herself; it was nonsense. He wasn't her child and, when Jack was eventually ready to date, someone would come along. He might re-marry and Toby would have a stepmother. Where would that leave Nancy, if she got withdrawal symptoms after one morning away from the child? It was just her biological clock ticking or something. She'd realised she wanted a family and he made her feel a bit broody, that was all.

Unable to stand the silence, she switched on the radio in the kitchen and listened to a medley of Christmas songs, chirping on about snow falling all around – even though it absolutely never arrived as promised on the big day itself; at least, not in this part of the world.

The toast she made seemed bland, like her taste buds hadn't woken up. It felt like she was going through the motions all morning. She wanted to see her dad more than anything in the world. What she didn't particularly feel like doing was visiting the man who now inhabited the shell of John O'Brien's body. He wouldn't say *nollaig shona duit*, Merry Christmas to you, in Gaelic, as he'd always done on Christmas morning when she was a child, or tell her stories of the potato famine, or sing the folk songs he'd loved so much, especially in his maudlin moments after a drink or several, when he'd always seemed to miss the 'old country' most. And he'd never dress as Santa to entertain the children of St Nicholas Bay again. He'd more than likely stare at her blankly or, if she was lucky, talk about something totally unconnected with her visit, no more realising that they were a day away from Christmas than he did that she was his daughter.

Taking him out would make things easier. Borrowing her mother's car and getting him out of The Pines might at least register, somewhere in the dark recesses of his brain, as a special occasion.

The carpark of the care home was almost full. Duty visits and those born out of love combined on Christmas Eve, so Nancy had to negotiate carefully to squeeze Ruth's little Nissan into the last remaining space.

The smell of cabbage hit her as soon as she opened the car door and memories of her grandmother's Christmas dinners flooded back. Nan must have started preparing the cabbage at breakfast time back then, and the thought of swallowing that stuff made her throat close up.

The main lounge was busy and some families were already handing over brightly wrapped presents to residents who wouldn't remember receiving them.

'Dad.' Nancy put a hand on his shoulder, recognising his head even from behind. There'd been so much knowledge in there, so much wisdom. How could it have escaped like water through a sieve, so quickly and without resistance? She felt a stab of guilt that she hadn't brought him a present, even though she knew it didn't matter to him. After all, what did you buy the man who had nothing? Not even the memory of his own existence.

He turned and smiled at her. 'Hello, me-darling.'

For a second her heart leapt, as if he might suddenly have remembered who she was. But he was just grinning at her blankly, as he would have done to anyone who smiled at him.

'Do you fancy going out today? I thought we might drive to The George?'

He nodded and she let herself pretend he remembered the pub three villages away, which had always been a family favourite. They'd gone there to celebrate everything from Nancy's A-level results to her parents' pearl wedding anniversary, not long before he'd forgotten he'd ever been married.

He nodded amiably and began shuffling towards the door. Carpet slippers might not be normal attire for The George, which had just received its first Michelin star, but when she'd rung to book the table, Peter Grainger had remembered her and asked after John and Ruth. She'd been honest and Peter had sympathised; one of his uncles had apparently been lost to dementia, too. So the sight of her father in his Argyle slippers was hardly likely to induce a ban, even if the newer, more sophisticated clientele might not like it.

The George was a very old pub, half timbered, not in mock Tudor 1980s style, but the real deal, as though Henry VIII himself might have stopped off on route to an historical battle and ordered a flagon of ale. Nancy was desperate for a gin and tonic, but she ordered a Coke. Not diet, though; she had a distinct need for the full-sugar version. Her father was having a cider. Not something the care home recommended, but what the hell was the point of abstinence to prolong life in his circumstances?

'Do you fancy a rack of lamb in a raspberry and peppermint jus?'

Nancy read from the menu and her father nodded.

'Or perhaps the salt-and-pepper squid with sweet potato fries?'

He nodded again.

'Or how about albatross neck, stuffed with minced hippopotamus?'

He nodded for a third time and she sighed. Maybe this wasn't such a good idea. Was seeing her dad really worth it any more?

'I think I'll just order us both the Dover sole.'

She scanned the menu. Fish was supposed to be brain food, and if there was something they could both do with, it was that. Being more adventurous with the starters, Nancy ordered them both the razor clams with seaweed and bacon. John O'Brien had always been a plain food sort of man and had tangled with her mum on more than one occasion over the inclusion of garlic to flavour a roast dinner. After a year and a half of dining at The Pines, though, he had taken to eating whatever was put in front of him.

When the food arrived at their table, Nancy began to relax a bit. There was less need to try to make one-sided conversation with her dad once they were eating, and the ambience in the pub meant people-watching and listening in on other people's conversations was perfectly possible and discreet. Her father was having one of his quiet days, which she supposed was better than a day when he could rant and rave with frustration. Those were becoming less and less frequent, as if his mind had come to terms with its forgetfulness and no longer raged against itself. He seemed content wherever he was now. Occasionally he would pick up the menu and read a couple of lines from it, not with any particular purpose.

'Enjoying your food?'

It wasn't the waiter speaking. She would have known that voice anywhere.

'Fraser.'

Turning to look at him, she felt something flip in her stomach. He'd caught her by surprise when she was teaching and she'd been more annoyed than anything at the thought of him spying on her. Yet now, looking casual but annoyingly handsome in a navy-blue roll-neck jumper, and with his blond hair ruffled, he looked much more like the old Fraser.

'Can I sit down? I hadn't realised Peter had got himself a Michelin star in my absence and it would be impossible to turn up and just grab a table.' Fraser smiled, the crease between his eyebrows deepening, just as she remembered.

'Of course. Are you eating?' Nancy indicated the chair next to her. John smiled at the new arrival, but didn't say anything.

'I think I've got to now I've seen that delicious starter.'

Fraser picked up the menu and a waitress walked past several other diners to make a beeline for their table. Nancy wasn't the only one to notice that Fraser still had it.

'What can I get you, sir?'

The waitress had what looked like a platinum wedding ring on the fourth finger of her left hand, but she leant in so close to Fraser that Nancy could see her pink bra.

'I'll have the venison cooked in hay with the roasted celeriac, if that could be brought out at the same time as my friends' main courses, please?'

'Of course.' The woman definitely smiled at the use of the word 'friend'.

'What are you doing back again? I thought you weren't going to grace us with your presence until the New Year.'

She tried to keep her tone as nonchalant as possible.

'Since Maisie's decided to spend Christmas with you so she can go gigging, she can't make it down to Mum and Dad's new place in Cornwall. So I said I'd bring them up and they've taken her out to lunch. We'll probably be driving through the night to get back down there, but Mum's got half her family staying right through until New Year. It's worth a trip back anyway, as I wanted to drive by a couple of the houses I've got estate agents' details for to see if it's worth going to see them after the holidays.'

Fraser gave her one of the smiles that were the first thing she'd noticed – and loved – about him.

'To buy?'

She couldn't really believe he was going to settle in the Bay again. His parents had followed him down to Cornwall, but now it seemed he was considering coming back for good.

'If things work out like I'm hoping, then yes.'

'Things? At the college?'

'Yes, there.' He looked at her so intently she was forced to look away. 'And elsewhere too.'

'I didn't think the Bay would ever be enough for you.'

'I wasn't sure it would be either, but that old saying that the grass isn't always greener is truer than I ever thought. I've missed you, you know.'

He placed an arm along the back of her chair and she was suddenly acutely aware of their proximity. It felt strange, although not unpleasant, to be so close to a body that she'd once known so well. She could close her eyes and picture him naked, remember what it felt like to touch him. The memories were still there, no matter how much she didn't want them to be.

'It was your choice to go.'

'I had no choice, you know that.' Fraser gave her a rueful look.

'Sweetbreads and chestnut pulp.'

Her father had picked up the menu again, choosing another item to read out loud, and Nancy laughed.

'Do you know, Dad, I couldn't have put it better myself.'

She turned to Fraser and raised an eyebrow. 'He's right, you know. Although I might have put it a little less delicately and said bollocks. Of course you had a choice.'

'Well, if I had a choice, then we both did, and maybe I made the wrong one.' He looked away for a moment. 'Seeing you now with John, I can understand why you stayed. Even though I had no idea why at the time. I'll admit it, I couldn't see the point.'

'And you can now?'

'Of course. He might be locked inside his head, but he's still your dad.' Fraser shrugged. 'I've realised a lot lately. I haven't been able to stop thinking about you since I came into the college and saw you again. Maisie told me what happened with David and that you and Jack are just housemates. She told me not to get involved and mess you around again, but she didn't say I had no chance.'

'You can't just turn up here and say you want to pick up where we left off. You might have been thinking about all that for the last couple of weeks, but it's been the last thing on my mind.'

Making a mental note to kill Maisie for blabbing about

Jack, she didn't know what else to say. There was so much shared history. He'd known her father when he was still the real John O'Brien, when they'd spent evenings with her parents in this very pub, the four of them laughing and talking. Maybe that was a big part of the pull she was feeling. She couldn't imagine building a life with someone who'd never really known her dad.

'I'm not going to rush you, but I really loved you, Nance. It's nowhere near as easy to forget that now I'm back in the Bay.' He smiled. 'You don't think it's a coincidence I just turned up here and found you, do you? I went to The Pines and they said you'd taken your dad to your favourite restaurant. How many people would know that about you? Know exactly where to find you? I know you better than anyone, Nance, I really do.'

'We were together a long time.'

She didn't want to say any more; he was too close to her and the restaurant was crowded with people celebrating. It was hard to work out what was real and what was just a memory. He smelt great, though, and so familiar. If they'd been somewhere else and he tried to kiss her, she'd have let him and *hated* herself for being so weak. Whatever her true feelings now, he was the only man she'd ever really loved. Her attempts to settle for David had been unfair to them both, and any animosity she'd had towards him had all but evaporated. She'd cheated him just as much as he'd cheated her.

'I'm not going to say anything else for now, but I had to put my cards on the table.' He stood up. 'It's Christmas Eve and, if nothing else, we're friends again. That's a great start and we should get something expensive from the bar to celebrate. The best champagne they've got.'

He grinned and there was no doubt the Fraser she'd fallen in love with was in the building. 'Well, the best that won't bankrupt me, now that this place has gone all up market. I don't want to have to resort to a toasted cheese sandwich for lunch!'

Nancy returned his smile and another little piece of her heart thawed out.

CHAPTER TWENTY-FIVE

'How was your dad yesterday?' Jack pushed the buggy out of the front door and turned to see Nancy struggling with two bags of presents. 'Are you sure you don't want me to take the car?'

'No, it's fine. It's only this last bag of presents. I've already dropped off the rest and I think you're going to need a drink to get through Mum's endless charades this afternoon.' She smiled. 'Sorry, what were you saying?'

'I was asking how things were with your dad yesterday.' Jack took one of the bags and rested it on the hood of the buggy. 'Nothing breakable in here, is there?'

'No, it's mostly for Toby.'

She smiled again. There hadn't been time to talk about what they'd both been up to on Christmas Eve. Jack hadn't got back from London until late. The morning had been a frenzy of present unwrapping for Toby or, more accurately, for Jack while Toby took more interest in the wrapping paper than the presents themselves.

'Dad was okay.'

'Did you take him to the pub?'

'Yes and it was fine. He wasn't having one of his shouty days; in fact, he barely spoke. So I was quite glad it wasn't just the two of us in the end.'

'Oh?' Jack hadn't missed the shift in her tone and his

hands involuntarily tightened around the handles of the buggy.

'Fraser turned up at the pub when we were in the middle of lunch.'

'Out of the blue? I thought he wasn't due back until the New Year.'

Why it should bother Jack if it had been pre-arranged he didn't know, but it did.

'It was a surprise to me. He was on a flying visit to see Maisie.'

Nancy's face didn't give anything away as they walked further up the hill towards Ruth's place.

'But he said he'd gone to The Pines knowing I'd be there and they told him I'd taken Dad to our favourite restaurant.'

'And he knew where that was?'

'We've been going there to celebrate since long before it was as successful as it is now, and he'd been there with my family a few times over the years.'

'So, are you …?' Jack hesitated. He wasn't an idiot, and the way she'd spoken about Fraser had always been different from the way she talked about David. For all he knew she could be about to move out. The thought of that stopped him in his tracks and he couldn't finish the sentence, turning to look at her again.

'Together? No!'

There was something reassuring about her emphatic response.

'There's a lot of history, but I don't know. Something's just not the same and I can't work out yet if that's a good thing or a bad thing.'

'It's early days yet.'

He could have kicked himself as soon as the words were out of his mouth. He didn't want her to leave. He didn't want anything, their friendship included, to change. It wasn't that he wanted to be with her – the last few days had convinced him he could never do that to Alice. But he had to admit that his and Toby's lives were better for having Nancy in them. So why the hell was he telling her to give things with Fraser some time?

'I suppose.' She shot him a sideways glance and seemed to pick up the pace a bit. 'What about you? How were things with Pam?'

'As you might expect, at first. She was tearful and angry about all sorts of stuff, but after we got to the cemetery she seemed to calm down and we actually had a nice lunch remembering Christmases with Alice. After that I popped in to see Craig and Selena, before they headed off to her parents' house. They were loved up to the point of nausea!'

He laughed. In some ways it had been a bit painful to witness, but he was pleased for them and oddly grateful that their getting together had inadvertently come out of Alice's death – something that made it all less pointless and unnecessary.

'How are the plans for the wedding coming?'

'They're having a small engagement party on New Year's Eve. Nothing fancy, just a few close friends. I was going to ask you if you'd mind keeping me company?'

He could do with a friend, but with Fraser back on the scene she might well have other plans.

'That would be great. It has to beat sitting up at The Pines and celebrating the start of another year when Dad is just going to drift a bit further away.' Nancy shook her head. 'Sorry, I shouldn't bring the mood down today.'

'You can say anything to me, you know that, don't you? It's not like you haven't had to listen to me bang on about my misery often enough!'

'I've grown accustomed to your face … even on the really miserable days!'

She laughed as he took one hand off the buggy to nudge her.

'Yeah, and I've somehow got used to your out-of-tune singing. I wouldn't mind if you restricted it to the shower.'

There was that surge in his chest again, the painful mix of desire and guilt. The thought of Nancy in the shower was an image he couldn't quite shake.

Nancy turned the roast potatoes over and swore under her breath. It must have been a quirk of her mum's oven but the potatoes were absolutely refusing to brown. In the meantime the turkey was turning to the consistency of a flip-flop with every second. She took all her complaints about teaching being stressful back. Cooking Christmas lunch – even for only four and a half people – was much more panic-inducing. She couldn't count Toby as a whole person, given the amount he'd actually consume, and the added bonus was he wouldn't pass any comment about the potatoes being a bit on the *al dente* side.

Ruth had not long been back from The Pines and she'd come straight through to the kitchen to see if she could help. Red faced and flustered, Nancy had poured her mother a large glass of wine and ushered her straight back into the front room, where Maisie and Jack were safely ensconced. Maisie could keep them entertained with the latest saga in her love life and, if Nancy kept topping up the glasses, maybe no one would mention just how long it was taking for lunch to arrive.

There was a sudden roar of laughter from the front room and she couldn't resist any longer. Leaving the potatoes to their own devices, she grabbed another bottle of wine by the neck and joined the others. Toby was happily bashing pegs into a series of holes with a wooden hammer, but he stopped as she came in and his whole face lit up when he smiled at her.

'Hello, darling.' She put the wine on the table and knelt down to play with him.

'Nmm, Nmm, Nmm.'

The word was indistinguishable, but Toby's babbling put a smile on her face all the same. Who gave a damn about anaemic potatoes?

'He's trying to say my name!'

'I think you might be right.' Jack grinned and shook his head. 'It's no good. I've definitely got to start working harder on the dad, dad, dad bit. I can't have him saying Nancy's name before mine!'

Ruth raised an eyebrow. 'If it's any consolation, my darling daughter's first word wasn't Mum or Dad, it was "cat".'

'Apparently mine was biscuit, which explains a lot.'

Maisie smoothed her top down over her plump midriff. A few extra pounds didn't make her any less attractive. She had more than enough personality to make her beautiful.

'Rubbish, you look great.' Jack leant across and took the bottle to top up Maisie's glass before turning to Nancy with a smile. 'Anyway, we're all going to need a few biscuits if Christmas lunch takes much longer.'

'Oh, shut up, you, or you'll just get a plate of sprouts!'

She took a seat beside him, in the space he'd made for her on the sofa, leaving Toby happily banging the pegs further into the holes.

'So, come on, what were you all laughing about before I came in? It can't all be about my cooking!'

'Maisie was filling us in on her latest date.' Jack grinned. 'I keep telling her she should ditch the online stuff and go old school.'

'*Old school*?' Nancy raised her glass and her eyebrows at the same time. 'You have seen where we work, haven't you? Most people meet their other halves at work. Our place is full of marrieds and misfits. There's no way Maisie is ever going to find anyone there, there's not a decent guy among them. Present company excepted, of course.'

'Well, thanks, I think.' Jack narrowed his eyes. 'Sounds like you've given this a lot of thought.'

'I've looked into it.'

The words were out before Nancy had a chance to stop them and she clapped her hand over her mouth.

'So are you thinking of giving it a go, too?'

Ruth looked at her daughter and the heat rose up Nancy's neck.

'I haven't ruled it out. But I'm not on the lookout to get involved with someone else any time soon. Not after David.'

She wasn't about to tell any of them that seeing Fraser again had made her wonder if they still had a shot. Jack was the only one who knew how confused she was and, until she'd worked out exactly what it was she felt, she wanted to keep it that way.

'I think it would be great!' Maisie bounced up and down on one end of the sofa. 'We could profile scan together!'

'Really?' Jack's response was sharp. 'You were only telling us a moment ago how weird some of the guys are.'

'Okay, so my last date had more gold around his neck than Mr T and the one before that said he liked me because I looked like his mother.' Maisie shuddered at the memory. 'But, hey, I've had loads of horrendous dates with people that I've met "old school" as you put it. There was Gary who couldn't go five minutes without digging in his ear for treasure and then wiping what he found on his shirt. Then there was Tony, who was seeing at least three other girls at the same time, not to mention the boyfriend he had waiting at home. And I know Fraser's my brother, but he didn't exactly end up being Prince Charming for Nancy. And as for David ...'

'Doesn't give men in general a very good reputation, does it?' Ruth shook her head. 'And with the likes of Daniel Chapman on the singles market, I can get what you girls are up against.'

'Daniel's not so bad. In fact if I was ten years older, five even, I think I'd be pressing my number into his hand like there's no tomorrow.' Maisie took another swig of her wine and grinned. 'After all, big car, big bank balance, big ...'

'Maisie!' Nancy shot her a look; there were some conversations she didn't want to have with her mother around.

'He could have the world's biggest bank balance and he'd still be a pig.'

Her mother was already bristling.

'Anything specific this time or is it just the same old thing?'

Nancy couldn't help herself. She'd grown to really like Daniel and her mother's resolute refusal to see any good in him was becoming more and more difficult to cope with.

'Oh you know, another grand gesture, as empty and meaningless as his heart.' Ruth's face twisted like she was trying to swallow a whole lemon. 'He brought OTT presents into The Pines this morning and not just for the staff. There were ridiculously expensive gifts for the residents and even for some of the more regular visitors.'

'He brought you a present?' Nancy was genuinely shocked. It was certainly brave for Daniel to have done that – Ruth had hardly hidden her feelings. 'What was it?'

'Van Cleef and Arpels perfume.'

'That's your favourite!'

'It *was*. I won't ever be wearing it again, knowing he bought that perfume with your father's blood money!'

'Come on, Mum, that's not fair.'

'So, what are your plans for New Year's Eve, Maisie?'

Jack cut across the conversation as if he hadn't even heard it and Nancy could have kissed him. The last thing she wanted was for Christmas Day to be ruined by another row about a man they would never agree on – at least not for as long as she kept her father's secrets.

'I'm not sure. I've got three dates lined up between now and then. I've just about managed to squeeze them all in between gigs and the panto.' Maisie giggled. 'And, if more than one of them looks half decent, I might even be able to sort out a double date for my mate over there. I don't want her sitting home alone on New Year's Eve.'

She gestured towards Nancy.

'She's already sorted for New Year's Eve.'

Jack didn't quite pull off the casual shrug that went with his words.

'Ooh! Are you two going on a date?'

'It's not a date.'

Nancy and Jack spoke at exactly the same time.

'What are you up to then?'

'Some friends of Jack's have just got engaged and they're having a bit of a get-together.' Nancy fixed her with a warming look. 'So don't start getting any ideas.'

'Okay, chill out. I wasn't about to ask if I could be a

bridesmaid!' Maisie grinned again. 'And don't worry, if all the dates turn out to be decent, I'll pick the best one and keep the other two on ice for you until the New Year.'

'Well, there's a generous offer!' Nancy leant across Jack and clinked glasses with her friend. 'But before then we've got to get through the panto. So I want your mind on the job and not the millions of men you've got clamouring for your company.'

�֍

The potatoes finally complied and turned a gorgeous, crispy golden brown; even the turkey had somehow held on to a bit of moisture. Conversation came easily around the table, and Toby sat like an angel in the wooden high chair that Ruth had brought down from the loft. The knock on the door that came just as Nancy had brought in the flaming Christmas pudding was an unwelcome interruption.

'Please tell me that's not Jehovah's Witnesses! Just because they don't celebrate, it doesn't mean they have a right to knock on my door today of all days.'

Ruth was already half way up from the chair, but Nancy held up her hand.

'It's okay, Mum. I'll get it.'

A small knot of fear tightened in her stomach. What if something had happened to her dad and The Pines hadn't wanted to break the news over the phone? Why else would anyone knock on the door, unannounced, at lunchtime on Christmas Day?

'Oh my God, Mark!'

Seeing her brother on the doorstep was so unexpected she had to lean against the door frame, not sure whether to punch him or throw her arms around his neck. In the end, by the narrowest of margins, she decided on the latter.

CHAPTER TWENTY-SIX

Ruth's glass hovered in mid-air for a moment; how it made it back onto the table without shattering into a million pieces on the floor she'd never know.

'Mark?'

It was definitely him, but it still came out as a question. After all, it had been almost two years since she'd last seen him. Nancy was standing behind him in the doorway, the look on her face mirroring Ruth's shock.

'Happy Christmas, Mum.'

He leant towards her and pecked her on the cheek, the woody scent of his aftershave still familiar after all this time, like nothing had changed. She'd washed his shirts thousands of times over the years and they'd always been heavy with that scent.

'What are you doing here?'

If it came out sharply she couldn't help it. What did he expect, to return like the prodigal son he was – no questions asked? For all she knew, he could have been dead. The unwanted thought, which she'd been suppressing in the months of silence, twisted something in her gut and she grabbed his arm, her eyes filling with tears.

'I emailed you, to let you know I was coming back.'

'I don't read my emails any more.'

It sounded stupid when she said it out loud, but she didn't feel like she owed him an explanation. If he'd stuck around then he'd have known why she couldn't bear to read all the smug news from old friends. Anyway, that was hardly the point. An email? After all these months? Despite herself, she pulled him towards her, not sure if she'd ever be able to let him go again.

'It's okay, Mum. I'm home.'

His messy red hair still stuck up in all directions, just as it had done when he was a child. There was that same rueful grin, too, as if he was bringing home yet another school report suggesting he 'could try harder'.

'Do you know what?'

Jack, who was sitting opposite Ruth, pushed the long-extinguished Christmas pudding into the centre of the table.

'I think I could do with a walk before dessert, and Toby could do with some air too. Maisie, do you fancy it?'

Maisie, whose mouth was hanging open at the sight of Mark, seemed to jump at the mention of her name.

'Oh, yes, yes, of course.'

Despite her words she seemed reluctant to drag herself away from the table. But, within seconds, Jack had passed Maisie her coat and was strapping Toby back into his buggy.

'Right, see you later.'

He called out from the corridor and Ruth made a mental note to thank him later. Why couldn't all men be like him, instead of like the Daniel Chapmans of this world?

Nancy still hadn't spoken. The three of them needed time alone and Jack hadn't needed telling. If it had been left to Maisie, Ruth suspected she'd have sat herself in the

256

middle of the action, turning her head from side to side, like she was watching a game of beach volleyball instead of a fractured family trying to put itself back together.

'Where have you been, Mark?'

When the others had gone, Ruth turned to the head of the table where her son had taken a seat. He was pouring wine into someone else's empty glass, not seeming to care that it was second-hand.

'Ibiza, mostly. I know I slipped off the radar for a bit, but I couldn't handle the emails any more. You asking when I was going to come back.' Mark gestured towards her. 'And Nancy having a go at me for worrying you, when she knew better than anyone why I couldn't come home.'

'Mark, don't.' Nancy's face had clouded. 'It doesn't matter why you left now; you're home.'

Ruth's stomach contracted at her daughter's words. Nancy knew why Mark had disappeared and they were keeping something from her. Whatever Mark's reason for leaving and whatever he'd been doing all this time, it couldn't have been worse than her darkest fear that he might be lying dead in a ditch somewhere.

'I've already put it all in the email to Mum, Nance. I couldn't come back here unless I got it all out in the open.'

There was a muscle going in Mark's cheek, and there was so much Ruth wanted to ask, but she wasn't nearly as sure she wanted the answers.

'But we promised.'

Nancy looked from her brother to Ruth, her eyes darting between them with something close to terror.

'Because he didn't want to worry Mum, but it's nothing in the big scheme of things. She's survived having a husband who doesn't know his own name. I'm sure she can cope with the truth.'

Mark's fingers were drumming on the table as he spoke and Nancy looked like she wanted to stab a fork into his hand.

'She's fragile, Mark. You know that and so did Dad!'

'Stop talking about me like I'm not here!' Ruth suddenly found her voice. 'I brought you two up, so I can't for the life of me work out what it is you think I can't cope with. What's so terrible that my own children can't tell me?'

'That's the whole point, Mum. It's not that terrible at all.'

Mark stood up and moved to crouch beside her.

'It's just that before Dad got ill he wanted us to protect you and Nancy still thinks you need that. Because of everything that happened after Nan died, and Nancy giving up uni to look after you, she thinks you can't cope with the truth.'

'The truth about what?'

Ruth was barely resisting the urge to scream now. The remnants of Christmas crackers strewn across the table were so at odds with the conversation they were having.

'About the business.' Mark stroked her arm. 'Dad made the two of us and Daniel promise that we wouldn't tell you just how bad things were when he sold up. There wasn't even enough to cover the debts after the sale, even though Daniel paid us way over the odds. Dad had been running things on a shoestring and spending more than he earned for years. There was a massive tax bill he couldn't pay for a start. He didn't want you to know. He was terrified the worry would trigger another breakdown, and Nancy was just as worried that she might have to pick up the pieces all over again.'

'Don't put words into my mouth!'

Nancy was up from her seat, and for a moment Ruth was taken back to when they were kids and physical fights would regularly break out between them.

'Tell me you aren't terrified of going back to how it was after Nan died, and that you haven't sacrificed more than you really wanted already to look after her, when she's perfectly capable of looking after herself.'

Nancy eyes looked black. 'Don't be an arsehole, Mark. It's normal to make sacrifices for the people you love.'

'So you want this life, do you? Not being free to go where you want in case Mum needs you. I never had you down as a martyr, Nancy, but maybe I was wrong.'

'Just because all you ever cared about was the business.'

Nancy's barbed comment made Mark flinch and Ruth watched them, like a bitter game of piggy in the middle.

'Stop it!'

Both of them turned to look at her as if they'd forgotten that she was there.

'Are you saying Daniel Chapman didn't rip your father off?'

'He was more than generous. Dad nearly lost everything, and without Daniel he would have.' Mark's voice was much quieter all of a sudden.

'And you didn't tell me any of this because you think I'm too fragile to deal with it?'

She turned to Nancy this time, who was shaking her head.

'It's not that, Mum. It's because you've been ill before and we didn't want to risk it. Before he got too ill to understand what was going on, we promised Dad that we wouldn't tell you about this. Maybe it wasn't the right thing to do, but we really thought it was at the time.'

'So you were all just lying to me?'

'I asked myself over and over again if we'd made the right choice, but it wasn't something I could take back or talk through with Dad any more. Keeping that promise is one of the few things I've been able to do for him since he got really ill.'

'It still amounts to the same thing: everyone's had to carry me when I'm supposed to be the mother. I'm supposed to be the one looking after all of you!'

Ruth's voice cracked on the words, the burning sensation in her throat nothing compared to the one in her chest. She'd failed them – her family – because she was so weak. Mark had left rather than face her, and Nancy had been *forced* to do her duty. Again.

For a second she thought about Daniel and all the things she'd said to him, heat flushing her cheeks. She was pathetic and everyone had known it. Everyone but her. Her one wish had been to have both children home for the holidays. Some happy bloody Christmas this had turned out to be.

'Are you okay?'

Nancy was marching so determinedly towards Jack he thought for a moment she was going to walk straight past him.

'No.'

By the time she spoke, she was close enough for him to see tears streaming down her face.

'Shall we go home?'

He'd been heading up the hill to Ruth's house, having been dumped by Maisie pretty early on when she'd got a better offer.

Nancy nodded and he turned Toby's buggy around without saying anything else. If he'd been in the mood for writing anything much these days, this would all have been grist to his mill. Abandoning Christmas dinner after the arrival of a long-lost relative was like something out of *EastEnders*.

'Where's Maisie?'

Nancy didn't speak until they were almost back home, and she hadn't seemed to register her friend's absence until then.

'She got a call from one of her internet dates, inviting her over this evening. Not the one with the Mr T jewellery, you'll be pleased to hear. I told her it was a booty call, which she seemed absurdly pleased about. She said she needed a couple of hours to get ready and shave off her winter coat!'

'Gross.'

Nancy managed a half smile and Jack squeezed her hand, steadying the buggy with the other.

'You don't have to talk about any of it, but I'm here if you want to. You know that, don't you?'

'Sometimes I think you're the only person I can rely on lately. Weird, given I've only known you a while and I thought you were a bit odd when I first met you.'

'I was a bit odd when you first met me.'

It was Jack's turn to smile. He was still a bit odd, he knew, but losing your wife tended to have that effect.

'Let's get inside and I can tell you all about the *Jeremy Kyle Show Live* we just had at Mum's. Then you'll see how normal you are.'

Toby was sound asleep in his buggy. Jack wheeled it into the front room and laid him down flat, loosening the blankets around him so he wouldn't get too hot.

'Drink?'

Nancy, who had curled her feet up underneath her on the sofa, shook her head.

'I'd rather have something hot and comforting. I think this calls for tea. I'll make it though.'

She was up before he could protest and clattering cups out in the kitchen. He'd have been so lonely if he hadn't invited her to stay.

'Here you go.'

She put a mug down in front of him.

'Come on then, tell me all about it.'

'Oh, you know, just a normal family get-together with a brother you're thrilled to see because you've been missing him like crazy and been worried sick for months when he stopped emailing. Then ten minutes later all you want to do is to plunge a knife into his chest to shut him up.'

'Sounds fairly standard.'

Jack had to fight the urge to move next to her when she smiled at him. Being virtuous was bullshit.

'I take it things came to a head with your mum too.'

'Spot on. He blurted out everything about the business and Daniel bailing Dad out.'

'Did she take it badly?'

'I think she could have coped with the bit about the business. It's all ancient history now and she's had far more to worry about with Dad since. Mark was right about that. But it was the way he did it … Maybe it was to offload his guilt at not sticking around once the business was gone and Dad really went downhill. He put the blame at her door and hung me out to dry at the same time.'

'What did he say about you?'

'More or less that Mum had ruined my life before and we were all worried about her doing it again. That I only stuck around out of guilt, that sort of thing.'

'Shit.'

'That about sums it up!' Nancy took a sip of her tea

and pulled a face. 'Not only am I a terrible daughter, I also make God-awful tea.'

'You're far from being a terrible anything. You're lovely.'

He'd have to watch himself; her vulnerability was fast wearing down his good intentions.

'To your mum, I mean. And your tea's not the worst I've ever tasted.'

'Don't be too nice to me or I might cry.'

She might have been joking but the glassy look in her eyes suggested it was close to the truth.

'The look on Mum's face was awful, she was so hurt. We might have started out trying to do the right thing, but it coming out like this is much worse than it would have been if Dad, or one of us, had told her the truth in the first place. I couldn't stop to try and make things right, I just had to get out of there.'

'It was probably the best thing to do. She'll need time to process it, make sense of why you did it. I'm sure she'll understand in the end.'

Jack gripped the mug, the warmth strangely comforting. Maybe that was why everyone was so keen on tea in times of shock.

'I hope so.'

She looked at him for a long moment before standing up to cross the room.

'I don't know what I'd have done if you hadn't invited me to move in, Jack.'

She kissed him softly on the cheek. A totally innocent kiss that set about a chemical reaction in his body which was anything but.

'It was one of the craziest decisions I've ever made,' Jack said, pulling a pillow on to his lap as she sat beside him.

He pulled a pillow onto his lap as she sat beside him. His pathetic weak-willed flesh was in danger of betraying him.

'But it was one of the best. We're both a bit messed up. Maybe that's why it works.'

'Well, I'd recommend it to anyone in the same boat.' Nancy laid her head on his shoulder and, try as he might, he couldn't convince himself he wanted her to stop.

CHAPTER TWENTY-SEVEN

Ruth woke up on the morning of Boxing Day, drenched in sweat despite the sudden drop in temperature in the last twenty-four hours. She must have fallen asleep eventually, but she'd left the radio playing for company and she'd still been awake for the 5.00 a.m. news. .

She'd replayed the conversation with Nancy and Mark from the day before so many times. Mark had stayed after Nancy left, apologising for the bluntness of his revelation. He'd put it far better in the email, or so he'd said; she hadn't been able to bring herself to read that too.

She'd said it was okay before Mark had gone to bed, announcing he was off to stay with a friend for a couple of days in the morning. But was it really okay? Usually she'd have begged him to stay, especially after so long an absence. Only now she wondered if that would reinforce his sense of her as a weak and clinging mother. Nancy had texted to say she was sorry too and that she was ready to talk as soon as Ruth was. Nancy had nothing to apologise for. She was just doing what she thought was right, what her father had asked her to do. Yet it still felt like the rug had been ripped out from under Ruth's feet. She wasn't sure of anything anymore. Did Nancy relish the time they spent together, like Ruth did, or was she only there because she felt she had to be?

There were so many questions and she couldn't face any of the answers. She didn't want to see anyone, so she sent Nancy a quick message saying everything was fine, no need to talk, with one of those ridiculous smiley-faced emojis and two kisses. That would have to do for now.

The sound of Mark contentedly snoring as Ruth padded down the corridor towards the stairs caused a frisson of irritation. He'd turned up and changed everything. As wrong as it was for a mother to think that way, part of her wished he hadn't come home at all. Ignorance really was bliss.

Pouring herself a strong coffee, Ruth mechanically went about loading the dishwasher with the plates from Christmas dinner. Had it really been yesterday? It seemed like a lifetime ago. She even made toast, not that she was hungry, but her movements were automatic.

She took one bite of toast and pushed it away. Before the fall out, she'd agreed to take Nancy's turn to visit John today so Nancy could organise some things for the pantomime. Had she really relied on Nancy to visit her father so often while she held down two jobs? She'd exceeded even those expectations, not just visiting on the alternate 'duty days', but often popping in on her way to work to give him breakfast. Ruth couldn't deny it. She'd taken too much from her daughter, and the burden Nancy had shouldered with John was just a part of that.

The Pines seemed to have twice as many residents as normal, and Ruth raised an eyebrow as Barbara hunted out a spare chair for her.

'Sorry, we've got a load of extras in this week for respite. Daniel couldn't seem to say no to anyone, said he wanted the families to have a break over Christmas. So almost all of our respite clients seem to be here at once. It's cost him a fortune in overtime and for agency workers, what with it being Christmas and all.'

Ruth bit back the comment that had been on the tip of her tongue about Daniel raking in the cash with that much respite. It wasn't fair to criticise him any more, but she'd hated him for so long it wasn't going to be an easy adjustment to make.

'Are you working all day?'

She took the hard wooden chair from Barbara and smiled in thanks. An uncomfortable chair was all she deserved.

'Yes, but I had yesterday off. Daniel came in to supervise, so I could spend Christmas with my daughter and her family.'

'That's nice.' Ruth pursed her lips. Daniel was a regular saint.

'It was lovely. Carys did me right proud with the spread she put on. Seeing her manage her family so well, I felt guilty moaning about not seeing much of her. One day with the kids wore me out!'

'Sounds like you had a great time.'

Ruth watched John from across the room, nodding along to a tune that must have been playing in his head.

'It's a wonderful time of year to be with the family, isn't it? And I bet your Nancy did you proud too.' Barbara grinned. 'We're lucky women, you know, Ruth.'

'That we are. I'd better go and see John now or I won't be ready to help dress the hall for the panto this afternoon and I can't leave it all to Nancy.'

The irony of the words echoed in her head and she had to blink back tears as she walked towards the man who had once been her rock.

Ruth sat on the uncomfortable wooden chair for two hours, but John seemed to have drifted further away from her than ever. His striking blue eyes stared into the distance, focusing intently on something that wasn't there.

'Are you okay?' Daniel stood in front of her, immaculate in a dark blue suit and a white linen shirt with the top two buttons undone. She'd have said he looked sleazy the day before out of spite, but it had never been true. What she couldn't understand was why he still spoke to her. She'd been so horrible to him, yet he kept trying and he'd always kept John's counsel. She wondered if he'd die of shock if she suddenly threw her arms around him.

'I'm okay.'

Her voice betrayed her and a hot tear escaped, despite her efforts to blink it back.

'Is it John?' His arm was around her shoulder as he moved beside her, and for once she didn't shrug him off. 'You look terrible.'

'I …' She didn't know where to start, but he might be the one person she could talk to about this. He was the one other person who'd known the whole story about John's plea to protect her, without the family ties that clouded every conversation.

'Do you want to come into the office so that we can talk privately?'

Ruth managed a watery smile. 'I think we could trust this lot to keep our secrets, but it's probably a good idea. I don't want to scare anyone if I start sobbing.'

'That bad?'

Daniel had really kind eyes. She'd never noticed that before.

'No. It's worse than that.'

'Thanks for coming down with me.' Ruth stood outside the old community centre with Daniel. She shivered, but it had nothing to do with the cold.

'I told you before. I made John a promise to look out for you.'

'I don't want to be a burden to you, too. I seem to make a habit of it.'

She sniffed, the tears that had flowed in his office after they'd finally talked things through still not far from the surface.

'You aren't a burden. Anyway, you know me, I'll do anything to make myself look good!'

'I'm so sorry.' He was only trying to lighten the mood, but the words still stung. 'I've been a bitch, haven't I?'

'I told you not to apologise any more. I figured if blaming me helped you cope with what was happening to John, then that was okay.'

'How have I had you so wrong for so long?'

The warmth of his hand closing over hers as she spoke didn't feel odd. If he hadn't been there, she wasn't sure she could have crossed the threshold into the building at all. Even as she entered the lobby, it was as though there was some magnetic field between her feet and the parquet floor – every step felt like she was walking on the moon.

She couldn't let the rest of the world see her holding Daniel's hand – God, the gossip mongers of St Nicholas Bay would love that one – so reluctantly she uncurled her fingers from his.

Nancy had her back to the door as they entered the hall. Her hair was pinned up casually and, as she waved her arms around to direct the preparations, loose curls began to escape.

'Can I do something to help?'

Approaching her daughter's shoulder, Ruth managed

to stop herself placing a hand there. Daniel was right. He'd told her in the office to take it slowly, not to come on too strongly to try and sort it all out – they had to find a new equilibrium somehow.

'I think we're fine out here, thanks.'

Anyone who didn't know Nancy really well would have thought everything was normal. Her words were nothing out of the ordinary and even the tone of her voice was light. There was no doubting she could still act when the need arose. Only her smile was tight and forced, her back rigid.

'I think they could do with a hand out back, though.'

'Okay, I'll do that then.'

Ruth took a step back. If she'd allowed herself the fantasy that there'd be none of the awkwardness between them she'd feared there might, then she was in for a disappointment. Baby steps. She forced the silent mantra to repeat in her head. Causing a scene by pushing to resolve everything there and then, and possibly opening up another can of worms, wouldn't help anything. It would just be one more example of Ruth O'Brien being needy. Daniel had been right. Again.

CHAPTER TWENTY-EIGHT

'Have you spoken to your mum yet?'

She knew what Jack was really asking, but acting as though she didn't was the easy way out.

'You know I have. I saw her on Boxing Day, when we dressed the hall.'

'That's not what I meant and you know it.'

Anyone who said that men couldn't multi-task obviously hadn't met Jack. He was managing to give her a lecture at the same time as feeding a reluctant Toby, who was ducking and weaving away from the spoon with all the ease of a championship boxer.

'We haven't talked about what happened on Christmas Day if that's what you mean. If I'm honest I'd rather just gloss over the conversation and pretend it didn't happen. But Mark wants us all to meet for lunch after New Year. God knows why, but I said I would.'

'You haven't forgotten about Toby's birthday party on the second, have you?'

He looked suddenly panicked and she realised how hard it must be to face all these firsts without Alice.

'Only I can't bear the thought of it being just Pam and a load of people I hardly know from the nursery. I told Aunt Josie not to come over; it takes nearly a week on the boat and she'd have to travel from LA to New York first. I'd rather she waited until the summer so she can spend longer with us.'

'Are Craig and Selena coming down?'

Nancy packed up a few more of the props that she'd brought home to check over and which had left their tiny cottage looking like a junk shop for the past few days. There was a top hat, a long blonde wig and a sequinned wand still balanced on the scrubbed pine table.

'Apparently they're having a few days in Paris after the engagement party.' Jack sighed. 'Not bad if you can. Don't suppose I'll go back there for a long time; it's not the sort of place I could take Toby.'

'They've got Disneyland there, sounds pretty child friendly to me.'

'I would say they're going for something a bit more cultured than that, although knowing Craig you might be right!'

'Where did you and Alice have your honeymoon?'

She was never sure if Jack liked talking about Alice or not, but she wanted to know more about her, get a handle on the woman whom Jack had loved.

'My Aunt Josie invited us to New York. Alice was desperate to go; her biggest ambition was to perform on Broadway and at the time she thought going there would be the next best thing. I didn't want to, though. I had a feeling they'd both spend the whole time working on me, telling me we should move out there for good. We had a big row about it, but in the end she agreed to a week in St Ives. Not quite the same, but I promised I'd take her to New York one day.'

Jack met her eyes for a moment and the dark shadows that seemed to have lifted lately were instantly back.

'Only she died before I could and now it feels like I robbed her of that dream, just because I couldn't face finding out if she was like my mum.'

'What you went through with your mum would affect anyone. She must have understood that?'

Nancy wished she could make him feel better. Sometimes he was so weighed down with guilt she could almost see it.

'Did she know how bad things were for you growing up?'

'I told her, but she'd brush it off. She was ambitious, but aren't all performers?' Jack wiped some food off Toby's chin. 'Sometimes I could see how badly she wanted it and almost all of our rows were about Aunt Josie. She could have made things happen for Alice, or at least given her a big leg up, but I was determined we'd only make it on our own merits.'

'That's not a bad thing.'

'But it wasn't really about taking the moral high ground. I did it because I was frightened of losing her, like I did my parents. I should have put her first. What I worried about didn't matter enough to rob her of that chance.'

'You can't regret it, Jack, not when you've got Toby. You might not have had him if you'd done things differently.'

The little boy grinned at the sound of his name and Nancy wanted to scoop him into her arms.

'He ended up without a mother, though. Just like me.'

'You could never have anticipated that.'

'If I had, I'd have done so much differently. It's worth remembering, Nancy. Sometimes there aren't any second chances.'

'Okay Yoda.' Nancy grinned, glad to break the tension. 'I get the hint. I'll talk to Mum and clear the air properly when we get back from Selena and Craig's engagement party. Things will be too crazy before then.'

Jack watched Nancy simultaneously soothing nerves, running through lines with Dilys, Kate and Maisie and checking whether the lighting was going to cast shadows on the edge of the set, where some key pieces of action would be taking place.

He felt nauseous, there was no use denying it. The realisation that his work was going to be put on public display, in front of his new friends and neighbours, had hit home. He just hoped they didn't have unrealistic expectations.

As the audience filed in, Jack began to pace. Unable to settle down in his seat in the front row, he was in the way when he went backstage. Claire and Neil from the college were babysitting again, but he wished Toby was with him. Keeping his son quiet and content would have been a welcome distraction.

'You look rattled.'

Dilys was at his side. She could be quite stealthy for a woman of her size. It was probably what made her so lethal on the rugby pitch.

'Just feeling the first-night nerves.'

'First night, only night. That's the good thing about it. If everyone hates us, at least we're a sell-out tonight and we haven't got to try and flog any more tickets when the word gets out.' She laughed heartily and slapped him so hard on the back it made him cough.

'I suppose that's a good point, but what if they say the writing's crap?'

The crippling doubts he sometimes had about his writing had held him back in the past, stopped him doing more with it. Alice had never had the same worries about her acting – she'd always been sure that stardom was waiting for her.

'It's a good panto, Jack.' Dilys squeezed his shoulder with a gentleness he hadn't expected. 'It'll be our acting that lets you and Nance down if anything. But we've had a good time and that's the main thing, isn't it?'

'It is. Thanks, Dilys.'

He leant forward and kissed her cheek, feeling the heat as she coloured.

'I'd heard about all you theatre types kissing each other all the time, but it's still an unexpected bonus.' Dilys grinned. 'Do you think Nancy will mind Bernard making a little announcement about Olivia at the end of the play? Apparently they let her home from the hospital yesterday.'

'If we get through that far, I don't think she'll care what you do, and no one is going to object to him sharing good news. You could strip to your undies and pogo-stick across the stage for all I care. I'll just be glad when the play's over.'

'I'll bear it in mind.' She grinned again. 'Although I might save the naked pogoing until we need to clear the hall – that'll make sure none of the audience outstay their welcome!'

Jack still couldn't settle in his seat even when the lights were dimmed. So he stood at the back of the hall instead, where he was free to run outside if he wanted to. Despite Dilys's words of comfort, he couldn't bear to look at other peoples' faces as they watched the play, or hear their comments and try to judge if they were reacting as he hoped to the parts where they were supposed to laugh. Sometimes he hated being a writer, putting himself up for judgement, but he couldn't seem to stop. Maybe it was in the genes – something else Aunt Josie had given him.

The audience was made up of the family and friends of cast members, a big group of their colleagues from the college and locals from both St Nicholas Bay and the surrounding villages. It was hardly the West End and it wasn't as if it was the first time one of his plays had been put on, but he hated the thought he might let Nancy down.

His seat in the front row had been filled by Olivia's mum, Louisa, which seemed odd since Olivia had just come home. Nancy had mentioned how smitten Bernard seemed at the hospital, and it looked like the feeling might be mutual. Louisa clapped and whooped like a twelve-year-old at a One Direction gig every time he appeared on stage and he kept grinning inanely at her, even in the scenes where his character was supposed to be chastising Cinderella. Jack smiled despite himself. Whatever the critics thought, at least two people were enjoying the panto.

As it turned out, they weren't the only ones. He couldn't take all the credit. Nancy had worked miracles with The Merry Players and her direction ensured that the comic timing was spot on. When the curtains on the stage juddered to a close and then opened again just as jerkily for the cast to take their bow, the audience rose to their feet as one and a lump formed in Jack's throat.

Maisie was smiling so broadly it had to be hurting her face. Relishing her role as star of the show, she stood on a trunk which she'd dragged from the edge of the stage and clapped her hands together.

'Thank you, everybody! But please sit down.'

Maisie was a natural, although most lecturers he knew liked the sound of their own voice.

'I think you'll agree the cast and crew have been fabulous tonight.'

Maisie paused and there was another thunderous round of applause, and some of the audience even stamped their feet.

'Thank you all so much!'

Maisie gave the audience a coy smile, lapping up every minute of her moment in the spotlight.

'However, there are two people without whom all of this wouldn't have been possible.'

Louisa had got to her feet and was whooping again.

'Nancy, our brilliant director, producer, coach and comforter, and Jack, who wrote this fabulous panto.'

Jack saw Louisa land back on her seat with a thud. She had obviously been expecting Maisie to thank Olivia too. Nancy was being dragged, with great reluctance on her part, from the wings and on to the stage. Jack didn't move, but some of the audience turned around to look for him and, after spotting where he was, a few even began to chant his name. He'd never felt more British than at that moment, caught by a mixture of pride and mortification.

As he made his way slowly towards the stage, Nancy rolled her eyes.

'Everyone, I give you Nancy O'Brien and Jack Williams.'

Maisie stood back and let the applause take over for a moment. Someone in the crowd shouted 'Kiss'. Before Jack could respond and give Nancy a simple peck on the cheek, half of the audience had begun to chant the request. They were clearly far too into the spirit of audience participation after getting involved in the usual 'he's behind you' shout-outs.

The only way to shut them up was to give them what they wanted. Jack casually shrugged his shoulders and moved towards Nancy. Right up until the last moment, he'd intended to go for her cheek. Only, up close, her lips were full and rosebud pink, with a light sheen of gloss. Somehow he was drawn in, his lips brushing hers for the briefest of moments – a jolt of recognition from his traitorous body.

'Well, that's all great.'

Bernard's booming voice brought Jack back to earth.

'But let's not forget that there is someone else who should have been here today, someone who was a huge part of making this all happen and who has battled back to health, but still been there for me and helped me get over my nerves before tonight's performance. I'm proud that she's part of my life and I'm sure all of you are too, so let's have a standing ovation for Olivia Merry.'

Bernard was giving Gwyneth Paltrow's Oscar speech a run for its money. Louisa got to her feet and the rest of the crowd obediently followed. Maybe it was Jack's imagination, but there seemed to be an awful lot of half-hearted clapping.

'Everything all right?'

Jack stopped loading the costumes and props into his car and Nancy jumped at his words, realising she'd been staring vacantly into space and doing very little at all to help.

'Sorry, I was thinking.'

She reached down to pass him the box that was at her feet as she spoke.

'Trying to justify to myself why I haven't been in to see Olivia lately.'

'You don't need to justify anything. In your shoes, not a lot of people would have done what you did when she was first attacked. She's home now, Dilys told me. In fact, Bernard was supposed to mention that in his speech.'

'You knew about the speech?'

'Dilys mentioned it just before the show. She asked me if I thought you'd mind. I said no, of course. Oh God, you don't, do you?'

'No, I just feel bad that maybe I should have said something. It's like she's some sort of saint and everyone thinks I'm hogging the limelight.'

'Anyone who says that about you needs their head read.'

Jack's dark eyes searched her face. It was probably because he was a writer, but sometimes there was such intensity in the way he looked at her, as if he could see right into her soul.

'Thanks. Maybe it's all the stuff with Mum, but I feel like I'm letting everyone down at the moment and doing a hundred things badly, rather than one thing well.'

'That's bollocks.'

Jack placed his hands on her upper arms, the memory of his lips on hers taking her by surprise. Okay, so it had only been to stop the audience chanting, but she couldn't deny she'd like to do it again. Perhaps not in front of a crowd, though.

'What's bollocks?'

'You saying that. You've never let anyone down in your life. All you try to do is to make everything right. If you feel like a failure, it's only because you're trying to do the impossible.'

'Whoa! That was almost as passionate as Bernard waxing lyrical about Olivia.'

Nancy tried to make light of it, but his eyes darkened further.

'Alice drove me crazy by trying to win some sort of popularity contest with the world and look what it cost her in the end.'

He slammed down the boot of the car so hard it made her ears ring.

Jack had driven them home in silence and she didn't want to push him further. To make the silence less awkward, she took her phone out of her bag and switched it back on. There were a few *break-a-leg* messages, which had arrived after she'd switched her phone off. She was glad of something to distract her.

'I'm sorry.'

Jack's voice broke into her thoughts as he brought the car to a halt outside their cottage. Hot air had cleared most of the windscreen, but there was still an archway of glittering frost framing the edge.

'I was out of order shouting at you, but I've felt so guilty myself lately. I guess you just hit a nerve.'

'Guilty about what?'

She gripped her phone, wondering if he was going to tell her he was seeing someone.

'Guilty that I'm getting more used to a life without Alice and that I'm somehow betraying her as a result.'

'You've got to make a life for yourself and Toby, but that doesn't mean you have to forget her. Somehow I doubt that would ever happen. She's part of you, Jack. It's obvious every time you mention her name.'

A hollow feeling accompanied her words. Would she ever have that?

'I shouldn't compare you to her, though. I think Alice doing stuff for other people was always about validation. She longed to be loved.' Jack sighed. 'She was a far better mother than mine, but there was still some of that narcissism there, if I'm really honest. I don't think that's why you do it, though. You're not just trying to be popular.'

'Are you saying no one likes me?'

She shot him a quizzical look, hoping he got the joke.

'Not at all, but I see your motivation is different from Alice's, and when I snap at you about stuff, sometimes it's because I'd love the chance to shout at her. Tell her what an idiot she was to think all that was more important than being with Toby. But it's not fair on you.'

'I don't mind being your whipping boy, if it helps you get through it all.'

'There you go again, Nancy, being just about bloody perfect.'

He turned to face her, the warmth in his brown eyes replacing the troubled look of earlier, and something in her that she'd been fighting for weeks shifted outside of her control.

If things had been different, if their pasts had never happened, they'd have been more than friends – every inch of her was saying so. Yet the past enveloped them in its own agenda, like a brick wall forcing them apart.

CHAPTER TWENTY-NINE

Ruth woke herself up sobbing on the morning of New Year's Eve. It had been such a long, painful year. John was more lost than ever and her children thought she was too pathetic to face the truth. What was the point of her even getting up, let alone seeing in another year? Tears slid into her hair and her throat burnt like she'd been crying all night. Maybe she had. Even her bedclothes were knotted into a tangle that mirrored her emotions.

Forcing herself out of bed and downstairs, she flicked on the kettle and caught a warped image of herself reflected in the stainless steel cooker hood. Even the distortion couldn't hide the haunted look in her eyes. She looked at least a hundred and felt twice as old. She hadn't had a chance to talk to Nancy after the panto; if she was honest, it had been the perfect excuse to avoid it.

A knock on the door stirred her from her apathy, half of her hoping it would be Nancy so they could talk things through properly, the other half scared to death of what else she might find out.

'Daniel, I can't …'

She would have been powerless to stop him, even if she'd really tried. But despite her hideous state, she wanted his company. Someone's company.

'Let me make you some breakfast.'

He moved past her into the kitchen as easily as if he'd lived in the house for years, finding the things he needed without having to open ten cupboards first, and she wondered briefly if he'd always found things in life that easy. But for once she didn't resent him for it.

'I look a wreck and the house is a state.' Ruth was wittering, but she couldn't stop herself. 'I just haven't had the energy to tidy up since Christmas Day and it all feels so pointless all of a sudden.'

'What you look is exhausted, and you *need* to eat to have energy. When was the last time you bothered with that?'

Ruth shrugged. 'I wouldn't panic, it's not as though I'm about to waste away.'

She yanked at the bottom of her pyjama top, suddenly self-conscious about covering her bottom as completely as possible. Daniel was immaculate as always and the subtle scent of his aftershave made her want to stand closer to him, until she remembered she hadn't taken a shower since before the panto. It had been hot under those lights and she'd spent most of the performance with a back view of Daniel as he took centre stage. She went hotter still at the thought.

'Have I got time for a shower?'

He was deftly chopping up tomatoes and whisking eggs in a jug she hadn't even known she owned.

'Yes, but don't be too long. I don't want any more excuses. You'll feel better when you eat something.'

Her bedroom was relatively tidy compared to the rest of the house, but Ruth still straightened the covers on her bed and sprayed some perfume into the air. Not that Daniel would see the room, of course, but it made her feel better all the same.

The torrent of water from the shower stung her skin, even when she adjusted the flow, as though it was deliberately set to liven up her senses and clear her mind. She could see now that Nancy had become her everything and that was too much pressure, even for her. Mark had been right to set things straight.

She'd have to make a new life for herself, and a new year was the ideal time to start. She squeezed lemon-scented shower gel into her hand and the zing on her skin made her feel more alive than she had for days. She and Nancy would get over the awkwardness Mark's words had caused in the end. But things couldn't and shouldn't ever go back to the way they were. Ruth had to change for her daughter's sake … and her own.

Even in the steamed-up mirror of the bathroom, she could tell she looked better. The wild curls she shared with her daughter were damped down, and her lightly freckled shoulders were not slumped as they had been for days. Daniel was some sort of miracle worker.

Wrapping herself in a white fluffy towel, she stepped out of the en-suite and into the bedroom. A knock on the door made her start for the second time and she clutched at the towel, which had threatened for a moment to drop.

'Yes?'

'Just checking you were okay. You've been a while and I wasn't sure if I could start cooking.'

Daniel spoke from the other side of the door, his voice deep and warm.

'I'm fine. I just *really* needed that shower.'

'Can I come in?'

'Yes.' It was as simple as that. Maybe he just wanted to chat, but her body stirred in response to his question all the same.

He crossed the space between them in two strides, his hands on her bare shoulders, and it was all she could do not to launch herself at him.

She stood on her tip toes, brushing her lips against his neck, and then his mouth. Before she could stop herself, her hands were unbuttoning his shirt with a haste she suspected was indecent, but she didn't care.

'God, I've wanted to do this for what feels like for ever.'

Daniel's breath was hot against her face as he spoke and she placed her hand in the centre of his bare chest, pushing him backwards onto the bed and falling with him.

For the briefest of moments, as she closed her eyes, an image of John flitted into her head. She forced it out because the John she knew was gone for ever and the man left occupying his chair at The Pines would neither know nor care what she was about to do. She *had* to hold on to that. Opening her eyes, she gazed at Daniel, wanting to focus on him, keeping everything and everyone else out. He was beautiful.

'Ruth, are you sure you want to do this? We don't have to.'

Silencing him with a finger to his lips, she sighed in anticipation. Her body was taking over now and there was no going back.

Lifting her body upwards briefly, she lowered herself down until he was inside her and she was lost to something she'd never had before. It had always taken much more to give her pleasure, but with Daniel it was different.

Lying in the crook of his arm afterwards, she knew she hadn't been wrong. Daniel Chapman was indeed a miracle worker.

CHAPTER THIRTY

Nancy pressed the send button and immediately felt better. Telling her mum she missed her and wishing her a happy new year was the first step to getting back to normal. Words that were hard to say in person without releasing a torrent of emotion were much easier by text. Jack had been right, life was too short to wait for the perfect moment to make things right. Things would be different, and Mark's solution might have been clumsy, but maybe it needed to be.

'Are you ready?'

Jack came into the front room and she did a double take. Although he was undeniably good-looking, he looked like a teacher and a writer most of the time – casually dressed, as if he spent more time thinking about plotlines than he did worrying about his appearance. So seeing him in a charcoal-grey suit and a smart black linen shirt had shocked her. He was still too slim, heartbreak having taken its toll over the past months, but he looked great.

'Looking good!'

She said and he took a bow.

'Well, thanks, you don't look so bad yourself.' He gave an appreciative whistle and she smoothed down her dress. It was ages since she'd taken so much care over getting ready, but Selena and Craig's engagement was a reason to celebrate and there hadn't been too many of those of late. She was wearing a strapless pastel pink dress, fitted over the bust, which floated across the rest of her body. It was pale enough not to clash with her red hair and the soft grey angora wrap that went with it coordinated well with Jack's outfit. It was almost as though they'd done that thing teenage girls sometimes do and rung each other up to check what they'd be wearing to the party so they could match. Toby looked incredibly cute too, but that was hardly out of the ordinary.

Nancy tried not to think about what the New Year might bring. With Fraser back, she wasn't sure what she wanted any more, but one thing was certain – she wanted Toby and Jack in her life.

'You have now reached your destination.'

The satnav's automated voice announced their arrival as Jack pulled into the carpark, which was flanked by buildings on two sides. Craig had kept the venue itself a surprise but it looked like there were a couple of possibilities. The first was a packed pub, with New Year's Eve revellers, keen to make an early start, already spilling outside, drinks in hand, singing and shouting. It was only 8 p.m. and Jack hoped it wouldn't be there. Even in a private function room, it would be a nightmare venue on New Year's Eve and not the sort of place he would have brought Toby if he'd known.

Across from the carpark was a budget hotel, where Craig and Selena had recommended guests book a room so they could all have a drink, but it wasn't the sort of place to have a function room. That left only one other alternative, a boat he could see moored to the left of the pub.

'I hope it's not in there!'

Nancy gestured towards the pub as a very drunk looking women caught hold of the man nearest to her and stuck her tongue down his throat, accompanied by a chorus of whoops and cheers.

'Me too.'

Jack lifted Toby out of his seat, while Nancy got out the buggy and nappy bag. They were such a well-oiled team these days that sometimes it was hard for Jack to remember a time pre-Nancy.

'Let's try round the front by the river. I'm keeping everything crossed that even Craig wouldn't book a pub for an engagement party on New Year's Eve.'

They rounded the front of the building, which would have been beautiful without the raucous crowd. It was half-timbered and had obviously stood on the banks of the river for hundreds of years, the heavily leaded windows watching vessels come and go.

The boat moored in front of the pub had an open deck circled by patio heaters, where strings of fairy lights danced on the light evening breeze. Jack could smell the woody aroma of a barbecue. The other half of the boat was undercover and there was bunting made from pink hearts strung in loops around the inside of the windows. It might have been an odd choice for a December night, but it looked lovely.

'Mate!'

Craig suddenly emerged from the small throng of people on the open deck and leapt onto the riverbank to help them on board, even though there was a perfectly good ramp just to one side.

'It looks fantastic.'

Jack couldn't help grinning. There were three small palm trees in one corner, surrounded by a small bank of sand, a nod to Craig's Aussie heritage with a toy koala bear clamped on to the trunk of one of the trees.

'Only you would have the balls to risk a barbecue in December.'

'Jack, you know there'd have been a barbie on the beach back home if we'd had the party there. So this is the next best thing!'

'And did Selena get a say?'

Jack raised an eyebrow as Craig laughed.

'She's all good with it, mate. Easy going, you know. Part of the reason I love the girl so much, I think.'

Craig had a look when he spoke about Selena that left Jack in no doubt he meant every word.

'Congratulations, it's lovely to see you again,' Nancy said, leaning forward to kiss Craig.

Her wrap slid off her shoulder and halfway down her arms. Her skin was creamy white and so perfectly unblemished it didn't look real. Jack shook his head. He had to stop looking at her. If he needed a physical release as badly as he'd felt he did of late, it wasn't going to be with Nancy. Casual was all he wanted. He wasn't going to lose her friendship like that.

'You two look great. Life on the coast suits you.'

Craig handed them both a drink from a tray balanced precariously on a table next to the barbecue. It was a bit warm and Jack smiled again. He might not want to be, but Craig was almost British now, serving the warm beer he'd hated so much when he first arrived.

'Where's Selena? We've got a little present for you both.'

Nancy pulled the wrap back around her shoulders as she spoke.

'She's still getting ready, over in the hotel. Wants to make a big entrance or something.' Craig grinned. 'You know women, though. I'll go and give her a shout now that everyone's here and we can set off. You couldn't keep an eye on the barbie for a minute, could you, mate?'

Without waiting for an answer, Craig leapt off the boat. Never the easy option of the ramp for him.

'I'm glad I didn't bother with a tie!'

Jack took his jacket off and laid it over the back of Toby's buggy. Standing that close to the barbecue was warm, even in his shirt sleeves.

'Thank God it's not raining.'

'Do I look ridiculous, dressed like this?' Nancy fiddled with her wrap again. 'I'm beginning to wonder if I should have worn board shorts and a Hawaiian shirt!'

He was tempted to tell her she'd look good in a sack. Christ, he needed to rein all this in, and soon.

'You look great and it sounds as though Selena will be dressed up. I've never seen her without make-up or even remotely dressed down, so I wouldn't worry about it. I should have known that Craig would do something like this, he's never been exactly what you'd call conventional.'

Toby started to complain about being strapped in and Jack watched Nancy deftly take him from the buggy. Her wrap slipped again and this time she took it off, letting it rest on top of his jacket. Toby immediately settled in her arms and made several grabs for the beads she wore around her neck. He finally managed to get hold of them and put them straight into his mouth; Nancy didn't complain, even when he started to dribble as he ground his gums against the wooden beads.

'He really loves you, you know.'

Jack couldn't look directly at her as he spoke, so he

concentrated on turning over the chicken kebabs.

'The feeling's mutual.'

He looked back at Nancy as she responded. Toby was balanced on her hip and the urge to wrap them both in his arms was almost overwhelming.

'Ladies and gentleman!'

A voice over the boat's tannoy system broke the spell and for that he was grateful. The voice continued, 'Let me have your attention, please. Welcome on board the happy couple – Craig and Selena.'

They were grinning from ear to ear as they walked up the ramp hand in hand. Craig took the microphone and couldn't speak for a moment or two, overwhelmed by the emotion of it all. Jack noticed the ramp had been lifted up and the boat started to move slowly away from the bank.

Craig finally managed to start his speech.

'I'm glad you're all applauding and not throwing stuff from the barbie at us for taking you out on a boat in the middle of winter. Our best mates are all here tonight.'

The guests began to cheer and Craig broke into another grin before holding up his hand.

'You're all so special to us and we want you to party. This last year has been the best of my life and I've met the love of my life too. We hope that the New Year will be just as good for all of you.'

For a second his gaze caught Jack's before he looked away.

Craig turned to Selena and took her in his arms. They looked like a couple from the pages of a wedding magazine, but Jack was surprised to find that he didn't feel the crushing pain in his chest he'd had when they first got engaged. Glancing at Nancy and Toby, he didn't

292

doubt why, and he hated himself a little bit more.

As Craig and Selena broke off from the kiss, 'The Way You Look Tonight' filled the air around them. When they took to the deck, it was obvious Jack's no-nonsense Aussie best friend had taken some dancing lessons. Jack wouldn't have believed it if he hadn't seen it for himself and he felt himself welling up. Thank God for the barbecue smoking away behind him. It gave him an excuse to turn around and a reason for the tears in his eyes if anyone asked. Maybe that's why Craig had given him the job – his old friend knew him better than he knew himself.

'I'm going to take Toby away from the smoke a bit.'

Nancy's voice was soft. She must have seen his reaction, but she never pushed him to talk.

'Probably a good idea, thanks.'

She went to sit under one of the patio heaters with his son. He'd join them in a bit, take some food over and make casual conversation. He just needed a moment first. One minute he felt guilty about not missing Alice enough and the next he was crying like a baby – grief was a fickle bastard.

Jack hadn't noticed the music stop.

'You okay, mate?'

Suddenly Craig's hand was on his shoulder and Jack turned round to give him one of the man hugs they'd perfected over the years, curling their hands into fists and thumping one another on the back at the same time. It somehow seemed less girly that way and, despite the new side he'd seen of Craig tonight, it was them all over.

'I couldn't be happier for the two of you, honestly.'

'I wanted to check if you felt up for the job of being best man when the time comes. After everything that's happened, I wanted to give you the chance to opt out if it's too hard. But I wouldn't want it to be anyone else.'

There were tears in Craig's eyes too. What the hell had happened to the two of them?

'Thanks, Craig, it means a lot and, like I said before, I'd be honoured.'

'Everything will be okay, mate, you know that, don't you?' Craig thumped him on the back again and Jack just nodded, not trusting himself to speak.

❋

Jack came over to join Nancy and Toby as soon as the other guests began to collect their food from the barbecue. He'd obviously needed some time to himself and Nancy had been glad to have Toby to take care of. There was a heightened sense of emotion on the boat that was tangible in the air.

The food was surprisingly good and alcohol was in ready supply. The night was incredibly mild for the last day of December and the patio heaters around the edge of the open deck meant they'd been able to stay outside longer than she would have dreamt possible. Toby was now wrapped up against the night in a sort of ski-suit all-in-one. He looked like the Very Hungry Caterpillar or one of those uber-cute Anne Geddes portraits. He also made a pretty effective hot water bottle. Still, about twenty minutes before midnight, Nancy gave an involuntary shiver, and without saying a word, Jack put his arm around her shoulders and drew her and Toby towards his chest.

'Do you think we can hold out until midnight?'

'Hold out for what?' Was it wrong of her to be thinking about kissing him? It was a New Year's tradition after all.

'Hold out here, in the open. The temperature's

dropping fast now.'

'I think Toby's quite cosy. Snug as a bug in a rug, although he is cuddled up to me like a puppy.'

'Lucky him.' Jack looked down and caught her eye. 'Being so snug, I mean.'

'I can hold out if you can.'

'It's a deal.'

She stayed there, pulled in close to his chest, as the hands of the clock hanging from a beam at the end of the boat ticked round. They seemed to be moving faster than normal. Just before midnight, Craig and Selena took to the floor again and this time they danced to Snow Patrol's 'Chasing Cars'. The person in charge of the sound system on board was a genius – the song faded perfectly into the twelve chimes signalling that New Year had arrived.

All around them, other guests were kissing, hugging or shaking hands. Nancy planted a kiss on the top of a sleeping Toby's head. Jack did the same and they lifted their heads together, their faces only inches apart. It was the most natural thing in the world, not forced like the kiss after the show had been.

Toby was cossetted between them as their lips met. For weeks she had been telling herself that what she felt for Jack was friendship. She loved Toby and increasingly she knew she relied on his father for support in all aspects of her life. Now, though, she couldn't deny that the truth was in that kiss. It wasn't some over-the-top display of passion, but she felt it right down to her toes and it changed everything.

They strolled back to their hotel when the boat docked. Toby was back in his pushchair and they walked close together, so Jack could sense the heat from her body. But they didn't touch. He wanted to touch her, more than anything, but there'd be no going back from that and he needed her friendship more. Nothing else they did could last, not when so much of him still belonged to Alice and felt so tortured about the thought of moving on. It was too soon and rubbish timing to meet someone so totally perfect when he wasn't ready. It was harder than he'd thought possible to turn to her at the door of the hotel and tell her why they couldn't be together. In the end he bottled out, glad of the excuse that Toby gave him.

'You know that kiss meant something to me other than the start of the New Year, don't you?'

He put a hand under her chin and she looked at him shyly, as though they'd just met, rather than lived together for the past four months.

'Yes, I know. Me too.'

'I don't want to rush things, though, and with Toby here tonight, I couldn't, we couldn't …'

Somehow the words wouldn't come. He wasn't quite able to shut the door on the possibility altogether.

'It's okay, I know you're not ready for this and I'm not sure I am either. With Fraser back to confuse things and everything so raw for you, the timing's off, isn't it?'

She smiled and he almost changed his mind. Every fibre of his body told him to scoop her into his arms and worry about tomorrow when it came. He had to stop himself.

'Good night then, and happy New Year.'

'Happy New Year.'

As she turned and pushed the hotel doors open, he sighed. It had bloody well better be a happier new year than the one before. He just hoped he hadn't started it by making one of the worst mistakes of his life.

CHAPTER THIRTY-ONE

Ruth woke up in Daniel's arms and enjoyed ten glorious seconds before the guilt started to creep across her skin, leaving a trail of goosebumps in its wake. The day before had been the first for as long as she could remember when neither she nor Nancy had visited John. She'd rung Barbara at The Pines to explain that she had an awful cold and didn't want to pass it on to John or any of the other residents or carers. Daniel had laughed at her fake 'I've got a cold' voice and said it was exactly the same one that his staff used on hangover Mondays. She'd laughed too, temporarily buoyed up by their lovemaking and the thought that she deserved to feel like a woman again.

The first frisson of guilt had come when she'd got Nancy's text wishing her a happy new year, saying she missed her, and asking her to give her father a new year's kiss, because she'd be in London with Jack and Toby. She'd pushed the guilt away. What Nancy didn't know wouldn't hurt her, and it wasn't as though John was going to spill the beans, was it?

'What are you thinking about?'

Daniel swept her hair from her face as she turned towards him.

'You don't want to know.'

'Oh, but I do.' His brown eyes looked serious. 'You're

not about to run out on me, are you?'

'Hardly.' She tried to laugh, but it caught in her throat. 'It's my house after all.'

'Otherwise you would. Is that what you're saying?'

'I've got to go and see John.'

The guilt took a stranglehold as Ruth said her husband's name. The John she'd married would have yanked Daniel away from his wife by the scruff of his neck and hung him from a coat hook if he'd known what they'd done. Now she could confess and he'd just look at her with his watered-down eyes, which didn't really see her, and nod with the same inane smile she'd get if she told him what she'd been watching on telly. Yet that didn't make what she was doing right, even though the last twenty-four hours had made her happier than she'd been in years.

'Do you have to go? Can't you ring up again?'

Daniel began to run his hand up her leg. Only it didn't feel sexy any more, just sordid.

'I *want* to see him.'

She stood up, yanking the sheet with her, not caring if it left him exposed. Better that than for him to see her tired old body in the harsh light of a winter morning. She used to laugh at films where, after a sex scene, the heroine would wrap herself tightly in a sheet. What was the point when they'd been at it all night? But now she knew why. Abandon might carry you away the night before, but cellulite and stretch marks were good reminders to cover up when you came to your senses.

'What about later?'

Daniel got up too, but she had to look away again. He might be only five years younger than her, but it might as well have been in dog years based on the difference in their bodies. What man of his age had a six-pack for

Christ's sake? He had no inhibitions about being naked in front of her. She must have taken leave of her senses.

'I don't know.' She hesitated as he moved towards her, unable to turn her back on him. 'It's complicated for me, you know that, and it's all happened so crazily quickly. I'm sorry, I just don't know …'

'It's okay, I understand.'

He kissed her forehead and wrapped his arms around her, but it wasn't sexual, it was loving – and that made it all the harder to walk away.

Neither Nancy nor Jack mentioned the kiss from the night before during the journey home. They'd spoken about almost everything else, though, from the plans for Toby's birthday party the next day to their likely timetables at college when term started again on the fifth.

'I don't want to think about that.' Nancy shuddered at the thought of it. The holidays were what had kept her in the job for so long, when bureaucracy and Ofsted inspections had long since taken all the joy out of teaching. All that was what had driven her to set up the business.

'Fraser will make sure you get whatever timetable you want, surely?'

The tight smile Jack was wearing made him look like a shop dummy.

'He won't involve himself in minutiae like that. Far too busy empire building.'

She didn't want to think about Fraser being in charge any more than she wanted to think about the start of term. Her feelings about her ex were confused to say the least. Part of her wanted to kiss him and the other part wanted to push him over the nearest cliff. Or at least forget that he'd ever existed. Unfortunately neither of these was a viable option, given that she had to spend half of her working week with him effectively being her boss. Or, more accurately, her boss's boss – which made it even worse.

'Do you ever wish you'd gone with him – when he left the Bay, I mean?'

'I did sometimes wonder if I should have.'

She sighed. She'd thought about it a hundred times, sitting in The Pines with the stranger her father had become. Wondering if she was actually doing any good by hanging around.

'And then when I found out how upset Mum was about us lying to protect her, and staying behind out of guilt, I felt like I'd been an idiot not to go.'

'You shouldn't feel like an idiot. You were just trying to do the right thing and I for one am glad that you didn't go with Fraser.'

He touched her leg for the briefest of seconds before returning his hand to the steering wheel and she tried not to want so desperately for him to do it again. Maybe they could be friends with benefits and go back to just plain old friends when they'd got it out of their systems. Trouble was, she wasn't sure if she'd be able to put those feelings back in a box if she let them out. And what if one night was enough for Jack? What then? He was right to have put the brakes on the night before.

'Despite everything, I'm glad I stayed too.'

She and Jack might just be friends, but the memory of her time with Fraser suddenly felt as remote as if they'd never been close at all.

They approached St Nicholas Bay along the coastal road, and as they rounded the bend Nancy caught her breath, as she always did. Why would she ever want to leave this place? The sand was a pale gold in the winter sunlight and, without anything or anyone to spoil it, the beach was even and unblemished – the tide having smoothed it out to perfection, except for a few strands of seaweed which the waves had left as a parting gift.

Jack slowed the car as they approached the narrowest part of the road and Nancy spotted Olivia sitting on the bench looking out to sea. Jasper and Sophie were playing football on the grass of the clifftop just in front of her, but she wasn't alone on the bench. Bernard was sitting beside her, one arm around her shoulders, their heads pressed together.

'Were they kissing?'

Jack's voice startled Nancy. There was something about the way Bernard and Olivia had been positioned which could quite easily have given that impression.

'I don't think so. Bernard is definitely not Olivia's type! And last thing I knew he had his sights set on her mother. But whatever they were talking about looked quite intense.'

'You don't think that things have kicked off with Miles again, do you?' Jack was clearly exasperated by the thought. 'Maybe that's why Bernard was so worked up and emotional when he made the speech after the show. I thought he was just trying to impress Louisa, but it would make sense.'

'Maybe.' Nancy bit her lip and silently prayed that, whatever was going on, no one was going to get hurt. Sophie and Jasper had been through far too much already.

CHAPTER THIRTY-TWO

A Facetime call came through alarmingly early on the morning of Toby's first birthday and Jack knew exactly who it was before he looked at the screen.

'Josie!'

'Morning, darling boy. I wanted to ring before I hit the hay as Toby's big day will be half over before my alarm goes off.' She was wearing false eyelashes and a cocktail dress, a stark contrast to the image of him in the corner of the screen, looking like he lived in an underpass. Sleep hadn't come easily the last couple of nights; he kept thinking about the night of Craig and Selena's engagement.

'I'm afraid the birthday boy is still sound asleep.'

'Oh, never mind, hopefully I'll catch him later and you can tell me all about the party.' Josie screwed up her face. 'This thrombosis is a bloody inconvenience! I wish you'd let me get the boat over there for his birthday, though.'

'And have you miss out on all those New Year's Eve celebrations?'

'It would have been worth it to see my boys. I'd give anything up for you two.'

Josie blew him a kiss in the exact same way she'd done when putting him to bed every night as a child.

'You already did.'

His aunt had had a few boyfriends over the years, but Jack had always known he came first. She'd once told him that none of her suitors had been good enough to be a father figure to him. He had to set the same standards for Toby. If his son couldn't have his real mum, there'd be no settling for second best for him either.

'No word from your mother over Christmas, I take it?'

Aunt Josie was shaking her head in response to her own question. She knew the answer as well as he did.

'No, nothing, but why change the habit of a lifetime?'

'It's her loss, Jack, and one day I'd like to thank her for it, for letting me have you all to myself.'

'Me too, Auntie J, me too.'

'I love you and I'll call you later. Tell Toby to save me some cake.'

'We'll freeze you a bit until the summer.' Jack blew her a kiss this time. 'Night, Auntie J.' As the call disconnected, the sound of Toby stirring next door crackled on the baby monitor. He could be Mum and Dad to Toby, no problem. After all he'd had the best role model imaginable.

Pam turned up an hour early and was getting in Jack and Nancy's way as they tried to make room in the tiny cottage for Toby's birthday party. Six of his little friends from nursery and their parents would be there, as well as Pam, Ruth, Jack and Nancy. Kate and Will, who'd appeared in the panto, had also been invited. Jack got on really well with them and their work gave them plenty of common ground. After all, no one but another teacher could truly understand the ever-present threat of an Ofsted inspection. Pursuing this potential for friendship was one attempt at lessening the intensity of his feelings for

Nancy. He needed more people in his life down in the Bay – that was all.

It was hardly a cast of thousands but, even so, Pam's interfering was making heavy weather of it. They'd already watched Toby open his presents and Pam had cried a bit about Alice missing it all. Jack pushed down the lump in his throat with hot coffee, Pam shooting Nancy the odd resentful look, as if it were somehow her fault that Alice wasn't there. Maybe he was imagining it, but Pam seemed not to be satisfied with anything Nancy did. Even when she set out a tray of cupcakes he saw Pam glance at her surreptitiously and then rearrange the display. She didn't say anything out loud, just pressed her lips together so tightly they almost disappeared.

'Why don't you take Toby out for a little wander around the bay in his pushchair, Pam? He could do with some air before the party and he'll probably have a nap, so he'll be much more cheerful later on.'

Jack was already in the hallway putting up the buggy before she had a chance to object. Her mouth opened and closed like a fish several times but, sighing heavily, she took the handles of the pushchair and headed out of the door without saying another word. The atmosphere immediately lifted and he turned towards Nancy.

'I'm sorry about that. She still gets really emotional at times like this.'

'It's okay. It must be really hard for all of you.'

She touched his hand as she spoke, their kiss immediately on his mind. Nancy had helped him to get through so much, but in a way he wished he hadn't met her – at least not yet. If it had been a year or two down the line … but now they'd never know.

'It is hard, but you being here and being such a great friend has made more difference than you'll ever know.

305

So please don't let Pam make it feel like you shouldn't be here, because you should.'

He couldn't risk kissing her again, even though it felt like it would be the most natural thing in the world.

'You know you and Toby have got me through a hell of a lot, too. I didn't know Alice, but I do know that she would have been prouder than anyone to see the way you and Toby are together.'

'Thank you, that means so much.'

He couldn't help himself. She understood him and Toby so well, like the third piece of a jigsaw puzzle. Most people would call it wrong, barely half a year as a widower, but love had found him and it was no good pretending. Kissing her again, he wasn't thinking about Alice , only Nancy. And it felt more right than anything had in a long, long time.

Nancy busied herself answering the door as the other guests began to arrive. She couldn't make eye contact with Jack, and the dagger looks Pam had been giving her all morning seemed all the more pointed. On New Year's Day she and Jack had spent the evening on opposite sides of the room. She hadn't wanted to sit next to him, sure that he'd regretted their kiss from the night before and all the time aching to do it again. Only the kiss they'd shared earlier hadn't been some accidental boiling-over of emotion on New Year's Eve. It had been deliberate, slow at first, but then Jack's hands had moved up her back, touching the bare skin beneath her shirt, and they'd been on the sofa in seconds. Months of pent-up emotion were in that kiss, and she had a feeling it would have gone a lot further if there hadn't been an energetic rapping on the door. Ruth calling out 'Yoohoo, it's me!' was enough of a mood killer for anyone.

'You're early.' Nancy couldn't keep the accusation out of her voice. What if this had been their only chance? Maybe they'd be over each other after one time, or maybe Jack would find a way to deal with the guilt of them being together. Now, though, he might just stuff it all back into the box whose lid they'd both been sitting on for weeks.

Her mother couldn't quite look her in the eye. 'I wanted us to have a chance to clear the air before everyone else turns up. It is still all right for me to come, isn't it? Only Jack invited me before Christmas, but with everything that's happened I'll understand if you want me to go, if now's not the time for us to sort things out.'

Nancy's desire for Ruth to leave had nothing at all to do with the row at Christmas.

'It's good to see you, Ruth.'

Jack stepped out from behind Nancy and gestured for her mother to follow him through to the lounge.

'Can I get you a drink? You might need one to put up with my mother-in-law bending your ear all afternoon.' He seemed keen to get her mother inside. Maybe he'd been grateful for the interruption.

Jack disappeared into the kitchen and she turned to face her mother.

'So how have you been?'

There was something different about Ruth that Nancy couldn't quite put her finger on.

'I've been okay thanks, but I've been thinking a lot too, about how much I've put upon you.' Her mother gave a half smile. 'I know now why you felt you had to lie to me.'

'We shouldn't have kept on with it, not once Dad got as bad as he did. Keeping his secrets shouldn't have been more important than trusting you with the truth, it's just …'

'You were worried I'd fall apart again, like when Nan died? And that you'd be the one left to pick up the pieces?'

Ruth looked directly at her and all she could do was nod.

'It's all right, Nancy, I know I've leaned too hard on you over the years, but I'm a tough old boot now. Maybe going through everything with Nan helped me to cope this time, helped me prepare for this with your dad. It's a rubbish hand to be dealt, but I'm coping. In my own way.'

'I know you are, Mum. We should have seen that, and I think Mark coming in and shooting his mouth off was a good thing after all.' Nancy laughed. 'Not that it will stop me having a go at him when we meet up for lunch next week. He could have been a damn sight more tactful about it.'

'He could, but I finally read the email he sent before he came home and he handled it all a lot better there. He just doesn't have your way with words.'

Ruth held out her arms and Nancy moved into them. Any resentment about her mother's knock on the door faded.

'Do you think Mark will stay in the Bay?'

Nancy's voice was muffled against her mother's head and Ruth drew back to look at her again and nodded.

'He's staying local. Daniel has offered him the chance to manage the new O'Brien's store in Copplestone. He could have taken over Marley's Chains again, but Mark felt a fresh start would be better, and it was always Dad's dream that he'd run a second store by himself.'

'I still can't believe you're saying Daniel's name with a smile on your face!'

Ruth's cheeks had flushed with colour and Nancy could only imagine how embarrassed she felt at the way she'd treated Daniel in the past, now that she knew the truth.

'Me neither! But he's done so much for all of us.'

'He's a lovely man.'

'He is.' Ruth took Nancy's face in her hands. 'But not nearly as lovely as you.'

'Thanks, Mum.'

Folded into her mother's arms again, Nancy breathed slowly. Jack's mother-in-law had been testing her patience all morning and once or twice she'd come close to snapping at her, but she understood her better now. She and her mother might have had a rocky patch since Christmas, but a simple hug was enough to sort it out. Pam would never have that with Alice again.

Pam's return to the house had driven Nancy to stand in the hallway and welcome the rest of the guests. When she had her back to Pam, it felt like the older woman's eyes were boring into her, and when she turned round Pam was watching her every move. Thank God Alice's mother wasn't staying the night or she'd have to sleep with one eye open.

The mums from the nursery, one dad with his daughter, Kate and Will all arrived. The teachers were soon being interrogated by a woman who wanted to know the details of their latest Ofsted report, even though her son was barely a year old.

Nancy kept herself busy going backwards and forwards with drinks and nibbles, while Pam, Jack and Ruth kept the children fed and entertained. One of Toby's friends, an angelic-looking little girl called Daisy, picked up two fistfuls of jelly and threw them at the birthday boy. He looked startled for a moment and Nancy was sure he was about to cry, but instead he started to laugh and it spread around the room like a Mexican wave.

'Time for cake, I think.'

Jack disappeared into the kitchen and Nancy reached for the wet-wipes, clearing the worst of the jelly off Toby and the area around him. He looked up at her with big, dark eyes and broke into a grin.

'Mum, mum, mum.' Toby could just have been sucking his gums, but it sounded like something else and Nancy shot Pam a furtive look to see if she'd heard it too. Thankfully, she was deep in conversation with one of the other parents. It didn't mean anything, but she was still glad Pam hadn't heard.

Jack came back into the room with the caterpillar cake they'd picked out together and the room broke into a noisy rendition of happy birthday. Unlike jelly in the eye, the out-of-tune singing made Toby start to sob.

'Oh darling.' Jack put down the cake and lifted Toby out of his high chair, jigging him up and down to stop the tears. The little boy arched his body away from Jack for a moment and held out his arms to Nancy.

'Mum, mum, mum.' This time there was no mistaking the sound, even when the shriek from Pam had drowned him out.

'Was Pam okay by the time she left?'

Nancy had disappeared soon after Pam dissolved into even noisier tears than her grandson and Jack had been grateful for that at least. His mother-in-law had been beside herself, ranting about how she'd known this was always going to happen. That Alice's memory had been tarnished and it was only Pam who still cared she was gone. The rest of the party had cleared pretty quickly after that.

Perhaps it was the guilt of the two kisses he'd shared with Nancy and the feelings he couldn't deny having developed for her, but he found himself agreeing with Pam and making a promise he didn't want to keep.

'She was still crying and threatening to take Toby, saying it was the only way to keep Alice's memory alive.'

'I can understand why she's upset, but what are you supposed to do? Toby doesn't know any different and it was just a sound he was making. He can't know what the word means.'

Nancy was so upset, he didn't want to make that any worse, but he had to. And he had to do it quickly, like ripping off a plaster.

'I've got to do something I really don't want to do.' He couldn't look at her or he'd change his mind, but he owed it to Alice. She'd wanted to be famous, to be remembered more than anything. Toby calling someone else mum felt like the ultimate betrayal of that. He'd let his own feelings get in the way and he deserved the pain he was about to inflict on them – even if Nancy didn't.

'Jack, you don't have to …'

'I'm sorry, Nancy, but I do. I need to ask you to move out. All the time you're around so much, Toby is going to be confused.'

'But …'

For a moment he'd thought she was going to beg or argue. If she'd got angry it might have been easier to take.

'If that's what you really want, I'll be out by this time tomorrow.'

'You don't have to do anything that quickly.'

Jack looked at her, something twisting in his gut. He

didn't want her to leave so quickly. He didn't want her to leave at all, but he *had* to stop thinking about himself.

'I think we both know I do.'

Nancy met his gaze, her eyes glassy, as she turned to leave the room. He had a horrible feeling she was disappearing out of his life. And who could blame her?

CHAPTER THIRTY-THREE

It was like the worst kind of déjà vu when Nancy found herself sitting in the beach-front café, homeless all over again, just as she had four months before. Only now it was a grey January day and already dark outside, whereas it had been an Indian summer back in September and breakfast out in the sunshine meant things hadn't felt quite so overwhelmingly sad. At least that's what Nancy tried to convince herself – that her current depression had nothing to do with her feelings for Jack and Toby and everything to do with the dingy view from the steamed-up windows, and the peeling Formica in the near-empty beach café in the depths of winter.

If she could have faced being honest with herself, she'd have admitted that September was when she *should* have been heartbroken, finding out that her best friend and fiancé had cheated on her in the most public way possible. Yet she didn't remember it feeling anything like this. Watching Gav's famous fry-up grow cold on her plate, she thought that never had an all-day breakfast looked less inviting.

A tap on the window made her jump and she narrowly avoided landing the whole plate of food in her lap. A second later the door to the café burst open.

'Nance! I thought that was you. What on earth are

you doing in here?'

Fraser looked ridiculously out of place in his Hugo Boss town coat, like he was trying just a little bit too hard.

'Not eating my food.' She hesitated, wondering whether to bite the bullet and tell him. Term started in three days and by that time it would be all over college, so she might as well confess. 'And waiting for Maisie to get back from band practice so she can let me into her flat and I can resume residence on the world's most uncomfortable sofa.'

'Shit.' Fraser did his best to look sympathetic, but there was a hint of something else as he pulled out the chair opposite her and sat down. 'Am I allowed to ask what happened?'

'You already have.' Nancy took a gulp of cold tea and barely resisted the urge to spit it out.

'I take it something happened with Jack?'

'More Toby really.' Nancy ripped another strip off the paper napkin, which she'd been fiddling with for the past twenty minutes.

'You didn't run off with the baby, did you?'

'Of course not!'

She snapped at him, not wanting to remember the conversations they'd once had about how their life together might pan out. Especially now he felt like a stranger – despite the brief moments when it felt as though the last eighteen months apart had never happened. She didn't need any of that right now.

'What then?' Fraser ignored her reaction, fixing her with a serious look.

'Toby called me mum.'

'Is that all? I thought maybe you'd gone out and left Jack's precious baby unattended or the two of you'd had a one-night-stand that didn't seem quite such a good idea the next morning. Why the hell has he chucked you out just for that?'

Fraser leant back in his chair, his words about a one-night-stand forming a knot in Nancy's chest. She wished to God that had been the reason. At least she'd know for sure whether all the pain she was feeling really meant something.

'Jack lost his wife, remember. *Toby's mum*. She was the only person who had the right to be called mum by him and Jack can't bear to see anyone take that away from her.'

'But she's dead. It's not like she's going to know, is it?'

Fraser's mouth was moving, but Nancy wasn't sure that she was hearing right any more.

'*He'll* know, and his wife's mum will know. Jack's torn up with guilt about what she's missing and I understand that. Any normal person would understand that.'

The tears were threatening again and she had to take another swig of cold tea, the colour of dishwater, trying to push the urge to cry back down her throat. Why couldn't she fall in love with no complications for once? It was love. Toby had landed in her heart from day one, and Jack had crept in beside him in the months they'd lived together. Now she had no idea how to get them out again. Cold tea was helpless at holding back hot tears.

'I'm sorry, babe, I hate to see you so upset.'

Fraser placed a hand over hers and she wanted to snatch it away, but he wasn't letting her.

'Why don't you come and stay at the apartment I'm renting? I've got a spare room and it's got to be more comfortable than Maisie's sofa.'

'I don't think that would be a good idea.'

She wrenched her hand free. If there'd been a remnant of doubt left about Fraser, it was gone. Jack was the one – well the *two* with Toby. Nothing was ever going to happen between them, but getting involved with Fraser again would be an even bigger mistake than getting engaged to David had been. Her track record for sharing a house with someone as a knee-jerk reaction to a break-up was hardly glowing.

'Hey, there's no pressure. Just as friends! I'm not going to pretend my feelings for you don't go further than that, but we can take it slow. You're worth waiting for, Nancy.'

The words 'you'll be waiting forever' longed to escape, but she kept them in. She couldn't afford to burn any more bridges at work, and it wasn't Fraser's fault – this time – that her heart had been broken all over again.

'Thanks for the offer. I'll think about it.'

It was a lie, but it seemed to satisfy him. Maisie's sofa would be a stop-gap for a day or two and then she'd probably have to go back to her mum's, which wouldn't do either of them a lot of good. Maisie had better have wine back at the flat, and plenty of it.

'We shouldn't be doing this.' Ruth stretched out her naked body against the silky sheets on a four-poster bed in the Merryworth Hotel, just four miles from her house. It felt like she was having an affair, and, technically, she was.

'Oh, but we should.'

Daniel handed her a glass of champagne and slowly ran a hand down her upper arm, stopping to circle her nipple with his finger. How he found her tired old body so desirable she'd never know. She soon stopped thinking altogether and the champagne glass slipped out of her hand as she lost herself to his touch yet again.

Ruth had fallen into the habit of dozing in Daniel's arms after they'd made love. It felt so odd now that she'd hated him for so long, when the only place she truly felt comfortable these days was right there, lying against his chest.

Her phone buzzed and she wanted to ignore it, but she was still too much a mother to let it ring. What if it was Nancy? The drama at the birthday party the day before had hurt her daughter, she'd seen that, but she'd been sure that Nancy and Jack would find a way forward. They were great friends, good for each other. Everyone except Pam could see that Toby was happier for having Nancy around. But what if things hadn't worked out and Nancy needed her?

Ruth extracted herself from Daniel's arms.

'Mrs O'Bri ... I mean, Ruth?' Before the caller even said her name, Ruth knew who it was. 'It's Barbara here, from The Pines. I'm afraid it's John.'

'Oh God, is he okay?' Ruth sat bolt upright in the bed, suddenly horribly aware of her nakedness as the silk sheet slipped down to her waist.

'He's had a fall. We're not sure how serious, but the ambulance is on its way and I think you should head straight there. Just in case ...'

'I'll be there, thanks, Barbara.' Ruth was already half out of bed, for once not concerned about covering herself up.

'Is it John? What's the matter?' Daniel was at her side, his own nakedness making her flinch as shame prickled her skin.

'He's had a fall.'

She turned away from Daniel, refusing his comfort.

She didn't deserve it. Pulling on her clothes as quickly as she could, she picked up her phone and scrolled down to Nancy's number. She and Nancy had promised each other there'd be no more secrets between them, but she didn't think she'd ever be able to explain where she'd been when she'd taken Barbara's call.

CHAPTER THIRTY-FOUR

'I don't like to be personal, Nance, but you look shocking.'

Maisie appeared at the end of her sofa about three seconds after Nancy got the phone call from her mum.

'It's Dad. He's had a fall. They don't know how serious.' Nancy's voice was monotone. She seemed to have frozen, unable to react in the way she would have expected. She'd had about as much as she could take, and maybe that's why she didn't move, all sense of urgency having drained out of her.

'Oh God, Nancy, I'm sorry.' Maisie sat next to her on the sofa, showing the sort of emotion she should have been showing or, at the very least, feeling. 'Shall I drive you to the hospital?'

'That would be useful. Thanks.' Monotone was all Nancy could muster.

Maisie pulled up in the drop-off only zone. 'Do you want me to come in?'

'No, thanks, it's fine. It's good of you to bring me, but I expect they're limiting it to family only.'

Nancy turned towards her friend and didn't miss the look of relief on her face. She couldn't blame Maisie;

John was her father, and even she didn't want to go in.

'Call me if you need anything.'

Maisie shouted the offer as Nancy closed the car door and forced herself to walk towards the entrance. She didn't need to stop at the reception desk, which was manned by three harassed-looking middle-aged women surrounded by outpatients and relatives queuing for information. Nancy carried on towards the Mann Ward on the third floor where Ruth had said her father had a bed. There was no excuse for delay. Signs pointed her clearly in his direction. She didn't want to see him weak and broken – another sight to erode the memory of the man he'd been.

'Darling!' Her mother, who'd been standing near the top of the stairwell, spotted Nancy first and flung her arms around her with such strength she almost knocked her flying.

'How is he?'

Nancy's toes curled over in her boots as she asked the question, guilt that a part of her wanted him to let go making every muscle in her body tense while she waited for the answer.

'He's broken his hip.' Her mother's face was tear-stained and pale.

'Have you spoken to the doctor?' She followed her mother down the corridor.

'Yes, and they did a CT scan as soon as they brought him in. They want to operate later today, but he was getting really distressed because he didn't understand what was going on and they were frightened he'd do himself more damage, so they've given him some drugs to make him sleep. That's why they've put him in a side room and not on the ward.'

Nancy's legs had stopped moving. She didn't want to

take another step. Wasn't it bad enough that she'd been forced to watch her father slowly disappear? She didn't want to see him lying on a bed, his mouth hanging open.

'I can't do this.'

'I know it's hard.'

Suddenly Ruth's hand was in hers, as it had been when she was a child, and its warmth drove her on.

The machines surrounding her father were noisy. He was so fragile in the bed, in the midst of tangled wires and tubes, like a baby bird that had fallen out of its nest way before it was ready.

'We're going to lose him, aren't we? Older people die from fractured hips all the time.'

Nancy looked up at her mother, who slowly shook her head.

'He'll be okay. His body's still strong and I'm sure he'll make it through the op. He's not even that old.'

'That's why this is so unfair! He's been through enough already.' Nancy had wondered if there were any tears left, but they seemed to be an endless supply lately. 'He doesn't deserve to go through all this pain and trauma, just to end up back in the state he was.'

'I said the same to Barbara when I got up to The Pines as the ambulance arrived. I wanted them to leave him alone. It all seemed so bloody pointless when they can't really fix him at all. But then Barbara said something to me, about how your dad was the day before the fall. Daniel had organised for an Irish folksinger to come in and play for everyone. She said John was joining in all the songs and didn't stop smiling the whole time. She said although he sometimes gets distressed, there *are* moments of joy still to be had. All right, so he doesn't remember them ten minutes later, but he's living in the moment and maybe that's not a bad thing for all of us to do.'

'I don't want this version of him, though. I want my old dad back.'

'I know, darling, we all do, but if there are still moments left for him to enjoy, we have to want that for him, don't we?'

'I suppose.' Nancy sounded like a sulky teenager, but she couldn't help it. She didn't want this, none of it. And the one friend who'd always really understood – Jack – was out of the picture too.

'I need to tell you something.'

Ruth came back into the room with two cardboard cups about an hour and a half after John had been taken down for his operation. Neither of them wanted to leave, so they had resigned themselves to drinking endless cups of machine coffee while they waited for news. Mark had been and gone, still less able, or willing, to cope with any trauma. The two women in the family had promised to phone him as soon as there was anything new to report.

'Oh God, I'm not sure I can stand many more revelations.'

Nancy reached out and took the drink, bracing herself.

'I promised you no more lies, but this isn't going to be easy for you to hear.'

Ruth took the seat on the other side of the bed from Nancy and her hands were visibly shaking.

'If you're about to tell me you and Dad aren't my birth parents or something, then now really isn't the time.'

Nancy's forced laugh died in her throat as she looked over at her mother, the fear in Ruth's eyes making her shiver.

'I was with Daniel when they phoned me and told me about your father's fall. We were in a hotel. Together.'

'Together? You mean *together* together?'

Ruth nodded.

'No, no, no.' Nancy stood up. None of this made sense. 'You hated him until a couple of weeks ago.'

'I can't justify how things changed so quickly and I won't see him again. Not now, not with all this.'

Ruth hadn't moved from her chair. Nancy didn't know how to react; she couldn't even begin to get her head around it.

'When did this start?'

'On New Year's Eve, but Nancy, if I could go back and change it then I would.'

'I can't believe it.'

She looked at her mother as though seeing her for the first time, unsure what to say, unsure how she even felt about it. Daniel and her mother together was unfathomable.

'I'm sorry, I can't deal with this right now. I need to get out of here.'

❋

Nancy left the hospital room without a backward glance, and Ruth silently promised to give up Daniel if her daughter could forgive her. She owed Nancy that, after all she'd put her through. But she wasn't daft enough to think it would be easy. It turned out love and hate really were two sides of the same coin.

Ruth was still on her own when John was brought up from recovery. Looking across at the tangle of wires crisscrossing her husband's body, she was overwhelmed with the need to say sorry. Not just to Nancy, but to John. To tell him that part of her had finally let him go. A man she'd loved for over thirty years. Yet it seemed less painful than the thought of saying goodbye to Daniel – a

323

man she'd loved for less than a fortnight. Perhaps it was because her pain had been drip fed, little by little over the last few years, each forgotten memory on John's part another scar on her heart. She'd loved him more than she'd ever believed she would, but he'd left her, and Daniel had come along. She felt guilty, but still glad that Daniel had been there. If she had to give him up, she would, but he'd reminded her that *she* was still alive, and for that she would always be grateful.

'John?' Ruth raised his hand off the bed slightly and took it in hers. 'Thank you. Thank you for loving me for thirty-four years and for letting me love you, and for being the best husband and father you knew how to be.' She let go of his hand and leant forward to rest her forehead against his. 'I'll never forget you, my love, and deep down, I know you'll never forget me either.'

Only the sound of the machines whirring broke the silence, and Ruth lay there waiting, but for what she wasn't sure.

CHAPTER THIRTY-FIVE

Jack agonised for ten minutes over how to end the text to Nancy. He wanted to put lots of love, or at least a couple of kisses, but he couldn't muddy the water any further. He wanted to tell her that he'd do anything for her, anything that lightened her burden, but of course that would have involved a rider. One which said he'd do anything for her as long as it didn't sully the memory of his wife.

He'd barely eaten or slept since he'd asked Nancy to leave. He'd never imagined how painful it would be, almost worse than Alice dying in some ways. That decision had been taken out of his hands, so he'd *had* to live with it, but he'd chosen to lose Nancy and it was so hard. When he'd heard from Maisie about John's fall, he'd wanted to run to her, to somehow make it all right, but he'd sent her a bald little text instead – telling her he was thinking of her and that he'd cover any of her classes if she needed him to.

Thank God Craig and Selena were due to arrive on their way home from Paris. Even their loved-up newly-engaged presence was preferably to the hours of aching silence when Toby was asleep.

'You look like you've had a rough night, mate!'

Craig crushed Jack into a bear hug at the door, all that Aussie exuberance bursting to come out as soon as he arrived.

'Actually, it's been a rough week.'

Jack hugged Selena, who smelt of the same perfume as Nancy, so he had to force himself to let her go.

'Come on through, I'll get us all a drink.'

'Where's the lovely Nancy?' Craig's grin was threatening to split his face in two. 'You've no idea how stoked we were to see you two getting so close on New Year's Eve, mate, and to actually see you smiling again.'

'She's gone.' Jack swallowed hard and forced a smile. 'It was for the best.'

'How the hell can that be for the best? I haven't seen you that happy in ages.' The smile had melted off Craig's face.

'I've got no right to be that happy, though, have I, Craig? I buried my wife less than eight months ago and Toby and I were getting far too close to Nancy.'

'Jesus, mate, how did you work out what was *too* close?' Craig sat heavily on the sofa, his head in his hands.

'I never gave Alice the chance to live her dreams. I stopped us going to America and using Aunt Josie's connections that could have given her the career she wanted. I got Toby in exchange and I can't take that away from her, too. He's the only legacy she got the chance to leave behind.'

Did Craig think that all of this had been easy for him, either? For Christ's sake, he'd loved Nancy. He still did, but that didn't make it right, did it?

'I'm sure she'd have wanted you to be happy.'

Craig looked up at him, but Jack shook his head.

'Selena, you're going to have to tell him. Make him see that Alice's life would have gone on if things had been the other way around.'

Craig turned to his new fiancée, whose eyes widened in horror. She looked at Jack and shook her head.

'Oh no, Craig, you promised. You can't expect me to do this …'

❈

'He's going to be all right. The hip replacement went really well.' Ruth looked up at Nancy as she entered the hospital room. 'As long as nothing unexpected happens, and he's not too distressed when they get him off the medication, they'll try to get him up on his feet in the next few days.'

'That's great news.'

Nancy took the seat next to her mother, not ready yet to talk to her about Daniel. Understanding why it had happened was enough for now. It had taken three laps of the hospital grounds before she'd been able to begin processing it. Her mother's life had been on hold for years and Daniel had shown her nothing but kindness, even when she'd thrown it back in his face. What was it Barbara had said about her father living for the moment? Didn't her mother deserve the same? Who was she to judge anyway? She'd have been with Jack if he could let go of Alice and live in the now. The details were still too much for her to cope with, though, so slipping her hand into her mum's was an unspoken sign of understanding. She hoped that would be enough for Ruth for now too.

'You should go home soon, darling, get some rest. I can stay with your dad until they tell me to go for the night. I'll ring you at Jack's if there's any news.'

'I don't live there any more.'

Nancy's throat burnt with the words, the involuntary squeeze of her mother's hand something else to focus on.

'Because of what happened at Toby's party?'

Ruth's voice was gentle and all Nancy could do was nod, leaning into her mother for support. Neither of them needed to say any more.

CHAPTER THIRTY-SIX

Selena clutched a pillow against her body as she looked at Jack.

'There was no performance on the night Alice died.'

'What do you mean? There had to be, she was killed during the preparations for the show. Helping out a stagehand.'

'It was a party night. For friends of the theatre. Some agents and directors had been invited. The performance was part of the entertainment, not a ticketed show.' Selena frowned. 'There was one guy, he was on the Friends of the Old Granville committee, and he was the one who organised the event. He wanted some volunteers from the cast to meet and greet and, of course, Alice put herself forward.'

'So she didn't have to go that night?'

Jack could still recall the look on his wife's face as she'd agonised about having to leave Toby when they'd been so sure he was going to crawl. She'd said she'd do anything not to have to go to work so she could see it. And he'd promised to get Toby to sleep and keep that experience to share for another day. Only she'd had a choice all along. There'd have been no gap in the cast without her there. She was a much better actress than he'd ever realised.

'No, she didn't *have* to go. But she and Greg – the guy who organised it – were good friends.'

An unreadable expression crossed Selena's face and she quickly glanced towards Craig, whose arms were folded across his chest.

'Friends?'

There were connotations in the word that Jack could hardly bear to think about, given the look on Selena's face.

'Was she having an affair?'

'No!' Selena shook her head vigorously. 'It never went that far, but they emailed each other. He was a theatre groupie, I suppose, and was always hanging around after the shows. He had plenty of money. I think he was into property development or something, so he almost always had a front-row seat. He always wanted to take photos of Alice too, kept telling her he was her biggest fan and that she'd make it big one of these days, and that he'd be able to say he knew her before she was famous.'

'Sounds like a dickhead to me,' Craig interjected, throwing the words out like a grenade.

'He used to give me the creeps.' Selena paused. 'I hate saying this about Alice, but she liked the attention. He put the party on mostly for her I think, and the fact he'd invited some directors and agents … Maybe she thought she was on the way, that his money might give him the sort of connections that would help.'

'So he gave her what I never did?' Jack eyes met Selena's and there was an almost imperceptible nod of her head. 'How do you know they never slept together?'

'I found a box after the accident of the emails she'd printed off and a stack of photos he must have sent her too. They were love letters from him and, yes, she flirted back, saying he meant a lot to her, but she always refused his requests to meet outside the theatre. The two of us always travelled back together after he left. She didn't really love *him*, it was the adoration she loved. But I know she loved you and Toby too. More than anything.'

'She did, mate, I'm sure of it.' Craig had moved towards Jack. 'And we weren't ever going to tell you any of this. I didn't think you needed to know, but I want you to realise she had a life you weren't part of, and now you need to let yourself have one.'

'Right.' He couldn't say thank you and he couldn't turn the clock back to before they'd told him either. Maybe he'd wake up in a minute and discover the conversation he'd just had with Craig and Selena hadn't taken place. How was he supposed to feel about anything now?

The feeling of numbness continued into the following week. Jack coped with going through the motions at work. He managed to brush off Maisie when she asked if he was okay, and nobody else there bothered him much. If Nancy had been around it would have been different. She would have seen right through him, known that something was wrong. Only Nancy wasn't around. She was just coming in for classes and then disappearing back to the hospital, without coming down to the staffroom. Maybe it was a good thing; he had no idea how he'd react to seeing her.

When he finished work on Friday, the house felt emptier than it ever had. Toby was asleep by seven and he flicked through about sixty TV channels not finding anything he could bear to watch. He wanted a drink, badly, but if he went down that route there was every chance he might end up the sort of father to Toby that his dad had been to him. Instead he got up to look for a book he knew he had somewhere about coping with loss – some well-meaning gesture from a colleague at the university following Alice's death, which he hadn't read at the time. Now he was desperate to read it, because he'd lost everything. Not only his wife, but so much of what he thought they'd had together suddenly seemed less sure. And now he'd lost Nancy too.

The bookcase was a mess – paperbacks doubled up on the shelves and stacked on top of one another. He started tossing them to one side as the hunt became more frustrated, like a burglar ransacking a house for the valuables he knew must be hidden somewhere.

When it wasn't in the bookcase, he searched around the house. the dresser there was a group of Alice's photographs confronting him. The smile he'd loved so much seemed to be mocking him, telling him he'd never given her what she wanted. He couldn't bear to look at the photos of the three of them together; despite what Alice had said, he was convinced now that he and Toby would never have been enough for her.

Snatching one of the photographs, he threw it against the wall with such force that the four edges of the frame separated and the glass hit the slate floor, shattering into a thousand pieces. For a split second, he felt better, and it was that glimmer of relief that drove him on – smashing frame after frame until they were all broken.

Daniel was waiting in the small front garden of Ruth's cottage and she started as he stepped out of the shadows.

'You look exhausted.'

'You frightened me to death!'

Her tone was sharp. She hadn't wanted to see him like this, not now. She didn't have the strength for a big scene and she certainly wasn't going to give her neighbours the satisfaction of seeing it all played out on the doorstep – she was quite sure there was enough gossip going round already.

'As you're here, I suppose you'd better come in.'

'That wasn't quite the reception I was hoping for, but since you've been ignoring all my messages, I guess it's better than nothing.'

He stepped into the living room and she closed the door behind them.

'Why are you here, Daniel?'

'To see how you are. Make sure you're okay.'

He took a step towards her and she held up her hands.

'Don't make this any harder than it has to be.' She shivered, despite the fact that the central heating had come on while she was out. 'I've only come home for a few hours and then I've got to get back to the hospital. There's a reason I haven't answered any of your messages.'

'Don't do this, Ruth, *please*.' Daniel looked downcast, almost unrecognisable as the cut-throat businessman she'd cast him as over the years. 'I know we can't see each other right now and I'd never put any pressure on you, but I don't want you to make any decisions while all this is going on either.'

'I made my decision over thirty years ago, when I married John. I should never have let any of this happen.'

She couldn't look at him as she spoke, focusing instead on a seascape that hung on the wall behind him, feeling just like the boat in the picture – being tossed and buffeted by an angry sea.

'Is it Nancy? Did you tell her? I can understand why she's upset by this, but she'll come round eventually.'

'That's just it, she already has. I told her and I expected her to be angry. God knows she had every right to be. But we've talked about everything over the last couple of days and she told me life's too short not to grab a chance of happiness when it comes along.'

Ruth sighed heavily. If anyone deserved happiness it was Nancy, not her.

'That's great, then.'

Daniel's eyes were shining. She was going to have to turn out the light behind them, hurt another person even though that had never been her intention.

'Is it? I don't think so. It's like Nancy *expects* me to put my happiness first and so she just goes along with it. How do I know if it's what she's really feeling or if she's just saying what she thinks I want to hear? She's spent so long putting me first and that's my fault, because I've let her.'

Ruth was every bit as exhausted as she looked, but she needed to say this, needed to make it clear to him that she couldn't do this to John – despite Nancy's reassurance that she understood. It was time to stand on her own two feet. Leaning on Daniel was just moving on to another support.

'So you're ending this to punish yourself for what you've done in the past?'

'I don't deserve you, Daniel, and I don't deserve to put myself first any more either. Things didn't work out for Nancy at Jack's, so she's coming home to me and I need to make things up to her, even if that takes the rest of my life. There's no room for anything else.'

'Please, Ruth.'

Daniel's eyes pleaded, but she just shook her head. She couldn't make it better for him. Instead she said nothing and watched him leave, her tears falling in silence.

It never ceased to amaze Nancy that the teenagers she taught could transform with the right motivation. Sadie was seventeen and thought everything was 'sad'. If you asked her to read for a part she'd act so nonchalantly that any emotion she was trying to convey was squashed, her fringe hanging so low there was never any danger of her eyes giving any feeling away. More than once Nancy had been tempted to ask her why on earth she'd chosen to study drama. Yet surround Sadie with a bunch of six-year-olds and she was suddenly in her comfort zone, whipping them up into a frenzy of excitement as they pretended to be jungle animals. One of the little boys had a spot-on impression of a chimpanzee.

'What now, Miss?' Sadie turned towards her, her eyes sparkling, just like the group of primary-school kids she was supervising. 'Shall we do the alphabet game?'

'That would be great. I think Chantel is going to start that with her group. Maybe you could join up?'

Nancy gave her a questioning look. That sort of request would normally elicit a disinterested shrug of the shoulders from Sadie at best.

'Okay, Miss. It should be fun with a big group of them.'

'You're doing a great job, by the way, Sadie. Well done.'

'Thanks, Miss. I think it comes from having five younger siblings. I'm used to entertaining kids.' There was a flash of that smile again and, even though Nancy couldn't see them, she was sure it had reached the young girl's eyes.

Kate, who was the teacher in charge, crossed the room to talk to her as Sadie led off the group of children like a puddle of ducklings.

'This is brilliant, Nancy, thanks so much for

organising it.' Kate squeezed her shoulder. 'The kids are loving it. Look at their faces!'

'Almost as much as my teens. They weren't enthusiastic when I mentioned that your year twos were coming over for a morning's drama workshop led by them, but it's really bringing out the best in them. We should do this again.'

Even as she said the words, Nancy's smile went a bit wobbly. She wasn't sure if she'd last out the term the way things were going.

'Are you okay?' Kate dropped her voice slightly, but there was no way any of the kids could have heard their conversation, not with eight of Nancy's teenage students in charge of twice as many six-year-olds. The noise was steadily building. 'I heard what happened with Jack. Will told him he's being an idiot, for what it's worth.'

'I miss Toby so much. Sometimes my arms ache and I can't work out why. Then I realise it's because I want to hold him.'

She hadn't guarded herself enough against falling in love with the little boy. At least with Jack she'd stayed cautious, tried to keep her emotions in check. But she'd fallen hook, line and sinker for Toby, without holding any of herself back.

'Oh God, it must be hard.' Kate grimaced.

'I wish I could still see him, even if Jack doesn't want to see me.'

Nancy tried not to think about how the little boy had been affected by her leaving. Had he missed her even a fraction as much as she had him?

'And Jack?'

'He's made his choice.'

'But it can't be easy seeing him every day? Working together?'

'Luckily I've managed to keep a low profile so far and I haven't seen him.'

Tears pricked her eyes at the thought, especially if Toby was with him the next time they met. Two people she loved, suddenly so off limits, and she had no control over it.

'I'm not sure I could deal with it.' Kate shook her head.

'I'm not sure I can either.'

Nancy had been trying to pretend she could cope when things went back to normal and she went back to sitting at her desk in the staffroom, just across from where Jack sat with pictures of Toby pinned to the shelf. Fraser constantly checking on her and renewing his offer of a room in his apartment didn't make it any easier either. She didn't want the whole world to know how she felt about Jack, but the longer she stayed at the college, the more of a risk there was of that. Or, even worse, of making an idiot of herself over him.

'Maybe you're right – maybe it's time I moved on.'

'Oh no, Nancy, please. Don't listen to me. I'm not sure I've ever felt that strongly about anyone.' Kate looked horrified at Nancy's response. 'What would I know about the best way to deal with it?'

'Don't worry, it's nothing you've said, Kate. I've been feeling as though I can't breathe properly here since I came back after Christmas. I need to be somewhere else if I'm going to get myself back on track, and it'll be better for Jack, too.'

'Just don't rush into it, Nancy. Promise me that?'

Nancy nodded, but her mind was already made up. The right decisions weren't always the easiest ones, but she'd finally run out of options.

CHAPTER THIRTY-SEVEN

'Toby, just give me a minute, darling, please, there's someone at the door.'

Jack's son was clamped to his leg. It was no good trying to convince himself otherwise: he'd been far clingier since Nancy had left. The poor little sod obviously had no idea why someone he was so attached to had disappeared so suddenly from his life. Whoever was knocking on the door was as determined as Toby, though, and in the end he scooped his son up, the little boy hanging on to him like a koala bear. God knows how he'd manage to get away when he dropped him off for his next nursery session.

'Well, if it isn't my two favourite boys!'

Aunt Josie standing on his doorstep, with a case on either side, was the last sight Jack had expected to greet him.

'Josie!'

Other than a Californian suntan, she looked exactly the same. Thank God she hadn't got into Botox or had something unthinkable lifted or plumped. She'd always been cuddly and he'd never been more grateful for that as she pulled him towards her.

'Are we going in, then?' When she let him go, he nodded, picking up her bags.

'Why didn't you tell me you were coming?'

Judging by the weight of her Louis Vuitton cases, she was planning on staying a while.

'Because I'm staging an intervention.' Josie gave him a knowing look. 'Craig phoned me after he saw you. He told me what had happened with you and Nancy and I got myself booked on to the next cruise.'

'Why didn't you just phone and give me an earful?'

He knew that was exactly what he was in for. She was already peeling a reluctant Toby away from his side, but the little boy had no idea who she was.

'Because there are a few other things I need to sort out while I'm over here.' Josie jigged up and down to sooth Toby's complaints. 'But I'm starting with you. As soon as you've made me a proper pot of English tea. I've missed it almost as much as my boys.'

'So you're telling me that you've given up the chance of being happy because you felt guilty?'

Aunt Josie was on her third cup of proper tea by the time they were getting to the crux of the conversation.

'It's not really about me and Alice any more. I've worked through how I felt when Selena first told me about her and that guy at the theatre. I'm not angry. We both made mistakes – me in trying to hold her back by not taking up the opportunities you offered and Alice in getting involved with him as a result.'

'I don't think you can blame yourself for that. But maybe the two of you should have talked a bit more about what you really wanted.' Josie broke a ginger nut in half, remembering after the second cup of tea how much she'd missed English biscuits too. Cookies were all right, she'd said, but you couldn't beat a nice, crisp ginger nut.

'That was our problem, we weren't honest enough about that. Maybe we'd have sorted it out and still found enough common ground to go the distance. Who knows? But after Selena sent the box of emails and photos down to me, I'm convinced there was nothing sexual in it. Not for Alice at any rate. It wasn't that she wanted another man more than me, maybe just another life more than ours.'

'And that isn't enough to give yourself the green light to change your own?' She fixed him with a level look, the one she'd always used when they'd played rummy together, trying to read behind his expression to see what cards he was holding. 'It's perfectly normal to mourn, but a time comes when you have to cross that line and have a life of your own again. Life's for the living, Jack. You can't do anything for Alice any more, but that doesn't mean you have to stop living too.'

'It's not just about me, is it? Toby *had* a mum. I can't take that away from him.'

'Oh, so what am I, chopped liver?' Three deep creases stretched across Josie's forehead as she frowned. She'd definitely given the Botox a miss. 'Are you really telling me that when your mum walked out, you'd rather I hadn't stepped in to take her place? That you'd have been happier without a mother figure?'

'I'm not saying that. I couldn't be more grateful for what you did, but this is different. My mother had a choice, Alice didn't.'

'That's right, she didn't, and neither did Toby, but you do have a choice! For Christ's sake, Jack, half the world has two mums or two dads, or both. The days when everyone was a neat little first-time-round family are long gone. By the time he's at school, half his class will probably have a stepparent. Toby doesn't have to forget

Alice just because he has someone else he can call Mum. You're being an idiot.'

'You're the third person to tell me that.'

Jack couldn't help but smile. He'd heard more or less the same from Craig and his new friend, Will.

'Yes, and I won't be the last.'

Josie snapped another ginger nut with considerable force and Jack was glad she was taking out her frustration on the biscuit.

'Even if I did think you were right, what's to say Nancy feels the same way? Not only have I pushed her away, but she has enough of her own baggage to worry about. She might never have been interested in anything long term, and I only want someone in Toby's life if they're planning to stay.'

'I know you, Jack, despite what you're saying. I can tell by your face that you wish you'd taken the time to find out.' She waved a finger at him. 'Don't you?'

'Of course I do.' Jack felt overwhelmed with tiredness all of a sudden. 'But it's too late.'

'It's never too late.' The smile was back on Josie's face, the ginger nuts safe for now. 'I'm going to London for a couple of days tomorrow and I want you to have found your balls by the time I get back and have spoken to Nancy.'

'And there was me thinking you hadn't gone all Californian on me.' Jack returned her smile, even as nerves fluttered in his stomach. She was right, he had to take the chance, but the fear that it would all be too little too late wasn't easy to shake.

'They're going to let Dad out next week.' Nancy greeted her mum with the news as Ruth entered his hospital room.

'He's just finished with the physio and if he keeps up the good work, he'll be able to go back to The Pines.'

'He's made of tough stuff, your dad.' Ruth sat next to Nancy on the side of his bed, John in the vinyl-covered armchair at the side, staring vacantly out of the window. 'Has he said much today?'

'No, he's still quiet, but I've been playing the CD of that Irish folksinger's music that Daniel sent in for him.' Nancy gestured towards the CD player on John's bedside cabinet. 'He was humming along for a bit. The music definitely seems to make him happier.'

'That was nice of Daniel.'

Ruth's tone had lost all the sarcasm when she spoke about him and Nancy just wished she could make her mother see sense.

'He really *is* nice, Mum. In fact he's one of the best. I never wanted you to give up what you'd found with Daniel and I keep hoping you'll change your mind. Everything that happened with me and Jack has taught me one thing – life is too short to hold on to ghosts from the past. Dad will be back sitting in a world of his own in that chair at The Pines soon. He doesn't remember that you are married, otherwise we wouldn't have had so many calls about him being in bed with the vicar.'

Nancy managed a rueful smile and squeezed her mum's hand again. 'You punishing yourself about Daniel won't change any of that. You'll just make two more people unhappy and I really don't want that to happen.'

During the time they'd spent together around John's hospital bed, they'd spoken – really spoken – more than they had for years. They'd talked about the effects of the Alzheimer's, the mistakes they'd made with each other along the way, as well as how grateful Nancy was that she'd never followed Fraser out of the Bay. Nancy had admitted how strongly she felt about Jack and that, if she wanted him to let Alice go enough to give them a chance, she could hardly begrudge her mum the same.

'I can't see Daniel any more. It's too difficult to keep these things secret and, although you might understand, not everyone is going to feel the same.' Ruth smoothed her hair. She'd been straightening the faded red curls lately to a silky curtain. Things might be over with Daniel, but he'd given her a new lease of life. He was a great guy and Nancy didn't want to believe there was really no chance for them. Her mother would just have to ignore everyone else, but right now Nancy was too tired to argue. It was one problem that could wait for another day.

Nancy had got into the habit of walking around the hospital grounds to clear her head when the stifling atmosphere of her father's hospital room got too much. Ruth had headed off for a few hours' break and the nurses had come in to wash her father, giving her an excuse to escape for a while.

The weather was crisp, the grass crunching beneath her feet as she cut across one hospital path and on to another. She'd emailed Fraser the night before to give him her notice and Mark had offered her a job to tide her over, working at O'Brien's tools in Copplestone with him. So okay, it wasn't how she'd envisaged her life panning out, but it would do for now. She'd emailed Olivia too, asking if she wanted to step up and take some of the drama groups when they started up again in February. She hadn't heard from her old friend in a while, but by all accounts she was on the mend and still spending all her time with Bernard.

She wouldn't stay at O'Brien's for ever, but she could

save some money while she was back living with her mum and maybe then she'd even leave the Bay for a bit. Home would probably always call her back, but it might be time for a break at least. She wasn't as scared of telling her mother any more, either. Ruth could cope; she'd dealt with much more than Nancy had given her credit for and been strong enough to give Daniel up. Sadly, Nancy was nowhere near as indispensable as she'd once believed. Trying not to think about how easy it had been for Jack to say goodbye, she headed up to the orthopaedic ward.

CHAPTER THIRTY-EIGHT

The nurse gave Nancy a disapproving look when she got back to her father's hospital room.

'Your mobile's been going crazy.'

'Sorry, I thought I'd switched it off.'

She picked up the phone from the table beside her father's bed. There were three missed calls from a number she didn't recognise.

'You really should, you know.' The nurse gave her another schoolmistress-type look, scribbled something in John's notes and marched out of the room.

Nancy listened to her voicemail. It was from Toby's nursery. There'd been an accident and he was being taken by ambulance to the Kent and Coastal hospital's accident and emergency department. Nancy thought her heart had stopped. She was obviously still down as one of Toby's emergency contacts and something bad enough had happened for A&E to call her. Whether Jack wanted her to be there or not, she had to go down to A&E. If he sent her away, she'd deal with that, but there was no way she could sit around waiting and wondering. If Toby didn't have one of them there, he'd be even more afraid, and if he was in pain ... She couldn't even bear to think about that.

Nancy ran along the corridor to the top of the stairs

and took them two at a time all the way to the accident and emergency department on the ground floor.

'Apparently my nephew's being brought in as an emergency. His name's Toby Williams.'

It was the easiest lie she could think of. She could hardly explain that she was his former childminder who happened to be madly in love with his dad – a man who'd all but sacked her a week before.

'Yes, he's already in.' The receptionist looked at the computer screen. 'He's in cubicle seven with his father, if you want to go through.'

Nancy's legs were like lead. Toby was in a cubicle, though. That had to be good, didn't it? He wasn't in resus or whatever they called it on *Casualty*. He hadn't been rushed straight to ICU. It would be all right, it had to be.

Thank God, she could hear the familiar sound of Toby crying. She'd have recognised it anywhere. Pulling back the curtain, she saw them both there – the loves of her life. Jack looked up at her from the trolley, Toby in his arms.

'Is he okay?' Nancy was crying, a mixture of relief that the baby looked okay and terror that he might not be.

Jack managed a nod, holding out one arm and pulling Nancy towards them both. Toby held up his chubby arms towards her and she silently prayed he wouldn't utter the fateful M-word. There was an egg-shaped lump on his forehead, but other than that he looked okay.

'It's all right. He's going to be okay.' Jack kissed her on the forehead, soothing her tears just as he might have done Toby's.

'What happened? The nursery left me a voicemail, but they didn't say much and I didn't want to waste time ringing them.'

'One of the students didn't shut the stairgate to the staff area properly and somehow Toby got through it and made his way half way up the stairs before falling. He must have hit his head on the way back down, maybe when he hit the floor. I thought I'd lost him and it would all have been my fault.'

Jack's eyes were like dark pools in a face drained of colour. Toby's tears were subsiding, but he was still taking shuddering breaths as they ebbed away.

'Of course it isn't your fault.'

Nancy wouldn't let him think that. No one could want for a better father than Jack; it was something she'd recognised in him from the start.

'Mr Williams?' A young doctor entered the cubicle; he had thick-rimmed glasses and a serious expression. 'We're going to send Toby for an X-ray, but it's more of a precaution than anything. The fact that the lump has come out is a very good sign that any swelling the fall might have caused is on the outside.'

'Oh thank God.' Nancy felt Jack slump with relief as he spoke. 'And if there's nothing on the scan?'

'You'll be able to take him home.' The doctor smiled and it lit up his whole face. 'I just need to ask a few routine questions before the scan. Is Toby epileptic or is there any history of epilepsy in the family?'

'No, there's none of that in the family.' Jack still had one arm around Nancy and she was scared to move in case he suddenly remembered she was there and let her go again.

'That's good. And is he allergic to any drugs that you're aware of or is there any allergy to iodine in the immediate family?'

'I don't think so.'

'Great. And does he seem his normal self to you?' The doctor looked from Jack to Nancy and back again.

'He does to me. What do you think, Nancy? Does he

look normal to you?'

Jack hesitated, looking at Nancy until she was forced to drop her gaze.

'The same gorgeous Toby, apart from the tears. And the egg-shaped bump, of course.'

'Well, all that sounds reassuring too.' The doctor smiled. 'We'll get the tests ordered as soon as possible.' He pulled the curtain closed as he left, and for a moment the three of them sat in silence.

'I'm so sorry for asking you to leave, it was the worst thing I could have done.'

Jack was the first to speak.

'That doesn't matter now.'

Nancy looked at Toby again, the little boy holding his arms up for a second time. He hadn't forgotten her.

'It matters to me.' Jack cupped Nancy's chin with his hand. 'I'm in love with you. You know that, don't you? I've felt that way almost from the beginning, but I fought it every step of the way because of Alice.'

'Don't say anything you might regret later because of how you're feeling right now.'

Nancy gave him a serious look. She couldn't stand to have him promise her things, only to snatch them all away again when he was less emotional. As long as Toby was okay, there was time for the rest later.

As the young doctor had predicted, Toby's scan was clear, and by the time Ruth had arrived back at the hospital, they'd been told they could take him home.

'Will you come back with us?'

Jack held out his hand and Nancy couldn't say no. She was desperately trying to slow things down but she didn't seem able to stop herself. She couldn't be sure if his feelings for her were real or a knee-jerk reaction to Toby's accident, but she loved them both too much to do anything else.

Back at the cottage, they put Toby to bed and watched him sleep for the first half an hour before they finally felt safe to leave him.

'I meant what I said, you know.'

They lay side by side on the tiny single bed in her old room.

'But I don't understand what's changed.'

She had to know he meant it, even as she struggled not to reach out and take his hand.

'Everything. Everyone was telling me what an idiot I'd been to let you go and I realised they're right. Being with you is all I want, for me and for Toby.'

'What about Alice?'

'I can't change what happened to her, but not being with you for her sake makes no sense. And you not being in Toby's life doesn't either. I didn't realise how ridiculous that was until you walked into the hospital today.'

Jack turned to look at her so their faces were almost touching.

'I saw the expression on your face, the way you looked at Toby, and I could tell you love him as much as I do. What right have I got to deprive a little boy of that? I had it with my aunt when my mum disappeared. Doesn't Toby deserve it too?'

'But what about you? Do you want me, or someone for Toby? I couldn't take it if this was a lie, Jack, even if you don't mean it to be.'

'I missed you from the moment you walked out of the door, long before Craig and Selena tried to talk to me. Will did his best too, but it wasn't until Josie turned up on the doorstep that I really began to see sense. I've felt guilty for months because of my feelings for you. I felt the scum of the earth for falling for someone else so hard when I'd only just lost Alice. I kept telling myself that she'd never do anything like that to me, if things had been reversed, and that I owed it to her to wait a decent length of time before I allowed myself to feel anything. But there's nothing I can do for her now. Josie gave it to me straight: life is for the living and I want to share it with somebody.'

'Any somebody?'

'No. I'm afraid only Nancy O'Brien will do.' His breath was warm on her neck. 'But you haven't told me how you feel yet. Now that Fraser's back, do Toby and I still stand a chance?'

'I love the Williams boys like I've never loved anyone. Fraser never stood a chance against the pair of you.'

'That's the second fantastic bit of news I've had today.'

His lips brushed her neck and she tingled in response as they moved slowly down her body. Even if she hadn't believed he meant every word, she wouldn't have stopped him – she wanted this so much.

'Just promise me something Jack: you're not going to cry again, are you? I don't think I could take it.'

Her breath caught in her throat as he reached her belly button, her body arching as he stopped for a moment to answer her question.

'I promise I won't cry.'

'That's good.'

She gasped again as he resumed the sweep of his lips down her body.

'Because I just might.'

CHAPTER THIRTY-NINE

Jack pushed Toby's buggy along the promenade and looked down at the beach. He could just make out the pier in the gloom of late afternoon in January. The days were very slowly starting to lengthen, but it was still dark by five and the cold air could take your breath away when the mood took it.

Only ten months ago, he and Alice had strolled along this pier with their tiny son and sat on the beach, making sandcastles for him while Toby attempted to eat handfuls of sand. Now Alice was gone and he wasn't sure how well he'd really known her. It seemed like another lifetime. Part of Alice had always been hidden from him, but Nancy wore her heart on her sleeve and he loved her for it.

'I want to say something to you, before Aunt Josie arrives and we don't have a chance to talk properly.'

He turned to Nancy and stopped pushing the buggy.

'What is it?'

Her eyes widened and he was sorry for not coming straight out with it. He'd put her through enough already.

'I just wanted to let you know that if being deputy manager of a DIY store is your dream, then I won't stand in your way. I've learnt my lesson on that front.' He grinned, Nancy nudging him playfully in the ribs. 'But I won't be the only one who'd be sorry to see you go from the college. Your students think the world of you.'

'Much as I had my heart set on a personalised tool belt with a special wrench pocket, I think I can let go of that one dream.'

God, she was gorgeous when she smiled.

'Luckily Olivia has already replied to say that she's sorry but she can't take on the drama groups and she can't be involved any more either. She said she'd tell me why next time we meet.'

'Are you planning on seeing her?'

'Not for a while. Right now everything in my life is close to perfect and I don't want to get pulled back into Olivia's drama just yet.'

'That's good to know. Perfect eh?' He pulled her into his arms and kissed her softly on the lips. Maybe not perfect, but it was close enough for him. 'What about the college? Can I look forward to walking hand-in-hand to work with the woman I love?'

'Fraser wouldn't accept my resignation, so if you're lucky I might even let you carry my book bag.'

'Does that mean we're going steady?'

He couldn't stop smiling.

'I'll think about it.' Linking her arm back through his, she pulled him forward. 'Now let's go and meet your aunt, or we'll be late.'

'Do you know what? I don't think she'd mind.'

'Lovely to meet you at last, Nancy.'

Josie had cheeks like apples and the sort of smile that immediately made you feel welcomed into the family. Jack really had been a lucky boy to have her in his life. He seemed to realise it, hugging her tight and taking her overnight bag when she got off the train.

'How was your trip? Did you get everything done that you needed to?'

Nancy took the handles of the buggy, and the older woman put a hand over hers.

'I did indeed and I'm glad to see my nephew took my advice while I was gone.'

Josie had a ready laugh and Nancy warmed to her immediately.

'So what was so pressing that you had to head up to London the day after you got here?'

Jack raised an eyebrow and his aunt laughed again.

'I went to see Pam.'

'You did *what*?'

Jack clearly wasn't happy and the lightness of Nancy's mood began to ebb away at the mention of Pam's name.

'It's all right. She wasn't too pleased to see me at first, but we sorted it out in the end.'

Josie tapped the side of her nose, but there was no way Jack was going to let her get away with that.

'What do you mean you sorted it out?'

'I told her she couldn't keep punishing you because she'd lost her daughter. We rowed, she cried, and then we spent half the night talking and looking at old photos.' Josie gave a shrug, as if it had been the most natural thing in the world for her to do. 'She even took me to her grief-support group this morning. There's a widower there who's desperate to take her out for dinner, but he told me she keeps turning him down.'

'Josie, you didn't!'

Jack's eyebrows shot up again.

'*What*? I just gave them a bit of a push in the right direction, that's all.' Josie was smiling now. 'I told her what I told you, she needs to start living again. It might lead to nothing, but it's a start.'

'You're like a fairy godmother.'

Nancy turned to the woman who'd brought up the man she loved, certain they were going to be friends.

'Sometimes love just needs a bit of a helping hand and sometimes it finds its own way.' Josie laughed again. 'Look at those two up ahead, they don't need anyone's help.'

Nancy followed her gaze to the couple illuminated by a street lamp a hundred feet or so up the road, locked in an embrace.

'Isn't that your mum and Daniel?'

Jack shot her a quizzical look. She hadn't had a chance to tell him about that yet. And now it looked very much like they were back together.

'It certainly is.'

She smiled; things were just getting better and better. Love could take the scenic route sometimes, but Josie was right, it always found a way.

CHAPTER FORTY

On Easter Saturday, Nancy and Jack decided to go for a walk on the clifftops before meeting Ruth and Daniel for lunch. They were bringing John too. Daniel had got him a wheelchair so they could take him out for a decent walk without putting too much strain on his hip. Happily-ever-after wasn't always as neat as you might want it to be, but these things were worth working for.

'Did you send my aunt some flowers for Easter?'

Jack stopped pushing John's wheelchair to look at the text message that had come through on his phone.

'Yep. She's already messaged me to say thanks and she's going on another date with that accountant from the film studio. She said it was high time she took her own advice.'

'What would I do without you, Nancy O'Brien?'

'If you play your cards right, you'll never have to find out.'

They carried on up the headland until they reached a large wooden beach-hut, selling ice-creams and soft drinks, which only opened from April until September to cater for the summer tourists. Nancy sat on a bench in the spring sunshine, next to her dad in his wheelchair, while Jack went inside with Toby to get an ice lolly.

The couple walking up the hill towards her were

visible from a distance, but she didn't recognise them until they got much closer. When she did, there was no mistaking it this time – they were definitely holding hands – Bernard and Olivia.

'Nancy, great to see you!'

Bernard beamed and, as Olivia released his hand, almost pulled Nancy off the bench into a bear hug.

'It's great to see you both too.'

If it was a shock to see them together, something instinctively told Nancy that this was a good thing.

'Would you like a drink? I'm going to get Livvy one. What do you want, my love?'

Bernard turned towards Olivia who grinned in response.

'Surprise me, you know what I like.'

'So can I get you something, Nancy?'

Bernard smiled again and Nancy shook her head, saying nothing until he'd disappeared inside.

'How have you been, Liv?'

She turned to look at her old friend. If the expression 'glowing' was overused, it was apt on this occasion.

'I'm great. Really happy.'

'I can see that.' She couldn't help smiling. Bernard had clearly brought something amazing into Olivia's life. 'So I take it you two are an item now?'

For a split second it had crossed her mind to say that she'd once thought Bernard was involved with Olivia's mum, Louisa. But even if he had been, it clearly didn't matter now and it wasn't her place to say.

'A bit more than an item. I'm pregnant.'

Olivia's hand immediately moved to her stomach, her smile never wavering.

'Oh my God, Liv. Congratulations. Are Sophie and Jasper thrilled?'

'They are. They're at an Easter egg hunt today with some friends from school and they've both said they'll be saving their biggest egg for the baby, although I've told them it will be nearly Christmas again by the time the baby's here. Bernard's brilliant with them, too.'

'I'm so pleased for you all.'

'It's a shame not everyone sees it like that. Some of the kids in Jasper's class have been teasing him about Bernard being his granddad. But I couldn't give a stuff what anyone thinks. Everyone thought Miles was a golden boy when I married him and look how that ended up.'

'You know what? I couldn't agree with you more. What other people think shouldn't stop you being happy.' Nancy thought of Toby. A lot of people might say it was too soon for her to be in his life, or for her and Jack to be in love.

'Bernard makes us all feel safe and I've never felt more accepted for who I *really* am.' Olivia placed a hand on her arm. 'I treated you badly, Nancy, and I never got to say thank you for what you did for Jasper and Sophie when Miles put me in hospital.'

'It's in the past now, and perhaps all that stuff with David did us both a favour in the end.' She got to her feet and gave Olivia a brief hug. There might be no going back to a real friendship, but Nancy really did have a lot to thank her for. 'Will we see you at the old community centre soon? At least in the audience?'

'I hope so.'

Olivia took the seat Nancy had only recently vacated. Perhaps some things would never change.

'I'll see you then.'

She pushed her dad's wheelchair towards Jack, who had emerged with Toby and an ice lolly, and they walked along the coastal path to where they were meeting Ruth and Daniel.

They might not be a conventional family and they wouldn't always get things right, but love was the glue that held them together and that was all that mattered in the end.

The End

Coming soon…

The Gift of Christmas Yet to Come

Surrounded by friends she has had since childhood, with a job she loves, as a special-needs teacher at the primary school in beautiful St Nicholas Bay, Kate Harris has it all … well, almost. As Christmas rolls round once again, she longs for a child of her own to share it with.

In a town where Christmas is big business all year round, it turns out Santa Claus isn't the only one with mysterious powers. When a psychic reveals that the answer to her future will come in red and white, Kate follows this sign. It leads her to disastrous dating agencies and demoralising dead-ends until, finally, the answer seems to be revealed.

Her search for the missing piece of her family might end happily but has it made her blind to another kind of love?

**For more information about Jo Bartlett
and other Accent Press titles
please visit**

www.accentpress.co.uk